TWIXT

DIANE J. REED

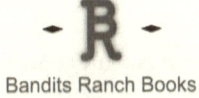

Bandits Ranch Books

CALL OF THE RAVEN

I have loved her from before time.

This love may seem impossible,
the way a bird who becomes more
than a spirit blessed with wings defies logic.
Such notions are the ether of fairy tales and
    dreams.
But one thing I have learned—
the harsh light of reason never made love any
    less real.

It all started long ago,
on an island off the west coast of Ireland.
I cannot tell you the date, of course,
for that is the work of those who weigh and
    measure the world.

But I can tell you this: I warned her. I protected
    her.
And I tried with all my might to guide her.
In doing so, I fell in love with her.
Any soul guardian would.

They say when you gaze upon the sea,
it shifts and changes with every glance.
Ages can pass in the flicker of an eye,
only to return again, unawares?
This tale is as old as it is new.
Though she wings through history like a bird
    testing flight,
her path too often marred by a dark shadow,
her heart remains eternally the same.
And so does my love for her.

This is our story…

PRELUDE

1847: Connacht, Ireland

A raven pierced the horizon, a silent presence. He cut a wide swath along the edge of a field, then turned to trace a silhouette on a row of potatoes below. Another raven joined, then another. Their shadows formed a ring around Ailís O'Dannan as she tilled the ground. The lead bird called to her, sharp and insistent, voice raw above beating wings. Yet after two more ravens gathered, and their shadows stained the earth, nothing could stop the steady rhythm of Ailís's hoe—until she saw their circle unravel.

Ailís gazed up at the late afternoon sky over the island. The clouds had splintered into thin white threads, and the birds' loose circle stretched into a line over her cottage, their shadows splitting it in half. The wind began to swell on the knoll with a sickly whine that whistled in her ears until it shattered her thoughts. Ailís took a deep breath, knuckles white against her hoe. She stared at the dark patches of fungus on the potato leaves—they were the same shape as the ashen clouds she'd seen earlier that day. Usually the forms she saw in the sky made sweeter impressions: patterns spoke of births and reunions, new loves and old friends. But today, not even the sky could comfort her.

As the baying of the hounds began to echo behind the knoll, Ailís could feel her heart rending in two. She stumbled across the potato rows to her nine-year-old daughter, Corvine, who glanced up with green eyes clear as water. The black-haired girl was so thin from the famine that she looked to her mother like a ghost. Ailís swiftly dug into her skirt pocket for her diary and held it up for Corvine to see. The cover was filled with suns and moons, herbs and animals: the drawings of an illiterate woman that bore record of her wisdom. Ailís pressed the diary into her daughter's hands, then cupped both palms around her cheeks. "*A thaisce*," she said as if holding her soul for safe-keeping. In the blink of an eye, colors shimmered around the girl, and the raven landed beside her feet. The bird let out a fierce caw, tossing his scarred beak. "I'm trusting her to you now. Guard her!" Ailís pleaded before the colors waned and the bird took flight. Then she wrapped her arms so tightly around her daughter that she nearly crushed her breath. "Hide," she insisted, just as the dogs appeared over the horizon.

Corvine scurried across the field, her path haunted by the raven's wings. She reached a neighbor woman who grabbed her by the hand, and together they hid behind a wagon. Mrs. Brogan tried to bury the girl's face into her skirt, but Corvine peered past the folds to see three men on horseback surrounding her mother while dogs snapped at her flesh. The men carried whips and shouted angry demands: "More rent, more crops—no more magic!"

But what they didn't know was that the magic wasn't entirely under her mother's control. Ailís couldn't force her will on the birds or the clouds—they attended her and those she loved with the capriciousness of shadows. And it was no use trying to manipulate them. It would be like trying to catch a rainbow or harness starlight. Still, whenever the landlord tried to squeeze more money from the O'Dannan widow, his cattle were drummed by hail and his pastures flooded. And each time investigators came around to uncover insurrection, they were pummeled by thunderstorms and pursued by lightning.

These events were commonplace to Ailís's neighbors, not worth more attention than a remark about the weather. It was no secret to the locals that Ailís was "fairy 'twixt"—a descendent of the ancient Tuatha de Danann race and their liaisons with Irish mortals. The townspeople had always murmured she was born of air spirits, and in her blood ran the force of tempests. What else could explain her eyes of green fire, black hair unruly as wild roses, or the uncanny way she inspired the elements to protect those she loved?

This knowledge was as indecipherable to the English landlord as the locals' Irish tongue. Ailís's neighbors never spoke aloud of her gifts, referring to the spirits around her as the "good people." It was bad luck to utter such things, for one might risk offending the fairies. Besides, there were enough advantages to being Ailís's neighbor that warranted keeping your mouth shut. All you had to do was lend the widow a helping hand—quietly fix a fence or mend a roof once in a while—and you could rest assured that the spring lambs would be healthy and the hearth fires would burn long and warm.

Everyone on the island knew these favors followed the seasons. A good deed in spring yielded a full harvest in fall, as long as you weren't greedy or impatient. And above all, you should never speak ill of Ailís or her daughter Corvine. So, like the early frosts in autumn, it was no surprise to the neighbors that the landlord's herd of pigs dashed over a cliff on the night of the first full moon after he'd held up his fist and cursed the O'Dannan name.

Later, the countryside gossip said he blamed Ailís for setting the swine loose, and the landlord grew tired of hearing rumors that he got what he deserved. Word had spread about how he followed the pretty O'Dannan widow at twilight, whispering her name in shadows until his longing boiled over like a teakettle. Soon, laughter erupted behind every sheep pen, for the landlord couldn't admit his yearning for a 'twixt woman had driven him mad. Finally, after Ailís kept refusing him, and her ravens hurled stones upon his head, the landlord decided he'd had enough. The O'Dannan acres weren't yielding a profit anyway, and there were plenty of starving workers willing to take her place. But more than that, he was determined to rid the area of Ailís's influence, of the ridiculous fairy superstitions that put her on a pedestal and helped her neighbors maintain their pride. Local pride didn't yield a profit, he said. Nor did it explain why he'd lost an entire swine herd. As far as the landlord was concerned, it was time to bury the past and start again with a new order.

Above the din of hounds, Corvine heard the ravens call out a death knell. She broke free from Mrs. Brogan's grasp and ran to her mother, but all she could see were flashing fangs and shreds of flannel. Hooves sliced beside her as Corvine flailed at the dogs, until a bloody hand grasped her ankle and pulled her to the ground. Panicked, Corvine saw her mother's face washed in crimson. "Go!" Ailís cried. "We will be with you—go."

Lightning struck the ground with such force that it knocked a man off his horse. Before Corvine caught her breath, another lightning bolt exploded. Corvine blinked— colors were inverted, black as white and white as black. She glanced at the ravens on the ground, their wings pale as albatrosses. Then she rubbed her eyes—all sound had ceased but the ringing in her ears. The dogs' faces lay embedded in the dirt, and nearby a small mound looked like the belly of a man.

Through the smoke Corvine searched for her mother, when an arm wrapped around her and pulled her away. Corvine recognized Mrs. Brogan, her eyes wide in terror. The Brogan widow babbled incoherently and pointed at the sky. As Corvine's vision readjusted to color and light, she saw a face emerge from the clouds. Ailís appeared, alone against a rainbow, her black hair sweeping across the sky like a veil. Yet her features seemed different somehow—smooth and unlined, before time and famine had weathered them with sorrow. A soft breeze caressed the girl's cheek, gentle as a mother's fingers, and the raven returned to her side. The bird stood tall and bowed his head. Corvine heard a voice gliding on the wind:

Go—we will be with you. Go.

The long passage across the Atlantic was dark and wrought with fever. Corvine huddled against Mrs. Brogan in the hold of the coffin ship, fearing they'd never reach land. After her mother had passed, Mrs. Brogan pitied Corvine and took her in, and later they accepted the landlord's offer for a free trip to America. No one was fooled by his generosity. Without Irish tenants, it would be easier to import fresh workers who hadn't been weakened by famine—and who'd never heard of the likes of O'Dannans. Yet in spite of their burned-out cottages and empty stomachs, the people of the island clung to their dreams like holy relics. For them, this was a chance to start new in America, perhaps acquire land. If they survived.

When Corvine and Mrs. Brogan finally arrived in Boston with haunted eyes and hollow cheeks, they discovered the Irish were treated like a pestilence. Notices were posted in windows warding them away: *No Irish Need Apply.* Fortunately, Mrs. Brogan's talent for bargains convinced the Sterns, an affluent family living on Boylston Street, to take her and Corvine in for domestic help. "Two for the price of one!" she insisted, and she made Corvine hold up her hands to her future employer. Though thin, Corvine's hands were wide and large knuckled, and her black hair gave her a serious cast that gained Mrs. Stern's approval. Behind all the velvet and lace, silver and linen, the Stern's household was run with military precision, and Corvine's day of housework always began before dawn.

Mrs. Brogan, on the other hand, connived her way into the

kitchen, even though her cooking skills were limited to potato soup and scones. At night, Corvine opened her mother's diary and the two of them pored over the symbols for the secrets of kitchen magic. Beside pictures of hens were images of rosemary and pepper. Next to cows were drawings of onions and sage. Their clandestine recipes met with unusual success, and each evening Corvine tiptoed out to the back garden to leave milk and fairy cakes to pay respect to the "good people."

"Are there any good people in America?" Corvine asked Mrs. Brogan one night. The woman sighed and hugged the girl. "We have full stomachs and firm beds," she chastised. "That's proof enough! Don't let curiosity tempt our luck." Corvine stirred a kettle of soup with a sharp look, as if she might discover something in the broth. She bit her lip and turned to Mrs. Brogan, who was kneading dough. "You saw my mother, didn't you—up in the sky that day? Lately, I've spotted her raven in the back garden, the one with the scarred beak. Do you think the good people are watching over us?" Mrs. Brogan's cheeks lost their color, and her flour-dusted fingers pushed away the diary before she cleared her throat. "*A Thiarna déan trócaire*," she muttered, patting Corvine with a trembling hand. "Some things are beyond our understanding, dear. Now mind your soup—we have work to do."

Nevertheless, Corvine couldn't help asking questions in her heart, and she often snuck out at sunrise to the Stern's back garden to gaze at the sky, wondering if her mother's pledge remained true in a new country: *We will be with you.* Then she cradled the tender roses along the walkway and inhaled deeply, cherishing her mother's words, "Fragrance is a fairy's blessing." Corvine liked to return the blessing, so she caressed the plants and dropped carrots for the cottontails that darted at her feet, until Mrs. Brogan would appear like clockwork at the back door. "Mark my words, child," the woman always scolded, shaking a wooden spoon. "That soft heart will be your undoing! If the mistress catches you wasting rations, she'll throw you to the streets."

Aside from her brief garden comforts, Corvine's skin still tingled whenever a storm was near, and her breath would catch with the sound of thunder. On particularly stormy nights, she ran to the windows, hoping to see her mother's face illuminated by a lightning bolt. She searched her pockets for the diary, and sometimes she held it to the moon to draw down its power. But as clouds shifted in the sky to reveal fleeting colors, all she could ever count on for company was a raven at her windowsill, marked by a scarred beak. The bird often brought trinkets to cheer her: shiny coins and buttons, a silver locket or shells that smelled of the sea. Once, he even arrived with a potato in his claw, small and dark, the kind they used to harvest on the island. The sight brought tears to Corvine's eyes. Cocking his head, the raven gazed at her with such a deep and ancient knowing that it made her gasp, as if her soul had been laid bare for all to see. Corvine trembled from her head to her toes, until he lifted his beak and gently unfurled a tangle in her hair, then skipped across the ledge to make her smile. "Ah, if only you were a man," Corvine sighed wistfully, running her fingers through his feathers, "then one day, we could be married."

With that, the bird settled a wing upon her shoulder, and Corvine could have sworn she heard him whisper *Believe*. Yet despite his faithful presence over the years, Corvine's heart couldn't help yearning for human solace. As she blossomed into young womanhood and watched the Stern's daughters marry, the ache of loneliness slowly made her numb to the raven's murmurs. Even Mrs. Brogan refused to abide her notions about fairies anymore, and Corvine's faith in the "old ways" naturally began to waver. By the time she reached her twenty-fifth birthday, a spinster by anyone's standards, the only hope she had left for her future was in the thrilling tales she'd heard of treasures out west.

Late at night, Rory O'Brien, Mrs. Stern's carriage driver, had taken to whispering to Corvine about the discoveries in Idaho Territory. "I've got a secret," he confided, pulling her close behind a cleaning closet when no one was looking. At first, Corvine didn't know whether to be flattered or frightened. She'd seen him spying on her for weeks, his reflection hesitating on the parlor window, or his long shadow seeping into the floorboards of the pantry. But Rory gently took her by the hand. "There's gold out there—haven't you heard? Rivers of it!" His voice lilted with echoes of Ireland. "We'll need a *currach* to row across." Rory's hair was a mirror of the sun, brighter than Mrs. Stern's brass candlesticks, and his eyes burned with a fever that made Corvine blush. His words had the same intensity of the men back on the island when they used to talk of overthrowing the landlords. "Don't you see?" Rory prodded Corvine, "If you go with me, there'll be nothing holding us back anymore. We'll be rich beyond our wildest dreams."

Rory's uncles had gone to the California gold fields in '49, and he said he'd be damned if he missed this opportunity. Between stolen kisses, he told Corvine that her liquid green eyes transfixed him, and her pale skin was a blank page upon which he could write new legends. "Wild rose of Boylston Street, what are your talents worth to the Sterns?" Rory taunted, his fingers igniting sparks up her spine. The heat of his hands made her quiver, feeling more alive than she had since she'd left her beloved island. And with each kiss, his eyes flashed like stars, studying her face as though it were a map of a new land. "Mrs. Stern will keep you trapped in her parlor, telling fortunes till you shrivel up and die," he warned, pausing to savor her lips. "Let's live, Corvine—really live."

Years spent in service for the Sterns had already made Corvine a peculiar young woman, the kind who caused the neighbors to whisper. Rumors had spread about the lovely Irish maid who read tea leaves on Boylston Street. To Mrs. Stern's delight, Corvine's modest celebrity enhanced her social position, and made her the most sought after hostess for afternoon tea. But what Corvine didn't tell them is that she never read the leaves at all. She simply stared into the teacups as if they were the sky, and she let the murky impressions act upon her mind like forms in the clouds. Then she whispered "O'Dannan" while she secretly stroked her mother's diary that she always kept in her pocket. Suddenly, patterns in the tea would become clear. Shapes of acorns spoke of prosperity, outstretched wings meant new love. The guests often became so giddy that they forgot themselves and hugged the Stern's servant with the fervency of a long-lost friend.

To her disappointment, however, Corvine found she couldn't read the future for herself. Whenever she stared into a teacup with a burden on her heart, all she saw was her own reflection, eyes filled with wonder. And if she consulted her mother's diary for her own fate, the pictures merely blurred together, only adding to her confusion. Frustrated, Corvine weighed Rory's possibilities the way Mrs. Brogan weighed kitchen ingredients. Did he have the power to unleash her future like he promised, far from the stale old maid she had become in Boston? She knew he talked fast, moved faster, and his passions were fierce. But sometimes, after a long work day, when Rory stumbled to stack hay or hang harnesses in the carriage house, Corvine would see his face light up as she walked by. He would glance at her across the grounds in her uniform, crisp white in the sunshine, and she would see him stand a little taller, his eyes embracing her as if she were a vision—his *aisling*. Then he would quietly dip his head in surrender, as though he might collapse without the sight of her for sustenance. In those moments, Corvine realized he needed her, just like he needed his dream, and that thought filled her with a euphoria that rivaled the bloom on her mistress' cheeks from nipping laudanum. Not even Mrs. Stern's liaisons with her afternoon lovers could compare to the heady draw of Rory's longing upon Corvine's heart. Suddenly, she could see a place for herself in the world—not just as a mere cleaning girl, but as the light of a man whose hope would only be matched by the West itself.

Was that love? How could she know for sure? Week after week, Corvine's endless rounds of dusting and polishing ate at her soul. She stared at her hands, pale and chaffed from her ornamental prison. Even the kindly Mrs. Brogan had become bitter over the years, and all Corvine knew for certain was that their lives at the Stern's would never change. So, in spite of the raven's violent thrashes against her window on that bright night when Rory tossed pebbles at the glass, Corvine quickly gathered her belongings. She paused to tear a heart from her mother's diary and laid the page gently on Mrs. Brogan's pillow before kissing the sleeping widow good-bye. Then she ran down to meet Rory O'Brien in the Stern's back garden. There, ignoring the clatter of ravens, Rory and Corvine locked hands under a full moon and pledged their eternal loyalty to one another. After a long, exhilarating kiss, Rory proudly knotted a scarlet bandana around his neck. He vowed they would make it to Idaho territory, even if it killed them.

~

1863: Idaho Territory

The wind howled across the land like a banshee. With each step, Corvine felt dust grinding at her feet, her scalp, her teeth. She grasped an edge of the wagon and stared at the mules' ears flopping in rhythm with their hooves, hides powdered gray. Before them were the ghostly tracks of the Oregon Trail made twenty years earlier, now scoured by tumbleweeds and patches of grass that the wind whipped into waves. Corvine recalled the sea she had known as a child, the way its cool spray beckoned to her of heroes and legends she could almost see in the mist. But out on the southwestern edge of Idaho Territory, the dust funnels spoke only of demons and *sluagh*— creatures that screamed and licked your bones clean until even your memory dried up and blew away.

Corvine didn't mind letting go of the past, especially the lonely years in Boston. With every mile she traveled west, hope burned in her chest as bright as the sunsets she saw bleeding over the hills. And each morning at sunrise, Rory consumed her in kisses, assuring her she'd never been more beautiful—though her skin had tanned to leather and her clothes had worn to tatters. His desire was sometimes so strong that it bordered on delirious, and he would stop their wagon to seize her on the trail, his affection roiling over at a fever pitch. Yet as days passed into weeks and weeks into months, Corvine saw the light slowly fracture in his eyes. He became angry at her for little things, disappointments she couldn't change—a pond filled with algae, too sour for drinking, or a stone blocking the wagon wheels. "Couldn't you see that coming?" he'd fume as he kicked the dirt, fists tight, "I thought you were a fortune teller."

Corvine realized the hot sun and wind were enough to drive anyone mad, though she'd tried to admit her shortcomings many times. "I-I told you, I can't see the future for myself," she'd reply as dust devils consumed her words, or Rory cut her off, too tired to listen. But later, beside their campfire, Rory always held her close to the point of trembling and whispered a dozen apologies. Then he stared into the flames, and his eyes flickered again with the need she craved. "We are one heart," he'd say desperately. "Do you hear, Corvine? Never leave—promise me." Corvine nodded, and Rory eased his head onto her lap and drank whiskey until they both drifted off to sleep. Then, in the middle of the night, she would hear his voice, tender beside her. "Mountains of gold," he'd whisper, "bigger than Croagh Patrick," and he'd cling tightly to her until he slipped back into slumber. In those moments, Corvine pressed her cheek against his chest, treasuring the fullness of his breath. As long as the dream is still alive, she thought, we will survive.

Five and a half months after she and Rory left Boston, they stopped beside an outfitter's corral next to the Boise River to swap their wagon for more mules. The couple were parched, bone thin, and so dusty gray their eyes shone white as eggs. Anyone who didn't know Corvine would have thought her to be an old woman. Corvine was secretly glad. Rory had told her there were far more men than women where they were going, each one voracious to the point of insanity. "They'll kill you for gold," he warned, looking her up and down, "and anything else they can get their hands on." Most of the prospectors were veterans of the California goldfields, still hungry for more, and they could spot two newcomers in a heartbeat. "Don't say a word to anyone," Rory instructed as they loaded the pack train to head for the mountains. "There are no friends in gold country."

The two of them rode along a narrow trail that climbed to the heart of the Boise Basin. At twilight, they finally descended on Ophir Creek, a dark hollow between several ridges that twinkled with a thousand miners' lamps. Navigating their mules around a sea of tents, they were careful not to step near dogs that guarded miners' supplies with rabid ferocity. All around them, Corvine saw lean men with eyes of want, as ravenous as what she'd seen on the coffin ship. Only this hunger was different. It was not the hollow cravings of the body, but the fierce and insatiable desire to find gold. Corvine shivered, drawing her mule closer to Rory's and feeling fortunate to have a man beside her—any man. To her relief, they soon reached an opening at the end of town, and Rory dismounted and settled their packs onto the ground. Then he grabbed several stakes and stomped them into the dirt with his boot. One by one, he tied up the pack animals, except for the mule ridden by Corvine.

"Ready?" he said.

Corvine rubbed her eyes, craving sleep. "What?"

Rory gave a tug on the reins. "Let's go."

Despite her protests, Rory insisted on leading Corvine's mule away from camp, convinced they should look for gold before sunrise. "If people see you in daylight," he warned, "they'll jump your claim before you can register it. This is the only way, Corvine."

"Your mind's bedeviled!" Corvine argued, trembling with exhaustion. "We can't find anything in the dark—we don't even know where we are."

Rory dug his hand into Corvine's arm and yanked her from the mule. She landed in a heap on the ground. He pulled her to her feet and slapped her.

"*Damnú air!* Why do you think we crossed two thousand miles? If you can read tea leaves in Boston, you can tell me where the gold is." Rory shoved her forward. "Now move."

Corvine felt blood rise to her cheek. Her mule bolted for the trees, and she turned to dart from Rory when he grabbed her by the collar. As she twisted to break free, she heard a metal click, felt a barrel press against the small of her back. Her vision clouded with panic, a haze of dust and tears that burned her eyes. He's gone mad, she thought, as Rory mumbled between curses. The pistol burrowed into her spine. "Start walking—now," he demanded.

Corvine held her breath, stepping forward into darkness.

Above her, the stars were obscured by campfire smoke, and it wasn't until she'd walked for several minutes that she could even spot the moon. Instinctively, she followed the white glow up a hillside to the top of a ridge, until Rory tugged at the back of her coat. His hand spun her around.

Shiny streaks of sweat lined Rory's forehead in the moonlight, and his eyes had hardened to sterling beads. Corvine stared at the wayward blonde hair she used to comb with her fingers, purring tenderly over each curl, bleached silver now like an apparition. Then she searched his eyes, so absent of the piercing affection that used to overwhelm her, and she wondered what she had ever found in him to love.

"*Damnú*—where's the gold?" he insisted.

Gazing at the sky, all Corvine saw was a slate of black. There were no clouds to decipher, no winds to whisper directions. Only tall trees charred from lightning strikes that stood around them like sentinels. She quickly rubbed her mother's diary in her pocket until it grew warm, her heart pounding.

"R-Rory," she stammered, "I-I've tried to tell you a hundred times. I can't see fortunes for myself—my heart is blind."

Rory smiled and shook his head. He reached up his hand to stroke her neck. "Ah, my wild rose," he said, "of all people, you should know. We see what we want to see." He caressed her throat, searching her green eyes as if they were tea leaves, but then his fingers closed firm. His face became oddly serene, and in his gaze Corvine thought she saw the ocean—a gray, limitless horizon that blended with the sky. It was the kind of space you could get lost in, like the heavy mists of Ireland, where you might wander aimlessly for years, or drown without ever knowing what happened.

"My, you're beautiful, aren't you, my rose?" Rory's lips were so close she could feel his breath.

His words fell deep inside Corvine, and they sounded peculiar, as if she'd heard them from the bottom of a well. Rory's voice rippled within her, seeping into every vein and sinew, an echo she feared might last for centuries. Her body began to tremble in waves as Rory squeezed her throat, pressing against her skin with his pistol.

"Well, if you won't find our gold," he whispered, turning her face to the moonlight, "I'd be a fool to let you find it for anyone else, now wouldn't I?"

Rory devoured her in a kiss. Each time she struggled, the pistol pressed harder against her neck. His beard scratched her lips, her throat, until she thought it would tear her to pieces. Corvine cried out, her voice swallowed by a wild, screeching sound. A chaos of claws and feathers enveloped her, muffling her screams. She dropped to the ground to cover her head. When she glanced up, she couldn't tell where the wings ended and Rory began. A raven dove at him furiously, wings drumming as it ransacked his flesh like fresh carrion.

Corvine crawled along the forest floor that smelled of smoke from recent fires. Shaking, she pulled her mother's diary from her pocket and held it to the moon, daring to hope the elements might intervene. Rory stepped before her with his pistol raised, his other hand waving savagely at the bird. Closing her eyes, Corvine whispered "O'Dannan." Suddenly, thunder intermingled with Rory's gunfire, and bullets sparked off nearby rocks. A slice of light exploded between them as a wild cry erupted—so deep and raw it seemed to come from within the ridge itself. Soon, all clamor ceased and the night fell into silence.

Pressing her face against the earth, Corvine murmured prayers to the soil. When she gathered the courage to look up, she saw a familiar raven on the ground, blood dribbling from his scarred beak. Rory's body lay next to the bird, his head struck by a ricocheted bullet. Stumbling over to them, Corvine steadied herself, bewildered. Her hand trembled uncontrollably as she stroked the raven's head and felt his blood seep between her fingers. Then she reached down to unravel the bandana from around Rory's neck. She cradled the red fabric as if it were his heart.

"*Dia ár sábháil*," she whispered, the words rattling in her throat. "*Dia ár sábháil*, Rory—"

A brittle cold pierced her chest as though her soul had splintered into a thousand pieces. Without warning, a magpie swooped down and landed at her feet. The bird strutted beside the fallen raven as if in victory. Then it cocked its head and traced strange circles in the soil as it waved its white wing bands to the moon.

It's not over, Corvine heard Rory's voice haunt the edges of the wind.

It's never over between us.

You made a promise to me in a garden—eternity is a heartbeat, you'll see. There's no gold without ore, no white without black. Forever you'll run, and forever you'll need me.

The Present: Highway 95, Nevada

Rose peered through the truck windshield at the black birds, their shadows weaving over the highway in a broad figure eight.

"See the birds, honey?" she asked her daughter Crystal. She traced an infinity sign on the glass. "Just like the ravens from the legend—they're supposed to be our protectors, right?"

Her voice cracked a little as she recalled her great-great grandmother's tragic end. Drawing a deep breath, she cleared her throat. "You know, people in Ophir Creek say our ancestor found a fortune after all," she said hopefully. "Folks claim that when a blue moon rises over Rook Ridge, all those who are pure of heart can make a wish in the O'Dannan name and find gold."

Setting her hand down on the old, threadbare diary

between them, Rose couldn't help rubbing it for good luck. "Remember how we used to lay on your bed at night, honey? And look up at the stars and dream about fairy gold?"

She reached over to stroke an ivory lock along Crystal's cheek, but her daughter didn't flinch. Rose lifted the diary for her to see.

"Can you say book for me, sweetie?" she urged with forced gaiety. "C'mon—give it a try. Booooooook?"

Crystal's green eyes registered nothing. She stared with empty saucers at the wide Nevada sky as they headed north on Highway 95 from Winnemucca. Rose sighed and set the diary back down on the truck seat. Then she wriggled an old cloth free from the corner of the dash to rub the dusty windshield, but all she managed to do was spread her fingerprints into smears. Frustrated, she wiped her forehead and rested the red fabric on the steering wheel. Her fingers began to tremble as she recognized its hearts and diamonds, clubs and spades.

It was Jake's.

Five months ago, she'd brushed a fiercely blonde lock from his forehead for the last time, unraveling the bandana from around his neck before they closed the casket. Rose leaned forward on the truck seat, tempted to inhale the scent of the fabric, to absorb the man-smell of Jake again that was once laced with possibilities. She drew in a hesitant breath, allowing the familiar aroma of suede and dried sweat to seep inside her. Wincing, she almost wished she could conjure that old adrenalin between them that used to substitute for courage. But when she glanced down, she noticed her tears had dampened the cloth with stains the size of poker chips. Her cheeks flushed and she swallowed hard, letting the bandana fall to her lap.

"Time to fold," she whispered as she brought the red corners neatly together. Rolling down her window, she released the bandana to the wind.

Rose brushed away her tears and scanned the still, dry landscape, a page she figured hadn't changed in a thousand years—it had simply endured. The road before her was a silver line that stretched past Bloody Run Peak to Boise, Idaho, where she would pick up another highway before reaching the dirt road that led to Ophir Creek. It had been five years since Rose took this route, since she'd promised her half-sister Laurel she was starting a new chapter in her life.

"We're going to get married!" she'd smiled on that hot afternoon while Laurel had folded her arms and refused to help pack the truck. "Don't worry," Rose added cheerfully, "I'll work in a casino while Jake starts his business. He's got a knack for money, you know." Her face beamed as she held up her barmaid apron and threw it in the trash. Then she gave Laurel a big hug, startled by the darts of envy in her eyes. For once, Laurel was no longer the golden cheerleader and junior potato queen—it was Rose who shined brightly. Raven-haired Rose who'd won the attention of the handsomest man ever to cast a shadow on Ophir Creek. She shuffled her boots and tried to ignore Laurel's wisecrack about "taking off with a stray" along with the callous gaze of her husband Tom, a former quarterback and potato executive who'd aged to the thickness of a tuber. But when Laurel sniped that she'd be back in a heartbeat with her tail between her legs, Rose was forced to shake her head.

"Can't you just be happy for me for once?" she pleaded, stung by her sister's disdainful sigh. "At least I'm finally breaking out of this town."

At that moment, Jake walked around the truck and stretched his arm over her shoulder, making her feel shielded for the first time in her life from Laurel's criticism. Then he gave her a gentle kiss on the cheek, his eyes such a tender blue and his tousled hair so shiny that for an instant she forgot all about her sister's sneers.

"Let's go, honey," Rose finally decided, averting Laurel's indignant stare. "Just like you always say—sometimes you gotta bet everything to rake in the chips."

Rose never dreamed the price of her gamble would mean losing her daughter to a realm of silence and shadows. Jake's "business" turned out to be speed—ecstasy, crystal meth, a little "gold dust" cocaine. Anything that made you move quicker, talk faster, fly higher than the next guy. "Stimulation addict," they called it at the Narcotics Anonymous meetings, after Rose convinced Jake to attend with her in good faith. Yet no matter how many times they repeated "codependent no more," it was nearly impossible to escape the pull of Jake's appetite. When he was high he made love to her like a God. Rose swore he had the power to draw her soul from her body, releasing her to a place where she shone blistering white, as if she'd been consumed by the sun itself. But when Jake came down, his paranoid words stung like nettles. He couldn't stand the sight of her, much less tolerate her touch.

Does a man have to be high to love me? Rose had agonized in secret. Yet so many times Jake pulled himself together for her—going cold turkey, holding down jobs for six months or more, particularly after Crystal was born. All the while, Rose struggled desperately to keep her family intact, to provide the kind of stability she'd never known in childhood, no matter what roll of the dice fate threw at her. But regardless of her best efforts, their lives relentlessly spiraled into rehab followed by roses, candlelight dinners after scrapes with the law, with Jake always insisting it was the last time.

Finally, after he slapped her one morning when she caught him stealing from her purse, Rose gathered his things faster than he could recite his Twelve Steps. Shaking, Jake spewed staccato apologies while she dumped his belongings from their apartment window. But then Rose grabbed a baseball bat and held it up until he surrendered his key and walked out the front door. As she slammed the door shut, Rose heard Jake fall to his knees and promise her every cherished dream she'd ever tucked away in the darkest corners of her lonely heart.

How on earth does he know all my secrets? she whispered to herself, bristling against the force of his words like a drug. Rose gritted her teeth and bowed her head, still feeling the sting of his hand against her cheek.

"Get help, Jake!" she demanded, bracing her bat against the door. "And for God's sake, get the hell out of our lives." Then she turned the handle on the brass deadbolt, determined to keep him locked out for good.

"Mommy," Crystal had asked her later that evening, while Rose was feverishly preparing her favorite pot pie for dinner from scratch, "do you have to go to work tonight? Can't you stay home and bake fairy cakes with me? Maybe then we can find fairy gold."

Rose turned around and hugged her daughter for all she

was worth. The truth was, nothing could possibly please her more than cracking open her great-great grandmother's diary and making treats to share with the "good people," the way her own mother used to do with her. She loved to hide trinkets around their apartment afterwards, from gold-painted rocks to glittery play rings, then watch the way Crystal's eyes sparkled while she uncovered "fairy treasure." But she'd already called half a dozen coworkers to cover her night shift at the casino, and no one was biting. Rose trembled as she swayed Crystal in her arms, feeling the guilt sear into her soul. She couldn't tell what bothered her more—the fact that her daughter had witnessed Jake's abuse, or the fact that Crystal hadn't shed a single tear when he left. She knew that by this point in her life, Crystal regarded her father as little more than a bothersome fly—someone to put up with on birthdays or holidays so her mother could still pretend they were a family.

"Oh, sweetheart," Rose whispered into her cottony hair, "in just a few more days, I can pick up my paycheck from the casino. Then we'll clear out of this town. No more night shifts, honey. I promise."

In spite of her assurance, Crystal remained sullen throughout dinner and the rest of the evening. But after the babysitter arrived, Rose squeezed into the cozy armchair beside her daughter and gently placed the old diary in her lap.

"Before you go to sleep tonight," she said tenderly, "I want you to look through these pictures and pick out any recipe you want." Rose flipped through the quirky drawings of Irish delicacies, her fingers pausing over a colorful page of edible flowers. Then she pointed to the living room window at the dark sky. "When you're ready, whisper your choice to the stars, and in the morning, I'll have it prepared for breakfast."

Crystal crossed her arms in a huff, still angry at her mother for going to work. But then her lips curled into a mischievous smile. "Raspberry tarts!" she giggled, hugging the diary to her chest. "With daisy petals on top."

Rose kissed her on the forehead. "Don't tell me yet!" she chastised, tousling her feathery bangs. "Let me see if I can guess."

Rose adored their silly game. It was a sweet way to feel connected, even when they were apart. Yet oddly enough, she'd always managed to pick the right recipe, regardless of whether Crystal chose something unusual, like strawberry-marigold porridge or pansy-walnut fritters. Rose had always chalked it up to motherly intuition—a simple byproduct of her closeness with her daughter. Nevertheless, as she drove her truck to work that night, she couldn't stop her thoughts from spooling in worry over Crystal, her mind jarred by the traumatic events of their day. And each time she spun the roulette wheel for gamblers at the Gold Strike casino, Jake's eerie voice came back to haunt her. Only this time, it wasn't the smooth promises he'd made to try and get her to open the door. It was the way he'd begun to laugh while her hand had gripped the deadbolt. His voice echoed with a long, harsh cackle, as raw as a magpie's, as if he were certain that this chapter in their lives was far from closed. The sound so startled Rose that for a second she leaned her ear up against the wood. It was then that she heard him whisper through the cracks.

"Go ahead, Rose, try to break free." His laugh was rough and slow, seeping through the hinges. "Just remember, soul bonds can't be broken. They only bend for a while."

Shivers ran across Rose's skin every time she recalled his words, and no amount of gaudy lights or clanging bells inside the casino could distract her from a nagging feeling that something in her world was still askew. Yet despite the phone calls she'd made throughout the night to check on Crystal, the babysitter had patiently assured her that everything was fine. Even so, when she stepped outside on her break and glanced up at the sky, she didn't see stars or clouds that reminded her of apple tansy pancakes or fairy bread pudding—the usual patterns that inspired her to make a whimsical breakfast for Crystal. Beyond the neon lights of the gambling hall, the clouds above her stretched as long and thin as knives. And strangely, a flock of ravens gathered in a circle in the parking lot, making a ruckus.

Curious, Rose stepped closer to see what unsettled them, but the birds didn't scatter all at once, like she expected. Rather, they lifted their wings one by one, forming a dark line across the full moon as if slicing it in two. Suddenly, she heard a shrill voice ring through the night air. It was Crystal, and she had cried "Mommy!"

Rose dropped the casino chips that were still in her hands from her latest tips and bolted for her truck. She bulleted home through a zigzag of side streets and screeched in front of her apartment building, just as the night sky was giving way to dawn. As she dashed through the parking lot and into the apartment complex, her eye caught the sight of something peculiar beside the pool. The chipped cement rim was soaking wet, as if there'd been a splash, and her great-great grandmother's diary was on the ledge, its smooth leather binding reflecting the gold of the rising sun. To her horror, beneath the ripples of the pool she spotted Crystal at the bottom, her tiny face a blank.

Rose shrieked and dove in, striking her head against a submerged step. Tumbling through water, she managed to reach the deep end and grab for Crystal, when her vision became hazy, as though she might pass out. Heart racing, she desperately clutched the chilled weight of her daughter against her chest, her legs struggling violently to push to the surface. But no matter how hard she tried, the water pressed upon her muscles like a vise. Soon, darkness closed in at the corners of her eyes. "No, not my baby!" Rose cried as her words bubbled into liquid silence. With one last thrust of her legs, she prayed from the bottom of her heart for a miracle to give her the strength to save Crystal.

All of a sudden, colors alighted around her, shimmering as they swirled through the water like carnival glass. Then, from out of nowhere, a tall, dark-haired man appeared before her in the pool. He blinked with big brown eyes as if bewildered. Rose had already swallowed so much chlorine she thought for certain she was hallucinating, until the man engulfed her and Crystal in his arms and shot to the surface. As Rose broke through water, she struggled frantically for breath. Soon, she sensed the hard cement beneath her shoulder blades. The man settled her and Crystal down carefully beside the pool, and Rose could hear him resuscitating her daughter. Yet try as she might, she couldn't will her hands or limbs to budge—all she could feel was the fire in her lungs and a fierce, shooting pain in her forehead.

To her relief, she heard Crystal sputter and gulp for breaths, and the man briefly leaned over to check on Rose. His eyes were as dark as chestnuts, creased with questions, and a deep scar ran across his nose that dipped into his cheek.

"I-I can't believe you're real," he gasped, cupping her face in his hands as if he could see straight into her soul. His expression appeared tender yet oddly stoic at the same time. "I've been searching for you—"

Rose blinked hard, startled by the intense intimacy in his eyes, like he'd known her forever, yet wondering if this was all a dream as the weak morning light began to fade from her vision. Her stomach lurched and the world swung topsy turvy, until it was difficult for her to tell which way was up or down. But strangest of all was the fragrance. Tinged with the bite of pool chemicals was the aroma of flowers everywhere, reminiscent of an enchanted garden, the kind depicted so lovingly in her great-great grandmother's diary. With that thought, the colors returned, bright as butterflies, their edges glinting with sparkling light. Rose heard the man's deep voice resound in her ears like a caress.

"It's all right now," he promised. "We've found each other." He grabbed the diary from the ledge and pressed it into her hands. "Believe—"

His fingers glided gently across her forehead, but when Rose tried to look into the man's eyes again, his form had melted into the colors, becoming nothing more than a shadow. Astonished, she clung to the diary, lashes fluttering. All that was left was his silhouette across the pool and a peculiar sound, like the echo of beating wings. Rose shook her head, and with every fiber of her being, she tried to sit up and reach Crystal, but her vision had become so blurry that she could no longer distinguish her daughter's blonde hair from the rays of the sun. After a few more heady breaths, she blacked out.

When Rose finally awoke, she discovered she was lying in a hospital bed. She scanned the room, but Crystal was nowhere in sight. Rose sat up straight and screamed. Within seconds a nurse arrived, calmly informing her that not only did her daughter survive, she was warm and safe in intensive care. The nurse went on to describe how the police reported that her husband had broken through a window two nights ago, then knocked out the babysitter and ransacked the apartment, looking for something. "Probably drug money," she sniffed as she took Rose's temperature. "No wonder he overdosed."

Rose felt like a mule had kicked her in the heart.

"You okay? You knew about it, right? They said the apartment door was open. His heart stopped and he'd collapsed at the threshold. I'm so sorry—"

Shaking, Rose dug her fingernails into the bed linen until she ripped the fabric. Despite all of Jake's near misses, till-death-do-us-part didn't seem real somehow. She wondered if it ever would. Perhaps he would still haunt her like a ghost, endlessly making excuses and seeking his next fix, then attempting to seduce her again with the power of his want. Confused, she clutched her forehead, trying to sort out the shocking finality of his death with the surreal vision she'd had in the pool. Was the stranger who'd rescued her and Crystal even real, or some kind of angel? Clasping her hands to stop her tremors, she cleared her throat.

"H-How's my Crystal?"

The nurse flinched and glanced away.

It was then that Rose knew her daughter was torn from her —still a million miles under water. One by one doctors arrived and filled the room with words that couldn't possibly describe a vibrant four-year-old who'd memorized all her shapes and colors and learned to trace the letters of her name. *Amygdala, hippocampus, cerebellum malfunctions*—to Rose these were ugly terms, hurled at her like insults. Finally, a specialist announced, "What it all comes down to is that your daughter has suffered hypoxic brain injury from the lack of oxygen. Her body functions are normal, and our tests show she has full use of her arms and legs. But she exhibits severe emotional withdrawal and communication impairment. She can see, hear, even walk around. She just can't respond."

"Can't?" Rose said. "Or won't? Maybe she's frightened—"

The specialist shifted his feet. "As hard as it is may be to accept brain damage, it's even more difficult for a single mother with few resources to provide the support she needs. At a minimum, she'll require testing and rehabilitation over many years. You're best off to consider a reputable institution—"

"I-Institution?" The words faltered on Rose's tongue. "D-Did you say institution?"

Bolting from the bed, she ripped out her IV and threw it to the floor. The metal stand fell with a crash.

"Where's Crystal?" She held out her bleeding hand to keep back the nurse. "Bring her to me!" she demanded with same ferocity of her last words to Jake. "I don't care what you say— she's my girl. Bring her to me NOW."

Rose shifted her truck into high gear and sped through a rugged canyon, stealing glances in her rearview mirror to watch its gaping mouth grow smaller and smaller. "See, nothing can get to us now," she promised Crystal, but she might as well have been talking to the dashboard. Crystal's head bobbed occasionally in her car seat when the truck hit a rut in the road, but she seemed unperturbed by the dark thunderheads that gathered before them. The early October sun shone silver through the clouds like a moon, and Rose shivered as the air thickened at the cusp of rain. Soon, indigo streaks cast a net over the mountains, spreading billows of dust on the desert plain like a giant broom.

"Clean slate," Rose murmured as drops began to clatter on the hood of the truck. She stretched her arm out the window, grateful for moisture, and wiped the cool water across her brow. She craved the forests and rivers of her childhood in Idaho like an ancient memory, and she pictured green trees and mountain ridges waiting for her, even if it did mean returning to Ophir Creek. Anything to forget the white-hot anvil of Winnemucca.

Pushing aside a bag of potato chips from the stick shift, Rose picked up a grease-stained letter. She smoothed out the paper and scanned her half-sister's precise handwriting, avoiding the usual chit-chat about her successes.

By the way, Rosie, I received notice that Dad's old gold-panning business in Ophir Creek has been condemned. "Lack of occupancy," the county said—the limit is five

years. There are still tourists around, though the town is
pretty shabby, but it's a free room for you and Crystal if
you're willing to fix it up. I don't have time to help with my
charity work, of course, but I think it would be perfect for
you two. Surely that's better than renting some dump in
Winnemucca, right? Heaven knows, you could use the
break.

— *XX, LAUREL.*

Rose sighed. Along with the letter had come a brass door
key and a coupon for a sack of potatoes. She knew moving
back to Ophir Creek meant tiptoeing through the minefield of
her sister's controlling streak. Even with her busy life in a
manicured Boise suburb, Laurel always had enough energy to
tell the whole world what to do, if it would only stop long
enough to listen. Rose braced herself, facing the fact that she
needed a new start and wondering how she might preserve her
sanity. She ruminated over excuses to escape Laurel's
intrusions—the dinner invitations designed to show off her
house, the offers of money to prove how affluent they were.
Oh, you're so kind! Rose practiced in her head, I've just got a
lot on my plate right now. Why thank you! But I'm doing fine
on my current budget. Worst of all, she had to prepare herself
for Laurel's reaction when she saw Crystal. It always took a
while for strangers to notice, but once they did, their sideways
glances said volumes. Usually, all she had to do was push her
shopping cart up the grocery aisle, or pretend to whisper at a
private moment with her daughter, as if she were merely soft-
spoken. But Laurel would sense the disability in a minute. She

had a radar for people's vulnerabilities that bordered on psychic power. Rose pictured the way Laurel would stare at Crystal, stalking all of her fears before she knew what hit her. Then she would say something cutting but undeniably sensible that would chew into Rose's soul for days.

Rose lifted her chin and imagined one of the storm clouds as Laurel's serious face. "Crystal's just a little shell-shocked, that's all," she muttered, watching the weather pattern shift in the sky. "She's been through a lot—we both have." The storm clouds appeared to grow darker with disapproval, ready to pelt her at any moment with a torrent of rain. Rose peeked at Crystal's blank stare, then gripped the steering wheel tighter. "Dammit, I don't care what the hell Laurel thinks," she said defiantly. "Nothing's going to make me feel ashamed of my girl—"

The sound of Rose's strained voice made Crystal turn her head. Her icy green eyes seemed like protective shields that filtered out more of life than they let in. Rose picked up a stuffed coyote from beside the car seat and bounced it up and down, making gentle yips and howls, but Crystal ignored her and gazed back out the window. Setting down the toy, Rose felt self-conscious, as if she'd been dismissed by a sphinx who had no intention of revealing her secrets.

A dust devil erupted nearby, swirling dirt and debris into a brown column that defied the scattered rain drops. Rose stared at the dark funnel and wondered if everything was her fault, if her daughter had already seen so much pain between her and Jake that she retreated inside to a safe haven—the pool was simply a sound barrier. Perhaps the accident was Crystal's way of crawling back into the womb, where life could be fluid and uncomplicated again. Rose lightly touched her belly, remembering the way Crystal shifted inside while she was pregnant, her tiny feet fluttering as if she were swimming. She wished she could join Crystal in her private sanctuary, and she imagined the two of them submerged in water, their thoughts transcending the currents like dolphin songs. Rose ached inside, wondering if they would ever communicate again, ever share the delight of sound and recognition. Maybe her daughter would only recall her father's lies, and the memory of his voice would keep them separated like smoke. Desperate, she reached over and clutched Crystal's hand.

"Where are you, Crystal?" she pleaded, as if calling beyond a veil. "Can you hear me? Can you hear Mommy?"

Nothing but silence.

Discouraged, Rose dug into her pocket for a crystal bracelet, smoothing the stones between her fingers for solace. She'd purchased it six months ago for one of their treasure hunts, but she hadn't put it back on Crystal's wrist since the accident. Holding it up to the windshield, she watched iridescent blues and greens light up the prisms in the raw sunlight that burst through clouds. All at once, Crystal's eyes appeared mesmerized by the colors. She flapped her hands excitedly and reached for the bracelet.

"Yes! Colors!" Rose nearly ran her truck tires off the road. Heart pounding, she swerved the wheels back toward the center line and clutched her chest. "Oh my God—do you remember colors, sweetie?" She handed her the bracelet. "Red? Blue? Greeeen?"

Crystal shrieked. Rose swallowed her words, afraid her enthusiasm had overwhelmed her daughter. The neurologist had warned her that brain-injured children couldn't handle much stimulation. Nevertheless, it was the first reaction she'd seen in Crystal in months. Biting her lip, Rose tried to remain calm, but her daughter shrieked again and again. Frazzled, she counted to ten to center herself, until she realized Crystal was smiling at the bracelet. Then her daughter lifted her gaze to the windshield, and her eyes appeared transfixed, taking in the horizon as if it held treasures just for her. Crystal began to laugh, wiggling her fingers at the glass. Up ahead, a rainbow arced over the sky. Its rich hues washed through smoky clouds and vanished into the fold of a mountain ridge.

"Look—a rainbow," Rose whispered, so as not to upset her daughter. She studied the overlay of colors that tinted the mountain tops, wondering where they might lead, what pot of gold they pointed to. "Oh honey, do you think those ridges might bring us luck?" She glanced at her daughter, her blonde curls nearly white in the sunshine, her gaze still electric. Thrilled, Rose closed her eyes for a split-second, keeping her hands firm on the wheel. "Make a wish before the rainbow fades to discover a fairy's fortune. That's what my mother used to say."

In her mind, Rose pictured a shining four-year-old, talking a mile a minute about preschool and bragging about what she'd learned. She envisioned her little girl crossing her arms impatiently while her mother tried to sort out which friends were real and which were imaginary. Rose smiled, clinging to a belief deep in her soul that such good fortune might come true. Oh God, she prayed silently, please give me back my daughter. I'll do anything—anything for you.

When Rose opened her eyes, the rainbow had disappeared

into the mountains, and the sunlight shone crisp over the wide desert. Up ahead, a thin line of dark birds flew along the highway. Their shadows traced the road in single file, and they looked to Rose as if they pulled an invisible cord leading her home.

2

The uneven dirt road curved through the Boise Mountains, and Rose gazed at the amber aspens that lit up the hillsides like wildfire. She hardly needed to watch where she was driving. Rose knew the contours of these ridges like her own body—Osprey Reach, Huckleberry Slide, Old Bear Peak. Each bend renewed her senses, and she rolled down the window to inhale the light vanilla scent from the ponderosas as the autumn sun warmed the sap in their bark. Sometimes she caught a whiff of sage, or the spicy aroma of buckbrush that always reminded her of gingerbread. She glanced at Crystal to see if she noticed the fall foliage, but she was silent in her car seat, fingering a butter cookie. Rose decided not to fret over her this time. It was enough to be among trees again, to see eagles spiral on afternoon thermals and to feel the breeze through her hair. It was enough to say goodbye to Nevada.

Guiding her overburdened truck up a rise, Rose listened to

its loose muffler shuffle over bumps in the road, and she reminded herself to get it fixed. As she descended on the other side, she saw dozens of rock mounds along a creek—the tailings left over from giant dredging machines that scoured for gold decades ago.

"Ophir," Rose whispered like a forgotten promise, recalling the school book she'd read about Solomon's mines as a girl. "Land rich in gold."

Passing more piles of dry rocks, she sighed. After the initial gold rush, there hadn't been fortunes found here for over a century. Rose knew her father's gold-panning business relied mostly on naive tourists who wanted to play miner for a day. Every summer, she helped her father lead them to the creek outside of town, and there he would point to his "special claim." It was fool's gold, of course—shiny flakes of mica tinted yellow from the iron-rich water, then pulverized into dust by the spring snow melt. But like a true showman, her father boasted of his discoveries until his audience was nearly ecstatic. Then, at just the right moment, he dipped his boot into the water and kicked up soil from the creek bottom, releasing hundreds of particles. In the bright sunshine, they always sparkled like magic.

Magic, Rose thought, feeling a catch in the back of her throat. She had no idea whether her father ever found real gold. After her mother died of cancer when she was nine, her father always claimed to have struck the mother lode in places he wouldn't mention, often disappearing for days at a time. Perhaps he ventured deeper into the mountains, or went prospecting in another state. Maybe he just haunted the bars. During his many absences, Laurel and Rose ran the gold-panning business on the weekends as best they could, though Laurel was always frustrated by her younger half-sister who gazed out the windows as if at any moment their father might appear. One day, when Rose was thirteen and their father hadn't been home for a month, seventeen-year-old Laurel sat her down beside the wood stove and explained that he wasn't coming back. "There is no gold," she said, her lips firm but her eyes welling with tears. "No magic either. We're on our own, Rosie. We've got to be grown-ups now."

The two of them already knew how to survive on cornmeal and beans, and they both held odd jobs to keep money coming in. Rose thought it was an adventure at first, not so different from those earlier stretches when their father was gone. The finality of his departure hadn't set in yet, and besides, they got to play at being real adults living in the apartment at the back of the gold-panning business. But it wasn't long before Rose realized that Laurel was not her peer. Laurel was her parent—far stricter and more neurotic than any she'd had before. "You will be home each day by five o'clock," Laurel warned with a raised spatula in her hand. "Got it? And if you don't have chores and homework done by seven, no dinner. Nothing's going to interfere with my cheerleading, and I'm graduating with my class. Dad might have been a loser, but not me. I'll be legally an adult in four months, so if anyone sees you running around like riff-raff, you're the one going to a foster home. We can better ourselves, Rosie—we just have to stay focused on our goals, like they say at cheerleading practice. All it takes is discipline and determination."

Rose nodded dutifully, but Laurel might as well have been

speaking a foreign tongue. The truth was, Rose worshipped her half-sister, with her lovely blonde hair and talent for turning any situation to her advantage. Somehow, rising to the top was Laurel's birthright. Yet no matter how hard Rose tried, she never got the knack of her sister's willpower. Rose was hopelessly dreamy, believing in superstitions and the meaning behind the weather, like her free-spirited mother—a fact that Laurel never hesitated to remind her of. "Your mother's head was always in the clouds, seeing things that weren't there, just like you. If she'd faced reality, she would have caught her cancer in time. It doesn't pay to daydream, Rosie. It only pays to do."

Do what? Rose had wondered, puzzled. As a child, she had no particular design for her future, no grand plans for success. She simply relished the company of her half-sister in their forest world, where the bows of pines dipped rhythmically in the wind and the fox and elk appeared at twilight. Each evening, Rose tiptoed out to leave treats for the forest animals and made wishes on the first star, hoping that woodland spirits might guide them. And she often hummed to herself at night, pretending that the gentle echo from the wall beside her bed was her mother's voice, reaching through time. "On a bird's wing, my heart brings, all my love to you," she would sing, until Laurel scolded her to stop. Then she would listen for ravens in the night and try to picture her mother's face, but all she could ever see were shadows.

Yet in spite of the gnawing heartache of her childhood, Rose adored their little apartment behind the gold-panning business. Everywhere she looked there were picks and pans, shovels and sluice boxes—prospector's gadgets just brimming with hope and imagination. These were the wares of dreamers, like her father and mother, and to Rose, each item carried with it the spark of chance and possibility. That is, until she reached adolescence and Laurel made certain that they never spoke of magic again.

Rose pulled down the visor as she rounded another corner, careful not to let her truck slide on washboard grooves in the road. The aspen trees quivered as she passed, their leaves dangling like gold coins. Up ahead, a handful of leaves swirled softly in the air and landed, only to be crushed by her tires. Rose swallowed hard. Am I just kidding myself? she wondered. What am I looking for here? She stared down the twisted logging road, pondering what she might really find in Ophir Creek. After all, her father's gold-panning business had been boarded up for years, and she didn't even know if it still had electricity or running water. What made Laurel think I could live here—did she start to miss the old place, or miss me? Rose bit her lip, afraid to presume too much.

Pine trees shadowed the road as she drove over the last hill before home, a welcome relief from the afternoon glare and the sky so blue she had to squint to look at it. Ahead, Rose spotted the old sign at the entrance of town: *Ophir Creek, established 1863, elevation 5,000 feet, population 2500*. The last two digits had been crossed off after residents had dwindled over the years. She steered her truck to the corner of Main Street and brought it to a halt, watching dust rise up to the windshield. Anxious, she stroked Crystal's hair, her hand absorbing the warm strands as soft as silk that always soothed her nerves. Tracing her fingers along the bracelet she'd put back on her daughter's wrist, she patted her hand.

"This is it, honey," she said brightly. "Are you ready? We're home."

Rose peered through the dust at the western storefronts and rustic boardwalks that lined the town square. A few signs had faded to bleached colors, and the edges of the buildings were chipped from sun and wind. Several buildings were boarded up with tall, black panels made of steel, the kind that were used to prevent fire damage during the gold rush. But otherwise, the old mining town looked the same as it did five years ago, as it probably did a hundred years ago, like it had been freeze-dried into place. Rose blinked, feeling strange, as though she'd stumbled into a peculiar loop in time where nothing ever changed—it simply waited. She scanned the familiar post office, city hall, and the old mercantile that overlooked the square. At the edge of town, kitty-corner from the Magpie Saloon along the road that led to Rook Ridge, was her father's gold-panning business.

"Well sweetie," Rose said with hope brimming in her voice, "let's check it out."

She drove around the square to the tan building with a sign out front that said *Rainbow's End Miners Exchange.* A set of scales were painted above the red letters, but the small mounds of gold that used to shine over the trays were no longer visible. On the door was a yellowed poster that read *"Free Gold Panning Lessons with Prospecting Trips."* Rose winced, wondering how many pans of water she'd swirled with phony pay dirt at the bottom, showing customers how to get the wrist action just right.

"Did you know that gold sinks, honey?" she said to Crystal as she cut the engine. She got out and walked around the truck to unbuckle her from the car seat. "It's heavy, just like you— sometimes precious things are like that." Rose nuzzled her cheek for a kiss as she hoisted her onto her hip, but Crystal pulled away. Disappointed, she fished into her overalls for the brass key and stepped across the boardwalk to wriggle it into the front door. Taking a deep breath, she gave the door a hefty shove.

"Oh my," Rose gasped as she ventured inside. Thousands of dust particles floated down in a band of sunlight, and everywhere she looked the dark room was washed of color, coated by years of gray dust. Rose felt her nose itch, and she set Crystal down on a small rocker before she sneezed. Wiping her eyes, it seemed to her as if she'd just cracked open a vault. She glanced at the shovels and pans on the wall, laced together by cobwebs—the same miner's tools she used to daydream about as a girl. But in the spare afternoon light, she could see their metal surfaces had been pockmarked by orange rust. Stepping forward, she heard a crunch. Rose startled at the broken skeleton in an old mousetrap beneath her boot, surrounded by a trail of droppings. The air around her suddenly felt cloying, as though the dust had seeped between the seams of her overalls and was burrowing into her pores. Fanning her face, she stepped outside and unlatched the bars of the steel panels to open the windows for more light. As she swung them wide, her mouth dropped open. All she could see, from the floor to the rafters, was junk.

Rose brought her hands to her cheeks, feeling the rush of panic. Her heart raced as she gazed at the cluttered room that looked like an abandoned museum. Digging into her overalls for the truck key, she was tempted to grab Crystal and drive— drive anywhere. But then a sick feeling entered her stomach: You've got no place else to go. Rose stared at the empty road that led out of town to more mountains—to more nowheres.

"Stop it!" she chastised herself, straightening her back. "It's just dirt—nothing to be afraid of." She paced in front of the old building. "Okay, so the place is a mess. But it's free! How can you beat that?" She paused and peered through the dirty window pane. "Everything you see can be fixed with a little elbow grease. You can do this—you can! You just have to be determined and give it a hundred and ten percent." Rose grasped her temples, shocked at how much she sounded like her half-sister. "My God," she muttered, "maybe Laurel's finally rubbing off on me."

"Rose?"

The soft, feminine voice from behind her nearly made her jump. She whipped around, expecting to see Laurel there, already checking up on her. But instead of Laurel's blonde, cropped hair and stern eyes, the woman before her had a tangle of shiny red curls that caressed her face like ribbons.

"Rose!" the woman squealed. "Oh my God, it's really you! I knew you were coming—I just knew it!"

The woman grabbed her for a hug, and Rose steadied herself as she realized it was her old girlfriend Amy. The hair was completely different—long red tresses instead of a pixie cut. But there was no mistaking the familiar freckles on her cheeks, or the overwhelming smell of jasmine and the jingle of the charm bracelet that she always wore to ward off bad omens.

"Amy?" Rose gasped after being released from her grip. She took a step back and studied her friend's willowy frame in a blue silk blouse scattered with stars. Shiny moons dangled from her earrings, and she wore a white lace prairie skirt over ruby cowboy boots. Rose blinked, wondering if Amy wanted to look like a cosmic cowgirl, or if she'd simply gotten dressed in the dark. She tucked her thumbs into her suspenders and smiled. "You look, um—amazing!" Rose giggled.

"Thanks!" Amy lifted her toes to show off the silver tips on her red cowboy boots. A gust of wind blew by and swelled her skirt, and for a moment Rose thought she might ascend to Oz. Then Amy grasped the belt buckle at her waist so that the murky gray stone at the center caught the sunlight. Sudden flashes of blue and green lit up from beneath the stone's surface, seeming to radiate from within.

"Labradorite," Amy said proudly. "Marvelous vibrations! It might look dull at first, but there's a lot going on underneath. Just like most people, really. They may seem kind of ordinary, but then you'll discover that they have the most remarkable past lives—"

"Past what?"

"Oh, sorry," Amy dug into her skirt pocket. "Here, let me give you my card."

Amy placed a stiff piece of paper into Rose's palm. At the top it read in large letters, *Eternity's Wings: Transmigration Therapy and Psychic Repair.*

Rose smirked, unsurprised by Amy's latest foray into metaphysics. As near as she could tell, Amy Tinker was the least psychic person on the planet. In high school, she'd tried out astrology on all her friends, only to get their forecasts confused and become dizzied by "so many stars." After graduation and a brief stint with Rose as a barmaid, she'd hitchhiked to the Southwest to join a New Age commune, with disastrous results. Although convinced she could read palms and auras and mix healing potions, her advice consistently tangled people's love lives or made their stocks crash, and her herbal remedies produced foul smells and rashes. Finally, Amy wrote a letter to Rose in Winnemucca when the commune kicked her out, claiming it was merely a patch of "bad karma." Rose could tell from the eager look in her eyes that Amy's confidence had remained undaunted.

"Well," Rose offered, "it's good to be home, right?"

"Sure—just like the old days!" Amy beamed. "Remember how you got me that job serving whiskey with you at the Magpie Saloon? You were always helping folks like me who were down on their luck. Oh, and then Jake came in and made you play blackjack? Who would have thought you two would run off and tie the knot?" She winked. "Guess night and day can't help following each other. Hey, is he inside the shop? Let me give him a hug—"

"Amy—"

"Better yet, I'll go to my cabin and grab you guys something to eat. You must be starving!"

"Amy," Rose clutched her friend's elbow before she could walk away. "Jake is," she paused, "well, we're not together anymore. What I mean is—"

Rose tried to say it, but the words snagged in her throat. It was the first time she had to explain to someone what had happened. Word had quickly spread to her neighbors in Winnemucca, and she'd simply enclosed an obituary in a card she mailed to Laurel. Shaking a little, Rose wrapped her arms around her waist and held herself tight.

"Jake's dead, Amy."

Amy's face went pale. She stared at the silver tips of her boots and curled a finger around a ringlet of hair, letting it fall and spring back into place. "I'm so sorry, Rose—"

"It's okay, really," Rose lied, putting on a brave front. "He was always, you know, headed in that direction." She shifted her boots in the dust. "I tried writing to you a few times, but my letters were always returned with no forwarding address. Guess we've both had our share of wandering, huh?"

Amy winced as Rose turned to grab a box from the back of the truck. "Here, let me help you," she insisted, her voice filled with apology. She hoisted a sack of potatoes in her arms and looked up eagerly at Rose.

Rose met her gaze with a kind smile. The two of them stepped inside the shop and looked over the shelves that had served as a general store for decades before the building became the gold-panning business. There were still remnants of local history everywhere: old tincture bottles and tobacco tins, burlap sacks and wooden barrels, even a couple of steamer trunks. Rose stepped around a weather-beaten saddle to her daughter who was swaying in the rocking chair. Crystal's quiet face looked like a porcelain doll's, her pink cheeks and yellow sweater the only bright spots in the otherwise gray room. For a moment, Rose watched the sunlight glint off her hair, her face peaceful but distracted, as though she were simply daydreaming. Rose kneeled down and looked into her eyes, their green color so liquid that sometimes she thought she could see herself, and she stroked her cheek.

"Is that Crystal?" Amy said excitedly, setting down the sack of potatoes.

Rose pursed her lips, preparing for Amy's reaction. This was the crucial moment—the dividing line when a friend either accepted her daughter's disabilities or got weeded out of Rose's life. Several acquaintances in Winnemucca had already fallen by the wayside: people who were too quick to look away, or worse, who hugged her and said "you must be devastated." Go to hell, Rose always wanted to reply, but she never did. Instead she simply left, and she knew she'd been leaving ever since.

Rose glanced at Amy, desperately hoping to keep her friendship and wondering how many more exits she could endure. She figured she might as well get it over with, so she took her daughter by the hand and gave her a gentle tug from the rocker. When Crystal stood up, her eyes immediately focused on the opposite wall like there was no one else in the room. Then she snapped her hand from her mother's grasp and began to twirl in place. Rose shrugged her shoulders. She was used to it.

"She always does that," Rose explained, "whenever she gets overstimulated. You know, when the lights are too bright, or there's too much noise, or she meets a stranger. The doctor said it's, um, typical. I mean, for children like her."

"Oh my," Amy stepped a little closer. She scanned the little girl up and down, her eyes growing wider.

A lump swelled in Rose's throat. Though she pretended not to care about people's reactions, it still hurt—hurt hard. A familiar knot twisted in her stomach, when she saw Amy's face break into a smile.

"She's so beautiful. Just like an angel. Oh Rose, you're so lucky."

Rose sighed in relief. Before she knew it, Amy had lifted her arms and was twirling in circles along with Crystal, lace prairie skirt skimming the tops of her red boots. Rather than recoil from her closeness, like she usually did with new people, Crystal simply began to hum. Her lips purred the same rhythmic note.

"Listen, she's chanting." Amy slowed herself to a stop. "I read once that whirling dervishes did things like that, way back in the thirteenth century. They had visions."

"Visions of what?" Rose stared at Crystal's eyes for some clue, but they seemed glassy.

"I don't know. Maybe of their ancestors, or of heaven. But I think it made them happy."

Rose felt the knot release at the idea that somehow, somewhere, in a place she couldn't see, Crystal might actually be content.

Amy gazed at the swivel patterns her boots had made in the dust. She was silent for a moment. "What happened to her, honey?"

The knot returned to Rose's stomach, twisting all the more from the genuine concern in Amy's voice—a rare commodity in her world.

"Jake happened."

Amy nodded, and Rose was grateful she didn't need to elaborate beyond a few phrases that included "overdose" and "pool"—Amy could do the math. Even back in their barmaid days, Amy was the one who'd warned her that men like Jake were comets. High flyers, born to live fast and expire. "A streak across the sky, that's all they are," Amy had said, convinced Rose was just having a fling. "But hell, why not grab good times by the tail when they come? Just know when to let go." At the time, Rose had dismissed Amy's words, given her sketchy track record with spiritual advice. Compared to the beer-bellied hunters and lumberjacks that usually stumbled into the Magpie Saloon, Jake's lanky grace and quick wit had seemed as fresh as a newly-minted coin. No one had expected Rose to lose her heart to him over a simple game of blackjack. But then, they had all underestimated Jake.

Rose ran her fingers through her hair and picked out some paper and crayons from inside a box. She set them carefully on the floor in front of Crystal, and waited. Although Crystal usually appeared intent on blocking out the world, certain repetitive motions always hooked her: the sway of a rocking chair, the spin of a top, or the endless circles she could create with her crayons. Crystal paused from her twirling, spellbound by the paper as if she could already see the loops and swirls she would draw. Rose dug into the crayon box for colors to go with the autumn season.

"So that's it." Rose allowed Crystal to remain on the floor to play. "A couple of months ago, Laurel sent a letter saying the Rainbow's End was up for grabs." She studied the miner's gadgets on the walls to collect ideas for her future, then squared her shoulders. "I've decided to run the gold-panning business again," she announced firmly. "I'll sell coffee and sandwiches for hunters and tourists, and the very best fairy cakes that money can buy. You know how crazy I get over cooking! The way I figure it, there's always a steady stream of people on the weekends, especially during game season. And the place is packed with campers in the summer." Rose chewed her lip for a moment, lifting her chin. "I'm going to make this work, Amy—I have to. And with any luck, it'll be bigger and better than my dad ever dreamed."

When Rose cautiously checked for Amy's reaction, she saw tears in her friend's eyes.

"The Blood Moon!" Amy brought her hands prayerfully together and her charm bracelet jingled. "I knew something like this was going to happen. That's how I realized you were coming back—the Blood Moon's full tonight."

"The what?"

"It's what brought us together again. Don't you see?" Amy gazed at the orange circles Crystal had drawn on a piece of paper and kneeled to trace one with her hand. "The Blood Moon of October stands for wholeness." Her finger completed the circle. "The ties that bind—things that change, yet somehow remain the same. Just like a reunion between old friends."

"But I thought it was for hunters. People who shoot things—"

"No, it's for seekers!" Amy insisted. "The Blood Moon lights the way home." She picked up one of Crystal's crayons and added silver rays beside her orange moon.

"Well, right now the only light that can help us comes from Idaho Power," Rose smiled. "C'mon, let's see if there's electricity." Scanning the room, she pointed to a stained-glass lamp on the counter. "See that cord? Give it a tug—but be gentle."

Amy stepped around a wagon wheel to the lamp, and Rose closed her eyes, bracing herself for the worst.

"Rose," Amy beckoned.

All at once, Rose heard the sound of clapping. She opened her eyes, only to see Crystal's plump hands coming together over the beautiful red and blue colors illuminated by the lamp shade. Tears welled against her lashes.

"See!" Amy blew dust off the shade. "It's a sign! Bright things are coming around the bend. After you clean this place up, I bet it'll be a success in no time. All you gotta do is have faith."

Rose headed to Amy and gave her a big hug, swaying her in her arms. "Thank you," she whispered, clutching her tightly, "for being a true friend." She let her head fall onto Amy's shoulder. For the first time in ages, she felt safe. The sensation was so foreign to Rose that it made her tremble. When the tears slipped down her cheeks, she feared they might dissolve her entirely.

"It's okay," Amy stroked her hair. "You made it, honey. You finally made it home."

3

S taring at the tiny flames in the cast iron stove, Rose stuffed another wad of newspaper in the back and held her breath. She'd found some old logs stacked in a corner of the apartment, and she prayed they'd be dry enough to warm her and Crystal through the night. A warm glow spread inside the belly of the old Foster, and Rose exhaled in relief. Heat, electricity, running water—what more could anyone ask for? Just like Amy said, she smiled, all you need is a bit of faith.

Rose walked over to the kitchen to slide a wet rag over the counter, just a few steps away from the wood stove and an enormous four-poster bed. Sighing, she gazed at the small living space. The apartment had seemed so much bigger when she was a girl. At least it's easy to clean, she mused, setting the rag down to pick up a bowl from the counter. Her daughter had only eaten half of the mashed potatoes she'd prepared for dinner, but Rose could hardly blame her. They were from an

old box of freeze-dried flakes that she'd dragged with her from
Winnemucca. Laurel had sent another coupon as an excuse to
brag that Tom had been promoted to manager of a
dehydration plant. Her letter never bothered to ask about
Crystal or Rose. Instead, she raved over the machines that
could absorb every drop of moisture so the potatoes would
keep for a thousand years. Is that a good thing? Rose had
wondered at the time. But right now, they'd been fast and easy
—and at least they had some nutritional value. She stared at
the faded corners of the box and cringed. Well, maybe.

Placing Crystal's bowl in the sink, Rose glanced through
the window at the Magpie Saloon, and shivers skittered down
her back. The sign with the cocky black and white bird hung
crooked now, its chains glinting in the moonlight, but the
clapboard building was still broad and white, too close, even
though it was boarded up. She ran her damp fingers over her
forehead and recalled the night she met Jake—collided with
him, really. Cigar smoke, dueling fiddles, the smell of beer and
Jim Beam—it should have been an ordinary Friday night.
Except Jake was a newcomer in town, playing poker for
anything he could carry: cash, cowboy hats, even hunting
rifles. He seemed to be on a lucky streak, with a Winchester
beneath his chair and a Stetson on his table. Rose had seen
him sitting alone, counting his winnings after another game,
and she figured he was trouble. But she couldn't help noticing
his flaxen hair and vibrant blue eyes on her way to pick up
drinks at the carved mahogany bar. He leaned back in his
chair and unfolded his limbs with the ease of a cat, his long
legs stretching into scuffed cowboy boots. Despite her better
judgment, Jake's sinewy good looks unnerved her, and she was

so intent on avoiding eye contact as she weaved around tables that she accidentally bumped into a chair, dropping her tray. Glasses crashed, sending shards sparkling across the floor.

"There goes her tips," laughed a lumberjack.

"Yep, probably her job," his buddy nodded. "Hey twinkle-toes," he held up his glass, "think you can refill my beer without breaking anything?"

Beads of sweat ran down Rose's temples. It was the second time that week she'd dropped glasses—and had her paycheck cut. She scurried frantically to clean the mess, hoping the bar owner didn't see. As she stooped to pick up the shards, she slipped on a puddle of beer, her legs buckling beneath her. To her surprise, Jake caught her by the waist. He held her close, and the scent of suede, sweat, and a pinch of sage enveloped her like incense. His aroma reminded her of Amy's ceremonial smudge sticks: traces of earth and smoke, mingled with subtle mysteries. Flustered, Rose grabbed her tray and pretended to take his order, too busy calculating her lost wages to really listen. Then she felt something cold and hard press into her palm.

"Don't worry, darling, you haven't lost anything." In Jake's eyes was an apology—the first she'd ever witnessed at the Magpie Saloon. After five years of mopping up late-night whiskey and cigarette butts, Rose thought she might melt. She looked down at her palm and saw a gold coin.

"Do you know where that comes from?" He sat in his chair, pulling her to the one beside him.

Rose shrugged, picturing pawn shops, poker games, maybe a fight.

"A crash, just like we had." Jake smiled slightly and ran his hand through his hair. "They say millions of years ago the stars collided. Their explosions were so powerful they sent precious metals throughout the galaxy. That gold piece in your hand—think of it as a calling card, from before time."

"What are you, an astronomer?" Rose smirked.

"No, just a card player. Helps if you know what you're gambling for."

Rose glanced at the five-dollar gold piece in her hand, dated 1863. She ran her finger over its surface, tracing the shiny eagle's outstretched wings. Once upon a time, her great-great grandmother would have claimed an image like that meant new love. Her heart fluttered a little. She shook off the feeling and handed him the coin.

"Take it—it's yours," Jake curled her fingers over the gold. "As long as you play blackjack with me."

"Oh no you don't!" Amy announced from across the bar. She tossed Rose an extra towel for the beer puddle. "Rose doesn't play anymore. Especially with drinks around."

Everyone in the bar laughed. The saloon's rules were no secret in the county. Word had gotten out about the pretty Ophir Creek barmaid who could look into a glass of liquid— any liquid, from a cup of coffee to a shot of whiskey—and ferret out people's cards. At first it had been a cute trick, something she did to keep customers amused. Until one night, Rose helped her old friend George, who'd been laid off at the lumber mill, rake in hundreds of dollars from unsuspecting hunters. Larry, the bar owner, was already mad at her for sneaking free food to him, so he drew the line. "If you do that again, you'll never see another paycheck in these mountains," he hissed, his hand gripping her shoulder until she winced.

Rose pulled away, but she knew all too well that jobs were tight in the county—and it was the last time she'd rolled up her sleeves to play with the boys.

"That whole story, it was just a coincidence," Rose insisted, keeping her eye steadfast on Larry. "Sometimes I peek into shot glasses and see pictures, that's all. Then I take a wild guess at what they mean. I can't see fortunes. People exaggerate."

"Don't let her fool you!" Amy called out between filling drinks. She smiled proudly. "Sure, Rose acts casual, but her ideas are always right. She's a bonafide psychic."

Rose cringed at the word, given her family's past, threaded with sorrow. After all, her great-great grandmother's life had always been marked by tragedy. What good were such talents when they only brought pain? "It's really a matter of chance," she emphasized. "Pure luck."

Jake eased his chair from the card table and patted his lap. "Then be my luck, sweetheart. C'mon, just one round."

Rose shook her head, setting the gold coin on the table with a clink. Jake had already won a new rifle and a cowboy hat—to help him any more now would be downright cruel to the regulars. She gazed at his cowlicked blonde hair, bright as the inlaid gold nugget on the mahogany bar counter. But what really struck her were his eyes—so blue and animated they were almost electric. Suddenly, without warning, she saw pictures floating there as if on a screen: shooting stars, swirled galaxies, a vast cosmos, full of glinting lights like a casino—a million light years from the Magpie Saloon. Paradise, as far as Rose was concerned. Jake shuffled the deck and paused, as though sensing what had passed between them. He locked his eyes on hers and dealt each of them two cards.

"Don't look at the cards, honey. Look at me," he whispered. "Make your best bet—who wins?" He touched her hand and Rose felt her cheeks flush.

"I really c-can't," she said, glancing back at the bar to see if Larry was watching.

"I'll tell you who wins." Jake covered her hand with his palm, skin warm but rough as granite. Then he wrapped his fingers in hers and flipped over her cards. Facing up on the felt card table she saw all red—the ace and queen of hearts. "You do."

"That's a card trick," Rose laughed uncertainly. "You've done that hundreds of times, right?"

Jake shook his head. He turned over his own cards—an eight of clubs and a ten of spades. "See, I told you. You're a winner." Despite her protests, he moved a stack of bills toward her.

"Still don't believe? Okay, this time no cards." To Rose's astonishment, Jake brushed the cards off the table. They pattered to the floor like rain. He leaned forward and stared at her, his eyes deep pools. "Tell me what you see."

Rose hesitated, picking up the gold coin on the table and rubbing it between her fingers. She knew better than to try and read anything for herself, to invest emotion in those ridiculous superstitions that only got her into trouble, even if it was just a game. Besides, all she'd ever done before was speculate on cards, not on personal impressions. But she couldn't help it this time—she glanced up.

It was then Rose felt an electric current pump through her. Sharp tingles charged up and down her spine, feathering out to her fingertips and giving her goose bumps everywhere. Yet she had a strange sensation of falling, tumbling end over end, plunging into deep space. Disoriented, she blinked and returned her gaze to Jake. His eyes were still, like the center of the universe, waiting on a power she couldn't name. The more she searched, the more those heavenly bodies she'd seen earlier raced toward her at lightning speed. Rose became dizzy, her entire being feeling caught in the gravitational pull of a massive star. Suddenly, a burst of light dazzled her vision with a white-hot glow. The Magpie Saloon disappeared—every cigarette butt and broken whiskey glass she'd ever wanted to leave behind vanished. Rose closed her eyes, trembling. All she could feel was Jake's breath in the hollow of her ear.

"Come away with me, honey," he whispered. "Together, we'll strike gold."

Rose turned from the kitchen window and folded her arms, feeling a chill. "I never did strike gold with you," she confessed, shaking her head as if Jake could still hear, "only fool's gold." Even the antique five-dollar coin he'd given her had been pawned ages ago, the first time their electricity had been cut off. Rose darted her eyes from the shadows in the kitchen, afraid his ghost might be lurking, and she turned on an extra overhead light for comfort. Beneath the bare bulb, her fingers shook as she fished in her pocket for a weathered envelope. Pulling it out, she gazed at the green bills inside, checking each one to make sure there weren't any distinguishing marks.

Five thousand dollars.

Rose had no idea who owed Jake before he died—who

stuffed who into the trunk of a car or was held up at gunpoint, all for a white powder that was probably laced with Comet. She was used to seeing cuts and bruises on Jake when he came home, used to not asking any questions, especially toward the end when they hardly spoke. But after he finally overdosed in Winnemucca, the envelope had been dropped through the apartment mail slot, which she'd discovered following her release from the hospital.

Rose had never told a soul about it. Blood money, she figured, or maybe it was a mistake—a strange, cosmic payback for all the grief she'd suffered. She tucked the bills back into the envelope and slipped it safely inside a dresser drawer. Wherever the money came from, it was hers now, and she was going use it to open up the Rainbow's End. She'd offered for Amy to be her business partner, to set up the shop with a cafe and teach people to pan for gold. They could share profits, Rose said, just like they used to split tips at the Magpie Saloon. Amy was thrilled over the idea, and as far as Rose was concerned, the five grand was their seed money for a new start. Besides, she thought, it was high time Jake paid something back.

Rose rubbed her eyes, rubbed away memories. Time to move forward with my life, she affirmed, keeping her back to the kitchen window. She stepped around the large bed to check on Crystal. Earlier, she'd set down sheets of paper she'd gotten from a therapist in Nevada with geometric designs for Crystal to color. They were supposed to trigger comprehension of shape and order in brain-damaged children, train neurosynapses to connect normally once again. But ever since the accident, Crystal rarely colored inside the lines. So each night before bed, Rose made a little ritual out of taking her by the hand and helping her, all the while affirming "triangle, rectangle, square." When Rose peeked at her daughter beside the bed, instead of coloring, she found Crystal sitting cross-legged on the floor, her fingers gathering little mounds of dust into piles. Her yellow sweater and green cords were smeared with dirt, and the white lace tops of her socks were black.

"Good grief—you're filthy!" Rose picked Crystal up and brushed her off, reaching for a wet rag by the sink to wipe her face. "C'mon sweetie, let's get you out of those clothes." As she headed for their duffle bag, she stepped on top of one of the dust piles. Crystal whimpered.

"I'm sorry. We'll play with more dirt tomorrow, okay?" Rose rolled her eyes. "There's plenty where that came from." She lifted the sweater over her daughter's head and slipped off her pants and socks, then reached into the duffle bag for a pair of pink pajamas with plastic feet. "It's time for bunnies—your favorite," she said cheerfully, referring to the rabbit pattern on the material. "No need to be afraid of a new place with these on, right? Bunny snuggles."

Rose stroked the cottontails and touched the soft fabric to her cheek, then to Crystal's, as much to reassure herself as her daughter. Crystal glanced aside, searching for her lost dust piles. She held up her arms.

Rose stopped breathing. She blinked several times, unsure whether to believe her eyes. Her heart skipped a beat—she dropped the pajamas to catch her breath.

"Good girl!" she cried, voice shaking. "Oh, good girl!" She pressed her hands to her heart, amazed her daughter had remembered to lift her arms for the pajama routine, even in a different setting. She hadn't done that since the accident. Rose wrapped her arms around her and gave her a big squeeze. "We're gonna put a bright gold star on your progress chart, the shiniest one ever. I promise," she whispered, gently rocking her. She glanced at the duffle bag, "As soon as we find it. Those doctors were wrong, weren't they? Just like we thought —big old dummies." She brushed the hair back from Crystal's eyes and gazed into their limpid green. "You knew that all along, huh? I bet you're going to surprise everybody. My miracle girl."

Rose closed her eyes. She dared to imagine her daughter laughing in the sun on a swing set, or sitting at school, learning to add two plus two. Wiping the dampness from her lashes, she gave Crystal another hug. Tenderly, she wriggled the pajamas onto her daughter's legs and arms, then zipped her up and lifted her onto the bed.

"Tonight we're going to sleep in something really special," Rose promised. She unlatched an old trunk and pulled out a large bundle covered with muslin and sprigs of sage. "See this old quilt?" She unfolded the crazy quilt and shook it out, spreading it across Crystal on the sheets. "Your great-great grandma made it—the one with all the ravens. That means it's an heirloom, a gift passed down for a really long time." Brushing off the sage leaves, she carefully tucked the edges of the quilt around her daughter's face. "It's extra cozy and warm, just for you."

Rose stared at the uneven hand stitching on the quilt patches. They zigzagged wildly in all directions through pieces of flannel, calico, even burlap. Some of the patches were clouds and lightning bolts, while others were forest animals—

birds and bears, sewn onto the fabric like strange totems. Rose wondered for a moment if Corvine O'Dannan had lost her mind, like some folks claimed when they recited her family's legend. "Of course not, she was just creative," she mumbled defensively, before she realized it. She glanced at Crystal, a little embarrassed. "Right honey? Our family's a bit different, that's all."

She leaned on the thick quilt and curled a lock of her daughter's hair around her finger, relishing its downy strands. "Different can be good sometimes, you know? It makes us unique." Rose fluffed up a pillow and gently set it under Crystal's head, kissing her soft bangs. "Goodnight, honey. Have a good sleeeep," she enunciated, voice slow and precise. "I love yooou."

She paused, waiting expectantly for words that didn't come. Rose searched her daughter's face for a hint, a glimmer of the girl who used to say "I love you, too, Mommy," even if it might be coded in her blinks. Since Crystal had remembered the pajama routine, anything was possible, right? She traced the iridescent stones on her daughter's play bracelet, then watched for an interminable minute as Crystal's eyes fell closed, resting into the evening silence.

Rose bit her lip and gazed at the old quilt. Running her fingers over the asymmetrical patches, she wished she could find a pattern, some sort of order that might make sense of the chaos of her life. No matter how hard she tried, the quilt patches always seemed random. She sighed and bent down to open her purse on the floor. Pulling out a color photo of Crystal with a thumbtack at the top, she pressed it hard into a wood post on the bed and adjusted the picture.

"Good night, darling," she blew a kiss at her two-dimensional daughter. Rose always felt a twinge of guilt when she did that, but she couldn't help it. The photo renewed her hope each morning when she woke up and saw Crystal's face, still perfect before the accident, as if everything else had been a bad dream. Sometimes she talked to the photo, made little confessions to the sparkling eyes that lit up on that day at Sears when the photographer held up a Snickers bar and snapped the picture. Crystal had just turned four then—it was on her birthday six months ago, and she was wearing her favorite red shirt, the one with the pony appliqué at the center. Rose recalled how her daughter had demanded fairy cakes for breakfast that morning. When her mother had been too slow drying her hair, Crystal had gone into the kitchen and stuffed broken eggs, flour and jelly beans into a bowl, returning to show her mother the mess she'd made with a big grin on her face. "Hurry up, Mommy," she demanded impatiently, "I don't have all day!"

Rose had burst out laughing. That was her real daughter: confident, bold, even sassy. She was the one hiding deep down inside, somewhere out of reach. Not this vacant toddler who'd taken her place, as if Crystal had been stolen by fairies and replaced with a changeling. Rose caressed her daughter's cheek, felt the tender, satiny warmth of her skin. Then she patted Crystal's chest, wondering if it was possible to feel her soul. "You're in there somewhere, baby. I just know it." She snuggled beside her, absorbing the heat of her body, the rise and fall of her breath. "Okay, kiddo, tonight we were lazy bones," she admitted more to herself than to her sleeping daughter. "But tomorrow it's a bath first thing. Then back to our schedule. Calisthenics, flashcards, and we can't forget our ABC's."

She sat up on the bed and studied Crystal's face. Though her daughter's eyes were lost to sleep, Rose refused to be daunted. A therapist had drilled into her that structure and persistence were essential for progress. You have to be patient, focus on movement, patterns, associations—things that helped realign circuits in the brain. Sometimes, even when Crystal was napping, Rose would sing her nursery rhymes or commercial jingles. Forget the odds, she decided. She was determined to be like those people who talk to their comatose relatives in the hospital, who hold entire conversations and holiday parties, regardless of the reaction. Someday, somehow, the person might wake up and remember everything that was ever said. And then they'd be eternally grateful, right?

"You've got a bright future ahead of you," Rose promised her daughter, keeping her voice low to let Crystal sleep. She looked around the apartment. "Once we clean this place up, anyway." She unlatched her overalls and kicked off her hiking boots, then crawled beneath the sheets. Taking one last glance at the photo on the bedpost, she turned to Crystal.

"Sleep tight, honey." She kissed her gently on the forehead. Pulling the cord on the bedside lamp, she sank her head into the pillow. "May the fairies sprinkle stardust on your dreams."

The scratching noise on the window sounded like nails on a chalkboard. It's probably from branches waving in the wind, Rose thought as she buried her head under her pillow. She'd forgotten how the forest came alive at night—how every creature that could yip, hoot or howl joined together for a midnight jamboree, especially when the moon was full. But what really irritated her was the insistent tapping, and after that, raspy caws.

"Dammit," she sat up in bed. She gazed at the window just in time to see a dark bird skitter away, wings flapping. Rose grasped her head, holding back a moan so as not to wake Crystal. Her sleep had been turmoil. In spite of her prayer for nocturnal blessings, she'd had the nightmare again.

It was the same dream each time, ever since Jake had died. She was driving across a desert, but she never reached the other side. A dust storm enveloped her, and before she knew it, her truck fell down a crevice into a dark hole. All she could hear was the screech of metal and her daughter's screams. She reached out desperately for Crystal, but her daughter had become slippery, like a trout out of water, her mouth gaping and her rainbow bands fading to gray. When the truck finally stopped, everything went black.

Then a lantern was lit, and within its glow Rose saw Jake —he was seated with her again in the Magpie Saloon. Only he'd changed: he was wearing miner's clothes with a red bandana around his neck, like a prospector from another century. Instead of poker chips, he measured out small piles of gold dust on scales to wager. He was still strikingly handsome, his eyes like fresh denim, his hair the color of sunlit honeycomb. Every cell in her body wanted to touch him, to taste him, to feel his skin and lose herself again in that golden confidence. Then Jake dealt them both cards and emptied an entire pouch of gold onto the scale. "How much to start over again?" he pleaded, eyes full of apology. "I miss you so much, Rose. We need each other—admit it. Just give me one more chance. Promise me." He held out his hand as if for alms. Rose always averted her gaze, but then she placed a trembling finger on his pulse—gambling again on that old electric surge between them. When she glanced down, she discovered her hand lay upon bleached bones. Screaming, she knocked over the scales. Gold dust fell all around her, changing in air to ashen powder.

Rose hugged her knees and leaned her face into the quilt. It was always a shock to see Jake again, even in a dream. She'd torn up pictures of him months ago, convinced she could forget what he looked like. She knew she shouldn't have glanced out the window at the saloon before bed. She was too tired, too fragile—a shot of brandy would have been smarter. Suddenly, Rose felt cold and empty and alone, and she wondered if this was why some people popped Prozac.

The light of the Blood Moon streamed through the window, striking a patch of red corduroy on the quilt like a stain. Rose unfolded her legs and glanced at her daughter's side of the big bed. The sheets were knotted and twisted like a wild animal had been writhing. Heart racing, she patted a wide lump in the quilt, shocked by its emptiness. Crystal was nowhere in sight. Panicked, she threw off the covers, hoping her daughter had simply gone to the bathroom. As she hopped out of bed, she noticed the walls. Wild crayon marks covered the wallpaper, zigzagging into lightning bolts—spirals—wings? Bewildered, Rose stumbled toward the bathroom and threw on the light—no Crystal. She rushed back and fell to her knees to peek under the bed. Nothing. Lifting the lid of a trunk, she saw only a pile of wool blankets. Desperate, she bolted to the kitchen to open the cupboards beneath the sink. "Crystal!" She peered into dark shelves that merely echoed her voice. Rose dashed back toward the bed, struggling to put on her overalls and hiking boots that she'd left on the floor. Then she ran into the shop and turned on the lights. "Crystal?" Scanning the room, everything looked precisely the same to her as it had several hours ago, except the front door was ajar.

"No, not my girl!" Rose recalled the horror of Winnemucca. She was certain she had locked the front door at nightfall. Perhaps the lock was broken, or her key had fallen to the floor and Crystal found it. "This can't be happening!" Rose grabbed a lantern beside the door. Fumbling to flip the knob, she heard the familiar kerosene hiss. Quickly, she reached into her father's old cigar box on the counter, grateful to find a match. She managed to ignite the lantern flame and darted out into the town square.

The full moon was so bright it cast a lattice of tree shadows on the edges of town, washing the buildings in shades of chalk and charcoal. Rose rubbed her eyes, feeling like she'd just stepped into an old tintype photo. She wanted to cry out for Amy, for angels, for anyone to help her, but her throat was too constricted by fear. It's because you moved her too soon! Rose berated herself. Crystal's scared—she doesn't know where she is yet. "Crystal!" she struggled to shout, unnerved by her own echo in the dark. A raven swooped down beside her, its black feathers glistening in the lantern's glow. Rose bristled at the bird's arrival, but next to its claws she noticed small depressions in the dirt—little footprints heading away from town.

"Get away from me!" She brushed aside the bird, dipping her lantern low to examine the soil. Fortunately, there'd been a brief shower that night, setting off any new tracks. With slow and steady steps, Rose carefully followed the footprints, the same size as her daughter's, as they paralleled the Magpie Saloon. Then the tracks veered, aligning with the path of the moon through a corridor of pines. Rose stopped, recognizing the trail—it headed up a rise to Rook Ridge. Heart drumming, she struggled to climb the hillside, her lungs swelling against her chest, unaccustomed to the high altitude after years in the desert. The October air was so cold and crisp that she felt exposed, as if there were nothing between her and the wide canopy of stars, no oxygen or atmosphere—she had only to reach up her hand to lose herself and everything she loved in deep space.

"Where are you, Crystal?" she called, disturbed by the long reach of shadows, the silver glints every time she rustled a branch. Gulping breaths, she pursued footprints past sage and buckbrush that whipped her legs. The tracks became so faint she had to drop to her hands and knees, eyes inches from the dirt, and crawl until the footprints became clear. Rose listened for any hint of her daughter's voice—a tiny cry or muffled sound, even a whimper. Only the wind whispered through quivering aspen leaves.

Ahead, Rose spotted trees charred from lightning strikes at the top of a hill—the silent spires of Rook Ridge. Tall granite rocks stood in a loose ring nearby, ancient monoliths cast by glacier rubble, as commanding as pictures she'd seen in grade school of Stonehenge. Rose observed the footprints had begun to fold back on themselves. Confused, she glanced behind one of the dappled rocks, wondering if her daughter had tucked herself behind it, chilled by the night air, or curled against a crevice to sleep. In the lantern's glow, she spied scars on the granite's surface, perhaps carved by elk antlers or a shoot-out long ago. A shadow caught the corner of her eye. Something passed between the stones.

"Crystal? Crystal, honey—IT'S MOMMY!"

A man in a long, black coat stepped from behind a rock, his towering height nearly matching the stone pillars. Panicked, Rose ducked behind a rock, watching as he began to walk in the same spirals as her daughter's footprints, steady as a metronome. In the moonlight, his long, dark hair tumbled past his shoulders and his beard skimmed his coat's lapel. He muttered repeatedly, appearing lost in prayer, yet his strides were measured and purposeful. While he chanted, the wind began to pick up, seemingly energized by his gait. Thunder rolled in the distance, and for the life of her, Rose thought she heard a deep groan coming from the earth itself, eerily matching the cadence of the man's steps. She shook her head, feeling like she'd somehow stumbled upon the soul of the forest, with this strange man as its conduit. Then he stopped and pointed past the tall rocks. He held up his fingers. Rose heard a raven's caw.

"One for sorrow, two for joy." His words were deep and resonant like river water over rocks.

Another raven sounded.

"Three for a girl."

Is he some kind of Druid? Rose wondered, studying the

circle of stones reflected under a full moon. Maybe he's doing a ritual, the kind my mother used to perform here on nights she believed were sacred. With that thought, a moist wind swirled around her, creaking the tops of branchless pines like old bones. The wind began to play curious tones through hollowed trees, making an enchanted type of music. Goose bumps alighted on Rose's skin, as if the notes were dancing up and down her arms. At the same time the air felt thicker, electric and alive with presence. Rose leaned against the stone, wondering if she'd stepped into a dream. Who is this man, anyway? And why did Crystal's footprints stop? Does he know where she is—could he have taken her somewhere? Spotting a large hunk of quartz on the ground, she set down her lantern to pick it up, clutching the rock as a ready weapon. When she stepped forward, a twig snapped. The man turned from his circle and stared at her, nodding as though he knew her.

Bravely, Rose fingered the cold edges of the rock. "Have you seen my daughter?" she demanded.

The man gazed up at the sky. Above him, Rose thought she saw colors, flickering in a wide circle like butterflies. She squinted, but they disappeared.

"Don't you hear me?" She raised the big rock over her shoulder to show she meant business. "I swear to God, I'll let you have it if you don't tell me where—"

Rose was about to complete her threat when the man walked off into the trees with lanky strides. She raced after him, keeping the rock firm in her grip. He was hard to follow, his black coat vanishing into shadows or blending with dark tree trunks. He quickened his powerful stride—Rose had to drop her rock and run to keep up. Buckbrush and pine needles whipped against her face, and she started to cry, an overwhelming sense of loss coursing through her veins. *I can't survive this*, she thought—*not again, not my baby!* Suddenly, she spotted the man as he descended down a gully toward a stream. Rose stumbled after him and fell, cheekbone meeting hard against the forest floor. Grabbing fistfuls of dirt, she tried to look up, too stunned for a moment to get her bearings. The man grasped her elbow and easily lifted her to her feet. Rose scrambled to step back, cursing as she yanked away her arm. She clenched her fingers, ready to strike.

"My daughter!" She took a swing.

The man leaned back and let her fist slice through air. When she swung again, he held her arms firmly to her sides with his large hands and stared her square in the face. Astounded, Rose peered through his knotted locks—she recognized that look. The dark, imploring eyes, able to steal a glimpse into her soul, the long scar across his nose that dipped into sharp cheekbones. Shuddering, she wondered if she was hallucinating again, like that day in the pool in Winnemucca. *He can't possibly be the same man—the same angel—*she thought, bewildered. *This must be some sort of flashback.* She scanned his dark hair that was long and matted now, his chin overflowing with a tangled beard. But there was no mistaking his eyes—deep, mahogany pools so tender and dignified that even in the moonlight they pierced her heart. Although he appeared scruffy, she could tell from his unlined skin that he was rather young, hardly much older than herself. In that instant, the man tilted his head and gazed at her with a bittersweet expression that surprised Rose, as though he'd waited throughout all time for this moment, and now he was grateful his wish had finally been granted.

Unexpectedly, a warm feeling suffuses her being, the way she often felt as a child when she snuggled beneath her great-great grandmother's quilt. Her breathing slowed and her heart throbbed to a more natural rhythm. Rose couldn't understand it, but in this stranger's arms, underneath the delicate canopy of stars, she suddenly sensed deep inside that Crystal was safe —that they were both protected and safe—and everything was going to be all right. Hesitantly, she allowed the muscles in her shoulders to release a little. The man let her go and pointed his long arm toward the mountain stream.

"Moonchild." His voice rippled in a low echo that made her tremble to her bones.

Rose turned. There was Crystal, sitting beside the water, her hair tousled white in the moonlight. Her daughter dug her hands into the stream bank and stared at the mud in her palms, watching the way mica flecks reflected the moon like fairy glitter. She threw up her fingers and let the mud hit the water with a splash, laughing at the sparkling magic.

"O-Oh my God!" Rose dashed over to Crystal. She scooped her up and squeezed so hard that for a second she thought their hearts might merge.

"You all right, honey?" She rocked her in her arms. "You okay, baby?"

A hundred kisses—Crystal's forehead, nose, and cheeks— left Rose hungry for more. She pressed her face against her daughter's, wishing she could swallow her whole and keep her safe inside forever. Uncontrollable sobs emptied from her chest, both from a gratitude and a grief that felt bottomless.

Body trembling, Rose stroked her daughter's forehead and brushed the hair from her eyes. "Don't you ever leave again," she scolded. "Do you hear that, baby? Don't you ever leave Mommy."

Crystal ignored her and stubbornly reached out her fingers toward the stream, wanting more glitter. Gazing at the moon's shiny reflection on the water, Rose studied the murmuring eddies and whirlpools, trying to discern what fascinated her daughter. All at once, she noticed the strange man's silhouette swaying in the ripples. For an instant, she thought she saw his dark image slip beneath the surface, then rise up again as a ring of colors shimmering on the water like the northern lights. She shook her head, assuming it was fallout from stress. But when she turned around to thank the man for finding Crystal, he was gone.

It was then Rose heard a voice trail a gust of wind, so low and resonant she could have sworn it rumbled the very stones.

I have loved you for longer than I have known my own breath.

❧ 4 ❧

Harness bells jingled as the front door slammed.

"Geez, you startled me!" Rose clutched her chest, glancing up from a bowl of batter she'd been stirring. There was Amy, standing inside the shop with a wide grin on her face, her floral-tapestry coat splattered by purple stains. "How'd you get in here?"

Amy held up a brass key. "You gave this to me, remember? When Dan came to fix the lock." She stuffed it into her jacket. "Why so jittery?"

"Oh, nothing," Rose lied, still concerned that Crystal could find a way to unlock the door, like she did on the night that she slipped away to the ridge. Sudden intrusions to the shop particularly unnerved her, but she'd been too baffled by the whole incident to tell Amy. Yet every time she allowed her thoughts to wander back to that mysterious man who'd found Crystal, she wondered if she'd imagined the whole thing.

"Well, you'd better lighten up!" Amy teased. "Deer season

starts today, and all those hunters who've been up since dawn are going to want coffee by the time we open. Luckily for us, there isn't another store for miles." She high-fived Rose and set her basket on the counter. "Look what I got—huckleberries! We can make pancakes. Customers will devour them like bears. Gotta fatten up before winter, you know."

"No, *fairy cakes*," Rose gently patted her bowl. With a tilt of her head, she studied Amy's basket the way an artist appraises a new canvas. "They're a lot like muffins, only we'll add huckleberries and pine nuts," she took a swift lick of batter, "and maybe a hint of wild geranium root. That way customers can take them to go."

Tracing her hand along her great-great grandmother's diary that she'd propped open on the counter, Rose felt tingles of excitement dance up her arm. She couldn't explain it, but ever since she'd returned from the ridge, she felt different somehow—more creative and energetic than she had in years—and she wondered if this was what her mother used to mean by "fairy struck." Folks in town had always laughed at the silly miner's wife who climbed the ridge every spring and fall, returning with a radiant smile and baskets of flowers or herbs, rambling on about "fairy power". But no one ever snickered when she offered them a serviceberry scone or her wild onion-elk chili. Her mother's cooking was legendary in Ophir Creek, and the smell of her recipes brought out more than a few reclusive neighbors and rangy coyotes. Rose smiled wistfully, hoping her efforts might do the same miracle for her shop—if only she could keep thoughts of that dark stranger from her mind. Quickly, she rinsed off Amy's berries and swirled them into her bowl, then ladled the batter into muffin tins and popped them in the oven.

"So!" Rose stepped from behind the counter. "What do you think?"

She gestured at the sparkling clean shop with pride. After Amy had left last night, Rose had stayed up well past midnight scrubbing, stacking, and rearranging, until everything was perfect for their big opening day. Like a whirlwind, the two women had already spent a fortnight clearing out the place and taking truckloads of trash to the county dump. All the while, Rose had a devil of a time keeping Amy's flighty energy on task. With every hat box or pickle crock she cracked open, Amy squealed and fluttered her hands, exclaiming over the "powerful vibes." Rose rolled her eyes and listened patiently to each past-life revelation, grateful for the company. But in the process, she'd discovered an entire treasure trove of collectibles, just waiting for artful display. Now, everywhere she looked there was color and twinkle—blue tincture bottles filled with rose water and sage oil, floral teacups atop handmade lace, vintage fabrics and spools of ribbon, even shiny spurs. Most of the items would only appeal to tourists and leafpeepers out for a day trip in gold country, intrigued by an old ghost town. But the glass case beneath the butcher block counter was filled with delectable tarts and hearty sandwiches that would tempt even the most stoic hunter.

"Oh my stars, I can't believe you finished all this last night!" Amy threw her arm around Rose for a squeeze. "Did you get any sleep?" She glanced at the last of the blue chicory blossoms that Rose had placed in a delicate vase by the window. Then she gazed at the tulle bows that Rose had fashioned into butterfly accents and the sparkly lights that she'd woven through shelves to add a touch of whimsy. "Oh honey, it looks just like a Wonderland in here now. All you need is a pair of wings."

Rose felt the tingles chase up her arms again. She hadn't consciously intended to create that kind of atmosphere, given the family legend and her mother's reputation in Ophir Creek. But even she had to admit the décor bordered on ethereal.

"Well don't forget," she pointed at the shovels and pans on a wall, "we're still a gold-panning business. And miners are very superstitious about October—they think it brings them luck. So I put Crystal to work on Halloween crafts after breakfast."

She nodded at her daughter sitting on the floor beside the front window, methodically dipping a potato stamp into a paint pot and plopping it onto orange paper. Rose stepped over and sweetly stroked Crystal's hair, then leaned toward Amy. "Halloween used to be her favorite holiday," she whispered. "I mean, before the accident. I was hoping fairy cakes and crafts might bring her out of her shell."

Rose omitted the fact that her daughter had refused to look at the therapist's flashcards ever since they'd come back from the ridge. It was as though that night had changed Crystal as well—making her more stubborn and headstrong than ever. She glanced at her daughter's progress chart on the wall. There was only one gold star.

Amy's eyes twinkled at the sight of Crystal's colorful stamps, and she hoisted up her prairie skirt and sat cross-legged beside her, staring at the clever bats and scaredy cats that Rose had carved from simple potatoes. "These are amazing." She dipped one into a paint pot and pressing it onto paper. "See honey?" she smiled at Crystal. "I've made a bat. Eee-eee!" She wiggled the potato in pretend flight.

"I'm so glad you're decorating for the season." Amy's charm bracelet tinkled as she picked up another stamp. "It'll bring us good fortune for Samhain."

"Saw-what?" Rose returned to the counter to brew a pot of coffee.

"Samhain—that's the ancient Celtic term for Halloween. It's the mystical hinge of time from the old year to the new, when the veil is thinnest between worlds. At midnight, the gate to the Underworld swings open, and you can contact the departed."

Rose felt a chill, and she opened the oven door to peek inside, relishing the warmth that enveloped her cheeks. "W-What if you don't want contact?" She tried to dismiss thoughts of Jake.

"It doesn't matter. The spirits come by whether we like it or not." Amy dipped a ghost stamp into white paint and pressed it onto black paper, gently waving it in front of Crystal. "See the spirit, honey?" She turned to Rose. "By the way, I've discovered that past-life regressions work much better in October. The supernatural tone of the season makes people more willing to cross boundaries of time."

Rose sighed at Amy's psychobabble as she scooped grounds into the coffeemaker and massaged her arm, gazing with longing at a bottle of horse liniment she'd found yesterday. "Is that what you mean on your card by Transmigration Therapy?" She figured it was better to let Amy vent now rather than hear her chatter to customers.

"Exactly! Most of our current problems come from things we've been avoiding, or even fouling up, for centuries. I tell you, when you dare to investigate your past-lives, it opens up a whole new consciousness."

Rose chuckled to herself, quite sure Amy hadn't changed a bit over the years, except for her hair cut. When the oven timer rang, she pulled out the golden cakes and set them on a cooling rack. Removing three from the tin with tongs, she placed them on napkins.

"Look, Crystal," she hoped the sweet aroma might make her turn her head, "I've got your favorite treat—fairy cakes!" Rose carried them over to the front window and sat down beside her, placing them next to her paint pots. "Remember how we used to bake these on rainy days, or when someone was mean to you on the playground?" She smiled and caressed her cheek. "And you always picked out the berries to hide under your pillow, even though it drove me crazy?"

Rose held her breath, watching her daughter's eyes for interest, her nose for a familiar sniff. "I wouldn't mind if you picked out the berries again," she promised softly. "And later, we could go on a treasure hunt."

Crystal remained oblivious to her mother, and Rose noticed he'd given up potato stamping altogether. She dipped her fingers into black paint and began to make swirls on a piece of white paper. Then, with knitted brows, her fingers zigzagged into lightning bolts and odd shapes that resembled wolves or bears. Tingles returned to Rose's arms, working their way up her shoulders and into her scalp. Only it wasn't excitement this time, but fear. These were the same kinds of pictures Crystal had drawn on the walls on the night she ran away, eerily matching the patches on her great-great grandmother's bed quilt.

"Look at those lovely drawings!" Amy pointed at the paper. "Rose, your craft idea has really sparked her creativity."

Rose nodded, unable to speak—and equally unable to confess she'd seen these images before. Anxious, she got up to pour herself and Amy a cup of coffee, hoping it would help soothe her nerves. When she returned with two mugs in her hands, her daughter was dripping a small amount of black paint onto the paper. Just as Rose leaned closer, Crystal stopped. She pressed her palms into the puddle and pasted her hands onto a fresh spot, fingers extending out like little wings. Carefully, she traced the head and beak of a bird, filling in the center between the wings with black.

Loud taps sounded on the front window, making Rose jump. A tall man with long, dark hair in a black, foot-length coat faced her through the glass. Scanning his features, she recognized the scar that ran across his nose and dipped into his cheekbone. Her fingers began to shake uncontrollably, and she dropped the coffee mugs to the floor with a crash.

"Yikes, what's gotten into you?" Amy grabbed napkins to swirl over the puddles. She gazed at the window. "Well I'll be damned—that's Chance Murphy." She gave him a wave. "I haven't seen him around for ages."

Breathless, Rose leaned her hands against her knees to swallow air. Her mind raced as she attempted to sort out her watery hallucination in Winnemucca with the bizarre experience she'd had on Rook Ridge. How can our angel be actual flesh and blood, she wondered, and be standing right in front of my shop? Bewildered, she rested an unsteady hand on Amy's shoulder for support. "Wh-who is he?"

Amy blinked, confused by Rose's erratic behavior. She picked up a couple of mug shards before rising to her feet.

"Aw, just another mountain man who lives in the woods. The Forest Service keeps him on staff to roam through the ridge and count tree rings. They say he's obsessed with them. Folks in town call him the High Priest of the Pines."

Rose studied the man's long, disheveled hair and beard, his coat speckled with stains. But what really seized her were his big, brown eyes—so large and arresting they enveloped her in his stare like a deep, dark cloak. His gaze slowly caress her face —along her forehead and cheek, down the curve of her nose and line of her lips and jaw—not with the curiosity of a stranger, but as though he knew her so well he could trace her features blindfolded. Then his brown eyes locked on hers. All at once, Rose felt like the glass between them had vanished, and she'd somehow become stripped bare—no longer anchored by mere flesh and bone, but liberated into a pure, vibrating spirit that joined his to hover between them. Rose began to tremble, cheeks warm, feeling that surely she'd known him somewhere before, quite possibly in a dream, when she caught the way his neck abruptly twitched in the morning light.

"A-Amy," she struggled to recover from the force his gaze, "he seems a bit, well—"

"Crazy? You betcha." Amy stepped over to the counter to grab a dish towel. "Folks claim he's downright fairy struck. He used to be a top forest scientist until he cracked last spring. Nobody knows why—maybe a tree fell on him or something. I didn't meet him till last summer, after he wandered into town by accident. But they say he used to be a real looker in his own quiet way—tall, dark, and rugged. Now he just walks around in circles and mumbles to himself, living alone among the trees. Harriet Brimley down the street claims he's fed by ravens, like an Old Testament prophet." Amy rolled her eyes. "But she's a Bible Thumper, if you ask me."

Chance held up a small bracelet to the window that clinked against the glass. Iridescent colors flashed from the stones in the early sunlight. He studied the colors as if they could reveal something. Then he stared at Crystal, mouthing the word "Lost."

Rose's face flushed. She recognized her daughter's play bracelet immediately. Crystal must have left it that night on the ridge.

"What's he saying?" Amy squinted her eyes. "Don't just stand there, let him in! He can be our very first customer."

Rose walked to the window to turn the shop sign to *Open*. She swung the front door open wide.

"H-Hello." She wondered if there was a proper way to greet an angel. Bravely, she reached out both hands and clasped his weathered palm, squeezing it between her fingers. He's for real, she thought, kneading his skin to test the ligaments and bones. "Would you like some coffee?" She felt silly—do angels drink coffee? With a kind smile, she grasped his elbow and led him into the shop.

Chance scanned the cafe like a wild animal accustomed to sizing up new territory. He squinted, appearing uncomfortable with all the color and shine—even the old prospecting tools hanging on the walls had been polished until they gleamed.

His large frame appeared cramped in the shop, and his weathered features looked even more untamed next to the feminine décor. Chance spotted Crystal on the floor, his gaze following the black swirls and forest animals she'd painted. He held up the bracelet again.

"Lost," he insisted.

"Thank you—thank you so much," Rose gushed, feeling a catch in her throat. She cupped her hands to receive the bracelet as if he'd returned a piece of her daughter's soul. Glancing into his eyes, she was surprised by the calmness in his gaze, the tender way he took her in, like he'd somehow wrapped his arms around her in an embrace. His big hand covered both of hers, and an odd sense of serenity swept through her, from head to toe, just like on the ridge. Rose had the distinct feeling that if she laid her head against his chest, his big frame could fold over her and absorb all the cares of the world. She blinked several times, quite certain she was imagining things again. But then the tingles returned, skittering along the bracelet she held between her fingers.

"W-Would you like to sit down?"

Rose eased from his grasp and stepped over to the table, pulling out a chair and patting the seat. Chance stared at the delicate, embroidered tablecloth and his body stiffened, resistant to such finery. Instead, he fixed his gaze on Crystal and the dark bird she'd made on butcher paper. He held up his fingers one by one.

"Five for silver, six for gold. S-seven for a secret that's never been told." He stared intently at Rose, as though she should have comprehended his meaning by now. His eyes ran over her black hair that fell past her shoulders, along a particularly wayward lock that had resisted her efforts to detangle it that morning. When he reached out a finger to unravel it, he hesitated, clenching his jaw in restraint. His arm fell back to his side.

"Bird rhymes," Amy shrugged. "Because of your dark hair, he probably thinks you're a crow or a raven. Like Harriet Brimley says, he's got a thing about black birds."

Chance eased himself down to sit on the floor. He began to rock.

Rose winced. Part of her wanted to hug him with all her might, to kiss his forehead and cheeks and pay him any amount of money for rescuing her daughter—not once, but twice! Another part felt pierced to the bone. It was hard to see a broken-down man doing the same repetitive motions as her daughter. Crystal's state is only temporary, she told herself. She's going to get better—she will! To her dismay, Chance folded his arms and rocked harder. He mumbled as if warding off a spell.

Rose's throat tightened. She busied herself by heading to the counter to fill a mug of coffee and grab a warm fairy cake. She set them down in front of him. It was then she noticed his smell—a mixture of pine sap and campfire smoke, as if he hadn't slept in a real bed in ages. His hair was so dirty it resembled mud, and the tips of his fingernails were black. I don't care, she thought, allowing her eyes to embrace him the way she would her own child. He's our angel. I don't know how or why he came into our lives, but he did. And I'm going to do everything in my power to treat him like gold.

Chance lifted the cake to his nose and sniffed, like a wary timber wolf. He took a test bite, letting the crumbs tumble down his coat. To Rose's amazement, Crystal stood and held out her palms, fluttering her black-stained fingers like wings. Her daughter hummed intently, as though she recognized him and was trying to get his attention. Chance nodded at her with a slight smile. He stood to his feet with a far-away look in his eyes, appearing ready to leave. Rose darted to the counter and filled a basket with fairy cakes.

"Chance," she blurted, still getting used to the sound of his name, "I'd be so grateful if you'd take these with you." She met him at the door and handed him the basket. "You can come back for more, any time. There'll always be a cup of coffee with your name on it. I promise."

Chance stared at her, absorbed by her face, as if he were about to embark on a very long journey and wanted to memorize how the light sparkled in her eyes. Tears welled against Rose's lashes. She wondered if she would ever see him again. Impulsively, she lifted her hand to cup his cheek—his skin felt as coarse as rawhide. "I-I can't ever thank you enough," she whispered, and she surprised herself by giving him a soft kiss.

All at once, warmth bloomed in her chest, seeping through her limbs as if her body shimmered in a soft, amber light, like the delicate flames that danced in the old Foster. Rather than be taken aback, Rose had the sense she could fall gently into that glow and it would fold over her, bathing her soul in comfort. She closed her eyes for a second, when Chance gripped her hand. He took one last look at her and let her go, turning to step through the front door. For reasons she couldn't explain, Rose's heart yanked in her chest. The harness bells chimed, and she watched him walk with the basket in his arm, taking long strides to cross the town square.

"What on earth was that all about?" Amy joined Rose at the front window.

She shook her shoulder a little, but to Rose, Amy's words sounded like they came from under water.

"I-I really couldn't say. It's just that, well, I feel like I've known that man all my life."

"Huh," Amy tossed her dish towel to the cafe table. The two women studied Chance working his way up a rise toward Rook Ridge. They squinted at the back of his black coat as he gradually blended with the tree shadows and disappeared into the forest.

Rose leaned against an old barrel to wipe her brows from cleaning up after the swarm of customers that had blown through her shop. She couldn't believe it—by early afternoon, every hunter and lumberjack for miles had followed his nose to her door, exclaiming over the exquisite smell that wafted through the mountains like scented bait. To Rose's delight, the morning had felt more like a reunion than a grand opening, for most of the men had remembered her big heart and even bigger sourdough biscuits from her barmaid days. Each time they took a bite of her fairy cakes and raved, Amy folded her arms with pride, convinced it was because of the fresh huckleberries. Rose knew better. She glanced at the O'Dannan diary still propped open on the counter and gave it a sly wink.

Somewhere in heaven, she mused, her mother was dancing in a circle, waving her arms and singing "I told you so."

Despite the thrill of their first sales, Rose remained dumbfounded by her encounter with Chance Murphy. *Is my mind playing tricks on me?* She picked up her broom and pondered the scar across his nose. *Maybe I just think I recognize him*—it wouldn't be the first time a woman projected silly ideas onto a total stranger after trauma. Rose kneaded her head where she'd gotten a concussion five months ago, and she cut her eyes to Amy, who was stirring a bowl of batter. She still felt too raw to share her thoughts with her friend, particularly given Amy's habit of translating everything into a cosmic spectacle. *No more drama,* Rose stiffly pushed her broom across the floor. *I've got a new life now and a busy shop to run. With a few good nights' sleep, everything should settle down to normal.*

At that moment, a bright yellow bus halted in front of the shop with a herd of school children piling out, laughing and screaming. A shrill whistle pierced the air. They hustled into single file, keeping their arms to their sides. "Wolf Pass Third Grade," a stern voice commanded, "indoor voices, indoor hands!"

"Look, more customers!" Amy clapped and smiled at Rose. She set her bowl down behind the counter.

"Oh my gosh," Rose stood her broom in a corner. "I swear that's Mrs. Dingle. Remember, from grade school?" She studied the slight stoop to the woman's shoulders and the hair that was much grayer now. But there was no mistaking her sunny blue eyes and dimpled cheeks, as well as the thrust of her chin that showed she meant business.

"Welcome to the Rainbow's End Cafe!" Rose said cheerfully as the group entered the shop. Mrs. Dingle waved from the back with a weary smile. Rose ran up and gave her a hug. "How are you?" She gazed into the woman's eyes like a favorite aunt.

Mrs. Dingle wrapped a thick arm around Rose's waist. "My dear," she glanced appreciatively around the shop, "Look at what you've done to this place! Your parents would be so pleased."

Rose blushed, recalling her old teacher was one of the few people in town who never made fun of her family. "It's so good to see you." She stepped over to Crystal to pick her up. "I've got a little girl now," she smiled proudly, until one of the school children rammed into her leg. Rose cringed while the group wove through the shop like feverish ants, their noise level climbing. Thinking fast, she pressed her daughter's face to her chest and moved behind the counter, pulling out paper and crayons from a drawer. Rose settled Crystal in a safe haven beside Amy's familiar red boots. Crystal had done remarkably well all morning when there were only adults mingling in the shop, but she feared the children's clamor might overwhelm her.

"Crystal's a bit sensitive to loud noises," she explained to Mrs. Dingle, curling a finger through her daughter's hair. "It's okay, baby," she whispered. "We're among friends."

Rose set her hand on the bakery case. "Would you like to sample our fairy cakes?" She pointed to a fresh stack on a plate.

"Or how about black cat brownies?" Amy held up a

chocolate square with a feline face etched into the vanilla frosting.

"Hot cocoa!" demanded a pigtailed girl, rubbing her hands beside the wood stove to keep warm.

"No licorice?" the tallest boy huffed. The group groaned in unison.

Mrs. Dingle maneuvered her way to the center of the room and held out her arms for the children to return to her side. "We'll take fifteen brownies and fifteen hot cocoas," she announced with the same warm authority Rose remembered from grade school. "You do have hot cocoa, correct?"

Amy panicked and turned around, shuffling through drawers beside the bakery case. Rose winked and handed her a cocoa tin, pointing toward the milk. Relieved, Amy beamed like she'd passed a test.

"Sure, we've got cocoa!" Amy said brightly. "And while I prepare it, each of you can sit in a nice round circle so my friend can show you how to pan for gold."

The children roared in delight.

"Third grade—zipper lips!" Mrs. Dingle sliced two fingers across her mouth. "Remember, the quietest one gets a prize at the end of the trip." She pointed at imaginary spots on the floor, and the children sat in a circle like ducks—fidgety, but manageable.

Rose headed across the room to pull a gold pan from the wall, emptying into it a package of paydirt she'd taken from a shelf. After Amy passed out brownies, she handed her a pitcher of water. Carefully, Rose dribbled liquid over the dark soil, making sure not to slosh any over the sides. At first she was nervous, wondering if she still had a gold miner's touch. It had been ages since she'd panned. Then she spotted a flicker of yellow, bright as sunshine—as hope itself—and the old excitement returned. It all comes down to magic, her father used to say. Feel the gold within, and let your heart lead you. Before Rose knew it, she was standing tall, a performer once again, slick as a carnie, amazed at how the anticipation never failed to exhilarate her. She circled the water expertly in the pan with a certain pride in the ease of the wrist action that had taken years to perfect.

"There are lots of minerals in here," Rose stated in a big voice, tipping the pan so the children could see. She waited for the darker particles to settle at the bottom. "Quartz, silica, hematite. But what we're looking for is very precious—only the best panners can spot real gold."

"I see something!" claimed a red-haired boy. The children began to fuss and crane their necks, palms pasted to the floor under Mrs. Dingle's watchful eye. "It's gold!" the boy cried.

"Well, actually," Rose corrected, "that's mica, stained yellow from iron deposits. I'll show you how to tell the difference. See the golden color of these flakes?"

The children nodded, now mesmerized.

"If you shadow them with your hand, they look dull, don't they? Sort of disappear?" She let several children try it. "Real gold never looks dull. It's always shiny, even in shadows."

"So where is it? Where's the gold?" pestered a tow-headed girl. She sipped her hot cocoa too fast and spilled her cup on the floor. Mrs. Dingle swiftly dropped a napkin on the spot, watching the white paper saturate to brown.

"Gold hides at the bottom—it's the heaviest element in the

pan," Rose replied. "And since we don't have all day to separate the gold from paydirt, we're going to cheat a little."

The children giggled and checked Mrs. Dingle's reaction, as if Rose were getting away with something. Mrs. Dingle folded her thick hands and gave Rose a knowing smile.

Rose grabbed a potato from the sack by the window and cut it in half with her pocket knife. "This is an old miner's trick from a hundred years ago. You take a sliced potato, insert it into the pan, and bury it in the dirt until you reach the very bottom. Then press really hard, so the dirt sticks to the potato pulp. Hold up your potato—and there you go!" The starchy white edges glittered with yellow specks.

"So treat your dinner potatoes with respect, okay? They just might make you rich someday." Rose grinned, dipping into a dramatic curtsy. The children's clapping thundered through the shop. Rose glanced at Amy to check on Crystal's reaction. Her friend gave her a thumbs up.

"What do you say class?" Mrs. Dingle directed above their noise.

"Thank you!" the children sang too loud, dashing out of the shop into the town square. They charged toward the City Hall museum down the street, where Harriet Brimley waited for them with a dour look on her face. Mrs. Dingle walked up to Rose to pay for their brownies and cocoa, but she waved her hand.

"It's on the house," Rose gave her another hug. "Isn't it nice to know I listened to you during science class?" She held up her gold-speckled potato proudly.

"Excellent job, my dear," Mrs. Dingle smiled. "And you can bet I'll spread the word about these brownies—you've got your mother's touch, you know." She squeezed Rose's elbow. "I always knew you'd make something of yourself."

Rose's cheeks flushed again. She patted her gently on the shoulder before Mrs. Dingle had to break away to catch up with the children, watching her wave a warm hello to Harriet Brimley in spite of the woman's sour demeanor. Turning to high-five Amy, Rose grinned in triumph, then plucked the gold from her potato to reuse in another sack of paydirt.

"You really are a marvel with a potato. I'll have to tell Tom," a familiar voice remarked.

Rose spun around to see her half-sister, Laurel, standing at the front door. She held a grocery bag and a pot of mums in her arms, and she was dressed in a sleek, ivory pants suit, cut so precisely to her waist and hips that it screamed custom tailoring. The mid-afternoon sun glistened through the champagne highlights in her hair, which fell in a flawless line to her chin. Instantly, Rose was seized by her solid stare—the same inadequacy she'd always felt as a child whenever her beautiful sister was present. She studied her creamy skin, delicate chin, and perfect nose that curved into a graceful arc. How dare anyone be so polished and walk on ordinary soil, Rose had often wondered, with a self-assurance that rivaled sunrise?

"Still using that old potato trick?" Laurel observed. "Good thing I sent you those coupons in Winnemucca. They're Idaho Gold, by the way, top of the line." She nodded at Mrs. Dingle waddling across the town square. "But let's face it, you'll never make any money until you start charging people."

Laurel strolled boldly to the counter and set down her

grocery bag in front of Amy like she wasn't there, holding up her pot of mums.

"Happy Birthday, honey." She handed her the plant. "And congratulations on the shop." Laurel swiftly assessed the room, nodding at the antique cups and saucers she recognized from childhood. Stepping over to a chipped teacup, she turned the defect to the wall. "Very impressive. You've done a lot of work."

"It's your birthday?" gasped Amy from behind the counter. "I'm so sorry, sweetie—I forgot."

"It's no big deal." Rose sneezed at the orange blooms that reached to her nose. She set the flowers down near Laurel. "H-how did you know we were opening today?"

"Oh, I have ways," Laurel sniffed. She pointed at the potato Rose had used in her demonstration. "So is that real gold? Or were you doing another charlatan number on those poor children?"

Rose bit her tongue, avoiding any hint of sarcasm that might set Laurel off—she'd never won a verbal battle with her yet. "Most of it's authentic," she defended. "I discovered Dad's gold pouch in a tin canister last week. It was under our big old bed, right next to his pistol. We sure could have used it when we ran the shop as kids, huh?" She laughed uneasily. "The gold in the pouch, I mean, not the gun. Anyway, I sprinkled some of the gold dust in the paydirt we sell."

Laurel stared at the shiny flecks on the potato. "Well you'd better recycle it—Dad's not exactly around to find you more gold, thank God." She leaned against a cafe table and folded her arms. "You know, with enough discipline and business smarts, this place might really turn a profit. I'd be happy to give you a few pointers—I coach Tom on management all the time. Did I tell you he has a new division now? We're doing better than ever." She pulled out her purse and began to write a check for Rose on the front table, smiling with the ease of a socialite donating to her favorite charity.

Rose stole a glance at Amy and rolled her eyes. "Oh, you don't have to do that! We've been doing fabulous today, actually. Here, let Amy pour you a cup of coffee while I bag up some brownies *for the road*," she emphasized. "We wouldn't want you to get caught in traffic and be, um, late getting home, right?"

Laurel stiffened, completing her scrawl across the check anyway. She slipped it beneath the flower pot and clicked her pen, dropping it into her purse. "Well, you might want to at least think about some state assistance. You know, like a small business grant for disadvantaged women. I could get you the forms from the welfare office in Boise."

Rose shook her head, placing a few brownies in a bag and picking up the mug of coffee Amy had poured. "Oh, I'm sure if we need help, we'll manage." Suddenly, she noticed a reflection in the coffee: two faces, Laurel's and Tom's, floating at the center of the mug. Their images changed to planets that spun away from each other's orbit. Then she saw another face, an auburn-haired woman she didn't recognize, like a moon circling Tom's planet. Stunned, she whispered the word *affair* to Amy and watched her friend's eyes widen. Rose shot a glance at Laurel's diamond wedding ring, large as a blanched almond, and handed her the coffee mug like she'd seen a ghost.

Laurel twirled her ring until the diamond hid beneath her

finger. Her eyes became unsettled, as if she recalled Rose's otherworldly gifts as a girl—the teacup guessing games they used to play where her sister was always right. Hesitantly, she accepted the mug.

"So where's Crystal anyway?" Laurel abruptly changed the subject. "Don't tell me you dropped her off at Fannie Thistlewaite's cabin for daycare. That woman's crazy—"

"No, she's just, uh, taking a nap," Rose fibbed, hoping to deflect one of Laurel's notorious outbursts. She knew the minute her sister spotted Crystal she would sense something was amiss and start to pry, using it as an excuse to dominate her life. "I don't normally disturb her at this hour of the day. She needs her rest, you know."

"Don't be ridiculous!" Laurel set down her mug. "I've never had the chance to break away from Boise to meet her, and she's my only niece. Crystal!" She walked toward the back bedroom, clicking her heels against the floor boards. "It's me, your Auntie!"

From behind the counter, Amy bent down to Crystal, who was still beside her feet, and scooped her up. "Shouldn't you go to the post office right now?" She handed her to Rose and gave her a soft shove. "We need, um, tax forms. I'll watch the shop—"

"Thank you," Rose whispered, squeezing her friend's hand. She smoothed her daughter's mussed bangs and scurried with her to the front door, doing her best to keep the harness bells from ringing while she turned the knob.

"What the hell is going on?" Laurel bellowed, returning to the shop. Rose could have sworn her voice made the china clatter. "What are you hiding?"

Rose's heart sank to her knees. She didn't want her sister's steel eyes judging Crystal, reducing everything that had happened to the brutal sum of her mother's failures. It was too late now. Letting go of the door handle, she clutched Crystal close to her heart. She turned around just in time to see her sister's hands rise to her hips.

"Crystal's right here," Rose announced defiantly, stroking her daughter's blonde hair. "But I've got an errand to run, and I'm in a hurry—"

Crystal began to squirm, and Rose could no longer maintain her grip over her slippery limbs. Reluctantly, she set her daughter down and grabbed her by the hand. "C'mon honey, let's go visit Postmaster Cleary. I hear he's got lollypops."

Crystal yanked her hand free and rocked from foot to foot. Drool dribbled down her chin, making Rose cringe.

Laurel's eyes narrowed to slits, scrutinizing the girl's face. "What's wrong with her," she said—a demand, not a question. Instantly, Crystal began to hum, her tone slipping into a high-pitched wail like a needle registering pain.

"Nothing's wrong—you've just upset her, that's all. Lower your voice," Rose urged.

"For Christ's sake, Rosie, she's drooling. This is from that pool incident, isn't it?" Laurel pressed, stepping forward. "You didn't tell me she was…damaged."

Crystal stumbled from her rocking into a spin. She held out her arms and whirled, her voice reaching to a tinny screech. Rose covered her ears, then kneeled and tried to mutter soothing words to calm her. She held up her hand to stop Amy from spinning with her.

"Oh my God, she's completely out of control!" Laurel cried. Her tense voice made Crystal spin harder.

"Can't you just let her cope in her own way?" Rose pleaded, pressing her hands to her temples.

"Cope? Look at her, she's miserable!" Laurel squinted like she'd already assigned a diagnosis. "You know, I play bridge with a fundraiser for the Sunshine Psychiatric Center in Boise. They have beds, meals, even visiting hours—it's a very exclusive program. She might put in a good word for her. After all, you can't throw away your life caring for her the way I did for you in high school, Rosie. It's best to consider her needs—"

Crystal lost her balance, veering toward the front window until she knocked into the table. The pot of mums Laurel brought teetered and crashed, sending black soil and orange flower heads racing across the floor. Rose gasped and closed her arms around her daughter, burying her face into her hair. Standing up, she turned to Laurel.

"How would you know what she needs?" Rose challenged. "What are you doing here, anyway? You never once visited us in Winnemucca! But now that your husband's always gone on business trips, you get lonely and come up here to try and control *me*?" She let go of her daughter and headed to the cash register. "Here, take this money for the groceries," she grabbed fistfuls of bills and thrust them into Laurel's hands, "consider it a down payment for all those years you wasted on me. I'm sorry I messed up your life." She walked over to the table and ripped up Laurel's check, letting it fall through her fingers. Rose watched her sister's cheeks suffuse with pink as her gray eyes flinched.

"Thank you," Laurel said quietly. She glanced at the bills

in her hand. "I'm so glad you cleared that up. You've never been grateful, Rosie—what was I thinking?" She walked briskly to the front door. Before she opened it, she hesitated.

"By the way, who did you think made sure the electricity and water were working before you got here?" Laurel swiveled to face her half-sister. "And where did you believe that five thousand dollars came from—the sky?" She leaned down to brush dust off her patent leather shoes and flicked a speck of lint from her suit. "You're just like your starry-eyed mother, Rosie, with your head in the clouds. Always in the goddamn clouds. Well, I hope next year your birthday brings a little more wisdom. You sure as hell could use it."

"She always wins." Rose puckered her lips and threw back a shot of whiskey. Patting her chest, she wheezed. "Didn't I tell you? *Always.* And I was just starting to feel good about myself and my new life here."

Rose thrust her glass down on a wooden crate and warmed her hands over the cast iron stove at the center of the shop. Leaning back in her chair, she peeked into the bedroom to make sure Crystal was still asleep.

"So Rose," Amy stared absentmindedly at the fire, "can you divine where gold is, like water witching? You know, aspens grow beside the creek. We could use their branches for wands—"

"Aren't you listening to me?" Rose buried her head in her hands. "I'm five thousand bucks in the hole, my sister just walked all over me, and you want hocus pocus?" She poured herself another shot. "I've told you a hundred times: I can't read the future for myself. If I could, I'd have won the lottery by now. And I sure as hell wouldn't have been broadsided by Hurricane Laurel this afternoon or been stupid enough to get mixed up with Jake."

"It was just an idea." Amy gazed into her whiskey glass, disappointed. "What about your friends? Can you see my future?" She held up her glass. "Maybe a hint?"

Rose rolled her eyes, swiping a brief glance into Amy's shot glass to prove nothing would come of it. Curiously, the fire's glow danced orange and yellow on the whiskey's surface, and she saw the colors tangle into a golden knot—a symbol of loyalty and enduring friendship. She smiled gently and squeezed Amy's hand.

"It's perfect," Rose confirmed. "You'll never have to worry about lasting love."

"Really?" Amy clasped her fingers together, her charm bracelet dancing. "Did you see a lover? A new man? You know that lumberjack this afternoon was awfully cute. I love the smell of sawdust on those guys."

Rose's temples throbbed with embarrassment. After Laurel had left the shop, the man had wandered in and looked at her, not Amy. That is, until he spotted Crystal rocking at her feet, drawing black crayon circles on her forehead. At first he had flirted a little, asking when the shop might close—maybe he could come by. But then Crystal made a wild, screeching sound, still distressed from Laurel's visit. Her behavior startled him, and he whispered under his breath about "baggage" as he left a quarter on the counter.

"Something tells me that lumberjack won't be back," Rose muttered distantly. She lifted her glass to her lips, then thought better of it.

"You know what your problem is?" Amy got up and walked to the counter in the dim firelight. She lit a match and returned with a fairy cake, a slim candle burning in its center. "You've forgotten how to celebrate. Happy birthday, dearie!" she giggled. "These were our best sellers today."

"Ready to bake five thousand more?" grumbled Rose.

"Oh, stop worrying! We had a terrific opening, and you'll pay Laurel off—someday." She twisted her hands. "Did you, um, really spend the whole five grand already?"

"Nearly." Rose turned in her chair to study the appliances settled in shadows. "There's the new convection oven, the refrigeration cables for the glass case, plus a heavy-duty mixer and supplies. On top of that was labor and installation." She rubbed her eyes. "Oh yeah, and I paid off some old medical bills and replaced the muffler in the truck. Scary how it all adds up."

Amy set the cake on the wooden crate and sat down. Crossing her legs in the old captain's chair, she fidgeted. "Well, all I know is you got a birthday wish to make, before I steal bites of that fairy cake. Did you try one yet? They're addictive."

Rose stared at the candle wax that pooled onto the cake's crust, her vision blurred from alcohol. Shaking her head, she licked her fingers and pinched the flame. "How can I afford birthday wishes when everything I touch lately seems to come back to haunt me?" She stared at the candle's sliver of smoke. "Including my half-sister, dammit. Maybe there really is a family curse."

Amy shrugged and pulled the dead candle from the cake, nibbling crumbs stuck to the wax. "It's probably not my business, honey, but I suspect Laurel means well. She just got stuck."

"Oh God," Rose moaned, "not the past life stuff again."

"No, I mean now, this life," Amy insisted. "Think about it. Everything she did to help you survive as teenagers—ordering you around, keeping a tight schedule, controlling every dime— it's the only way she knows how to show love. The way you two coped with your rough childhood is like yin and yang: you give everything away, and Laurel chains people to her in hand cuffs."

Rose tilted her head back, letting her long, black hair fall nearly to the floor. "No wonder Tom's having an affair," she mumbled, gazing at the fire's radiance on the ceiling. "Who wants to cuddle up with a prison guard? But damned if Laurel doesn't look good at company picnics. Did you see those shoes?"

"Rose." Amy took a wholesale chomp from the fairy cake.

"What? I can be jealous. She does the same thing to me, you know. That whole tirade about Crystal—Laurel's just angry because she can't have children. She hates me for that. Yet she'd never dream of adopting. They might not be perfect."

"Meow," Amy replied between chews.

"I mean it," Rose sat up straight. "Laurel's whole existence is perfect. She lives to improve things, and when she runs out of things to do, she tries to improve me."

"Maybe it's because she cares." Glancing at her shot glass, Amy dipped a corner of the fairy cake into the whiskey before popping it into her mouth. She licked her lips, satisfied, and washed down the rest of it with liquor, tossing the paper backing into the stove. "Call me a traitor if you want, but I think your comments really hurt her." She watched the paper curl and erupt into flames.

Rose opened the wood stove and buried the fluttering ash beneath coals with a poker. "Why are you defending her all of a sudden?" She set the poker back on its stand. "Laurel's always treated us like dirt."

"I know, I know," Amy sighed, pulling back her red curls and plaiting them into a loose braid. Her eyes began to sparkle, and she smiled wickedly. "Remember that time we convinced her your car broke down so we could take a joy ride in her Mercedes convertible? And we went off roading and got sagebrush stuck to the grill?" Amy bent over her knees, laughing. "When we came back after two hours, I never saw a woman so mad."

Rose couldn't help giggling. "Don't worry," she nodded, "Laurel had it coming. I distinctly remember her busting into the Magpie Saloon that afternoon and telling me that my life was going nowhere. Like I didn't know."

"Yeah, she's a case, I'll grant you that." Amy toyed with her charm bracelet, stroking a silver heart between her fingers, then jiggling a tiny bell. "But you gotta be careful, even when people are rotten. You don't want to step on Laurel's karma and have it boomerang on you. Besides, she's probably been a queen for at least a few past lifetimes, so you might as well channel her energy into something more constructive. Like finding us new boyfriends," she winked.

"Do you hear yourself?" Rose marveled. "If Laurel had anything to do with it, we'd be married off to corrupt lawyers —who'd cheat on us."

"That's okay. I know lots of hexes," Amy grinned. She hoisted her ruby cowboy boots up on the crate, relishing Rose's reaction. "Oh, don't be so serious," she teased. "With the way things are headed, there ought to be hundreds of customers this fall. We're going to rake it in!" She poured more whiskey into her glass and clinked it against Rose's for a toast. "And I bet there will be plenty of guys to choose from. Chance Murphy was certainly smitten with you this morning, even though he's crackers. But underneath all that dirt, he's kind of good looking, don't you think? Tall, dark, and mysterious?" she winked. "And then there was that lumberjack, checking you out. I'm not blind, you know."

Rose took a small sip and blushed, the veins in her head already pounding from alcohol. "That lumberjack left the shop awfully quick, Amy," she whispered, glancing at the back bedroom again. "I mean, when he saw Crystal. She, um, had an episode."

"Well, maybe he had to be somewhere."

"Yeah, sure," Rose swallowed slowly, her tongue thick as cotton, "anywhere but around a worn-out, thirty-year-old widow. With baggage."

She fingered the rim of her shot glass, replaying the rejection in her mind: the snide look on his face, the abrupt way he turned on his boot heels and left. A tight sensation rose in her chest, a familiar coil that had twisted around her heart for months. Crossing her arms, she wished she could squeeze it into submission, like a snake. But no matter how hard she tried, the slow burn of loneliness always managed to slither around her soul, sometimes crushing her to a panic. Rose gripped the arms of her chair, tears swelling against her lashes.

"Oh Amy," she said, "Is this it for me? Alone forever in this dusty old town?"

Amy turned to Rose and gazed at her damp green eyes flickering from the fire. "Look who's asking for fortunes now," she said quietly. She slipped her arm around her friend's shoulder. "Don't tell me you think you're old," she reprimanded. "I mean, in terms of past lifetimes, we're barely getting started—"

"Not to lumberjacks." Rose opened the stove door and tossed in her shot of whiskey, watching the fire explode into a bright plume, echoed by a hiss. She wiped her eyes on her shirt sleeve. "I might as well book dates with Father Time."

"That's it!" Amy clapped her hands and set her boots on the floor. "No more self-pity." She grabbed Rose's empty glass from the crate. "You're not the only one who's psychic around here. I took advanced classes in Spontaneous Elucidation, you know." Amy poured another shot. "It's all about making quick associations, unhampered by logic, so you can open your life to new experiences. You stare at an object and say the first thing that comes to mind." Amy scrutinized the surface of Rose's whiskey, holding it to the fire to watch the yellow reflections sparkle. Then she closed one eye and peered at the liquid. "Yep," she nodded, "I see a potato in your future."

"Oh please. Not Laurel's fat husband—"

"No, a *real* potato," Amy replied. She got up and went to a sack beside the counter and dug in her hand. "We're gonna make you a love spell. Take your mind off things."

"Absolutely not." Rose felt the words ring inside her head. "Look, I know you're being kind, but it's been a really big day, and I'm not in the mood—"

"I can't hear you!" Amy held up two potatoes and wiggled them over her ears. "This is my birthday present, honey, just for you. And there's no better moment. Do you know what tonight is?" She didn't wait for Rose's reply. "We are exactly two weeks from the most important full moon of the entire year: The blue moon. It's a perfect time for spells."

Amy put a potato down on the crate, her eyes ablaze. "Did you know that this is the first blue moon on Halloween in forty-six years? First ever in our lifetimes? With the legend about your ancestor, Ophir Creek should be flooded with gold seekers before you know it. Remember what they say: Those who are pure of heart will find gold." She stepped gaily behind the counter to gather more candles. "Maybe love, too! By the way, do you happen to have a cauldron?"

Rose rolled her eyes.

"Okay, okay, how about a ceramic bowl? The metal one I used today won't do."

Massaging her forehead, Rose groaned at the dull ache forming between her eyes as the room teetered and settled back down. She reached for the bottle of whiskey, then shook her head. "I'm only letting you do this because you're my friend," she mumbled, too weary for more protests. She pointed to the back apartment kitchen. "In the top cupboard above the fridge, you might find some old bowls and a mouse trap or two—I haven't cleaned it out yet. Be careful, and don't you dare wake up Crystal."

She watched Amy trot excitedly to the back apartment, her shadow bouncing on the wall. Rose prayed it would be too dark in the bedroom for Amy to notice Crystal's strange crayon marks on the wallpaper, which hadn't come off yet with cleansers. While Amy hummed happily, Rose listened to her pull up a chair to the fridge, clanking china from her cupboard inspection. Then she heard a snap, and Amy gasped.

"You all right?" Rose called out, envisioning dead rats or Amy's hand caught in a trap.

"Oh my gosh," she replied. "I-I think I've found something."

Amy's feet landed from the chair with a thud. Her boot taps grew louder as she scurried back into the shop.

"Don't you bring me anything dead," Rose warned, covering her eyes.

"Rose," Amy patted her shoulder. "Check it out."

Hesitantly, Rose peeled her fingers from her face. Before her, Amy held a chipped bean pot in her arms. She lifted the dusty brown lid.

Rose watched Amy pull out old trinkets: antique coins, a tarnished silver locket, a faded red bandana—all the things that her mother once told her had belonged to Corvine O'Dannan.

"Y-You don't think these are my great-great grandmother's, do you?"

Amy sat down beside her and clutched her arm. "This is big, Rose," her fingers trembled. "I think it's a sign—you know, that tonight is really powerful."

Rose picked up the locket, the one the legend claimed a raven had given to Corvine. Opening it, she saw a snippet of blonde hair inside, tied together by a tiny pink ribbon. A lump swelled in her throat, and she glanced again at the back bedroom where Crystal was sleeping. Folks in town had always said that Corvine O'Dannan bore a daughter after her lover died. But they also laughed that she wore a coat of black feathers and meandered through the woods, casting her charms and searching for fairy gold. Rose winced—she didn't need any more reminders that people considered her family crazy. Closing the locket, she placed it back into the bean pot with a clink.

"Wait," Amy said, jiggling her arm, "It's no accident we found this. Maybe your ancestor's going to help us."

Rose yanked away her arm. "Only if you buy into all that stuff."

"Well don't you?" The hope in Amy's voice begged for a response.

Rose studied the bean pot and swallowed hard. "Know what I believe?" She flinched, her eyes traveling over Corvine O'Dannan's belongings. "I believe my mother loved me, and Jake didn't. And my O'Dannan ancestors led tragic lives. But damned if they couldn't bake one hell of a fairy cake."

She peered hesitantly at Amy through dark bangs, then lost her gaze in the fire. "After everything I've been though, honey, that's all I can say for sure."

The glow from the fire cast an animated look into Amy's eyes. "Then what would it hurt if we tried to change your future? If you're not brave enough to enjoy your family's gifts, you can just relax and let me have my fun." She picked up the locket and slid it between her fingers. Then she held up the red bandana and showed it to Rose. "Besides, one tiny spell will hardly put a dent in the family curse, right?"

Rose's heart drummed heavy—the bandana reminded her of Jake. She was tempted to grab it and toss it into the fire, watch as it slowly burned to ash—so much for true love. But then she realized Amy was already setting up her spell. A potato sat on the slats with a candle poked into the center. Amy doused it with nutmeg, cinnamon and cloves and placed it in the bean pot next to the bandana.

"What are you doing?" Rose coughed at the cloud of spices.

"Cooperating with the universe. I've got the potato for a wish seed, a candle for inspiration, and pumpkin pie spices for abundance. By the time I'm done, true love is gonna hit you like a ton of bricks."

"Amy, has this spell ever worked before? I hate to mention it, but your reputation at that commune—"

"There wasn't a blue moon coming! You can't fault me for lousy celestial alignments. Have faith," she urged. "What's the worst that could happen? We open the shop tomorrow and see the same old beer-bellied hunters?" Amy lit the candle, running her palms in circles over the flame. Closing her eyes, she began to hum and chant soft words: "Wish I will, wish I might, I call my wish to being tonight. Wind so wild, wind so free, bring Rose's lover here to see." She opened her eyes. "Okay, sweetie. Your turn."

"What?"

"Repeat after me: Wish I will, wish I might."

"Wish my might, wish tonight."

"No!" Amy waved her hands. "You're getting it all wrong! You don't want to attract coyotes, do you?" She folded her arms. "What's this all about? Are you afraid of true love?"

Rose stared at the faded fabric of the bandana, wondering who it belonged to—Rory O'Brien, her great-great grandmother's lover, or just some broken-down miner who wiped sweat from his brow? She stroked the aged cloth, nearly pink at the edges. "Sometimes love goes wrong," she whispered, her voice dry and crackled, "terribly wrong."

"But red is for passion!" Amy gushed, paying no attention to her. She curled the red bandana around the potato. "Exactly what you need! Okay, visualize your new man and imagine the power of the moon entering the potato, blessing your wish seed with all the forces of the universe."

Rose closed her eyes for her friend's sake and listened to the wind that picked up outside, branches scratching against windows. "But what if I'm afraid, Amy. I haven't had the best of luck, you know."

Amy grasped her hands. "Don't think about fear," she coached, "keep your eyes closed and concentrate. Imagine someone nice, like, I dunno, your favorite crush recently, or that cute lumberjack."

Rose tried, feeling like a silly school girl. She took a deep breath, slowly expelling air from her lungs and clearing thoughts from her head. As the wind whistled through pines, all that came to mind was Jake's face from her recurring nightmares, begging to start over and conjuring his stale promises. She saw his golden hair tousled in the breeze, his blue eyes intense as a mountain lake. Even the memory of suede and sage curled with the power of incense around her soul. She leaned forward and gripped the potato tightly, trying her best to shatter his image, but it clung to her like smoke. Beat it, she demanded silently, yet his imprint lingered, indelible as a stain. "Oh God," she sighed through gritted teeth, "anything but Jake again."

All at once, a violent crack exploded outside. Rose opened her eyes, only to see the room flooded with searing light. A window burst open, and she felt the hair stand on the back of her neck.

Amy's eyes fluttered. She glanced at the goose bumps on her arm. The cold air that breezed into the room swirled around them as if it were alive and filled with kinetic energy. She watched in amazement as a flurry of dry leaves circled their chairs and settled on the floor.

"Well, I guess that's it," Amy remarked uncertainly, waving her fingers at the spire of candle smoke. Thunder rolled deep and heavy outside like a train.

"What do you mean?" Rose rubbed her arms against the cold.

"Once the candle's out, the spell's over, honey. Nothing you can do about it now. Hope you thought of somebody good looking." Amy got up to close the window.

Rose shivered, recoiling against her chair. "Sure," she muttered, staring at the dead leaves, "a real hunk."

"Terrific! Wonder how we'll recognize him." She glanced dreamily at the bean pot. "Maybe he'll bring you a sack of potatoes—or a red bandana."

"No!" Rose slipped the bandana from around the potato. "No more red bandanas." She opened the stove and tossed it in, watching it burst into flames. Ignoring Amy's surprise, she slammed the door shut and secured the latch with a snap. Then she slowly stretched her legs from the chair.

"Well, I guess if the mystery man has anything to do with your spell," Rose accidentally released a yawn, covering her mouth, "he'll smell like pumpkin pie." She stood up to give

Amy a weary hug. "Thank you for a great first day, sweetie—it meant the whole world to me. But now I really need to hit the hay."

"Okay, but don't forget to bury your potato outside the shop in the morning," Amy pointed at the bean pot with school marm resolve, "so your lover can find you." She screwed the cap on the whiskey and got up to set the bottle and shot glasses on the counter. Grabbing her coat, she headed for the door.

"And Rose—"

Rose paused at the curtain by the back bedroom, dreading more instructions.

"Happy Birthday."

6

A lightning bolt crashed on Rook Ridge, and a hundred million volts pulsed through Chance Murphy's body before escaping to the ground. The sound was a bomb going off in his brain. His eyes rolled back in his head as the world became a panoply of red. Ringing, like giant cathedral bells, engulfed his ears for minutes, maybe hours. Then his mind merged with the darkness outside.

When his eyes finally began to flicker, all Chance saw before him was night. He lifted his head, his senses filled with the smell of burnt hair and charred earth. A rhythmic roar echoed in his ears, and he reached out to anchor himself, feeling tiny grains of sand between his fingers. Chance sat up, spitting granules from his mouth. His coat was covered in sand, and a cool spray misted the back of his neck. He turned around, baffled by the massive body of water that blended with the night sky.

Yet his thoughts were singular and clear for the first time in months.

Astonished, he stumbled to his feet, watching sand spill to his boots like sugar. Where am I? he kicked at it in disbelief. He squinted to make out a long stretch of beach in the moonlight, embraced at the edges by jagged rocks. As his eyes adjusted to darkness, he noticed his coat had been burned in places, frayed into threads at cuff and hem, his fingernails charred black. Then he noticed his skin—dark feathery patterns wove up his hand and wrist like tattoos. Chance pulled his hand closer, bewildered, examining the strange design as if it were a pox.

"What's happened to me?" he whispered, his voice stolen by the ocean breeze.

Perhaps this is a new kind of madness, he thought, still amazed at the clarity of his mind. He stared up at the black sky that revealed no secrets. A flash of lightning split the horizon, and he stiffened, digging his hands into his coat pockets. Pulling out crumbs, he lifted his fingers. They smelled of vanilla and butter, pine nuts and huckleberries—warm, inviting scents that whispered promises of home. The smell clung to his hands like a fragrance, and a smile curved at his lip. Inhaling deeply, he allowed the sweet aroma to linger in his soul.

He remembered.

He had only meant to dream of her—the beautiful woman of Ophir Creek.

With her basket of fairy cakes by his side, he had laid down that night within the circle of stones, wrapping his coat around himself for a blanket. Gazing up at stars, he had recalled the black wildness of her hair, her skin smooth as river rocks, her eyes verdant like spring leaves. She didn't know it, but he had watched her from shadows ever since she'd arrived in Ophir Creek. How could he help it? Her face was a lyric from the forest itself, winsome as a mountain breeze—a song to ease the loneliness of a woodsman bound to walk his life in circles. Even through his tangled thoughts he could tell she and her daughter were wanderers, like himself. Wild birds here to build a new nest.

Yet there was more…

Chance shook his head and stared at the restless, churning sea. All his life, he had seen this woman in his dreams. When he was young, she had appeared to him as a little girl, laughing and chatting with a black bird at her windowsill as though they were old friends. But as he grew older, she matured as well, and her windswept hair and imploring green eyes haunted him like a lost love. Her gaze was marked by such sharp longing that he would reach out to her in his dreams, hoping to create a bridge between them. Then he would wrap himself tightly around her, and the two of them would melt into one another with a yearning so fierce that it bordered on sacred. In those moments, Chance felt deeply recognized by this woman—not for the persona he showed to the world, but for a hidden facet buried in his heart that was as ancient and wild as the sea. Yet each time he surrendered to the fullness of their dream embrace, his arms would mysteriously change to feathers. And no matter how hard he tried, she always slipped away from him and disappeared into the night.

That is, until the day he reached into the fairy ring. Only this time, it wasn't a dream.

Six months ago, on the first day in May, he'd been out at dawn like usual, studying old-growth stumps in the woods. His mind was clear back then, and he was a forest scientist—some argued the best in the Northwest. The wealth of secrets told by trees never ceased to fascinate him, from burn scars of forest fire to the ancient markings of animals and man. Each stump was a puzzle exposing centuries of time. Chance liked to remark among colleagues that their work involved more than analyzing mere tree rings—what they really did was peer into past lives.

Yet on that early morning in May, as the sun cast a soft light over Rook Ridge, Chance discovered a particularly large stump, much older than he'd expected for the region. Its wide base was sprinkled with flowers, their blue and yellow petals glistening brightly with dew. Was that the reason for the rainbow hues that appeared to hover around the stump? Curious, Chance leaned forward, tracing his finger along a thick band of growth. Just as he completed the circle, colors flew up in his face like butterflies. To his astonishment, they glinted at the edges like sparks and began to swirl. That's when the surface of the old stump changed—instead of rings, he saw a pool of water. At the center was a woman, her face agonized in fear, clutching a limp child against her chest. From the way their hair swayed in the murky depths, they appeared to be drowning. Chance saw the woman struggle fiercely with her legs, but then her eyes dimmed and she uttered a cry as if she would soon release her spirit for good.

How could he not reach into that circle? Surely anyone would have, to save their lives. But the second he dove his hands into the water, Chance could never have predicted what happened next. Quicker than he could blink, he was beside the woman and child in the pool. Thinking fast, he grabbed them both and shot to the surface, settling their bodies on the cement rim. After resuscitating the girl, he stepped over to check on the woman, who was still barely conscious. Staring into her exquisite green eyes, shock waves rippled through his body when he realized she was the same woman he'd dreamed of all his life. He was certain of it, for he knew every curve of her face, the blush of her cheeks and dark velvet folds of her hair—such knowledge was as deeply embedded in his heart as his own DNA. The moment that flashed through his mind, he cupped her cheek to speak when an electric current exploded in his brain. Then he found himself once again on Rook Ridge.

But this time, he was soaking wet. And his mind had shattered.

Now, Chance gazed at the stars above the ocean, his mind so clear he could reach out and trace his finger over the constellations, murmuring the names for each one. The sea echoed a melody in his ears, its spray whispering a soft tune like a lullaby. Puzzled, he looked across the water, searching the stars' reflections on the waves, when he felt a small hand snuggle into his palm.

Startled, he glanced down to see a tow-headed girl in the moonlight, smiling at him with dimples in her cheeks. Chance knew her—she was the child he'd rescued from the pool, the same one he'd found two weeks ago on Rook Ridge. He resisted the urge to pick her up and keep her warm, to take her to a place where she would be safe until her mother came, as he did that night in Idaho. He scanned her face, his mind filled with questions.

The girl kindly patted his sleeve. She tugged his hand and led him up the beach to where the turf extended toward dark hills. Ahead, he spotted a stone cottage with a thatched roof. A bonfire burned nearby, piled high with peat bricks and driftwood. Its flames illuminated several rows of potatoes by the cottage, making the leaves glisten a soft gold.

The little girl let go of his hand to check on the plants. Huddling beside them in her fisherman's sweater, she whispered tenderly and petted their fragile leaves. She stepped back toward the beach and picked up a stick, slowly drawing circles in the sand. Curious, Chance asked what she was doing.

"I'm listening," she replied, "to the potato leaves."

Chance shifted in his boots, feeling sand chafe against his skin. "You are? What do they say?"

"They're singing," she stood up and smiled. "A healing song."

The girl began to hum as if the leaves could hear her. She picked up a seashell, fingering its delicate shape and smooth curves. Then she held it to her ear and listened, nodding as though it whispered the same melody. She handed the shell to Chance.

Chance accepted the small gift and dropped it in his pocket, suddenly aware that her mind was clear here, too. Both of them had lucid thoughts, ideas that formed into words and sentences, no longer bound by their limitations in Ophir Creek. He stared at her sand spirals, remembering her finger paintings that morning at the Rainbow's End Cafe. Recalling, too, the black bird she'd made on a piece of paper, the one she'd embellished with outstretched wings. At that moment, he heard a raven's caw. He glanced apprehensively around the windswept island.

"Where's your mother?" he asked. "Does she know you're here?"

The girl lifted her hand to show him a crystal bracelet on her wrist. She studied the fractured colors that lit up in the firelight.

"Mommy's lost," she replied. "She can't find me."

The girl walked over to a stone well near the cottage. Grasping a teacup on the ledge, she dipped it in the water and stepped over to the potato beds to sprinkle the plants. Returning to the well, she leaned her hands against the stones.

"Mommy can't see me." She peered inside. "She can't hear me either." Holding up her bracelet again, she twisted her wrist to make prismatic hues scatter in the firelight. "She's broken inside, like the colors."

With that, the girl held out her arms and began to spin, humming as her feet sank into the sand. Her tune became a gentle song.

"On a bird's wing, my heart brings, all my love to you."

A breeze picked up and circled them with moist salt air, tinged with the mossy aroma of peat and wild roses. A voice, singing the same melody, drifted in from the sea.

"Longing at twilight, our souls take flight, echoes of love unfold."

A dark figure appeared in the sea mist like a shade that had suddenly taken on form. It was black, darker than the night sky, in the shape of a large raven advancing from the beach. As the figure drew closer, Chance could make out a woman, wearing a long skirt with a shawl over her head. In her arms was a bundle of driftwood for the fire.

The woman set her wood on the sand, her green eyes illuminated by the flames. When she loosened her shawl, Chance observed she had thick black hair, laced with gray, and her skin was pale in the moonlight. He gasped—her features resembled the woman in Ophir Creek, as though she'd been transformed into an older peasant. She bent down to scoop a handful of sand. Stretching out her palm to Chance, she let the granules slip through her fingers.

"Time moves in circles, *a thaisce.*"

Wrapping her arms around Crystal, a warm smile curved her lips. "Tonight we'll sing more songs, won't we, Crystal? To heal the harvest plants." She gave the girl a squeeze and kneeled to check a potato leaf, turning it over to examine its vigor. When she stood up, she took Crystal by the hand and walked toward the well, motioning for Chance to follow. By the light of the stars, he could see the old well had pieces of cloth stuffed between the stones.

"These are the prayers of pilgrims who have come here for centuries," she said, removing a rag. She held it to the firelight to reveal its red color. "This one's Crystal's." She dropped it into the well.

Chance gazed at the water and startled when he saw a dark-haired young woman—the same one from his dreams—driving across a barren landscape, dust devils erupting at her tires. Her face was etched in worry as she stared out over the long desert. The woman stirred the water with her finger, and amidst the rings he saw the young woman again, only she was in the moonlight on Rook Ridge, shouting for Crystal among the tall stones. The peasant woman stirred her finger yet again, and the image blurred to become a coffee shop. But this time, the young woman was focused on a candle in a potato, clutching the edges of a red bandana. Despite the hope in her eyes, a shadow darkened the well. Soon, the ripples began to swirl into a violent whirlpool, threatening to devour her and everything else in its path of sweeping black ink.

Chance's heart hammered against his chest. Like an old, familiar reflex, every muscle in his large frame snapped to attention, swift as a switchblade and ready to strike. Without thinking, he leaned forward to dive his hands into the water to help the woman when the peasant woman clutched his shoulder. *"Cuir uait!"* she reprimanded, shaking him. "Not until it's time."

Stumbling back, Chance felt like his breath had been knocked out of him. His entire body shook as he recalled that voice—that command—from a very long time ago, an echo that still resounded in his bones. Shaking his head, it took every ounce of willpower not to push past her and thrust his hands into the water, to grab for the young woman and hold her close as he had done once in the fairy ring. He turned his gaze to Crystal, realizing that those images had been of her mother. He searched the peasant woman's face for answers.

"My daughter's heart is adrift." The woman drew Crystal to her side. "She's forgotten how to hear us."

"Wh-Who are you?" Chance's heart was still pounding. He squared his wide shoulders, bracing for her reply.

The peasant woman touched his hand, her fingers soft as feathers. A warmth blossom inside Chance as if a blanket had wrapped around his heart.

"I am her mother," she said. "And her mother before that, and her mother before that. We are O'Dannans, but you know me as Ailís."

She reached up to stroke the scar across his nose. Flinching, Chance jerked away, when he spotted his own reflection in the well. Only his black coat was no longer fabric, but feathers. He squinted, realizing wings had formed at his sides, as though his body were molting into a bird's. Soon, all he recognized of himself in the water was his dark eyes and the familiar scar on his nose, which had transformed into an ebony beak. Then a black-haired girl appeared at his side, and as she darted across potato rows, he heard Ailís's voice cry out in terror to guard her.

Just as quickly, another image floated on the water. It was of himself as a raven again, perched on a windowsill, dropping a silver locket for the young woman to see. When she smiled, he tossed his beak and thrust out his chest in pride. The image faded until only the moon's reflection settled on the water. A gunshot rang out, and the bodies of a man and a raven appeared, blood dribbling from their heads. The woman leaned over them both, sobbing.

Ailís pressed her hand gently on his arm. "You have watched her throughout time, *mo stór.* And always you've been as close to her as her own shadow."

Chance swallowed hard, his throat dry from bonfire smoke. Troubled, he lifted his hand to skim the scar on his nose as if it were a thread connecting him to centuries. All at once, he remembered how he'd gotten that wound—it was from a battle, long ago, during a time recorded only in the rings of ancient trees. A blonde, unscrupulous man had tried to overwhelm his O'Dannan woman that day, landing a heavy sword across his head. Though it would prove later to be a mortal blow, he'd refused to give in. He continued fighting, making certain that by nightfall, his opponent would also be buried.

Flashes came to his mind of other dawns, other battles, but always he'd faced his destiny with a coat of feathers. Chance bowed his head, feeling the vast weight of history settle into his bones. A question still smoldered in his veins. He lifted his gaze to Ailís.

"Why am I a man now?"

Hugging Crystal close, Ailís leaned her chin on the girl. She tilted her cheek up to the moon and closed her eyes, waiting.

Chance studied the silver light that caressed her forehead and full lips, the ageless dignity that defined her jaw and cheekbones, so like the woman he admired in Ophir Creek. Pressing his hand to his chest, his heart was seized by a yearning that had been kindling for centuries. This time, he didn't need to peer into the well for answers. He settled his gaze on the bonfire and watched the flames rise high into the night, snapping gold and crimson, as bright as passion itself. In that moment, he knew as sure as his own heartbeat why he had always guarded the O'Dannan woman. It was the oldest song on earth, the same one his soul had been singing throughout the ages. And every note called out to her.

"It's because I wanted to love her," he confessed, his voice crackling like the fire.

Staring down at his hands, at his fingernails as black as claws, he cleared his throat.

"I asked for this, didn't I? To become human."

When his eyes drifted back to Ailís, she nodded.

It was then that Chance pieced together the puzzle of his life—his lifetimes—in the same way he'd learned to discern the mysteries of old trees. All those years he'd been searching for her, trying to trace a path back to her heart through the tree rings. Circle upon circle, his love for her rippled out into eternity. But where would this story take him now?

Ailís drew in a deep breath, and in her eyes he saw a reservoir of sorrow, stirred with a knowing as ancient and immeasurable as the sea.

"My daughter doesn't know that darkness pursues her," she said, her voice solemn. "He is a *súmaire*—a leech. A black vortex who drains her of power. That's why he shines for her so brightly—because without O'Dannans, he can never endure. And he's been doing this for centuries."

Above her, clouds collected over the moon to match her sadness. A lightning bolt flashed, washing the beach in silver light. Thunder rolled over the ocean, and Ailís nodded at the sky.

"Do you know what you are?"

Chance slowly shook his head.

She glanced at the horizon to where the sea met stars. "You are 'twixt—*bheith idir eatarthu*—between the worlds. And you are all that stands now between their two fates. Your form has been stolen by his spirit. And he will try to destroy you, along with my daughter, unless he is stopped." She picked up a seashell and cracked it in her hand, dropping the shards at his feet.

Chance's face grew hot. His muscles quickened and his

hands clenched into fists. The old surge of protection snapped within in him as swiftly as striking a match.

"Steady," Ailís warned, lifting her hand like a sword. "You have the ability to return to her," she assured him, "and to guard her as you have always done. But it will require more courage from you than the urge to kill. For you have crushed him many times throughout history, yet always he returns to feed off her soul. Now, you must show her how to embrace her power, and to choose her own destiny—even if she doesn't understand. For only then can she break the cycle to be free. Because this darkness won't stop until it swallows her whole."

With that, she began to chant in Irish, and Crystal joined in, the two of them echoing a harmony of low whispers. When they stopped, Chance felt Ailís's hand upon his wrist.

"Time to go," she said, nodding at the beach. "The oars are with the *currach*—follow the currents, and they will lead you home."

Chance turned, spotting a small, dark boat on the beach. Fingering the shell in his pocket that Crystal had given him, he took a bold step, then another, his pace becoming more impassioned with each stride. Soon, his determination pounded like a drum within him, a rhythm that had been resonating in his heart from before time. As he advanced toward the sea, he heard Ailís call out, her voice nearly extinguished by the ocean roar.

"We will be with you."

In the spare light, a thin wash of pewter cushioned the last moments between night and dawn. He made the change.

The sea mist felt so cold against his skin he was sure it must have seeped into his bones. Rocked by ocean waves, he had rowed and rowed for hours, arms laden by sea-drenched sleeves. Then feathers began to form—a soft, downy layer of warmth, just like he'd seen in the well. Glancing at his chest, he was shocked by its layered blackness, by the clothing that had fallen to the *currach* where his feet had become claws. An upswell of wind caught him by the wing, tossing him over in the small boat.

He righted himself and drew a deep breath, his heart racing like a bird's. A raven flew past him in the mist, its crown feathers mottled gray, and it fixed its gaze steadily on the horizon. It turned and circled the small boat, cawing at him to join. Chance moved his wings up and down, listening to them creak like rusty hinges. A gust of air lifted him, and he stretched out his feathers. Catching sight of Crystal's shell that had tumbled from his pocket, he clutched it in his claw for good luck. He rose high above the boat, above the sea itself, his path lit by the dawning sun.

Cool air poured over his wings, and he flapped harder, his heart swelling. I can fly! he marveled, gliding over currents in a way that felt strangely familiar. He let out a laugh, but to his surprise, his voice came out a raspy caw. Ocean waves that had punished the boat earlier became as small as ripples, and in the distance he saw mountains, or perhaps they were cloud banks, stained blue by rain. For all he knew, those ridges could be merely another dream, by a man some people in Ophir Creek called "fairy struck", now crazier than ever. Was he really headed home to his beloved forest, or simply venturing toward more wild imaginings?

Chance shook his beak in wonder. All he knew is that he would travel to the ends of the earth, his heart embracing each moment, if that's what it took to find his O'Dannan woman again. Following the path of the raven before him, he rode on a breeze toward a mysterious horizon. The only thing he could count on for certain was that anything was possible.

7

The sun rose and a sheen of gold spread over the treetops of Rook Ridge. A man in a black coat lay on the ground in a heap. Clutching fistfuls of dirt, he lifted his head and squinted at the rays of sun that sliced through pines. It was cold. All around him, dead leaves and dry needles lie dusted with frost. As the dawn warmed his cheek, he closed his eyes and felt the strange sensation of blood coursing his veins, tingling down to his fingertips and toes. It's peculiar to inhabit someone else's body, he thought, to feel sensations pulsing through another man's skin. Poor bastard, he smiled—that's what you get for being at the wrong place at the right time. Moving his fingers, he rustled brittle leaves, crushing them easily to dust. He stared for a long time at the town of Ophir Creek below, sleepy and unaware of its new visitor.

The sun soaked through ponderosas, and soon shadows began to circle the ridge, weaving in and out over tall, granite stones. Ravens cawed. The man's heart pounded fast. He studied their silhouettes with the steady gaze of a mountain cat. When he looked up, the ravens' circle broke. Screeching, they dove at him, their black wings flapping as they pecked his face. The man stood and grabbed a broken tree limb. He swung at the birds, batting them aside like balls.

"You can't guard her forever," he said bitterly, waving at any raven that dared to come near. "This time, I win."

He held up the branch like a torch, ignoring the racket from birds that took refuge in trees, their dark eyes following his every move. "Time to rewrite history," he insisted, stepping over to a large boulder. He placed his hand on a bullet hole etched in granite, circling the depression with his finger. "It's not over," he muttered, rubbing the stone until it grew warm. "It's never over between us."

Mica filtered to the forest floor, glistening at his feet. He stretched out his long arm and examined the lacy welts on his skin, his fingernails charred black. "Lightning," he winced, recalling the violent passage of his soul's return. "Price of admission." Tucking the branch under his arm, he headed down the mountain, his legs trembling at the memory of movement, his arms bracing against trees for balance. He stopped to steady himself on a boulder, gathering breath and strength, but the din of forest creatures followed him like shadows. Owls hooted, coyotes cried, and always there were the caws of ravens. The man cursed them, all of them, humming rounds of old gold mining songs to drown out their echoes.

When he reached Ophir Creek, its storefronts cast dormant by mountain shadows, he recognized the Rainbow's

End at the corner of the town square. Pausing, he stared at the old tan building, at the sign above its front door with a scale balancing a pot of gold, newly painted until it gleamed. He traced the gold in air with his finger, and a cold wind picked up, lifting newspapers and leaves into spirals. An old dog limped along the boardwalk, hesitating when it saw him. The man stared it down. With hoarse barks and frosted fur high on its neck, the dog skittered away. The man stepped up to the boardwalk and laughed, took a swing with his tree branch at no one there, admiring his own sinewy grace.

Wind howled through holes in the boardwalk, and the man turned to study the Magpie Saloon at the edge of town, boarded up with black steel doors. Spotting a small, uncovered window on the side of the building, he walked up and shattered the pane with his branch. Glass fragments burst at his feet, and he kicked them away, hoisting himself through the window. Inside the bar, he nodded at the familiar poker tables and chairs, at the dusty shelves lined with liquor bottles and snake oil. For an instant, he could almost smell the spilled whiskey and hear the fiddle music that used to permeate the bar. But that was a long time ago—years had somehow slipped through cracks. What was his name back then? Rory? Riordan? Maybe James, or perhaps Jake. He moved his lips, but the words eluded him like a faint melody played too far in the distance.

The man stared curiously at the mirror behind the carved mahogany bar. His reflection in the low light resembled a photographic negative: darkness inverted of life. He stepped over to the front door and unlocked it, swinging it open to the morning sun. Then he unbolted the steel window panels.

When he returned to the mirror, he studied the contours of the tall, backlit stranger who returned his gaze.

"My God, you're a dirty son of a bitch."

The man stroked his scraggly beard, littered with pine needles, and examined his matted hair and the sage that stuck to his black coat. He walked behind the bar and rifled through bins and shelves. Inside one drawer were old buttons and handkerchiefs, a long-handled razor blade and a garter belt trimmed with lace. In another drawer, boxes of matches were stacked on top of pomade jars, along with a Chinese tin of opium. The man pried the tin open and dipped his finger into the gummy cake, lifting it to his lips. Bitter, he thought, but he smiled and tucked it into his jeans. Then he reached for a box of matches to light an oil lamp on the bar. In the amber glow, he removed the razor blade from the drawer and gazed into the mirror. Opening a pomade jar, he smoothed the cream on his face, which reeked of eucalyptus oil and herbs. He held the razor blade to his cheek and took a deep breath as he scraped cold metal against his skin, again and again, watching his beard drift in dark tufts to the floor.

When he was finished, he grabbed the handkerchief and wiped his stinging face clean, admiring the striking, roughhewn features he'd revealed: the firm-set jaw and sharp cheekbones, the lush eyebrows framing big brown eyes that could make any woman wilt. Lifting his chin, he couldn't believe his luck, and he smiled at the handsome face that now adorned the glass. "A mountain man kissed by the Gods," he marveled. "Ready to break hearts."

The man laughed, patting his cheek in hearty approval. He glanced down at the old bar sink and turned the creaky, porcelain handles. Ice-cold rusty water spilled into the basin. He waited a few moments until it cleared and thrust his head under the stream, letting out a scream. Gasping, he was astonished at the rawness in his voice, at the cool transience of water, and he cupped his hands to drink greedily. Reaching for the pomade, he rubbed it into his scalp and forced his head back under the sink. As water rinsed his neck and temples, he grabbed the razor to hack off long matted locks, watching them tumble into the sink. He turned to the mirror and sliced at unruly cowlicks.

The sun had begun to seep across the mahogany bar, and the warm morning light danced off the dark wetness of his hair. Staring intently at the deep scar across his nose, he gazed with great concentration until his cheeks began to swell with a boyish confidence, and the scar slowly faded from view. Then he lifted his fingers to his face, carefully massaging his skin with an artisan's precision, and soon, his features looked slightly different—softer and more radiant—as though sculpted to reflect a more celestial air. Studying his warm, brown eyes, lit up in the middle with sparks, he blinked as they changed to a dazzling blue. The man smiled at his creation. He nodded at his cropped black hair, focusing his gaze with unwavering attention, until the strands gradually glistened to a burnished gold.

"Perfect." He turned his chin left and right, allowing the razor nicks to remain. "Just like a fallen angel."

The man ran his hand across the gold nugget inlaid on the bar and slipped off his long, dirty coat, letting let it fall to the floor. Moving to an old trunk by the wall, he dug through tin cups and gold pans, old flannel shirts and dungarees. He found a deerskin jacket, faded to the color of sand, and slipped it on. Underneath it was an old calendar, dated 1863. Flipping through the pages, a chill ran down his spine. The paper was yellow and brittle, its ink bleached gray, as if the calendar had been lying there for a century. The man's jaw tightened. What year was it? Did it matter? He pressed his palm to his pulsing heart. Then he traced his finger over the calendar dates and studied them as though they once held keys to different doors, now locked and sealed from entry. Clenching his teeth, he crushed the dry pages with his hands, letting them fall in pieces on the floor.

"Death is simply the middle of a very long life," he smiled. "When you rule the heart of an O'Dannan woman."

He kicked the trunk closed while a caravan of vehicles hastened down Main Street. The man walked to the front window and leaned on the glass, watching hunters roar by in dusty trucks with barking dogs. For a second, he puzzled over the steel trucks with rubber tires, clouds of exhaust spilling from their tail pipes. Images stung his mind—pack mules and wagons, picks and shovels, the noisy town square crowded with tents and miners' lamps. Which century could this be? he wondered, shaking his head. He closed his eyes and forced the pictures to dissolve. The remembrance of an old, blue truck surfaced in his thoughts. Ah yes—the smell of a warm engine, the slippery feel of axle grease and familiar cracks of leather seats. "Automobiles," he recalled, coiling his fingers over an imaginary stick shift, "gasoline powered."

When he opened his eyes, he saw a battered blue truck up the street, parked at the Rainbow's End Cafe. Nodding, he nipped opium again from his pocket and felt the bloom tingle at the back of his brain. Then, just like in a dream, he saw a beautiful woman emerge from the cafe with a shovel in her hands. She wore faded overalls and appeared nervous as she began to dig a hole at the side of the building. A raven landed at her feet, cawing and flapping its wings, but she brushed it aside. After she thrust her spade several times into the frosted ground, she lifted a potato from her pocket. Glancing around as if hoping no one saw her, she smoothed back her black hair. She dropped the potato into the hole and quickly covered it up.

"Ah, my rose," the man said with a smile, "you should have known I would find you."

Cracking his knuckles, he walked over to a poker table to sit down and stretch out his long legs. For a moment, he stared at the rusted, metal bear traps hanging on the wall, waiting patiently for their next victims. He glanced at a scale for weighing gold on the bar. Picking up a poker chip, he flipped it in air and caught it, tossing it onto the scale with a rattle.

"You can't help it, my rose." He turned to gaze at the woman across the street. Each movement she made sent sparks up his spine, as though her contours were embedded in his genetic memory, pulsing through every nerve and vein. "No matter how hard you run," he clasped his hands behind his head, "you bring me back every time."

❦ 8 ❦

The morning sun crept slowly over wooden planks as Rose swept the boardwalk in front of the Rainbow's End Cafe. A curl of wind rose up, scattering leaves across her feet. She clutched her broom and listened to the leaves' whispers, pulling her jacket tighter. She couldn't help it —she had a strange feeling this morning of being watched. Yet no matter where she looked, the same old western store fronts and pine trees stared back at her, nothing unusual. Rose shook her head, realizing she was self-conscious about burying that silly potato next to her building, the way Amy had instructed after their love spell. But what could it hurt? she thought. It's not like my love life can get any worse.

A bird cast a shadow over the clean spot she'd swept, and she leaned against her broom to sigh. Earlier, she'd set out a fairy cake on a plate for Chance Murphy, in case he was too wary to step inside the shop again. At least he could eat something nutritious, she hoped, and it made her feel good to provide more food for him. But now that pesky raven had started hanging around, cawing at her. Rose had heard that ravens could be thieves sometimes—ready to steal anything from picnic food to car keys. Great, she thought, just when I've gotten everything organized.

"What do you want?" she challenged as the bird brazenly strutted across her boardwalk. "That fairy cake?" Rose figured she could set out another one later for Chance, so she snatched it to take inside. "Tough luck, I'm saving this one for a friend."

The raven tossed his head and squawked. Rose was about to shoo him away when a gust of wind chilled her, as cold and moist as if it came from the sea. The bird lifted his wings to brace himself and stepped forward, staring at her with penetrating, obsidian eyes. Rose did a double take. Something about his gaze seemed familiar—a brooding intensity mingled with concern—so peculiar for a wild bird. She watched as he dropped a small seashell at her feet.

Surprised, Rose picked it up. She'd spotted migrant seagulls a few times along the Boise River, an odd sight in the mountains, hundreds of miles from any ocean. Could this raven have carried the shell from such a far away place? She fingered the pretty nautilus shape in her palm, wondering if Crystal might like it, so she slipped it into her pocket. When she turned to open the cafe door, the raven cawed.

"Oh, all right," Rose sighed, swayed by the intriguing look in his eyes. She broke off a big hunk of cake and tossed it to him with a wry smile. "But I'm only giving you this because your eyes are dreamy. And thank you for the seashell," she said, feeling like a pushover. "Now I need to get back to work."

She flicked her broom at the raven until he hopped from the boardwalk. Adjusting a scarecrow she'd set up by the door for Halloween, she braced a couple of large pumpkins to make it stand straight. "A lot of good you did," she teased the scarecrow, fluffing up its straw. "You're supposed to keep wild birds away."

All at once, she heard a chorus of caws from a flock of birds that had swooped into the town square. Rose turned toward the ruckus to see a group of ravens hovering over the Magpie Saloon. They dive bombed the building, dropping stones and pinecones and knocking paint chips off the siding. Then they flew in a wild, dark swirl like angry bees. Rose shivered, unnerved by their eerie behavior. There must be a predator around, she thought—a badger, or maybe a fox. She opened the cafe door, just as the raven leaped back onto the boardwalk and boldly strutted into her shop.

"Oh no you don't!" She batted at the bird with her broom, but he lifted his wings defiantly and hopped further inside. He flew to a high shelf, beyond her reach. The tufts of his black crown feathers rose to indicate threat, and he made knocking noises in the back of his throat. The bird picked his way along the shelf, shoving items onto the floor with his beak—an old box of Lightning brand baking soda, an antique tin of Devil's corn starch. The raven gazed at Rose with a strange steadiness, his head cocked to one side, expecting a response. Rose groaned and picked up the items, then headed for the door.

"Listen, mister, you can either go willingly, or I'll call county animal control." Her cheeks flushed that she'd tried to reason with a wild bird. Reaching for her spray bottle, she squirted window cleanser at him to scare him off, when she heard a soft voice coming from the back apartment. It was Crystal.

Stunned, Rose set the bottle down and ran to the bedroom, where she found her daughter still asleep, humming what sounded like a lullaby. She tiptoed to the bed, her heart racing, and leaned over their antique quilt. Crystal seemed lost to slumber, the quilt snuggled close against her chin. *Am I dreaming,* she wondered, *or did I really hear her voice?*

"Come on honey," she whispered, her eagerness getting the best of her. She brushed the peach-fuzz on her daughter's cheek. "Hum for Mommy again."

To her surprise, she heard a chortling sound, like a cadenced melody—the same lullaby her daughter had hummed. Rose leaned her ear to Crystal's throat, but the sounds weren't coming from her. *Am I imagining things?* Then she heard a gentle series of notes. She whipped around to see the raven at the foot of the quilt, nestled as comfortably as a house pet. He stared intently at Crystal and chortled the song. Rose rubbed her eyes. A forest ranger had told her once that ravens could be mimics, imitating radio static, car engines, even voices sometimes. But how could this bird have picked up the lullaby so fast? Before she could ponder an answer, she heard her daughter hum, barely audible above her own breath. Crystal moved her lips as if she knew the words in her dreams.

The raven cooed a melodic reply. Tears slipped down Rose's cheeks. She recognized the song—it was the lullaby her mother used to sing to her, the one Rose had always hummed at night for comfort. Trembling, she picked up Crystal and hugged her so close he feared she might bruise her limbs.

"Oh baby," she whispered. "Oh my baby girl. A song! You remembered a song! The doctors were wrong—I knew it could happen. I knew you'd come back to Mommy."

Crystal wriggled her arms free from her mother's grasp and yawned. She smiled, not at Rose, but at the bird at the edge of the bed, reaching out her fingers like they were friends. Holding up her wrist, she watched colors from her crystal bracelet leap in the morning light. The bird took a hop toward her, mesmerized. Then Crystal crawled from her mother's lap and stroked the bird. Rose crossed her arms, studying her daughter in amazement. Crystal was actually bonding with something—a wild creature she'd barely met. At that moment, harness bells jingled at the front door, and Rose peered past the bedroom curtain to see Amy walking through the shop. When Amy spotted them, she smiled.

"Hey!" she said cheerfully when she reached the apartment. Amy gazed at the raven on the quilt. "Looks like Crystal found a friend. What's your name big fella?" She patted the bird with the same lack of hesitation as Crystal, noticing the silhouette it cast over the bedspread. "Shadow?" She smiled at Crystal. "Is that what you call your bird buddy? You know, ravens are omens of the magical connection between our world and the next—"

"Amy," Rose clutched her friend's arm. "Crystal hummed a melody this morning in her sleep. A real song!"

"Oh my gosh!" Amy's eyes the colors that flashed from Crystal's bracelet and nodded at the bird. "Well, we shouldn't be too surprised—ravens do mean transformation. But be careful, northwestern tribes believe they're shapeshifters."

"Shapeshifters?"

"You know, beings who assume animal form, to come and help us."

"Right," Rose glanced down at her hand. "Well, all I know is that he brought this seashell."

"Ooh, an animal gift!" Amy clasped her fingers, her charm bracelet quivering. She plucked the shell from Rose's palm and headed to the bean pot on the kitchen counter. "You'd better keep this," she warned, lifting the lid to drop the shell beside the items they'd found the night before. "Animal tokens are very powerful, kind of like good luck charms. I bet we're going to have a banner day."

The harness bells jingled again, and Rose peeked past the bedroom curtain to see an old woman standing inside the shop. Her face was pinched and her hands were kneaded together, as though she'd brought in all of her worries along with a gust of cold, morning air.

"Guess it's time to find out," Rose said, feeling harried that a customer had arrived so early. "Would you mind greeting her? There's still some fairy cakes in the glass case that you can offer."

Amy nodded and slipped into the shop as Rose hustled to dress Crystal. All the while, she sang the lullaby her daughter had hummed, her eyes tearing up. She stared at Crystal's cottony blonde hair in the mirror, at the distracted, glassy eyes that never returned her gaze. You can't fool me, honey, Rose thought. I know what I heard. I bet you're just waiting for me below the surface—it's only a matter of time. Soon we'll laugh and talk and sing, just like we always used to. Everything will be perfect.

Rose opened a tube of toothpaste and helped Crystal brush her teeth and rinse, then pulled back her hair into her favorite butterfly barrette. She couldn't help but smile as she watched Crystal amble into the shop, her ponytail bouncing, followed by the raven at her heels. As long as that bird helps her remember things, Rose nodded to herself, I suppose I can put up with him.

"Good morning!" Rose announced to the customer as she stepped past the bedroom curtain. The grizzled woman sat across from Amy at the window table near the front door. She wore frayed jeans held together by colorful patches and a bright turquoise rodeo shirt with pearl buttons, her white hair pulled back by a rhinestone star. Rose chuckled to herself, wondering if this was how she was going to look in forty years —another Rocky Mountain eccentric, decked out like the sweetheart of the rodeo. The coffee maker gurgled loudly in the background as the woman nodded at Rose and held up a half-eaten fairy cake.

"Might tasty," she remarked. "Hits the spot."

"This is my client," Amy said proudly. "Belle Crawford."

"Client?"

"Don't you remember my card?" Amy dug into her pocket and handed another one to Rose. "I figured I could squeeze in a session or two before we open. Helps bring in customers."

Rose glanced at the logo: *Eternity's Wings: Transmigration Therapy and Psychic Repair*. "Oh yeah," she rubbed her eyes, unsure whether she approved of this sort of thing, especially at the shop. But if the woman bought breakfast, she could hardly complain. "How can you do past-life readings so early in the morning?" She yawned and stepped over to the coffee maker to pour them each a mug.

"Vibrations never take a break!" Amy insisted. She stared intently at a crystal ball on the table that sparkled in the morning light. Her eyes began to dance as though she were watching a movie. "Belle's past is utterly fascinating. Once, she threw herself into a volcano over a lost love. And in the next life, she came back as a gigolo to see how the other half lives, but it left her feeling empty. After that, we discovered she was on the rodeo circuit with Buffalo Bill. She could perform tricks with pistols and lariats."

"That's how I lassoed lovers," Belle smiled. She stared at the crystal ball and ran a finger along its curve with a wistful look in her eyes. "The trouble is keeping 'em."

Amy glanced up and patted her hand. "Don't worry, dear —you'll meet up with Carson again. Just be open. Cosmic law requires that any unfinished business will always come back to you, just in a different form. So you'll find true love," she smiled at Rose, "we all will."

Rose sighed and studied the two women, trying to decide which one of them was crazier. Is that all Amy's hocus pocus is —a lonely hearts club? A tingling sensation skittered down her back, and she felt embarrassed she'd gotten sucked into the love spell last night. Yet in spite of her resistance, her nosiness kicked in, and she found herself swiping a glance into the coffee mug that she'd poured for Belle. To Rose's amazement, a weathered cowboy's face stared back at her, his skin deeply lined and his old hat curled at the edges, but his eyes surprisingly bright. She shook her head, yet the reflection remained, tenacious as the well-worn patches on Belle's jeans.

Rose giggled a little and walked to the table to set down the mugs for Belle and Amy.

"Well, I guess anything's possible," she conceded, squeezing the old woman's hand. From a corner of the room, she thought she heard Crystal's raven chortle. It sounded like he muttered, *Indeed*.

Rose blinked a few times and shrugged, blaming it on the shop's acoustics. She stepped back over to the counter to pull out paper and crayons for Crystal, along with a jar of glue and a bag of sparkly stars. When she placed the craft supplies on the floor, Crystal came over like a magnet, the raven chasing closely behind her. As Crystal began to swirl her crayons, Rose searched her face, hoping for signs of words or a soft, vibrating hum—any trace that might repeat her morning miracle. Although Crystal pursed her lips with deep concentration, she made no sounds while she fashioned her usual loops and circles, her eyes glued to her designs.

"You know, Miss Tinker has some awfully good advice." Belle watched the way Crystal ignored her mother like there was plexiglass between them. "Maybe you should give a past life reading a try? Might help you connect with folks you've become, well, a little distant from."

"What do you mean?" Rose replied too fast, biting her lip.

Belle took a sip from her coffee. "Oh nothing. Just that it's nice to explore once in a while. You can't find true love if you're too uptight, you know. Speaking of lovers, did you see that new fella across the street?"

Amy lifted her mug and studied the coffee ring on the table as though there might be meaning in the stain. "What new fella?"

"The one at the Magpie Saloon. He was unlatching a window when I waved good morning, so I asked what he was up to. He said he was going to open the bar again, bring back more business to this town."

"You're kidding." Amy eyes grew wide. She set down her mug. "Is he good looking?"

"That ain't the half of it," Belle chuckled. "You gals had better watch out—I might lasso him myself if you don't pocket him first."

She reached into her jeans and placed a few bills on the table before standing up. Pausing, she laid her hand lightly on Amy's crystal ball, her fingers gliding over its convex smoothness, appearing hesitant to leave something behind. "Thanks for the chat, dearie," she nodded. "Helps put things in perspective." She walked to the front door and swung it open, making the harness bells clang. "You two stay out of trouble."

The instant the door closed behind her, Amy dashed to Rose. "Can you believe it?"

"Believe what?" Rose was busy adding flour to the morning's recipe—today's special would be pine nut cornbread.

Amy curled a lock of red hair around her finger. "Don't you think it's peculiar that a new guy comes to town, right after our love spell? You planted the potato wish seed, didn't you?"

Rose blushed. "Sure," she pointed a flour-dusted finger, "and that's how we got stuck with that raven over there. He followed me inside afterwards. Just my luck—we forgot to specify the right species."

"You're so impatient!" Amy scolded. "The magic's already working, right under your nose, and you haven't even given it a chance. By the way, do you have binoculars? I want to get a good look at the new guy."

Rose set the mixing bowl down. "Amy, you're becoming a voyeur."

"So what—we're not hurting anybody." Amy headed to a wooden crate beneath a shelf. Rummaging through it, she held up an old corset and smirked, then rifled through clothing and gadgets till she picked out an antique spy glass. "This will do." Amy dashed to the window.

When Amy clinked the glass against the pane, Rose felt a sudden chill. She remembered the ravens that swarmed over the Magpie Saloon earlier, their cries shrill and hostile. Her mother used to say that angry birds meant deception was near. What if the stranger across the street was hiding something? It wouldn't be the first time an unsavory character had moved to Ophir Creek to lay low from the law for a while. Rose braved a glance into her coffee cup, but all she saw were hazy, gray clouds, matching the brooding October sky outside.

"Oh my gosh!" Amy squealed. "He's gorgeous!" She whipped around. "I can see him inside the bar. He's wearing a fringed, suede jacket, and he's tall and handsome. Just like you ordered."

"I didn't order anything," Rose wrung her hands. "I just went along with the spell to humor you."

"Then I like your sense of humor!" Amy smiled. She grabbed Rose by the arm and pulled her to the window. "I told you. Good things are coming your way. Here, take a peek."

Rose's curiosity got the best of her and she snuck a look,

lifting the spy glass to the window. She spotted a tall, wide-shouldered man dusting off the mahogany bar, whistling. All at once, he stopped. He put down his towel and leaned casually against the countertop, limber as a cat, and stared at her across the street. He smiled like he knew she'd been peeking.

Rose's cheeks flushed, and she quickly handed the spy glass to Amy. Without warning, she heard a violent caw. Crystal's raven flew to the window and beat his wings furiously against the glass.

"What's up with the raven?" Amy shooed him away before he could hurt himself. He landed beside Crystal and gurgled fiercely. Wide eyed, Crystal gave him her full attention, seeming to understand his language.

"I don't know," Rose replied, fascinated by her daughter's response. When she turned to gaze outside, she noticed dark thunderheads had gathered over Rook Ridge. Glancing down, she spotted clouds on Crystal's sheet of paper. She assumed her daughter's crayon shapes must be random, but nevertheless, the drawing gave her goose bumps. "Maybe there's a bad storm coming," she whispered.

At that moment, two men walked through the front door. Rose immediately felt guilty, realizing she'd spent the entire morning chatting and hadn't gotten cornbread in the oven. At least the coffee was still fresh. "Hello," she said brightly, hoping there were enough fairy cakes left to tide them over.

"You the gold lady?" said one of the men. He looked Rose up and down and held up a miner's pick, brushing off the tip.

Rose peered at her watch and scratched her head. It was only a quarter to seven, a bit early for such a request. "Uh, sure, I can show you how to pan for gold." She set down her mug of coffee. "The demonstration is free if you order breakfast. Take a seat."

"Nope—no touristy stuff. I'm talking about real gold, the legend of Rook Ridge. A blue moon's coming in two weeks. You the gold lady?"

Rose's breath hitched. Wordless, she glanced at Amy.

"Of course she is!" Amy said eagerly. "And she'd be glad to lead you on a prospecting trip. Hundred bucks a pop. Now if you sit here a spell, we'll have some hot cornbread for you in no time." Amy scurried to pour Rose's batter into pans while the man and his buddy sat down.

"Deal," the man's buddy said. He nodded at his friend like he'd won a bet.

"Amy," Rose whispered, darting behind the counter. "I can't find real gold. Don't you remember—my father was a charlatan."

"How do you know for sure? The legend says your ancestor found a fortune."

"No, it says she *might* have—no one knows for certain. Besides, it's just a story, a fairy tale. We could mess up, or worse, get taken to court for misleading people."

"Not if you make it entertaining!" Amy grinned. "Just bring them to Rook Ridge, show the bullet scars on the rocks and tell a good yarn, then set 'em loose. Their imaginations will soar." Amy tapped her head. "Sweetie, you gotta start thinking like an entrepreneur."

Rose rolled her eyes. "Is that how you make money off being psychic? With lies?" She filled coffee mugs and took them to the men. "So," she attempted to say lightly, "h-how did you hear about the legend of Rook Ridge?"

"Honey," the man replied, "every gold seeker in the county knows that one. You ladies are gonna be swamped pretty soon." He sipped his coffee and nodded at the flavor, then cleared his throat. "You know," he leaned back in his chair, "that prospecting trip is worthless if you show the site to everybody. What would it take for me and my pal to have an exclusive tour? Before the blue moon rises, of course."

Sweat dampened Rose's forehead. She wiped her brow, feeling like a swindler, and refused to make eye contact with Amy. For a moment, she stared at the floor and noticed the raven hopping alongside the wall. He paused beside the wooden crate Amy had searched earlier and plucked out a coin. Rapping the crate, he flung the coin aside and it skidded across the room. Rose picked up the tarnished nickel and turned it over in her palm.

"Five thousand dollars," Amy butted in, giving Rose a wink. "No guarantees."

The man shook his head and laughed, long and slow. He pulled out matches and a cigarette from his pocket and lit up, taking a few puffs. "Too rich for me."

"But that's only twenty-five hundred a piece," the man's buddy prodded, "this could be the mother lode." He grabbed his friend's matches and lit up his own cigarette, folding his arms as he stared across the town square. "We'll think about it," he added.

Before Rose could chastise the men for smoking, Amy snuck up behind her and gave her a kick. "Sure, let us know," Amy smiled.

A dusty jeep rumbled past the store, and the two men got up, abandoning their coffee. "You ladies have a good day," the man said. He grabbed his pick and opened the front door. "We'll be in touch."

As soon as the door closed behind them, the raven swooped underneath their table and nibbled the crumbs, chortling happily after each one. Rather than berate the bird, Rose sighed, glad she wouldn't have to sweep.

"Did you hear that?" Amy burst. "They're going to think about it! We might make back all the money Laurel sent you."

"By cheating people?"

"No, by giving them hope. What's wrong with that?"

"I don't know, Amy," Rose slumped into the chair by the window and stared into a half-filled coffee cup, her fingers toying with a napkin. All she saw in the liquid was her own reflection, her eyes confused. "I just feel uncomfortable feeding superstitions about my great-great grandmother. Gold hunting only brought Corvine O'Dannan tragedy."

"Well, think of it this way," Amy moved to the oven to pull out cornbread, setting the pan on a cooling rack, "after just one prospecting trip, you could get out from under your sister's thumb. For good! Bye-bye Laurel!" Amy waved at Rose with her oven mitt.

Rose nodded, studying the tarnished nickel she still had in her hand. A dust devil picked up outside and swirled leaves onto the boardwalk with a scuffling sound. She scanned the wooden planks, annoyed at the debris, when she heard the raven begin to caw. He hopped up to the window pane and tapped angrily. Rose wondered if there was a stray dog or a loose cat nearby. She picked up the spy glass Amy had left by the window and searched the town square. On the porch of the Magpie Saloon was the attractive stranger seated on a bench, his long legs stretched into suede cowboy boots. He reached into his pocket and began to flip a coin that flashed in the morning sun. After tossing it several times, he caught it in mid-air and stared with singular focus at the Rainbow's End Cafe. Then he smiled as he leaned back on the bench and laughed.

9

Instead of doing dishes that evening, Rose sank into the old, Victorian rocker next to her bed with Crystal cradled on her lap. The velvet cushion beneath her was threadbare at the edges, but its cozy softness was like a balm after a harried day. The miners who'd warned her that morning were right—a flood of gold seekers had funneled through the shop. Each one demanded panning lessons or supplies, their hopes set on the blue moon in two weeks over Rook Ridge. Gold fever had already struck Ophir Creek, and to Rose's embarrassment, most of them had heard she was a descendent of the woman in the legend. Not only did they expect her to bless their wares with magic spells, one woman even snipped off a lock of her hair for good luck. Rose yelped in fright, but that merely stirred customers into further frenzy. Before she knew it, a man had swiped a fork and a spoon she'd touched, as if they might impart special powers, and another woman lifted a napkin from the trash because she'd sneezed on it.

"These people are crazy!" Rose gasped during a break in the flow. She could barely cook enough cornbread to keep up with them.

"Stop complaining," Amy smiled, holding a wad of bills from the cash drawer, "we're making money! Besides, it shouldn't startle you that miners are superstitious—didn't you say your dad skipped on one leg before he panned and repeated little jingles?"

"That's exactly what I mean!" Rose's brows beaded with perspiration. "He was nuts."

Nothing Rose said could make a dent in Amy's enthusiasm, and she was mortified when she saw her friend hand out past-life therapy cards to customers. Before she could stop her, Amy assured them all they'd probably struck gold in the last century and might do so again, just to keep them coming back.

Sighing, Rose nestled her head against the old rocker, gently swaying as she tried to forget the chaos of her day. She stroked Crystal's downy hair, her fingers untangling soft locks as she relished the rise and fall of her daughter's chest. Rose savored early evenings like this, when Crystal was too tired to be fussy, and her own mind was too numbed by fatigue to cling to the usual worries. Instead, they folded into each other's warmth, their bodies blurring the edges of where one ended and the other began. Though Crystal didn't sing again that day, as Rose had hoped, the morning miracle still gleamed in her heart like a jewel. Ten gold stars now brightened her daughter's progress chart on the wall, and several times during the day Rose visited the place on the bed where Crystal hummed, repeating the lullaby in her mind like a recording. She couldn't help staring at the photo she kept of Crystal before the accident on the bed post, the memory of her daughter's sweet voice filling her soul to the brim.

"On a bird's wing, my heart brings, all my love to you," Rose sang softly on the rocker, squeezing her daughter's shoulder. She hoped the tune might somehow bridge the divide between them—that excruciating wall of silence that separated her from Crystal. Patiently, she hummed as much of the song as she could recall, hoping her daughter might hear it in her dreams. As her eyelids grew heavy, she didn't notice the raven on top of the coat rack in the corner of the room. He hid in shadows, his black eyes watching the flames in the wood stove dance as the fire cast a soft glow upon Rose and Crystal. Soon, Rose nodded off to sleep, and the raven lifted his wings and glided to the rocker, perching behind her. Cautiously, he edged closer to Rose, at first taking in the wood-smoke smell of her hair, then lightly unraveling a wayward lock with his beak.

My God, you're beautiful. Do you know that?

Rose's eyelids fluttered. She opened them for a moment, but the room looked fuzzy, as if she were under water, too overcome by drowsiness to see clearly. She didn't notice the bird behind her, and she tilted her head to drift back to sleep with the slow creaks of her rocker.

The raven gripped the wood of the chair tighter with his claws. He chortled softly.

All my life I've tried to find you—and here you are! You're even more lovely than I imagined. Who would have guessed that a cloak of feathers would bring me so close to my dreams?

He studied Rose, his eyes following the line of her nose, the smooth contours of her cheeks and lips. Hesitantly, he reached up and caressed her with his soft wing tip. His feathers ran along her pale, slim neck and down to her delicate collar bone, then on to the swell of her cleavage that lay slightly exposed beneath her red flannel shirt. As the wood stove crackled, he felt a guilty pleasure from watching her in silence, bathed in amber firelight, but deep gratitude as well. After all, what would a woman like her want with him when he was in human form, fairy struck and crazy as a loon? At least this way, he could observe her freely, sit beside her without her even noticing. How many others have appreciated this woman from afar? he wondered. He dared to lift his beak and slip it through the sweeping blackness of her hair, pondering whether she, too, had been a raven once in another life. Treasuring her lush locks, he marveled that his thoughts were so lucid now, clear as mountain air, as though the former haze of his frazzled neurons had dissolved into a pure horizon. *This is heaven*, he realized, taking in her face as if it were a polished work of art. Then he turned to the window that faced the Magpie Saloon, where a light had come on and gleamed across the square. He could see the silhouette of a man moving inside.

The raven grew restless, shifting his claws to steady himself on the rocker. He leaned forward and placed his beak tenderly beside Rose's ear.

There's a robber in our midst, he whispered. *I don't know who he is, or what he is. But I know I've battled him before, and he's nothing but a thief. He stole my body, Rose, but not my soul. That handsome, rugged man you saw across the street this morning—that was me, before the madness twisted my thoughts into knots. I was a mountain man, a forest scientist—someone you could admire. Chance Murphy then. And now? A raven in shadows. I'm so confused, Rose. Yet I can see you, feel your beautiful hair. And I know you care, in spite of your worries. You gave me a basket of food that morning in your shop, though my symptoms frightened you. Be careful, Rose—that man wants something. And I think he'll do anything to get it.*

The raven hopped onto the arm of the rocker and nestled against Rose's free hand. Unconsciously, Rose stroked his feathers, her other arm wrapped around her daughter's shoulder, as if all three of them were connected by an imaginary string. When the raven glanced up, he noticed Crystal's eyes were open.

She doesn't listen very well here, Crystal noted matter-of-factly. She yawned and stretched out her arms, gazing at the flames that leaped in the stove, her eyes reflecting snippets of gold. *Her heart's too jammed with junk. If you want to talk, you have to take her to the other place. At night, when she's asleep, so she can hear you.*

The raven cocked his head, puzzled.

Crystal crossed her arms impatiently. *Just close your eyes and dream. Soon you'll be there. That's how I do it.*

Crystal edged down from her mother's lap, careful not to sway the rocker. She stood between the chair and the bed and lifted her arms. Closing her eyes, she began to spin. As her feet moved in circles, she gently hummed the lullaby. *See?* she opened her eyes, staring at the raven. *Wish hard and tell her to go with you.* Crystal patted her chest. *Inside, she might hear.*

The raven hopped from the rocker and attempted to swivel, fluttering his wings.

No, silly, Crystal reprimanded, bending down to pick him

up. She set him on top of the rocker next to her mother.
Whisper—into her heart.

The raven inhaled a deep breath and leaned beside Rose's
ear. He snuck a glance at Crystal and closed his eyes.

Come with me, Rose, he urged. *In your dreams—let yourself go.
We'll travel to the 'twixt place, where sea and clouds stretch to meet land.
Don't hold on to fear. For just a moment, hold on to me.*

Rose fidgeted in the rocking chair. Still asleep, she brushed
her fingers across her cheek like a wisp of wind had tickled her.
Then she nestled more comfortably in the rocker as the raven
sang the lullaby in her ear. When he was done, he hopped
down to the arm of the chair and burrowed beneath her hand,
his eyes brimming with expectation.

Slowly, Rose's fingers sank into his feathers. She began to
dream of softness, of pale clouds rising all around until her
mind was as blank as a page. Before her appeared a misty
horizon, and she could hear the creak of the rocker, only now
it became the creak of a raven's wings flapping in the wind.
She didn't know how or why, but she sensed she was soaring
on top of a massive bird in flight.

Looking down, she was astonished to see feathers—a
canopy of black that stretched into large wings and suspended
her in air. Exhilarated, she felt the breeze caress her hair, the
sway of the raven carrying her to an unknown horizon. Like
so often in dreams, she didn't react the way she would in
waking life, with her mind racing in alarm or her voice
breaking into a scream. Instead, she lost herself to the motion
of the bird's flight, undulating on currents of air, feeling like
her soul had taken wings. Suddenly, her heart was light, and as
the cool air struck her cheeks she laughed, her voice swallowed

by the wind. A streak flashed in the distance, and it startled her, as though her own joy had erupted into electricity. Long ago, she had heard her Irish ancestors' moods could influence the weather, and for a moment, she wondered if it was true. She laughed again, and to her surprise, another lightning bolt seared through clouds. The raven heard her giggle, and he gently dipped and swerved, seeking ways to amuse her. Rose gasped each time, her fingers gripping the arcs of his wings as she swallowed gulps of air. Before long, the raven glided into a wide spiral, and through an opening in the mist, Rose saw a beautiful green island.

Time moves in circles, a voice whispered on the breeze.

As the raven descended through clouds, Rose felt oddly peaceful. Her soul seemed stronger, the swells of air invigorating her. The two of them approached a golden strip of shore kissed by the sea. For a moment, Rose felt a strange lack of boundaries, as if she and the bird had become one being, unified in this space between heaven and earth—the clouds and wind were merely a conductor. Yet the feeling was serene—not like the scattered rush of adrenaline she used to experience with Jake, but centered, almost like she was heading home. The wind swirled in her ears, whispering and alive with murmurings.

A rainbow arced over a stretch of turf near the shore, and the raven swooped to slice through the colors. Below them, a woman wearing a wool shawl stood beside a cottage, her long, dark hair blowing in the breeze. She held the hand of a little girl in an ivory sweater. Drawing closer, Rose watched the child break free and step over to a well, stuffing a red rag between the stones. All at once, she realized the cotton-haired girl was her daughter. "Crystal!" she cried, teetering on the bird. Impulsively, she reached out her arms and lost her balance. Crystal stared up at her mother, then grabbed a fold of the woman's skirt.

"Don't fall, Mommy!" she called out. "Please don't fall again."

Rose tried to right herself, digging her hands into the raven's feathers, when she slipped and tumbled through currents of air. A voice on the breeze settled deep inside her ear.

Guard your power, aisling.

With a thud, Rose hit the turf hard and awoke. The smell of ocean spray lingered in her nose. When she looked down, she expected to see sand between her fingers, but she found herself staring at the bedroom rug, puzzled. She realized she had tumbled from the rocker, her cheek pressed against the floor. "Crystal!" She clutched the bedpost to stand, dizzy and mournful that she wasn't able to reach her in her dream. Where is she? Rose wondered, when she heard a clicking noise. Turning to face the kitchen, she saw her daughter at the breakfast table playing with the bean pot, the raven at her side. The bird hopped up and down, clicking from the back of his throat. He plucked a sea shell from the bean pot and set it on her daughter's lap.

Crystal held up the seashell to the kitchen light and stared at the warm glow that illuminated its swirls. She placed it on the table and began to clap happily. The raven cocked his head, watching her squeal in delight. He pulled over the old diary that Rose had left on the table and nudged it open with his beak. When Crystal saw the book, she examined the peculiar drawings. She made a smacking sound with her lips, as if she were trying to say something.

"Darling!" Rose rushed over to her daughter. She gazed at the sea shell and gave Crystal a squeeze. "I-I had the most amazing dream. I went to an island and you were there, beside a woman with long hair who reminded me of my mother." She kissed her softly on the cheek. "You spoke, honey—I heard you."

Crystal was too focused on the diary to pay attention to her. She glanced down, running her pudgy fingers over the pictures. Disappointed, Rose felt like a mere shadow that flitted across her daughter's life. She gazed longingly at the diary, wishing Crystal would connect as strongly with her as she had with the book's images. When her daughter let go of the diary, Rose picked it up, remembering how they used to try out the quirky recipes. It had always been a bonding time between them, full of laughter and joy—the kind of play she wanted to engage in with her now. "I'd give anything to hear you giggle again," she murmured, stroking her daughter's shoulder.

Rose scanned a sequence of drawings on the pages: a cluster of eggs, a scoop of flour, a stack of little yellow balls. She remembered the recipe—it was for the special lemon fairy cakes her mother used to make, the ones that were supposed to bring sunshine to gray days. And they did! Each time her mother made them, like clockwork, brooding clouds would separate, if only for a minute, and a few rays of sun would peek through, as if the sky obeyed her.

She smiled a little, recalling the silly tales her mother used to tell about their Irish ancestors and their effects on the weather. Well, we could use a bit of sunshine this week, Rose decided, pondering whether she had enough ingredients to bake them tomorrow. She flipped through the diary, half-hoping there might be clues about raven dreams as well. My gosh, she suddenly realized, I've become as superstitious as Amy. But then she noticed a picture of a raven drawn in black ink. Hesitantly, she touched her finger to its outstretched wings, and for a moment, she lost herself again to the feeling of flight. Rose closed her eyes, imagining the wind in her hair, the smell of the sea, the bird's gentle soar on currents of air. But instead of an ocean roar, she heard a strange shuffling sound. When she opened her eyes, she saw the raven dragging a green dress across the wooden floor.

"What have you found?" she said to the bird. Against the wall, an old box was open that Rose had set aside for junk she couldn't use in the shop. She'd heard before that ravens were scavengers, ready to raid anything, but she scratched her head at this new attraction. Perhaps he wanted the dress for a nest? When Crystal saw it, she leaped from the bed and clapped, to her mother's surprise. Crystal buried her hands in the vivid, green fabric as if it were finger paint that she could smear.

Intrigued, Rose walked over to her daughter. "Do you want to put it on, honey?" she asked, wondering if her daughter had confused the dress with her pajamas. "It's getting late," she frowned at her watch, "we should go to bed." But when she tried to pick up Crystal, her daughter held her arms stiffly at her sides, refusing to let go of the dress. Rose sighed. "Okay, okay," she relented, "you can play for a little while."

Rose released Crystal and glided her palms over the fabric, feeling the silkiness between her fingers and the tiny little flowers embroidered on the bodice. "It looks like a fairy gown," she smiled, trying to recall where it might have come from. The smooth, gossamer fabric seemed weightless—maybe it was a nineteenth-century trifle once sold in the shop, or something her kooky mother might have worn. It could even be Amy's. Rose unzipped the back, hoping to slip it over her daughter's head, the way she did with her pajama routine at bedtime. Yet when she held the dress above Crystal, her daughter began to flail.

"What's wrong, honey? Is the fabric too scratchy?"

Crystal grabbed the dress and shoved it forcefully at her mother. Startled, Rose tried to understand what her daughter wanted, curious she had any opinion at all. Crystal picked up a sleeve and slipped it over her mother's arm. "You want me to wear it?" Rose doubted it would fit. "Okay, sweetie—I can try. Mommy can play dress-up for you."

Rose slipped off her flannel shirt and overalls and attempted to squeeze into the outfit, delighted at her daughter's interest, but apprehensive as well. It had been years since she'd put on something so feminine, so completely unnecessary for work or motherhood. She closed her eyes and twisted her arm to lift the zipper up her back, afraid to look into the mirror. What if she appeared ridiculous and the dress showed every bulge? Or worse—she looked like a middle-aged woman arriving fifteen years too late for the prom? Well, anything for my girl, Rose sighed. She prepared to sneak a glance into the mirror, when she heard the raven caw. For the life of her, she thought she heard someone say, *You look wonderful.*

As Rose opened her eyes, Crystal spun in circles and the

raven hopped beside her, flapping his wings. Rose peeked into the mirror and giggled. The vibrant green dress fell to her ankles, matching her eye color perfectly. She tousled her dark hair, creating a mass of tangles that looked blown by a sea breeze, and she stared at her reflection as a flush of pink rose to her cheeks. All of a sudden she appeared wild—not like a woman burdened by the fallen dominoes of her life, but like someone who had a future ahead of her, who might be capable of magic.

"Magic," Rose whispered, running her hands down the bodice, comforted she still had a nice curve to her waist. She kicked off her hiking boots and stared at her bare feet, ready at any moment to run off to the woods where something wonderful might happen under a bright moon. She hadn't felt this free in ages, and she drew a deep breath, relishing in the moment, when she sensed a tug at her dress. Crystal stood beside her with her hand buried into a fold of the fabric, staring at its luster.

"Isn't it lovely, honey?" Rose picked up her daughter. "If only we had matching dresses—we could be fairies together." She twirled around and hummed her mother's old lullaby, imagining what it would be like if they were both adorned with feathery wings. Perhaps I could try making a pair for Crystal for Halloween, she thought. As she swayed her hips to her hum, Crystal stretched out her arms, and though Rose wasn't entirely sure, she thought she saw her smile. Rose bent her face to her daughter's cheek, feeling their hearts beat together like one person. Maybe we can connect after all, Rose hoped, like we used to when we baked fairy cakes. Just two

souls, knit within the same space, sharing the same delights—
no demands or worries anymore.

Rose stared at the fire in the wood stove, Crystal snuggling
against her, and all at once she felt brimmed with gold. It no
longer mattered to her whether she and Crystal weren't perfect,
the way Laurel had cruelly pointed out. The only thing she cared
about was that they were together, here and now. Rose glanced
down at the raven nestled in front of the stove, at the firelight
shining off his black feathers. She wasn't quite sure how, but she
knew her dawning peace had begun with that bird's arrival.
Perhaps my dream is a hint of what's to come, she thought, a
time when Crystal and I can grow closer. But then her daughter's
words from the dream came back to haunt her. *Don't fall, Mommy*,
Crystal had said mysteriously. *Please don't fall again.*

Outside, one of the steel panels banged in the wind, and
Rose feared it might break a window—she had a hunch she
should have latched it tighter that afternoon. Reluctantly, she
set her daughter to her feet, then slipped on her hiking boots
and grabbed a denim jacket from the coat rack. "This will just
take a second, honey," she promised, annoyed that something
had broken their spell. "I'll be right back."

Rose flipped on the lights in the shop and headed to the
front, throwing on her jacket. When she unlocked the door
and creaked it open, a stranger was there—the new man from
across the street. His big blue eyes appeared nearly as
surprised as hers.

"I, uh, I noticed that your steel panel was swinging, so I
thought I'd latch it before it did damage."

He glanced down at his cowboy boots, and Rose thought

she detected a blush on his cheeks in the weak porch light. Had he forgotten his own name? It had been a long time since she'd made a man nervous, and she couldn't help being flattered.

"I'm, um, V-Vincent," he blurted, a bit flustered. "And you?"

Tongue tied, Rose suddenly realized how silly she must look in her green fairy dress, with hiking boots and a jean jacket, no less. She folded her arms in embarrassment, when she heard Crystal's raven break into shrill, pulsing caws, like the wild ringing of an alarm bell. Puzzled, she peeked back inside, but nothing appeared amiss with her daughter, so she gently eased the door shut. Swiveling on her heels, she took a deep breath.

"I-I'm Rose," she stammered, braving another look at his face. Vincent's blonde hair appeared tousled in the moonlight, and his cheeks had nicks and scratches, perhaps from an old razor. But he was handsome—drop-dead handsome by anyone's standard—and Rose fidgeted in her boots. "What are you doing outside this time of night?"

Vincent dipped his head, scuffing his boot self-consciously along a hole in the boardwalk. His lips curved into a shy smile and he gazed up at the piercing white stars. "Oh, just admiring heaven," he confessed. "In October, the stars are so bright they practically call your name." To her astonishment, he leaned forward a little, as if secretly hoping to catch a whiff of her scent. "And do you know what they say?"

"Um, no," Rose replied with caution, feeling the warmth of his breath skim her neck. Her skin tingled and she took a step back. "What do the stars say?"

Vincent reached into his jacket for a cigarette. It was thin and long, like he'd rolled it himself, and he lit a match off his boot and cupped the cigarette to the flame. For nearly a minute he said nothing at all, simply taking in her loveliness as though he'd lost himself in the sight of her. His silence made Rose feel unbearably awkward, and she was about to open the door again when he blew a slim line of smoke into the cold, night air. His eyes twinkled as he watched it curl around her waist, as if envying its touch.

"Eternity can catch up with you in the blink of an eye," he finally whispered, daring to reach for her hand. "Good to meet you, neighbor," he smiled with a gentle handshake. He studied the shimmer of her dress in the moonlight, the way it highlighted her eyes. "You look, um, nice."

Rose's cheeks grew warm, and her heart fluttered until she willed it to stop. Vincent offered her his cigarette, but she shook her head—she'd given up that bad habit after Jake. She'd sworn a dozen times she'd given up on men as well. But sometimes at night, even when she thought she was too exhausted to feel anything at all, the ache of loneliness still clenched around her soul, leaving a hunger that seemed bottomless. And now here she was, craving the touch of this stranger's hand again. Perhaps it's because it's been a while since I've had a man, she thought, or maybe because he seems carved from a dream. Rose swiftly glanced to the place where she'd buried the potato that morning after Amy's love spell. Closing her eyes, she made a silent prayer:

Oh God, just for once, let me have something fine and beautiful. If only for a little while, like the raven dream.

❧ 10 ❧

The next morning, Rose stirred a bowl of lemon fairy cake batter, losing track of the number of strokes. She still felt hazy, as if lost in a dream world, and when she glanced out the front window, a veneer of gold sparkled over the town as the sun inched across the mountain tops. Ever since she saw Vincent last night, she couldn't get his smile out of her mind. Colors seemed brighter, and the autumn dawn in Ophir Creek was crisp and clear, with a sky so blue she could almost dip her fingers into it, like a river. In spite of getting up early to do the day's baking and being industrious in every way, she found her mind wandering over the spell she'd cast with Amy, how a handsome man had appeared at her door within a matter of days. Could their hocus pocus possibly be real? And what was the meaning of that strange raven dream? Rose bit her lip, reluctant to invest in wishful thinking. When the harsh rings of the telephone scattered her thoughts, she stopped her stirring with a sigh. Reaching out a sticky hand, she picked up the receiver.

"Yes?" Rose swiftly remembered her manners and sputtered, "Rainbow's End Cafe, can I help you?"

"You're the one who needs help—and I've found just the thing!"

Rose set aside the bowl and groaned. It was Laurel. At barely sunrise, she already had more energy in her voice than most people could muster all day.

"Rosie—you there?"

"Sure, I'm listening," Rose lied, recalling Amy's warning to be nice. After all, they owed her money. She gritted her teeth. "Good morning."

"Oh, right. Anyway, I've found the perfect program for your daughter. Remember the facility I told you about in Boise? They have an opening, but we have to act soon—I'll bring by papers today. Just imagine, Crystal can get all the help she needs, and they even have visiting hours on Tuesdays and Fridays."

Isn't this the woman I kicked out of my shop? Rose marveled. She shook her head at Laurel's tenacity and tried to count to ten. Then she glanced at her daughter on the floor, happily outlining her hand on construction paper with the raven beside her, stealing crayons. "Crystal's doing just fine. She doesn't need—"

"Don't be silly!" Laurel cut in. "You can't let an opportunity like this pass you by. If you're worried about medical insurance, I know a social worker who could handle the case—"

Amy burst through the front door with a stack of mining

pans in her hands. As she kicked the door closed, Rose put the receiver on the butcher block counter and angrily stirred her batter.

"Who's that?" Amy set down her stack. She stared at the receiver with the voice chattering in air.

"Nobody." Rose fumed. She took a lick of batter and added more flour.

Curious, Amy held up the receiver to listen. "You know, we owe your sister a fortune," she whispered. "The least we can do is babysit her ideas once in a while."

"Hang up," Rose insisted. "We'll rob a bank. Here, I'll cut the cord."

Rose tried to reach for a pair of scissors when Amy set down the phone and wrestled her arm to make her stop. Laughing, Amy picked up the receiver again.

"Look, honey, everything you say is wonderful," Amy chirped. "Why don't you come over and help us decorate for Halloween? We'd be so grateful for your flair. See you later," she gently hung up.

"Have you lost your mind?" Rose gasped. "Why'd you do that?"

"Because your sister loves you. Hasn't it ever occurred to you that her childhood was difficult, too? That she gets lonely once in a while, like the rest of us? She just wants to belong, Rose. The way you treat her reflects the way you treat yourself —she's your soul mirror. And with her husband probably cheating on her, she needs you more than ever."

Rose rubbed her hands, lost for words.

"We get people in our lives for a reason," Amy pointed out.

"If we don't treat them right, they keep coming back. You don't want to deal with Laurel in the next life, do you?"

Rose shook her head.

"Then give her something to do. Let her love you the way she knows how. And don't be afraid to spread a little joy around. I swear, you two could conjure enough bitterness to turn candy sour."

"But you don't understand," Rose set down a baking pan on the stove, "she wants to lock Crystal away in a program. She's said she's going to bring papers and everything—"

"No she doesn't." Amy crossed her arms and smiled. "Laurel just wants your attention. And if that doesn't get a rise out of you, something else will. Boy, for a girl who reads tea leaves, you sure can be blind sometimes."

"I *don't* read tea leaves!" Rose replied, exasperated. "I just see reflections. Hunches is all they are." In spite of herself, she snuck a glance at her coffee cup, where she saw a grinning jack-o-lantern floating on swirl of cream. Rose relented and looked around the shop. "Okay, okay—maybe we could use a few more Halloween decorations. Laurel's good at that."

Rose briskly shaved lemon zest into the batter, still grumbling to herself, when she noticed that dark clouds began to collect outside. Oh great, she thought, there goes the nice weather, just in time to match my foul mood. Then goose bumps alighted down her back. What if the sky really does reflect my emotions once in a while, she wondered, like the clouds in the legend of my great-great grandmother? Rose dismissed the idea, realizing such thoughts were silly, when she remembered her dream the night before, how lightning flashed each time she laughed with the raven, as if her joy could spark electricity. She stared at her batter, made from a recipe that was supposed to insure sunny days. Just for kicks, she closed her eyes and whispered O'Dannan, the way her mother used to do whenever she wanted to improve the weather.

As she glanced up, a ray of sun broke through the clouds, lighting up the town square. Rose saw Vincent washing windows at the Magpie Saloon with the bright sunshine glinting off his blonde hair. For no apparent reason, he turned around and smiled. Surprised, Rose brought her hands to her cheeks, forgetting her fingers were sticky. Her heart fluttered and she swallowed several breaths to calm down. Coincidence, she told herself—those clouds just happened to clear up. Nevertheless, as she poured the batter into a pan, she began to whistle.

"What changed your mood all of a sudden?" Amy hung the mining trays on a wall rack. She squinted at the sunshine streaming through the windows.

"Oh nothing. Why do you ask?"

"Because you're whistling," Amy said. "A minute ago you were ready to tear Laurel's hair out."

"I guess it's from this batter." Rose scanned the cheery light that bathed the front table. "It's from an heirloom recipe, one that's meant to inspire sunshine." She held up the diary that had been propped open on the counter for cooking guidance. "You know, maybe you're right. Maybe there is something to all this magic stuff." The sky was clear now, as blue as it had been earlier, and Rose set the diary down and stepped from behind the counter to admire its perfect hue. "If I didn't know better, I'd almost say I'm a convert."

Amy spotted the saloon keeper across the street and caught

Rose's admiring gaze. "Convert, huh?" She watched Rose blush and avert her eyes. "Is there something you're not telling me?" Amy tilted her labradorite belt buckle to the sun and examined the flashes of blue and green on the stone's surface, as if they might reveal secrets. "That fella's cleaning awfully early. He's gotta be up to something. I wonder what his past lives were like—all of them handsome, I bet."

"Oh, he's not so great looking," Rose replied casually, trying to convince herself more than anything. "I met him last night and he had razor nicks all over his face."

"You *met* him? What do you mean, you met him?"

Rose returned to the oven to peek at the rising cakes. "Oh, we just chatted a bit. He seemed rather shy, actually."

"You talked with him?" Amy could barely contain herself. "I knew it," she clasped her hands. "The magic's working! Did you know that if you sprinkle dried apple on your oatmeal in the morning, it will make you a better lover?"

"Amy! You've practically hooked us up already. I think I should get to know him first." Rose's eyes narrowed. "And don't you do anything behind my back."

She opened the diary on the counter to a page for lemon icing. Beside the drawing of a bee hive and a milk pail were lemons and little girls with wings. She took out a small bowl and blended honey with a pat of butter, then added a few dashes of lemon and a couple dollops of cream. After stirring her concoction, she ran her finger across the spoon for a greedy lick. "Did you know that my mother believed this lemon icing could help you see fairies?" She hoped to lure Amy onto another topic. Curiously, Rose's eyes began to flicker. When she stared at where the raven was perched beside

Crystal, all at once she saw a tall, dark-haired man in a long, black coat. Rose blinked, but he was gone. She shook her head. Must have been the sugar rush, she thought.

"Ooh, fairy icing?" Amy dipped her finger into the bowl and swallowed a large sample. She glanced around the shop, disappointed that it looked the same, without a fairy in sight. "Okay, don't change the subject on me—exactly how did you meet our new neighbor?"

Rose fidgeted and tried to think of a way to skirt around the issue. After all, her skin still tingled whenever she remembered the delicate green dress against her skin last night, the way Vincent's hair shone in the moonlight, his remarks about stars. Against her will, a blush warmed her cheeks.

"Oh look!" she said brightly to deflect Amy. Rose pointed to a station wagon that had parked in front of the shop. A group of passengers filed out, and she could tell from their skimpy picks and shovels they were here because of the gold legend—typical amateurs, probably eager for a panning lesson. Quickly, she braided her hair and tied it up in a bun so they couldn't snip souvenirs.

Despite Rose's sidestepping, Amy leaned forward on the counter to press for more answers. But when she opened her mouth, the oven timer bell rang, and Rose pulled the pan out and set it on a cooling rack with a clatter.

"Showtime!" Rose grinned, clapping her oven mitts. She removed the mitts and tossed them onto the counter. "C'mon honey," she wrapped an arm around Amy, "let's greet our guests."

By the time sunlight slanted across the butcher block counter in the Rainbow's End Cafe that afternoon, Rose and Amy were so exhausted their limbs felt as limp as ribbons. The shop had been a total circus. Each day that neared the blue moon over Rook Ridge brought throngs of tourists eager to fulfill their prospecting dreams. In spite of the rise in sales, Rose pitied them, realizing the pay dirt they bought to practice panning might be the only gold dust they would ever see.

"But that's not the point!" Amy chastised whenever Rose felt guilty for being a swindler, "They're supposed to enjoy the journey." Nevertheless, Rose winced with every map she sold of the region, and she was grateful no one pressured her for a tour of the ridge like those miners had a few days ago. Each time Amy brought up the idea to a customer, Rose gave her a swift kick. She'd resigned herself to a few charlatan tactics in the shop, but Rook Ridge unnerved her—especially after her daughter had gotten lost there among the stones. That was the place where Corvine O'Dannan was nearly shot by her lover, where she'd watched him bleed to death from a ricocheted bullet. Rose had seen the scars herself on a pillar of granite—permanent warnings against falling in love with an impetuous man. The last thing she wanted was a reminder of the bad luck she shared with her great-great grandmother.

Leaning against an old barrel in the shop, Rose kept a keen eye on Crystal, who was outside on a wooden swing that she'd hung for her on the porch. Although her daughter was expressionless, content to repeat her endless pendulum motions, the raven perched sternly on a bench nearby, appearing to guard her. Rose took a deep breath and glanced at the racks on the wall, now empty after so many customers, and she wondered where they could possibly find more mining supplies. Then she dared to scrutinize the condition of the shop—it was a disaster.

"Oh God," she kneaded her forehead, "we've got to clean this place up."

"No we don't," Amy smiled from a chair at the front table.

Rose couldn't tell what had gotten into her. She had the spy glass propped against a window pane, and she was giggling.

"We're going to get a drink!"

"What do you mean?" Rose yawned, brooding over what to fix for dinner. Maybe I could whip up omelets with bits of leftover ham and onions, she thought. Are potato skins considered a vegetable?

Amy's fingers were plastered to the glass. "Don't you see?" She waved at Rose to come over. "People are going into the Magpie Saloon. He's opened the bar."

"You can't be serious—already?" Astonished, Rose walked to the front window. Sure enough, the crooked sign in front of the saloon hung straight now with a cocky, black and white bird freshly painted on its surface. Rose spotted several old friends who were entering the building: George Brickman, a barrel-chested lumberjack with arms as large as tree trunks, Kyle Monroe, a smokejumper who was always a little on the manic side, and old Jim Trotter, a wilderness outfitter who felt more at home with guns and mules than women.

"Hey, do you think those old rumors about whiskey barrels buried in the cellar are true?" Amy said, scratching her head.

"We were too busy to search when we worked there." She suddenly became excited and tapped on the glass. "Look, there's my client!" She pointed at an old woman on the boardwalk. Rose and Amy watched as Belle Crawford advanced to the front of the building and opened the door. "You know," Amy winked at Rose, "Belle still remembers how to swing a lasso. We don't want her to snatch the new neighbor before we do."

"His name is Vincent," Rose said dryly, masking her interest. "And she can have him—I'm not looking."

"Well I am!" Amy replied. "C'mon, remember all the good times we had there? We've got to peek. Besides, it's after four o'clock—no one's going to buy coffee now."

Before Rose could protest, Amy dragged her onto the porch. She picked up Crystal from the swing and grinned like a bandit.

"You're not taking my daughter into a bar," Rose folded her arms.

"Who me?" Amy shifted her feet, balancing Crystal on her hip. "We're just going to stroll over and say a quick hello to the neighbor—kind of like Welcome Wagon."

Rose rolled her eyes, and against her better judgment, she burrowed into her pocket for the shop key. Amy could be impossible, especially when she got a bright idea into her head, and sometimes Rose found it easier to indulge her than to resist. Besides, she rationalized, it wouldn't hurt to step out of the shop for a little while to relieve their frazzled nerves. But the truth was, she was curious—so curious she could feel a fluttering in her stomach whenever she thought of Vincent. She huddled her arms against her waist and took a deep breath. I am in control of my emotions, she whispered to herself. We're just taking a break, nothing more.

Crossing through the town square, Rose shuffled her hiking boots through the parched grass, listening to the lazy swish sounds of her feet as she watched aspen leaves fall around them like loose petals. Although the mountain air was cool against her cheeks, the late afternoon sun felt warm upon her shoulders, and it gently seeped into tired muscles. Rose was nearly lulled into a welcome sense of relaxation when she happened to glance down at their shadows that stretched across the dry lawn. Their long silhouettes reminded her of gunslingers advancing toward trouble, like so many outlaws had in Ophir Creek's checkered past.

In that moment, for no reason at all, Crystal's raven started to caw. He swooped in circles around the three of them, diving up and down until Crystal began to fuss. Rose chalked it up to cabin fever—after all, they'd been cooped up in the shop most of the day. But when she and Amy reached the front door of the saloon, a clamor of screeches echoed across the square. Rose swiveled, spying black birds flitting between the town buildings like bats. A brisk wind blew along the boardwalk and goose bumps skipped down her arms. Was it simply the erratic birds? Or was it because they were meeting Vincent? A lump swelled in her throat. It was the same sick feeling she used to have when she came home to her husband, never knowing whether he was high or not. Rose glanced at the saloon door, blanched the color of driftwood, its wood grain corrugated from years of harsh weather. Then it hit her—this was the place where she had first met Jake, where she'd become entangled in the darkest web of her life. Rose paused and tapped Amy on the shoulder.

"Listen, Amy," she stared down at her feet, "I'm, well, I'm just not comfortable with this."

Amy rubbed the brass knob on the saloon door like a portal to fond memories. They could hear laughter coming from inside and traces of a light singing melody. "Sounds like they're having fun," she encouraged, but the look in Rose's eyes told her she was serious. Amy dropped her fingers from the knob. Nevertheless, the door swung open wide, startling them both.

"Welcome." Vincent's voice was brisk but warm. With his tall, lanky frame, he filled the entire doorway in a deerskin jacket, frayed jeans and suede cowboy boots. Rose blinked. His disheveled hair and nicked face seemed to belong to the weathered building, as if he'd arrived from another century, like a veteran from the frontier. She wondered if he stepped beyond the threshold whether he might crumble to pieces, like an old, sepia-toned photo scattered to the wind. But then his deep blue eyes glistened with boyish charm in the afternoon sun, and he smiled as if he'd been expecting her.

"I have something for you," he said in the same gentle tone Rose remembered from the night before. He ushered the two women inside with Crystal and shut the door before the raven could follow. Rose heard the bird cry out in anger, scratching its claws fiercely against the boardwalk, but Vincent appeared oblivious. "Look," he pointed to the bar with a gleam in his eye, "I found two bottles of old wine—from France. They were buried in the cellar beside dusty barrels of whiskey underneath a pile of cobwebs." He glanced at Crystal. "Don't worry about your little girl. For opening day, we're only tasting the wine until it gets dark, no hard liquor. Here, be my guest."

Vincent cordially pulled out two captain's chairs from a table and encouraged the women to sit down. Cautiously, Rose took a seat, already searching her mind for excuses to leave. She scanned the familiar but scruffy faces of the lumberjacks and miners who were perched on stools around the bar, wondering how many of them could possibly enjoy the nuances of a French wine—including herself. She'd never had a fine wine before, fine anything for that matter, and the idea seemed a bit ridiculous in a mountain town. Nevertheless, when Vincent placed sparkly wine glasses in front of her and Amy, Rose blushed. She felt flattered to be served in a place where she used to be the one wearing the barmaid's apron, dutifully mopping up beer puddles and cigarette butts. Now she was the guest, and in spite of her nerves, she found herself enjoying the warm banter and cheerful mood in the saloon. Just like in the old days, Kyle Monroe was trying to arm wrestle big George Brickman, which everyone knew was evidence that he was off kilter. And old Jim Trotter was talking way too loud, telling the same stories about his cantankerous mule as though no time had passed at all. Rose smiled. It's nice to see that some things never change, she thought, even if they are a bit rough around the edges. Slowly, the knot in the back of her throat began to release a little, and she glanced around, noticing the carved, mahogany bar was spotless, polished to a rich sheen worthy of its original glory. Rose marveled at how quickly Vincent had cleaned the place up. She gazed across the table at Amy and Crystal.

"That's him," she whispered. "That's Vincent."

Amy snuggled Crystal closer on her lap and grinned. "He's gorgeous. Just like he stepped out of an old western picture. We did good."

"We?"

"Our spell, silly—it worked!" Amy's eyes lit up as they followed Vincent's sinewy body while he chatted with guests like he was an answer to prayer. Rose could tell from her friend's expression that she thought he was stunning.

"I wonder where he's from." Amy squinted, sizing him up. "He's got to be local, with an outfit like that." Crystal fidgeted in her arms, and Amy slid a handful of poker chips in front of her to play with. "You know, he looks kind of familiar. Something about the way he moves, the electricity in those eyes." Amy abruptly grabbed Rose's hand. "Hey, do you think we might have met him in another life?"

Rose jerked her fingers free, praying she didn't mean Jake. It already bothered her how similar the two men appeared, with their broad shoulders, blonde hair, and the easy way they blended into a western setting. On the vast, unpredictable highway of life, she couldn't bear another wrong turn, and she feared this man had déjà vu written all over him. Yet as she watched Vincent stride to the bar, she noticed how delicately he handled the old wine bottle from the cellar, as if it were something precious. Carefully dusting off the antique label, he ran his hand over the faded script like the vintage was a year he could actually remember. Mysteriously, he closed his eyes, holding the bottle with the intensity of a man clinging to a rope. His lips moved briefly. Rose thought perhaps he'd uttered a prayer, or voiced the name of a lost love. What private memory could possibly exert such a hold on him?

Rose couldn't resist being drawn to his secret, to the puzzle of Vincent that might yield an intriguing picture, if only she could find the right pieces. Surely a man like that has more beneath the surface than an adrenaline junky like Jake, Rose thought, watching him brush a cobweb from the top of the bottle, careful not to break the cork. Nothing about him seemed rushed, the way her late husband used to be, and he moved with a casual grace like he had all the time in the world.

Vincent picked up another bottle, and Rose pondered how the wine had ever arrived here, if maybe it had been swapped a century ago for a gambling debt. She knew people dragged peculiar things with them across the Oregon Trail to gold country—fine furniture, heirloom jewelry, even china patterns —and a number of those cast-offs had ended up in her shop. Yet she was also struck by how similar she and Vincent must be, two crazy people who dared to open businesses in an old, dried-up mining town. Unable to quell her curiosity any longer, she snuck a glance at his face across the room. To her surprise, his kinetic blue eyes met hers, as if he'd tuned in to her radio frequency. Then she heard a soft voice inside her head, as tender as an angel's.

I remember you.

The hair rose on the surface of her skin. All at once, Rose felt static electricity surround her, and the distance between her and Vincent somehow evaporated. She couldn't explain it, but in the blink of an eye, his presence seemed closer, and she swiftly became uncomfortable. It was as if he had slid his body right next to hers, and he was holding her heart instead of that bottle of wine. A tingling sensation prickled her forehead, and she nervously patted her brows. Nevertheless, she found herself swiping another peek at him from beneath her palm. Vincent returned her glance with a slow smile, when a burst of lightning flashed outside. Thunder rolled through the town square, matching the flutters in her stomach.

"Rose," Amy tapped her arm insistently. "Are you daydreaming? Didn't you hear me?"

"H-Hear what?" Rose stuttered, disturbed from her trance.

"Do you think we could have met him in another life?" Amy stroked Crystal's blonde hair, eager for her response.

Rose bit her lip, determined to ward off the possibility. "Animal, mineral, or vegetable?" she joked in parlor game style, unable to take her eyes off Vincent.

"Ooh, I didn't consider that. Come to think of it, my widowed aunt once had the most devoted cocker spaniel. Maybe he was her husband Edward."

Another flash ripped across the square and thunder rumbled loudly enough to shake the front windows. Crystal began to squirm, flapping her hands haphazardly in agitation. Amy gently rocked the child and covered her ears to block out the noise.

"Funny how the weather changed so quickly," Amy remarked as rain began to patter against the dust outside. "There wasn't a cloud in the sky when we came in."

Rose shuddered with another rumble of thunder. At that moment, Vincent held up a wine bottle and the room fell silent. He cleared his throat.

"I'd like to thank everyone for joining me here today. And to celebrate the Magpie Saloon, each of you will taste this bottle of bordeaux. It's dated eighteen sixty-three, the same year gold was discovered in Ophir Creek. A lucky vintage, you might say. For that reason, I think the first samples should to go to the most beautiful women in town."

To their astonishment, Vincent bowed and stepped over to their table. Amy giggled while he carefully eased the cork from the bottle. Rather than make a loud pop, like Rose expected, the bottle exhaled a smoky waft of air, soft as a breath that had escaped from a ghost. The sight made her shiver. Vincent showed them the wine-stained cork and held it up to his nose and sniffed, nodding appreciatively. Tilting the bottle to their glasses, he poured the burgundy liquid. Rose glanced at the faded label that featured a lion on top of a castle tower with *Chateau Latour* written in fine calligraphy. It was so elegant it made her heart skip.

"Ladies?" he said.

"D-Do you have a liquor license?" Rose mentioned anxiously, not sure she was worthy of this kind of expense. What if she didn't like the flavor, or it had turned to vinegar?

Vincent leaned beside her, and she felt his blue eyes pour into hers. "Ma'am," he whispered, "who's going to rat on me in this old town? Besides, I'd be happy to pay the fine for you."

Her cheeks rifled with warmth, which she prayed wasn't visible. "Th-Then I guess we should toast," Rose muttered, attempting to sit up straight. She couldn't explain it, but somehow, with Vincent beside her, she felt more refined, as if he saw something deep inside her that was as rare as the wine. Not just the white trash daughter of a crazy miner and his spooky wife from Ophir Creek, but someone better than that —better than her reputation for bad luck and lost chances. The way his blue eyes held hers made her feel like she was in the green fairy dress again—pretty, with possibilities at her fingertips. Before she knew it, she was untangling knots in her hair, hoping to merit his approval. She pressed her hands over her flannel shirt and held up her glass to Amy's. "To the Magpie Saloon," she said shyly, "may all of us prosper."

A cheer erupted from the bar when the two women clinked glasses, and the handful of patrons raucously urged them to gulp down the wine in a drinking contest. Rose and Amy rolled their eyes, each taking a slow sip. The liquid tasted leathery, with a faintly sweet flavor of dark fruits, like plums or cherries, along with something sharp, similar to cedar. A masculine flavor, Rose decided, amazed she could distinguish its complexity. Just like Vincent might taste, she mused, if he were bottled. The thought surprised her, and she quickly shuffled it to the back of her mind.

"Did you see anything?" Amy's question made Rose jump.

"What do you mean?" Rose swirled the liquid in her glass before taking another sip, assuming that's what wine enthusiasts do.

"In the wine—did you see any pictures in the liquid? You know, for true love?"

Rose's heart leaped. Though she pretended disinterest, curiosity got the best of her. She'd never been able to perceive the future for herself, but part of her wondered if it could be possible. If she mustered enough effort, perhaps somewhere in the glass there might be a hint that real love was in store. While Amy wasn't looking, she stole a glance at the wine. All she saw was the liquid's dark red color, vibrant as blood.

Rose blinked and stared harder, hoping to conjure a small shred of hope, when Crystal began to thrash in Amy's arms, knocking poker chips from the table. Immediately, Rose pulled a crayon from her pocket that she kept for emergencies. Although Crystal's outbursts were always a potential hazard in the shop, her daughter had behaved well for weeks, even around strangers, and she was alarmed to see her so angry. She grabbed a bar napkin and began to draw energetic yellow swirls with the crayon. "Look sweetie," she said with fake composure, "I've got your favorite color—sunflower."

When she attempted to put the crayon between her daughter's fingers, Crystal jerked her hand away, toppling it to the floor. The crayon broke into pieces.

"Rose," Amy struggled to restrain Crystal, "what's gotten into her? She's gone haywire—"

Rose stood and reached for her daughter, keeping her eyes from onlookers as she wrapped her arms around her in a big Momma-Bear hug. It was the hold she had perfected for public places, the one where she folded Crystal's face into her chest to block out any light and noise. At that moment, she wished they could crawl into a cave—a deep, dark place where she and Crystal could hide from all the stares, especially Vincent's. With her daughter tight against her chest, their hearts beat together as fast as a hummingbird's, like the two had molted into one frightened creature. She nestled Crystal close to her chin, bracing against her fierce wriggles. Gradually, her daughter's breathing slowed and her heart began to regulate. "It's okay, baby," Rose gently rocked her. "Momma's got you now. It's okay—"

All around, Rose heard murmurings inside the bar. When she glanced up, she spied Vincent advancing with the caution of approaching wild animals. Her heart sank to her ankles. Of course—she should have known. He was going to tell her to leave. Tell her she was a lousy mother and a loser and that people like Jake had been right—she couldn't keep anything good in her life for long. *Who am I kidding? True love is a fanciful idea, invented by people with too much time on their hands who don't have enough sense to move on with their lives.*

Rose squeezed her daughter like a vise. "We're going to walk straight out that door," she whispered to Crystal. "Don't look to the right or left, honey. We'll keep our heads down, the way we always do in the grocery store. If we don't glance up, no one can hurt us."

It was a lie of course, and Rose knew it. In that moment, her whole body ached as she tried to avoid the pinched stares of everyone in the bar. With her heart in her heels, she took quick, determined strides to the door and opened it to the afternoon air. *Time to face reality,* she thought. She squinted at the pewter rain drops that fell randomly over the town square, when a hand gripped her shoulder.

"Rose," Vincent held her firm. "Here, he braced the door with his boot and pressed the unopened wine bottle into her hand. "Take this. I want you to have it—for special occasions."

The softness in his eyes made her heart melt. "Oh, I-I can't," Rose replied, staring at the bottle with the lovely castle on the label, like something from a fairy tale. She'd never possessed anything so fine before. *What if Crystal threw another fit and she dropped it on the way home?* Rose couldn't bear the thought, and she tried to push the bottle toward Vincent, but he closed his hand over hers. His fingers felt strong and warm.

"I insist." He smiled and stroked her daughter's cheek.

All at once, Crystal shrieked like a banshee and pulled away, knocking the wine bottle from Rose's grip. Glass crashed, and to Rose's horror, deep red puddles swelled in the doorway, staining the floorboards like blood. At that moment, she heard a peculiar, clicking sound that grew louder against the boardwalk outside, like the march of someone in high heels. A shadow seeped across the threshold.

"Out of control again?"

Laurel stood in front of the saloon, careful to keep her ivory pumps from the puddles in the dust. She held a clipboard in one arm, her other hand clutching a jack-o-lantern bag. Looking Rose up and down, she observed the white-knuckled grip she had on her daughter as something to be expected.

"Poor Crystal," Laurel sighed. "Guess I came at the right time. Hope whatever broke wasn't expensive." She navigated around the glass shards and thrust the clipboard at her sister. "Here, I brought papers for you to sign—for that program in Boise. Looks like you're ready for a change."

Anger welled inside Rose, ricocheting within her stomach like ping-pong balls. How on earth does Laurel always manage to show up, just when I feel the most vulnerable? In the back of her mind, she suspected that her sister had her wire tapped —she wouldn't put it past her. Drawing a deep breath, she felt nearly ready to burst, when Amy dashed to her side.

"Laurel!" Amy said brightly, snatching her Halloween bag. "I'm so glad you made it—let's decorate!" Before Laurel knew what hit her, Amy had spun her around and whisked her into the town square. She threw her arm around Laurel's shoulder and made her dodge rain drops as ominous clouds gathered overhead.

"But what about the program?" Laurel protested. It was no use—Amy had an iron grip as she maneuvered them toward the Rainbow's End Cafe. Even as her arms trembled, Rose continued to rock Crystal to keep her quiet. It didn't help matters that her pants were soaked in wine and everyone in the saloon was gossiping about her. She shook her head, watching Laurel try to lecture Amy on the way to the shop.

"God," she whispered, "sometimes I could almost kill her." Rose was so angry that the acid in her stomach curdled into marbles. Without warning, Vincent gave her arm a squeeze. Suddenly, the slices of rain outside hardened into white kernels and the saloon roof began to rattle with the sound of dropping rocks. Large hail stones pummeled the town square, punching divots into the grass as they grew to the size of tennis balls. Shocked, Rose hollered to Amy to hurry to the nearest overhang, when she saw her sister stagger and fall in a heap on the ground.

11

The townspeople stood in a circle around Laurel's body sprawled on the grass, staring at her with the startled look of steers at a rodeo. Flabbergasted, Rose handed Crystal to Amy and kneeled at her sister's side.

"Laurel!" she cried, but her sister eyes remained closed. Rose jiggled her shoulders. When Laurel didn't wake up, she took a deep breath, recalling first aid tips from high school, and locked her lips to her sister's for mouth-to-mouth resuscitation. After several puffs, Rose thumped Laurel's chest with both palms, noticing the ruddy marks that stained her forehead and cheeks. The welts made her look like she'd been locked into a ring for several rounds with a prizefighter.

"Call a doctor!" Amy shouted as Rose counted heart thumps, then gave her sister mouth-to-mouth again. Rose's pulse raced as she remembered an article she'd read once of a man who'd died in a hail storm, stoned to death by clusters of ice. Maybe it was just a tall tale, but tears brimmed her eyes until she suddenly felt a breath escape from Laurel's lips. She released her and stared at her pale face, expressionless as a wax figurine.

"Don't die on me!" Rose demanded, hardly able to believe her own ears—she never thought she'd say those words to Laurel. Yet here she was, begging her to come back. "I need you!" she insisted, feeling like an orphan girl with braids again— the one her sister used to threaten with a horsewhip if she didn't finish chores, always setting a timer beside her at the kitchen table while she watched over her homework like a hawk. Truth be told, Rose couldn't imagine life without Laurel, regardless of her bitter streak. At least she'd always been there, albeit a stiff pillar to lean on—the one person who didn't abandon her in childhood. Rose desperately called Laurel's name and slapped her on both cheeks as hard as she could. Rubbing her stinging palms together, she stared intently at her face.

Laurel's eyelashes began to flutter. She opened her eyes and squinted, attempting to focus.

"Get back!" Rose waved at the small crowd to allow more breathing room. "Laurel," she leaned her ear, "can you hear me, sweetie?"

Laurel raised herself on both elbows and rubbed her head. She stumbled to her feet and teetered for a second, resisting anyone who tried to help. Lifting her chin, she became strangely composed as she dusted off her cream wool blazer and skirt, as though her biggest worry in life was a wrinkled outfit with too much lint. Then she narrowed her gaze at her sister. Before Rose could inquire how she felt, Laurel took a swing and landed a blow on her left cheek.

"How dare you strike me! Of all the mean, horrible things you've ever done, Rosie, this is the worst. I will NEVER speak to you again."

"B-But Laurel," Rose stammered, "I didn't mean to hit you—it was the hail stones. I just slapped your cheeks to wake you up—"

"Oh right, Rosie. Look at the sky."

Rose glanced at the bright blue horizon. It was true—there was sunshine all around and the sky was as cloudless and clear as glass.

"Th-those marks," Rose pointed to the red welts on Laurel's hand. "See? On your skin? They're as big as tattoos, left by the storm." She motioned at the layer of white balls on the grass. "There was a freak hail shower, and you got struck on the head—"

Laurel pursed her lips, fists clenched, fuming too hard to listen. Before she could take another swing, George Brickman wrapped his large arms around her chest. Laurel wriggled and stamped her feet on George's boots, nearly throwing him off balance.

The small crowd began to laugh. When Jim Trotter brought around his truck and offered to drive her to the county health care center, Laurel adamantly refused to get in. Instead, she managed to break free from George's grip and promised lawsuits if anyone dared to touch her. Then she marched toward her ivory Mercedes convertible in a huff, slipping occasionally over the hail stones with her high heels. As she drove off, the papers she'd brought for the program in Boise swirled behind her in a trail of exhaust. They drifted past the spectators in the town square and scattered across the hail stones like feathers.

Rose shook her head, when she caught the sight of Vincent from the corner of her eye. He stood at the entrance to the Magpie Saloon, casually leaning his shoulder against the doorway. As Laurel's Mercedes sped out of town, he shrugged and flashed a shy smile. Then he lifted up the glass of wine in his hand and nodded at Rose for a toast.

The following morning, the sky was tinted watercolor hues at dawn, a soft rose at the base of the amethyst mountains, blending into a robin's egg blue where it met the last glimmer of stars. Rose lay in bed beside Crystal and stared out the window at the morning horizon, still thinking about the waxing crescent moon she'd seen last night that hung in the sky like a delicate slipper. Her mother used to say such a moon meant power was building, the kind of force that helped you see fairies or influence the weather. But this morning, Rose felt weak and shaky, as if something—or someone—had sapped her energy.

Her stomach braided into knots, and ever since the hail storm yesterday her ears hadn't stopped ringing. Maybe it's from stress, she thought, rubbing her forehead. She still felt terrible about what had happened to Laurel, and every time she replayed the event in her mind, she wondered if she was somehow responsible. After all, hadn't she wanted to kill her sister the moment a ball of hail knocked her unconscious? Rose knew the notion sounded crazy. Nevertheless, she clearly remembered Vincent giving her arm a squeeze, when she felt as if the wind had been knocked out of her. Then, in the blink of an eye, her sister lay on the ground, immobile.

Rose sighed. She'd tried desperately to call her sister all last night, but each time Laurel picked up the phone and heard her voice, she hung up. Feeling defeated, Rose gazed at the wispy clouds outside that reflected the pastel morning light, their delicate forms as fleeting as any hope she had of patching things up with Laurel. She rubbed her sore jaw and recalled the mysterious words from the dream she'd had earlier that week: *Guard your power, aisling.* Guard your cheek, too, she thought, pressing her fingers to the bruise.

Scanning the crazy quilt that draped over her and Crystal on the bed, Rose examined the stitches once made by her great-great grandmother. She and Laurel used to snuggle beneath this quilt when they were young, every time their father disappeared. Whenever they held each other's hands underneath its soft folds, they felt strangely protected, as if benevolent forces watched over them. Those were the days when I still imagined ravens could talk, Rose thought, if only I knew how to listen. Back then, solace seemed only a bird call away, somewhere in the soft stirrings of the wilderness at twilight. She rubbed her eyes, wishing hope could come so easily now.

Leaning over quietly, she smoothed her fingers across Crystal's bangs as she slept, noticing the quilt patch tucked under her chin of a black bird flying beneath a moon. "Ravens in moonlight mean luck is bright," she whispered with the lilt of a nursery rhyme. Rose smiled a little. Her mother used to claim that each quilt patch told a story—some valuable lesson for life, like fairy tales. Laurel scoffed at her, of course, protesting that such notions were ridiculous, just like the silly pictures in the diary. But her sister's words only made Rose's mother smile. "Yes dear," she would always reply, "I suppose the old ways do sound like nonsense—until you need them."

Rose ran her palm over the quilt patch that lay across Crystal's chest. It depicted a gold nugget fashioned from a piece of yellow wool appliquéd onto a feed sack. No miner's pick or pan lay beside it, only a big red heart. What did this one mean? She searched her memories, trying to recall what her mother might have said. Closing her eyes for a moment, she stroked the fabric, enjoying the feel of the old wool that helped keep her and her daughter warm. She heard a quiet voice, like a tender breeze tickling her ear.

Only love leads to true gold.

Startled, Rose opened her eyes. She glanced around the apartment, but no one was there. *Was I dreaming?* she wondered, scratching her head, nearly certain she'd been coherent. She shrugged her shoulders and gently tucked the quilt a little tighter beneath her daughter's chin, when she spotted the raven perched on top of the bedpost. He raised his wings and nodded his beak, then cawed. Annoyed, Rose swooshed the bird away, wondering if he'd gotten in from an open window last night. *He's probably hungry,* she thought, but she wanted to linger in bed a while longer before she got up to bake—no freebies for scavengers this early in the morning.

"Scoot." Rose tossed a spare pillow at the bird. He strutted away from the bed, flicking his tail, and sulked into a corner. Rose turned to gaze at Crystal nestled under the quilt, glad to see the raven hadn't disturbed her, and she resisted the urge to give her a kiss on the forehead that might interrupt her sleep. Last night had been particularly strange—Crystal was restless in bed, tossing and turning, sometimes even moaning in her dreams. Rose had awakened several times and pulled her daughter close to try and soothe her. Unfortunately, she recognized the pattern all too well. Crystal used to fuss the same way in her sleep whenever Jake came home after disappearing on one of his binges. He'd barge into the apartment at night and crash on the sofa to doze off the dark underbelly of his latest high. In the mornings, while her father snored, Crystal always berated her mother. "Why don't you kick him out, Mommy?" she would say at breakfast, with her little hands clenched on her hips. She'd point her cereal spoon at Rose. "He's no fun and he stinks."

Rose cringed. Why on earth hadn't she? She'd flogged herself non-stop for months, of course, exposing every nook and cranny of her own failures with the brutal accuracy of a prosecutor. She was weak and stupid in outrageous proportions—any idiot could see that. But deep inside, Rose knew there was more. The real reason she'd allowed Jake to linger was because she didn't want her daughter to grow up in a vacuum, without a father figure, like she had—even if he was terribly flawed. The loss of both her parents so young in life had riddled her soul with perforations that made her feel empty for as long as she could remember. Although her relationship with Jake had clearly failed, and he'd bounced in and out of rehab half a dozen times, Rose had hoped to keep him at arm's length—to turn him into a cardboard cut-out who showed up once in a while to sing happy birthday or to eat Crystal's favorite dessert, vanilla custard with caramel and lavender petals on top, the way her own father never did. Rose believed she could protect her daughter this way from loss, from that dark hunger for love that never sees light—the kind that makes you consume all the wrong people and all the wrong things, leaving you breathless for more. Instead, she had only created more nightmares.

"Oh baby," Rose whispered, delicately touching her daughter's velvet cheek, "If only I could make all this up to you. I would do anything, sweetheart—I swear." She turned to glance at the picture she'd hung on the bedpost, the one of Crystal taken on her fourth birthday. With tears welling in her eyes, she blew the sweet image a kiss, wishing with all her might that their souls could somehow touch. In the corner, the raven let out a long, raspy caw. She heard the voice again.

Would you be willing to heal?

Rose glanced around, surprised. She quickly scanned the room and took a brief peek under the quilt. Where had that voice come from? When she was little, she used to believe she could hear fairy words on mountain breezes, whispers of comfort and direction when she felt lost. But now, she clutched her head in her hands. Oh God, Rose thought, I'm so tired I'm actually hallucinating. She laid back against the bed and yawned, wishing she could sleep for two whole days. Stretching out her body, she nestled next to Crystal and surrendered to her drowsiness. We'll just rest for one more hour, she promised herself, still worried over her daughter's fitful sleep. Why had Crystal been so disturbed in her dreams? Did the hail storm yesterday frighten her? As she closed her eyes, she whispered the lullaby into her daughter's ear, "On a bird's wing, my heart brings, all my love to you."

Rose's eyelids felt like heavy curtains sealing off daylight, even though the raven kept chortling from the corner of the room. Drifting off to sleep, she sensed something warm and feathery slip beneath her palm. It was like a down pillow, only softer, and she found herself stroking what felt like wings. Before long, she heard the methodic roll of ocean waves. Rose let her mind fall, descending deep into the soothing rhythm of the sea.

In the darkness of sleep, she could feel the ocean spray kissing her cheeks. The scent of a turf fire wafted on the breeze, a mixture of peat and smoke and damp earth that blended with the sea—rich and musky, like an ancient incense. Rose drew a deep breath and opened her eyes. Before her, the ocean met the shore in shifting light, sometimes flashing pewter or sullen iron, when a ray of sunlight broke through the clouds and made the tides sparkle emerald. The unpredictable waves hugged the golden shore like a crease between two worlds—the one she had left behind and the one presented to her now.

"Twixt" Rose whispered, feeling as though her hand could reach across the ocean to the mountain forests of Idaho, while the other touched the soft Irish sand. The wind tickled her hair and caressed her cheek in whispers, and everything around her seemed alive. Rose was alone, and the capricious breeze made her feel windblown as it blew across the grass in rolling waves, rustling the blades. For the life of her, Rose thought she heard someone say *Open your heart*.

Glancing around, she saw holes in rocks by the shore,

carved out by the sea, that made fluted sounds. It's just a stray echo on the wind, she thought. But deep inside, the wind felt animated and purposeful to her, the kind of force that might whisper your past or foretell your future. Rose snuck a peek at the clouds, the way her ancestors used to do, wondering if the sky really could guide anyone. To her surprise, she saw a black bird circling above her, blocking the rays of light that emerged from the clouds separating from the sun. The sight made her shiver. The bird slowly descended in spirals, landing on the beach.

Rose squinted, and suddenly a tall man appeared. Startled, she wondered where the bird had gone, when the towering figure took strides toward her. He had on a long, black coat, ragged at the edges, with dark, thick hair that skimmed his shoulders. Rose's breath caught in her throat. He had the same contour of face and body as—Vincent. But his black hair reminded her of Chance Murphy, only it was clean now, and the beard was gone. Shifting her feet, Rose tried to put the peculiar puzzle together, but it was no use. Confused, she gazed at the sand.

Yet when she glanced up, she realized the man was staring at her as if he knew her, every inch of her—the soft lines of her face and shoulders, the swell of her breasts and hips, even the gentle hollows of her throat and collarbones—and she blushed at the intensity of his admiration. The wind began to rise, and for a moment he lifted his arms like a bird testing the breeze. Rose half-expected him to fly, but he took several determined strides and then paused. The wind pressed at her back, as though the very elements were drawing her to him, and she trembled when she approached the grass at the edge of the turf. She saw him smile.

"Welcome back." His voice was the roll of the ocean, much deeper and more authoritative than Vincent's, tinged with a smoky resonance. When he stepped closer, Rose realized his eyes were not blue—they were a dark, dusky brown, nearly as black as a raven's. And there was a deep scar that sliced across his nose, just like Chance Murphy's. As he drew near, he smelled of turf fire and wild grass. Rose inhaled the aroma like a fresh fragrance offered by the breeze.

"I am not him," he said solemnly, as if he'd heard her thoughts about Vincent. "I am not that man." His voice was so low and urgent it made her quiver.

He gazed at her with traces of intrigue in his eyes, the way people do who harbor a secret. Yet his expression appeared wise—someone who had witnessed the ebb and flow of life, an eternal restless churning, as constant as the waves of the sea. How long has he lingered at this shore, waiting for me? Rose wondered. A shiver ran down her spine. Something in her soul whispered, *Beyond time.*

"You know me." Rose could have sworn his voice pulsed into her veins. "I am as close to you as your own shadow."

He paused and gazed at a ring of soft silhouettes cast on the sand by the clouds. Then he stared at her with such piercing sadness and dignity—two qualities she had never before seen in a man. The wind swelled again and he leaned his head back, listening for something.

Rose studied his face—the roughcast cheekbones, eyes dark as burnished ebony, lips surprisingly tender. And there was that scar, a mysterious emblem that spoke of a story—perhaps even a battle —which she wondered if she would ever know. Rose couldn't tell why, but she had the most irresistible urge to touch him. I'm only dreaming, she thought with a whimsical smile, I can do whatever I like! She reached up her finger to caress the scar across his nose, watching his thick eyelashes dip in surrender, trembling a little, as if he cherished her touch. Yet he kept his spine rod-straight and his shoulders stiff as compressed coils, like a soldier prepared at any moment to strike. Rose admired his lean frame, and she ran her hand down a strand of his long hair. The lock was dark but brittle, as though it had seen months or even years of sun and wind.

All at once, the man wrapped his arms around her with a force that rocked her to her bones, enveloping her in a wild, reckless kiss. His breath warmed her cheeks, her chin, her temples as his lips searched every facet of her face till her soul began to lift. Inside, she was flying again—soaring so free her body felt weightless. Yet strangely, she felt her boundaries waver, as though a fire had ignited within her. For a moment, while his warm lips pursued hers, she wondered if the two of them had somehow blended into the morning sun. The feeling was so strong that when he pulled away, gasping for breath, she was surprised to see their feet were still planted on the beach.

"I can't help it!" He stared into her eyes with a look that seemed shocked by the enormity of his passion. Taking a step back, he turned sharply to study the sun's place on the horizon to gauge the hour of the day. A raven cawed and he shook his head, his desire so powerful that Rose saw his jaw twist before he choked it down. Another caw rippled through the air, and he winced.

"I know—I know!" he blurted, appearing pressed for time. He searched Rose's eyes with the haunted gaze of a man facing an oncoming storm. He seized her by the shoulders, his grip so tight it made her flinch.

"Oh Rose, don't you understand?" His moist breath caressed her face even as the strength in his hands made her quiver. "You did conjure love—you did! I don't know how, but you brought up the past and the future all at once. And the problem is—we both want you." He reached hesitantly to touch her cheek. His fingers felt rough but strong, and as they swept over her skin, they trembled in restraint. "We both long for you, but we have such different intentions."

"We? What on earth are you talking about?" Secretly, Rose wished he would just shut up and start kissing her again.

The man spotted a raven's shadow hovering on the sand. He took her hand as though time might be slipping. Kneading her fingers, he glanced at the sky.

"Don't you see?" He pointed to a pattern in the clouds that looked like a pair of wings. Absorbing her face again, he studied the shifting pewter light that poured over her features and made her eyes gently shimmer. "What if I told you I've watched over you for centuries, and I know your good heart?" His voice resounded in her ears like a deep gust of wind. "How could I help falling in love with you?" He curled her fingers into his as if he never intended to let her go. But then a ring of leaves swirled at their feet, rustling with auspicious whispers. "Oh Rose," he gazed into her eyes. "Could you believe me if I told you I was—*I am*—a raven? A shadow who never leaves your side?" He shook his head. "It's no use. No matter what I say, you'd think I was crazy. I mean, I *am* crazy in your world—fairy struck, they call it—but not here. It's as if I'm healed here. We all are. The very best part of us, our souls, shine through."

The sun broke free from clouds, and Rose shuddered at bright slices of light that cut across the beach. She searched the man's face, mind filled with a thousand questions. When she opened her mouth to speak, all that escaped was her own breath.

"I'm mad, I know!" The man fixed his eyes upon hers. "You think this is all just a dream, right?" He scooped a palmful of sand and placed it in Rose's hands. It felt smooth as it filtered through her fingers. "Does that feel like a dream?" He lifted a seashell from beside their feet and thrust into in her palm. "How about that?" Grasping her fingers, he ran them over a curve in the smooth shell. Rose studied its pink swirls etched into an ivory shape, when he clutched her shoulders. "Does THIS?" He wrapped his arms around her for another reckless kiss.

Rose felt her whole being surrender, falling into a pool of light—and again, that weightless sensation, as though time itself had ceased to register. In that moment, she could no longer feel the edges of her skin, hair, or bones. She could have sworn she and this man had merged into one soul, and she almost expected them to melt into the sunlit sky, simply evaporate, like so many dancing particles in air. Above her, ravens cawed in a chorus—only this time, it wasn't with strident warning sounds, like they usually did in the mountain forest, but with a harmony of calls that built into a slow rhythm, becoming a powerful, cascading melody.

The man pulled away, gasping, and glanced up. "I hear

you!" he shouted defiantly. Gazing into Rose's eyes, he grasped her temples. "You must listen to me, Rose, and remember what I say. This is the truth: I'm merely another mountain loner in your world—someone who lost his mind when he dove his hands into a fairy ring to save a woman he couldn't resist. But here, I'm whole. And after all I've been through, I've learned one thing: When it comes to love, my beautiful Rose, people either give or take. They heal or they steal. And that new man who came to town—he might look like me with blonde hair and blue eyes—but he's all about the latter."

He grabbed her by the hand with such urgency that it left her rattled. "Please come with me, Rose".

Trembling, she forced her legs to walk beside him to the cottage, its stones now bright in the morning sunlight. The man let go of her hand and stepped in a slow circle around the well, whispering prayers. For a moment, he reminded her of Chance Murphy, on that strange night on Rook Ridge when he found Crystal, and the thought unnerved her. Could he possibly be the same man? Of course not, this is just a dream, Rose told herself—there's nothing to it.

The man looked up as though he'd heard her. He pointed to the well, to small red prayer rags stuffed between the stones. Rose nearly expected him to say "Moonchild," the way Chance Murphy did when he'd pointed to Crystal that night. Instead, he dipped a cup into the water and walked to a potato bed. The potato leaves were green, yet their tips were gray, appearing to have recovered not long ago from a serious blight. Rose wasn't quite sure, but as he approached, she could have sworn she saw the leaves dance.

The man kneeled and dug his hands with great force into

the dirt, pulling out a small potato, roots and all. He brushed off the dark soil and cradled the potato in his palms as tenderly as an egg. Tilting his head, he stared at the pale sliver of a moon, barely visible in the morning sky, as though it strengthened him. Then he began to hum—it was the same lullaby Rose had known as a child. A moment later, a little girl in an ivory sweater stepped out of the cottage.

Rose's tongue felt trapped in her throat. She reached out her arms. "C-Crystal?" she managed to cry.

The little girl turned away and scampered behind the man's leg.

"Honey!" Rose implored. "It's me—mommy!"

The man hoisted her in his arms and gave her the potato. Clutching it in her palm, Crystal buried her head into his chest.

"What's wrong? Your mother's here now."

Rose stretched for her daughter, but the child pushed her away.

"I don't want her! I don't want to go back. You can't make me!"

A dagger slashed through Rose's heart. As astounding as it was to hear her daughter talk, even in a dream, the force of Crystal's words twisted inside, leaving her breathless. "But-But honey, I can hear you. We can finally talk and be together again—"

"No! You'll *never* make me go back!" Crystal pounded at the man's chest.

"Sh, sweetheart." He rocked her in his arms. "It's okay, you can go now. You're not really broken over there. You'll be fine—if you want to be."

"No I won't! She didn't keep me safe. She breaks everything—can't you see that? *She's* the one who's broken."

"That's not true—"

"Yes it is! It is true!" Crystal drummed his chest with the potato in her hand. She turned to her mother. "He's a bird—can't you tell? Can't you see anything? You know him, Mommy! And you know me too, and you can't catch me!"

Flailing her arms, Crystal wriggled free from the man's grip until her feet stumbled to sand. She ran down the beach, still clutching her potato.

Rose dashed after her. Her adult weight made her feet churn, and she felt helpless as her daughter easily escaped to the shore. She pressed on, wanting with every muscle in her being to grab Crystal, to listen to every word she might utter, even if it did turn out to be a curse or damnation. Her legs lost a step for every one she tried to gain, until she saw the silhouette of a bird skim past her. Exhausted, Rose halted in her tracks. A raven with gray crown feathers flew ahead and landed beside her daughter. When its claws touched sand, the bird became a peasant woman in a wool shawl. She scooped Crystal in her arms.

Rose shook her head, stunned. The woman turned and stared with her salt and pepper hair blowing in the wind.

"We are always with you." She hugged Crystal close. "Even when you don't see."

With that, they both changed into birds.

12

Rose sat on the front porch swing that morning with her head in her hands, sobbing.

It wasn't over the county assessor's bill she'd just opened, informing her that she owed back property taxes, even though she'd only been operating the cafe for a month.

Nor was it because of Crystal's refusal to look at her learning exercises that reviewed colors, shapes and letters. After breakfast, she'd run straight into the shop and climbed onto a rocker, pitching back and forth as though her mother were made of air.

These events had disturbed Rose, already grinding at her stomach lining before she'd finished her second cup of coffee. But the real reason she was in tears was because when she went to the back apartment to clean the breakfast dishes, she spotted a potato on the kitchen table. It sat beside the bean pot and her great-great grandmother's diary. Small and round, the potato was the size of a golf ball, with tender roots still attached. Crumbly dirt clung to it, as dark as coffee grounds, as if the potato had just been pulled from the soil—from *Irish soil.*

Have I lost my mind? Rose recalled her dream earlier that morning, her daughter's peculiar accusations. She fingered the potato in her hand, feeling deeply unsettled. It's because of stress lately, she rationalized, I just need a break. Yet even as those words spilled through her mind, she couldn't escape thoughts of the island, as though it were seeping into her consciousness like a persistent tide. After all, in spite of her daughter's bitter words, her dream landscape had cradled a miracle—Crystal had talked! Entire sentences! Her daughter was once again the sassy little girl she'd remembered, before the accident had dimmed her eyes and stolen her voice.

Rose's heart fluttered. Could she dare to believe such a phenomenon might happen? The doctors in Winnemucca had been reticent about Crystal's prospects, afraid to build false hopes. But a kindly nurse had slipped her a medical journal in the hospital, which claimed recovery from brain damage could be capricious—sometimes patients made unexpected leaps after months or even years of no progress at all. Though Rose knew it was merely a dream, her thoughts skipped alternately between elation and dread. To hear her precious girl's voice, so clear after months of agonizing silence, filled her heart to nearly bursting. Yet she remained pierced by Crystal's words: *She's the one who's broken.*

Rose held the small potato in her palm like a delicate egg and stroked its smooth, elliptical shape. "Broken," she murmured, more tears moistening her eyes. If she was damaged, so shattered by life that her daughter had to retreat to a wild and forgotten place to protect herself, how on earth was she supposed to fix her own soul? All her life, Rose had felt like a sieve, with holes punched into her heart, so that even when love did come her way, she couldn't hold on to it. It blew through her outstretched fingers like the wind.

"How do I heal?" she whispered, half-hoping the ponderosa pines might provide an answer somewhere in the soft creaking of their limbs.

Can you believe? a voice echoed on the breeze.

The hair stood on the back of Rose's neck. She heard a sharp caw and turned to see Crystal's pet raven on the boardwalk. His eyes were intense, a burnished ebony—the same color as the man's eyes from her dream. He tilted his head and gazed at her with a tender appreciation, nodding as if he understood her predicament. A shiver danced down her spine.

"Men—birds—birds—men!" Rose muttered, clutching her forehead with her hands. "Now I'm seeing things in ordinary animals. Maybe I really have gone off kilter," she considered. "Strange dreams and hallucinations—I'd hardly be the first person to walk around half-cocked in this town."

Deep inside, however, Rose knew there was a truth still lingering in a secret part of herself that she couldn't escape. No matter how crazy it might seem, she found herself yearning to touch that dream man's cheek again. Just one more chance to inhale the musky incense of his skin, to feel his tender, trembling lips, to yield herself to an enveloping kiss that could make even a lonely widow's soul take flight. A cool breeze brushed her cheek, whisking a lock of hair beside her ear like a mischievous lover. Rose clenched the potato in her hand.

"You're being silly." She shook her head to scatter dream images that clung to her thoughts like dew. "Love never happens that way. On a beach, with an intriguing stranger who somehow peers into your soul."

But she couldn't help herself—the dream had made her feel alive again, as if all she'd been doing for years was walking among shadows without even realizing it. Rose glanced up at the morning sun inching over the violet outline of Rook Ridge, with a dusting of snow on the peak that reminded her of sifted flour. She bit her lip. "You've got Halloween cookies to bake," she scolded herself, busying her mind with a recipe that called for orange icing and candy corn. She leaned her head on the porch rocker, feeling fragile, when she sensed a gentle tap on her arm.

The raven had flown to the porch swing and perched beside her on the wooden arm rest. For a moment, she could have sworn he smelled of the sea—a salty, musky scent, with traces of turf fire smoke that she remembered from the island. But there was more. The aroma filled her sense memory with something ancient and beckoning. Curious, she took a deep breath, hoping to capture its essence before the breeze stole it away, yet all she could smell was pine. She sighed at her own folly and stroked the bird's dark, shiny feathers, watching his eyes soften in delight. Why did this confounded raven seem so familiar? More than a bird, she thought, a guardian. From the very beginning, he had waltzed into their lives with a possessive attitude like he thought he belonged with them. Rose shrugged, unable to

cipher the odd habits of forest creatures. She gave the bird
one last pat and reached into her coat pocket to toss a hunk
of a cornbread onto the boardwalk that she'd intended to eat
for breakfast. It landed beside the scarecrow she'd set up on
the porch, and the raven eagerly glided down to peck at the
snack. He turned to her and cawed, dipping his head.
Somewhere in the air, Rose thought she heard a voice say,
Thank you.

"Good morning, sweetie!"

Amy's jovial voice made her jump. How does she manage
to be so cheerful at the crack of dawn? Rose wondered,
squinting at the bright amber wool coat she wore over a
flowing paisley skirt, the ruby cowboy boots that always made
her eyes sting.

"So, are you the greeting committee today?" Amy stepped
onto the porch and plopped next to her on the bench.

Rose glanced aside so Amy wouldn't see her red eyes. She
held up the county assessor's bill.

Amy scanned the brief letter. Her mouth dropped in
shock. "Oh my God, a thousand dollars in taxes! Honey,
between the money we owe Laurel and this, we're in the hole
for six grand." Slayed, she leaned back on the bench and tilted
her head onto Rose's shoulder. "Listen sweetheart, I know it's
not your first choice. But with the blue moon coming in a week
and a half, it looks like you'd better give those tours of Rook
Ridge after all."

Rose was silent. Amy sat up straight and squeezed her
hand.

"We can't afford *not* to." She studied Rose's swollen, red
eyes. "Oh honey," her voice softened, "of all the things to hit

us right now. And I bet you're worried sick about Laurel, huh? Have you tried calling her today?"

Rose shook her head. "I rang her over and over last night. Each time she answered, I told her how sorry I was and asked if she needed anything, but she kept hanging up without a word. I don't know if she's truly angry, or just trying to make me crawl." She threw up her hands. "It's hopeless."

Above the town square, a flock of geese flew by in a V formation, honking as they steadily flapped their wings. Autumn in Ophir Creek was the season when everything was on the move—elk, wild turkey, deer—all headed for lower elevations and easier access to winter food. Rose glanced around the old town, historically known for its restlessness. For the first time since she'd arrived, she wondered how she could possibly afford to stay. She slipped the potato into her pocket and pulled her jacket tighter, placing her hand on Amy's.

Amy noticed her fingers were shaking. "Oh dearie, everything will work out somehow," she gave her palm a squeeze, "we just have to believe."

"Believe?" Rose recalled the eerie voice she'd heard. The last thing she wanted was more gibberish about hope and faith, omens and luck. What she really needed right now was hard proof that she and Crystal would be okay—preferably in dollars.

"Sure! There'll be lots more tourists this week. And with my transmigration therapy practice building, more money will be rolling in. I've got a client this morning, you know."

"But that's not enough," Rose protested. "We need serious cash—fast."

The raven stood on a large pumpkin and cawed. Rose

winced, unable to get his piercing, dark gaze out of her mind. With all the things she had to worry about, she didn't need to be pestered by lingering dreams and a bird that reminded her of a mysterious man's eyes. Maybe it's better to face my illusions, she thought. Meet them head on so they can be cleared away for good.

"So Amy," Rose tried to sound casual, "in your psychic practice, have you ever dabbled in dream interpretation? Does it all come down to wish fulfillment?" She remembered Crystal's accusation in her dream. "Or maybe a guilty conscience? Or are dreams simply a weird by-product of something you ate?"

Amy's eyes lit up at the prospect of Rose as a convert. "Dreams are a whole new vista, sweetie!" She waved at the mountains above Ophir Creek, and her charm bracelet chimed. "A road map of unconscious material, just waiting to be deciphered. Nothing's by chance. Every image you see in a dream is a code, revealing your past, present, and future all at once. They're like psychic greeting cards!"

Rose rolled her eyes at the hogwash she'd unleashed. She knew better than to ask Amy about such things—the last person on earth who could be logical. Rubbing her brows, she caught sight of the raven from the corner of her eye, sitting on a pumpkin finishing the cornbread. The way he lifted his beak and relished the treat reminded her of Chance Murphy when she'd given him a fairy cake. In that instant, the raven hopped from the pumpkin with a caw, as though Rose should have stumbled onto something by now. Her temples began to throb.

"Amy," Rose mentioned hesitantly, "w-what do you think

ever happened to Chance Murphy? You know, that forester who came to our shop on opening day?"

"Oh, he's probably out in the woods counting tree rings somewhere," Amy yawned. "Why?"

Rose flinched. She feared telling Amy her secret, knowing her nocturnal journey sounded absurd. Although the man in her dream was groomed, his dark hair free of tangles and his face cleanly shaved, something about his solitary demeanor and long, black coat was reminiscent of Chance. The man had the same scar on his nose as well—and then there were those eyes. Both men had beautiful brown eyes, filled with compassion and tenderness, yet marked by a haunted awareness of lost souls wandering through time that seemed to escape ordinary people. The mysteries of the island baffled Rose, pricking her heart like a pin. Before she knew it, words spilled from her lips.

"Well, you probably won't believe this," she confessed, "but last night I saw Chance Murphy in a dream. And even though his hair was black, he looked a bit like Vincent—or Vincent looked like him. Oh, Amy," she twisted her hands together. "It's hard to explain. But I think he's dangerous."

"Who, Chance Murphy? Honey, he's just a misguided loner—"

"No—" Rose stared at the Magpie Saloon and slipped her hand into her coat, rubbing the potato, "Vincent. Chance warned me about him in the dream. He said he was a thief, and ever since Vincent touched my arm I've felt weaker."

"Oh I know what this is," Amy folded her arms with a knowing smile. "You're in love!"

"What?"

Amy gave her a big squeeze. "You're in love, silly! And you're putting up all kinds of subconscious road blocks because you don't believe you deserve a good man. Don't worry," she patted Rose's knee, "it happens to women all the time! And I have the perfect healing ceremony. You just stretch out on a bed, and I'll rub pine sap on your chakras to cleanse your aura—"

"But Amy—"

"No buts! You've gotta loosen up, Rose. Let go of your fears—there's a whole life out there waiting for you. And it wouldn't hurt if it included a handsome stranger or two." She chuckled a little. "As long as I can have your left-overs, okay?"

"But I mean it, Amy. There's something I didn't tell you. Just before the hail storm happened, Vincent touched my arm. I swear—he was like a conductor. The second he made physical contact, I felt energy drain out of my body. And then I nearly collapsed."

"It's called kinetic attraction, silly! Lots of people get goose bumps from the touch of a good-looking man."

"No—it was more. It was like he funneled the anger I had for my sister, maybe even preyed on it. You know, they say my great-great grandmother could influence the weather...but somehow I felt like that man influenced *me*. Like he knew the storm would happen when he touched my arm—and for some reason he wanted to get rid of Laurel. I mean, what's he doing in Ophir Creek, anyway?"

"Starting over, like the rest of us. Listen, even if he's got a few mistakes in his past, so do we! If we weren't misfits, honey, we wouldn't be in this town. Unless he's wanted for a capital crime, I think you're being a bit stuffy. And I also think stress is getting to you and you're becoming paranoid. You don't want to turn out like Fannie Thistlewaite who hardly leaves her cabin, do you? The last time I saw her, she smelled funny and told me about a new recipe for skunk."

Rose shook her head, embarrassed she'd brought up her dream, and she abandoned the idea of convincing Amy of anything. The wind picked in the square and sent aspen leaves across the boardwalk with a dry, scuffling sound, making the morning itself seem shrouded in whispers. Their clatter put Rose on edge, and she pulled her collar up against her neck.

Just then, a green jeep parked in front of the shop. A Forest Service woman in a khaki uniform and glasses stepped out. She removed her ranger's hat and gave a shy wave.

"There's my morning client!" Amy said cheerfully. She grabbed Rose by the hand and pulled her up. "C'mon honey, time to throw on a smile and open our door. We've got money to make."

Silk tablecloths, crystal balls, the usual heavy incense that always made her sneeze—Rose was accustomed to the exotic trappings of Amy's part-time vocation. Because Amy's clients always ordered breakfast, she turned a blind eye to her friend's indulgence, even if it did fill the shop with billows of smoke. Rose rationalized that the smell went along with Halloween decorations, adding a certain ambience to the fake cobwebs and giant spiders they'd hung for the holiday. But when Amy's young client claimed to have a mad crush on George Brickman, an aging logger who Rose had known for years, she couldn't help allowing curiosity to get the best of her. After all, this was better gossip than could be had at the post office. She pretended to be distracted by making coffee for the two women, when in reality she was all ears.

"I think," the fidgety young woman confessed at the front table, her voice verging on tears, "that it's a fatal attraction." She stared into Amy's crystal ball, examining her own reflection. "I mean, look at me—I work for the Forest Service! My job is to protect and preserve trees, while George cuts them down every day. Don't you think that's strange?"

"Well, Sylvie," Amy stroked her hand, "opposites do attract. Right Rose?"

Rose blushed, realizing Amy had caught her listening. She ignored her friend's gaze when she brought over mugs of coffee and scrambled eggs as an excuse to get a better look at the woman. Sylvie's hair was stringy and brown, cut short for efficiency, and her dark-rimmed glasses made her look hopelessly prim. She was hardly the sensual, earth-mother type to hug trees—more like a nervous scientist with a penchant for wearing neatly-pressed uniforms.

"You know, this is quite a special time for romance," Amy encouraged. "In a week and a half, the blue moon will rise on Halloween. Anything could happen."

"Really?" Sylvie brushed a lock of hair from her glasses. "Come to think of it, the tree rings have been rather unusual this year. Very grainy and wide, distinct from other rings. We haven't seen anything like it for decades."

"See!" Amy massaged the ball to pick up its energy. "There's good vibrations everywhere." She narrowed her eyes. "But you didn't come here to talk to me about tree rings."

Sylvie glanced down at her hiking boots. "The truth is, he doesn't even notice me," her lips trembled. "We first met a few weeks ago at the county courthouse. But I think he only has eyes for Belle Crawford—that old hag."

Rose chuckled and started a recipe for Halloween sugar cookies. Who would have guessed old Belle could still reel one in? As she sifted flour into a bowl, she noticed Crystal had fallen asleep in the rocker, her pink cheeks as sweet as an angel's, with her hands tucked beneath her chin. Because of her tossing and turning last night, Rose wanted to make sure she got enough rest, undisturbed by customers. So she dusted off her fingers and went to the rocker to pick her up, hugging her close for a kiss. Rose reveled in these sneak attacks of affection, whenever her daughter was too drowsy to protest. She pressed her face against Crystal's cheek, inhaling her sweet aroma of sleep, better than any fine perfume. Then she carried her to the back bedroom and tucked her carefully under the quilt.

When she returned, she noticed Amy had both Sylvie's hands in hers. "I think we should do a past-life regression." Amy looked intensely at Sylvie. "That way we can find out if you and George are truly good for each other—or, well, acting out bad karma. Are you ready?"

"Um, I think so," Sylvie's eyes were a bit uncertain.

"Good! Let's both clear our thoughts and gaze into the crystal ball. Focus really hard, tuning out everything around you." Amy blew at the incense so that it drifted into Sylvie's face, making her cough. "Just let your mind go and breathe in the essence of your past lives. Then simply be open to what you see."

Despite Sylvie's hacking, Amy released her hands and stared into the ball, scrutinizing the reflections for clues. "Ooh," Amy purred excitedly, "I think I see England." She tapped the ball, but Sylvie's brows merely kneaded together. "Rolling green hills, an old, stone mansion. And there's George on horseback." Her eyes sparkled. "Maybe he was a duke or something!"

"A duke?" Sylvie's voice sounded hopeful.

"Now it's your turn. What do you see?"

Sylvie squirmed in her chair. "Well," her eyes crinkled, "to tell you the truth, all I see are cracks in the crystal. Where did you get this, anyway—a garage sale?"

Amy glared impatiently.

"Okay-okay," Sylvie studied the ball. "Wait a minute, I think I see paws. Yes, in the grass. I seem to be following George and sniffing the ground. Ick—I'm tracking through mud."

"You're a hound! That's such a great sign."

"What? Are you implying I was his dog?" Sylvie twisted the ranger's hat in her lap.

"Exactly!" Amy didn't miss a beat. "Dogs represent camaraderie and faithful relationships. This is very encouraging—"

Rose's mouth gaped, and she turned to flip the electric mixer on high. Regardless of the delicious gossip earlier, this was always the part that amazed her. How on earth does Amy get twenty-five bucks a reading for such rubbish? Don't people know her imagination is running wild? Scraping batter from the side of the bowl, she cringed, realizing at least one of them was pulling in a few dollars.

Cracking an egg into the batter, Rose stirred vigorously before taking a lick. She brooded for a moment and grated orange rind to add more zest. Folding it into the batter, she happened to notice through the front window that Vincent was walking across the town square. Sparkles of mica glinted in the sun as his boots kicked up dust. Rose stopped stirring, afraid her heart might stop as well. For the life of her, she'd never seen anyone so radiant. His pale hair shone as bright as brushfire in the early light, and his mouth relaxed into an easy smile, like the sun rose just for him. Although a black bird circled over his head and swooped, Vincent ignored it, walking with confident strides. The bird began to dive bomb, and he paused to pick up a stone, pulling out a red bandana from his pocket. Using it as a slingshot, he hurled the stone at the bird with surprising vehemence. The raven bobbled in air, wings flapping until it righted itself and flitted off. Vincent cocked his head and laughed, whistling while he tied the bandana around his neck.

Rose searched through the front window at the porch, but Crystal's raven was nowhere in sight. Goose bumps alighted down her spine. What if it was the same bird? But Crystal's pet wouldn't attack anyone, she thought—it must have been a stray. Adding more flour to her batter, she reminded herself not to leave leftovers outside for wild birds—the cafe didn't need a nuisance that drove away customers. From now on, she would feed her daughter's pet inside.

When Vincent walked in the front door, the harness bells echoed through the shop in musical tones. In spite of the strange warning from her dream, Rose admired how handsome he appeared, with his broad shoulders and sun-kissed skin. In that moment he seemed aglow, like he was lit from within, and it nearly knocked the breath out of her. For a second, she was tempted to believe Amy's notions about auras —those mysterious coronas of light that revealed a person's character. Must be the sunshine from the front window, she thought, backlighting his body to make him luminous. She watched him unravel the red bandana from his neck and wipe dust from his brow, tucking it into his deerskin jacket. He gazed at her with a sweet expression, his eyes soft yet focused, as if worried about her.

He doesn't look like a thief, Rose thought, heart skipping a beat. In fact, he looked so much like the man in her dream, all she wanted was to kiss him. Her cheeks flushed, but then she noticed his eyes were blue—a vibrant cobalt—not brown, like the man on the island. And there was no scar across his nose. Maybe Amy's right, she considered. Maybe I have been getting all these men mixed up in my head because I'm afraid of love. Why can't I relax for once? Just take a deep breath and enjoy the moment? She tried to calm herself by giving the batter a few more strokes.

"How's your sister doing?" Vincent asked kindly, stepping to the counter. He sat down on a stool near Rose and searched her face.

Rose attempted to keep her composure and poured him a cup of coffee. "Well," she admitted, "Laurel hasn't spoken to me since yesterday. She's pretty high strung, you know."

Vincent nodded. "Time. Don't worry, everyone comes back around in time." He reached out and gently touched her hand, glancing into her eyes. For an instant, all she saw was silvery white, as if a light had poured into her and washed through her thoughts. She couldn't comprehend it, but inside she suddenly felt buoyant. Young and lithe—not the tired, working mother who was a little past her prime and deeply in debt. As quickly as the feeling had come, she slipped back into fatigue, the blood in her veins plummeting to her feet. Although she pulled away her hand, she yearned to touch him again, to feel that sweet exhilaration. Vincent smiled.

"But how can we find love if we're a different species?" Sylvie nearly shouted across the table at Amy. "I'm just a canine to him! Oh, it's no use." She slumped into her chair by the front window.

Rose blinked, recalling there were other people in the room. She leaned her hands on the counter when she caught Vincent's expression, puzzled.

She rolled her eyes. "Past-life regression," she whispered, as if the term might be impolite in mixed company. "It's another one of Amy's crazy business ideas. She's convinced that she has, well, special gifts."

Rose expected Vincent to laugh, but he sipped his coffee and appeared to listen to the two women. When Sylvie let out another frustration over romance, Vincent swiveled on his stool.

"Oh darling, *never* give up on love," he admonished. "After all, it's the only thing really worth living for." He winked at Rose and took another sip of coffee. "Besides, I have it on very good authority that George Brickman fancies you. Last night I heard him talking to Belle Crawford to get her advice on catching women." His lips curled into a smile. "She laughed and mentioned something about lassos."

"Really?" Sylvie turned to Amy. "What do I do now? Ask

him out? Flirt with him around the lumber yard? I could get fired—"

"Just be yourself. And let love in. If it's meant to be, not even wild horses can stop it." Amy stole a glance at Vincent before nodding at Rose with smug satisfaction.

"Thank you!" Sylvie grabbed her for a hug. Checking her watch, she laid a handful of bills on the table. "I've got to get to work." She slipped on her ranger's hat and turned to Vincent. "And thank you, sir. For, um—hope." With a timid smile, she darted out the front door, the sound of the harness bells chasing her heels.

"Well, well," Amy smiled at Vincent, "looks like I'm not the only one who believes in true love."

Rose measured more flour in silence. Her cheeks burned.

"Would you like some breakfast?" Amy asked him, stuffing the bills into her pocket. "Or how about a past-life reading? Something tells me there's a lovely dark-haired woman in your history." She shot a defiant look at Rose.

Vincent laughed. "To tell the truth, I find the future far more compelling. Like the blue moon rising over Rook Ridge." He stared at Rose. "Rumor has it that you give private tours. To find gold, I mean."

"That's not true," Rose protested. "Where'd you hear that?"

"From a group of miners. They came into the bar last night and tried to beat me at poker." He pulled out a money clip from his jacket stuffed with bills. "Mistake."

"Well I don't give tours."

"Except for special occasions!" Amy stepped to the counter and slid onto a stool beside Vincent, leaning her elbows on the wood. "They say there's still gold up there—if you know where to look. But of course, for the tour to be exclusive, you have to be willing to pay the price."

"Five thousand is what I heard," Vincent leafed through the bills.

Amy's eyes narrowed. "Six thousand. Up front—right, honey?"

Rose gulped air. Amy had lost her mind. This was nothing short of highway robbery—worse than the wild schemes her father used to dream up. Besides, with her luck, she wouldn't find anything but fool's gold. Then Vincent would turn her in for fraud and she'd be arrested. The shop would go bankrupt and Amy would have to raise Crystal alone until she got out of jail. Or worse—Laurel would sue for custody and win. Her mind reeled through a dozen doomed outcomes, till Amy slapped the counter.

"Let's write up a sales draft right now." Amy grabbed a pen and notepad. "When do you want to go?"

"Halloween, of course." Vincent fixed his gaze on Rose. "That's when the legend claims the magic happens, right?"

"There is no magic." A knot clenched in Rose's stomach. "There are only silly stories that people tell because they don't have anything better to do in this town." She glared at Amy. "Besides, the ridge will be packed that night with amateur gold seekers. And not a single one of them will find gold in the dark with a flashlight—that's crazy."

"You've got a point," Amy tapped her lip with the pen. "And other miners might stake a claim by then. You'd better go soon if you want to beat the rush. How about two o'clock, on um, this Monday?" She knew it was a day the shop tended to be slow.

"Two o'clock it is," Vincent counted out a wad of bills. "Tell you what, I'll give you a thousand now, and the rest when we actually find gold." He put the cash in Rose's palm. Her fingers trembled. "Deal?"

"Deal!" Amy grinned like she'd won the lottery. "But no funny business, mister," she warned. "If you don't pony up, just remember, we know where you live." She scribbled a bill of sale and handed it to Vincent.

Vincent slipped the receipt in his pocket and rose from the stool, turning to walk out the shop. When he opened the front door, a cloud of exhaust blew in from a tour bus that had parked in the town square. A dozen senior citizens piled out, advancing to the porch with canes and walkers. Vincent held the door for them.

"By the way, Rose," he mentioned in a low voice, buttoning up his jacket, "you owe me an apology."

Rose cringed, assuming he meant the expensive wine bottle that had shattered yesterday. There was no way she could afford to repay him, and none of the antiques in her shop were worth more than fifty dollars. She wiped the counter with a dishtowel when she noticed his coffee cup was still half full. Unable to stop herself, she snuck a peek. In a flash, she saw brooding clouds floating on the liquid, like a storm gathering. A burst of white sliced through, quick as a lightning bolt.

"You lied to me, Rose." He knotted the red bandana around his neck with a smile. "You know full well that magic exists. You always have."

13

Amy curled a wayward lock of red hair behind her ear and stared into her crystal ball, trying to concentrate. She'd already given half a dozen readings to the senior citizens who'd barraged the shop that morning, the strain showing in creases around her eyes. Most wanted to know whether they would reunite with loved ones in the great beyond, which of course, Amy kindly assured them would happen. But several individuals were more demanding. One woman argued with her, insisting she'd been a duchess in another life, not a lowly cobbler, as Amy had claimed. "Then why did I see so many shoes?" Amy protested. "They weren't exactly satin, either."

With enough persuasion, the woman settled for her modest past, as long as the reading was reduced to half-price. Another man had a different agenda altogether. Hooked up to an oxygen tank, he inhaled strained breaths and pressured Amy for the right horses to bet on for his racing form. Amy peered into her crystal ball. "I really couldn't tell you," she sighed and held up her coffee cup. "For guidance like that, you'll have to ask Rose."

Rose ignored the reference to her fortune-telling abilities, pouring Amy her fourth refill that morning. It took a lot of imagination and caffeine to keep up with this crowd, so when the bus driver finally came in to issue a last call, Rose threw back her head in relief. After all, they'd been more work than the last group of third graders, and no amount of coffee, treats, or spiritual insight seemed to be enough to satisfy them.

"Thank God," Rose watched the last woman with a walker disappear onto the bus. She wiped her brow and leaned against a saddle rack. "Now we can take a break." She glanced at Amy, who was placing her crystal ball into a velvet pouch, apparently finished with being psychic for the morning.

"You know, I don't get it," Rose observed, "I knew we'd have more tourists this time of year—but it seems like people have been flocking to your past-life readings."

"Guess I'm just lucky!" Amy chirped, kicking a piece of trash under the table.

Rose sighed, grabbing a broom to clean the mess, until Amy headed her off.

"I can do it—you sit down and relax!" She swiped the broom.

Rose shrugged, happy to delegate. Nevertheless, when she stooped to retrieve the paper, she caught the startled look in Amy's eyes. Glancing into her hand, Rose realized it was a brochure. On the front was a fairy flying past a blue moon among a scattering of stars. The brochure read, *Eternity's Wings: Transmigration Therapy and Psychic Repair. Discover your soul's purpose through the healing of past-life traumas.* Rose flipped to the inside—to her shock, the brochure recounted her great-great grandmother's legend. At the bottom, it said, *While you're at it, learn a few gold panning tips from a REAL DESCENDENT of Corvine O'Dannan before the night of the blue moon!*

"Amy!" Rose burst. "How could you? When did you start circulating this?"

Amy cringed. "Oh, about a week ago." Her fingers clenched the broom handle. "Didn't you notice everyone seemed to know about the legend?" She broke into a big smile. "It never hurts to advertise! Besides, ever since I started leaving them at county buildings, our business has doubled. Do you realize we've made fifteen hundred dollars since we opened the shop?"

Rose was dumbfounded—she'd been too exhausted to even look at the books lately. She'd simply stuffed each day's receipts into an envelope, hoping bill collectors wouldn't come knocking, or worse, Laurel's lawyer. Rose went behind the counter and pulled out a drawer to rummage for the accounts ledger. Flipping it open, she discovered all the receipts stapled together and totaled in Amy's familiar, loopy handwriting.

Amy must have added them up at night, she thought, *when I was busy tending to Crystal.* She turned to her friend, suddenly aware that this was the most responsible thing she'd ever seen her do, and her heart melted. Back in their barmaid days, Rose had always been the one to cover Amy's tracks— mopping up her broken shot glasses, finding her missing bar tabs, even putting out a fire she'd started once when she tried to make a Blazing Saddle and spilled flames across the bar. Yet now here she was, all red curls in the sunshine, beaming like a goodwill ambassador for psychic enterprise. For all of her kooky ideas, Rose knew Amy was the best partner—and friend —anyone could hope to have. She smiled, wondering for a moment who Amy might have been in a past life. Regardless of whether she was a peasant, a princess, or a free-wheeling bohemian, Rose could be certain of one thing: Amy had become one hell of a business woman.

Feeling humbled, she smoothed out the crinkled brochure and slipped it into her pocket. "Thank you," she wrapped an arm around Amy for a hug. "Let's just hope none of those gold seekers ask me for a fairy hunt."

"It's okay, honey, I'd be happy to make you a pair of wings," Amy winked. "Hey, maybe you could wear them when you see Vincent tomorrow."

The two women laughed. Even so, a nervous sensation riddled Rose's stomach. How could she go through with the outing when she didn't have a clue how to find real gold? As a child, her father had taught her clever melodrama, with just enough panning techniques thrown in to make it seem genuine. Rose dug her hand into her pocket, stroking the bills Vincent had given her. For a second she imagined his face, the strong lines of his jaw and cheekbones, the wheat-blonde hair she'd just love to run her fingers through. What if those radiant blue eyes get through to me, and I can't help telling him the truth? She shook her head to fend off his potent charms. I don't care what anybody says, she decided. On Monday, if we don't find gold within an hour, I'm handing his money back.

Rose's thoughts were interrupted by the harness bells on the front door. A forest ranger came in, walking with purposeful strides to sit down at the counter. His khaki uniform was as crisp as Sylvie's, with pleats so perfect Rose had to resist the urge to salute. He ran his hand through his gray hair and perused a menu, spying the jack-o-lantern cookies behind the glass case. Rose pegged him for a dessert man, so she set two cookies on a plate to tempt him. Those nickels and dimes were beginning to add up.

"I'll take a ham sandwich." The ranger scanned the shop. He didn't't seem the sort to buy teacups, and he certainly didn't appear idealistic enough to be a gold seeker. Curious, Rose kept an eye on him as she cut ham and cheese and set it on bread slices, offering him an array of condiments. The man shook his head, preferring his sandwich plain. Rose put it on a plate and watched him take a few distracted chews before he glanced at Amy.

"So, Sylvie told me you two know just about everything that goes on in this town. Have either of you spotted Chance Murphy lately?"

Rose shook her head, forehead rifling with warmth. Only in my dreams, she thought, recalling his windblown face on the island, the romantic kiss that nearly swept her soul to sea.

"Well, no one at the ranger station has seen him either. To tell you the truth, we're pretty worried about him. You know, before his breakdown, he used to be our top dendrochronologist, analyzing tree rings. A brilliant man—the best we had."

Rose puzzled over his words when she felt a tug at her sleeve. Crystal stood beside her, blonde hair fussed in all directions, wrapped in the family quilt. She must have dragged it from the bedroom, Rose thought, glad she'd gotten a bit more sleep. She pulled open a drawer with her daughter's crayons and worksheets and set them on the floor. Then she caressed Crystal's wayward hair—in a few minutes she'd brush it, as soon as the ranger left.

"How long has Chance been gone?" Rose's gut twisted in worry. She shot a glance through the window at Rook Ridge and checked her watch to estimate when she could leave the shop to help with a search. Would he recognize her voice if she called?

"Nearly a week. Every Tuesday we leave supplies for him in the woods—backpacker's rations, like granola and beef jerky—but he never takes them. Once in a while we spot him in tree shadows around dusk, like a wild animal. If we're lucky, he'll talk to us." The man glanced at the jack-o-lantern cookies Rose had set on a plate, with candy corn for the eyes and noses. He fidgeted in his chair. "By the way, he mentioned you once."

Rose raised her brow. "He did?"

"Yeah. He told me you gave him some, uh, fairy cakes, I think he called them—in between his other ramblings. It was the first time I'd heard of him accepting food from anyone in months."

The man hesitated before he reached for a cookie, then gave in and ate it with relish. He smiled as he studied Rose's face, the outline of her cheeks framed by her dark hair, as though admiring a picture.

"I didn't quite believe him a first." The ranger picked up his hat. "By the way he talked, I thought maybe you were a vision, another part of his imagination. But now I see he was right."

"Right about what?" Rose felt tingles dance up her arms, the way she did after the night she met Chance on Rook Ridge.

The ranger smiled and left money on the counter. "Well, the food really is delicious here—and you're every bit as beautiful as he said."

Blushing, Rose turned to wipe the counter in circles, though it was already clean.

"Let me know if you see him again." The ranger nodded at her and Amy and walked with clipped strides through the front door.

He drove off in a green truck, his words clinging to Rose's thoughts. For a moment, the dust from his tires hung in the air like a veil, reminding her of the sea mist she'd seen on the island. All at once, her dreams about Chance Murphy seemed closer, an alternate world that existed at her fingertips, if only she knew how to break through and touch it. The smell of the sea, the feel of his lush dark hair, even that long, black coat he wore, speckled with sand. In spite of herself, she ached for his touch again, and she knew if she shut her eyes, she could almost feel his tender lips against her cheek. Stop it—you're just lonely, she reprimanded herself. So you fill up your spare moments with daydreams like some foolish woman. Chance Murphy is simply a lost, unstable man who deserves your compassion. It's only your imagination that builds him into more.

Rose resolved to call wilderness outfitters she knew who were expert trackers to help look for Chance, as soon as she finished sandwich preparations. The minute she sliced a few pickles, she felt Crystal tug at her sleeve again. Instead of coloring, her daughter was pointed at the heirloom quilt on the floor. Rose thought it was a hint she wanted to go to bed for a while longer. But Crystal directed her finger along the border of a quilt patch, tracing the square. Rose's heart pounded. They hadn't done their circle-square-triangle exercises yet this morning, the one a therapist told her was mandatory to repeat each day. Could it be Crystal was identifying a shape on her own? To test her, Rose picked up an exercise sheet from the floor and pointed to a square, then a circle. Like usual, Crystal merely stared, her expression empty. When Rose waved her hand, her daughter didn't even blink.

A familiar knot constricted Rose's heart. She dearly missed the brassy little girl who always beat her at games, who could identify whole pages of geometric shapes before her mother pointed past the first ones. "Don't be so slow, Mommy—I'm a big girl, now," Crystal always bragged, flipping through pages to hexagons and trapezoids. This was the same child who could draw nearly anything after seeing it once, whether with paint or crayons, causing even her preschool teacher to whisper the word "gifted."

"Gifted," Rose murmured like a prayer. Part of her wanted to gaze into a filled teacup or Amy's crystal ball—anything to reassure herself of a bright future for her daughter. But another part of her felt deeply afraid. What if she only managed to conjure romantic notions about Crystal the way she had about Chance? Perhaps the reflection in the teacup might show her a reality she couldn't bear, and her mind might snap, like his did. Then there would be two crazy people walking around this town. Rose's thoughts were lost to currents of worry, when she felt a tap on her leg. Her daughter quietly pointed to a quilt patch of a raven with wings outstretched. It was the one Rose had noticed earlier that day, while she and Crystal were still in bed. Her daughter began to hum.

"Amy!" Rose whispered. "Did you hear that? Crystal's humming again."

Amy tiptoed behind the counter. "It sounds like a lullaby. Do you think we should try and hum it with her?"

Rose shook her head, reluctant to interfere. The two women listened as Crystal's small voice cadenced with the melody. Crystal stroked the faded, black wool on the raven patch. Barely above a whisper, she said the word "man."

Silently, Rose and Amy clutched each other's hands. Tears welled in their eyes.

"Oh honey, it's a miracle," Amy whispered.

Rose clung to her friend like a pillar, and the knot in her heart ever so slightly loosened. Amy bent down to pick up her daughter, quilt and all, and cradled her. Amy hugged them, and for a moment they were one being, shrouded in the warmth of the quilt. Amy smiled and broke away, stepping over to Crystal's crayon drawer to pull out the tin where Rose kept gold stars.

"You know what, sweetie? If you ask me, I'd call this is a twenty-star day." One by one, she licked the stars and placed them on Crystal's progress chart that hung beside a cupboard on the wall. Rose tilted her head, bemused. She knew Amy didn't give a damn about the therapist's grid for shape identification and motor skills—this was simply her way of celebrating. Amy added a couple of extra stars for good measure, until the progress chart glittered like a constellation.

Rose smiled, feeling her heart expand in her chest. No

matter how anything might look on the surface, she could always hold on to the fact that her daughter had communicated in her own small way—she even had a witness in Amy. Okay, so the word was probably random, but it was identifiable, with real consonants and a vowel! There was still hope. Somewhere in her daughter's brain, Rose was convinced she had retained language and memory. She briefly closed her eyes and swayed, feeling like the two of them were gliding on a calm sea. Then she picked up the corners of the quilt and carried her daughter to a rocker by the window where the sun warmed the wood, accentuating the smell of pine. Rose ran her fingers through Crystal's hair and eased the rocker into motion. As far as she was concerned, her daughter could rock all day if she wanted, as long as she kept on talking.

Rose returned to the counter and dutifully cut more deli meat for the lunchtime traffic, keeping a careful eye on her daughter in case her lips moved again. All the while, she sang her mother's lullaby, the one Crystal had hummed in bed, hoping it might help trigger her memory. The song made her feel warm inside while she let her hands fall into the familiar routine of dicing onions and tomatoes. By the time she reached for a head of lettuce, however, her voice was overwhelmed by a ruckus in the town square. A pack of hounds dashed in circles, ears flapping as they nipped each other's heels and barked at anything that moved. Amy rolled her eyes—Ray Beane must be in town. Wherever he went, he dragged his wild hounds in the back of his pickup, and they often jumped out to create chaos in town, tipping over trash cans and snarling at strangers. Wiping her hands on her apron, Rose spotted Ray walking outside of the post office with a stack of mail. He tossed the envelopes into his truck and beat a path to her shop.

"Quick, put away anything that's valuable!" she warned as he neared the porch. "Old man Beane is on his way."

Amy grabbed china teacups and silver spoons and stood on her tiptoes to set them on a high shelf, scanning the shop for anything else he might fancy. The Beanes were notorious for their sticky fingers and fraudulent schemes. With a gaggle of offspring that included nieces, nephews, and grandchildren as well, they lived in a broken-down cabin by Wolverine Gully in a remote section of the woods, and as far as Rose knew they'd been wanted by the feds for years. Tax evasion, pyramid scams, mail fraud—you name it, and the Beanes probably had their hands in it.

Ray burst through the door with one of his mutts by his side, followed by a cloud of dust. Rose ordered him to tie his dog on the porch, and she picked up Crystal and carried her to a back corner of the shop where she'd set up a play table. Unfortunately, Ray played deaf, and as she handed her daughter crayons, his dog trotted up to Crystal and licked her cheek. Rose expected her to fuss, but she merely smiled, spooling her crayons in circles. Ray didn't notice his dog's behavior or even Crystal for that matter—he was too busy lighting up a cigarette. Blowing a few puffs, he sat down at the counter and leaned on his elbows like a regular at a bar.

"I'll take a cup of coffee, a roast beef sandwich, and one of them cookies," he demanded to anyone who might listen. Rose's hackles went up. He'd always been pushy, the same man who tried to steal mining claims from her father, though they were worthless. Once, the two of them came to blows, and her father gave Ray a black eye that was the talk of the town for weeks. In all honesty, Rose was surprised Ray hadn't been shot by now—he had an amazing ability to annoy everyone he came into contact with. Even his smell was foul: he reeked of cigarette smoke mixed with the oily odor of hounds and something he'd skinned, like coyotes or raccoons. As his smoke wafted through the shop, Rose walked up to him and grabbed his cigarette, crushing it onto a plate with a hiss.

"What's the matter—ain't my money good enough for ya?"

"No smoking." Rose pointed to a sign. She slapped together the sandwich and set it down with a cookie in front of him.

"So, I hear you offer tours of Rook Ridge." Ray chomped at his sandwich. "To find gold, like your old man never did. Poor bastard."

Rose fought an overwhelming urge to slam him like her father had done. "Only one tour. And it's already taken."

"I can't believe anyone bought into that malarkey. And to think our government calls *me* the swindler. Well, it won't matter anyway. There's nothing you can do to keep a place like this open."

"How's that?" Rose's fists clenched her apron behind the counter where he couldn't see.

Ray scratched his armpit with an uneven grin. "Well, you'll never make it through winter, once hunting season's over and the tourists taper off. After all the talk dies down about the blue moon, I reckon you and that idiot who opened the Magpie Saloon will close your doors within a month. So, where's that little girl of yours, anyway?" He checked around.

"I hear she's backward—you send her to a foster home or something?" He spotted Crystal in the corner with his dog. She held up a piece of construction paper, pointing to a crayon spiral. The dog's ears perked up as she moved her lips without sound.

Ray began to laugh. "What, is she a monkey or something? Trying to talk? Here," he leaned over to the fruit basket on the counter, "give the squirt a banana."

"Don't you dare touch my daughter!" Rose exploded. For a moment, all she could see was a blur of his body ripped apart if he moved anywhere near Crystal. "You and your dog—get out of this shop right now."

Rose dragged Ray's hound by the collar, yelping, and set him down in a lump at his owner's feet. Just as quickly, Amy headed to the shotgun they kept beside a corner cabinet. She tapped the barrel slowly with her fingers.

"Well now," Ray laughed at the women, their cheeks red in anger, "don't you two make a sight." He dug into his pocket and threw a couple of dollars on the counter, kicking his dog to get up.

As they ambled out the shop, Rose felt a rage whirl inside. His cruel remarks about Crystal had pierced her heart, just when she'd dared to invest a bit of hope. She remembered all those lonely years after her mother had died when kids in town cruelly associated her and Laurel with people like the Beanes. "Mountain Trash" they jeered at school, poking her in the ribs and asking if she'd had possum for breakfast. Rose kept silent in shame, pretending she didn't hear, but Laurel took a more proactive approach. She made certain they never stepped out the door with a wrinkle on their clothes, much less a hint of

odor or any sign of dirt, and they did laundry religiously each
week in the sink, often pressing clothes into the wee hours of
the morning. "Over my dead body will people compare us to
the Beanes" Laurel used to say bitterly, but it was no use.
Everyone still noticed when creative patches or embroidery
helped keep their clothes together. Things finally came to a
head one day when Ray Beane drove through town and a boy
pointed at his loud hounds and sneered, "How come you
aren't in the truck with your brothers and sisters?"

Laurel hauled off and nailed him between the eyes

Rose smirked—he'd never dared to come near them again.
Guess Laurel's got a history of taking things into her own
hands, she thought, patting her sore jaw. She gazed out the
front window as Ray headed to his truck. He's gone now, she
reminded herself, you don't need to fight anybody—just let it
go. Then her eye caught the bills Ray had left for her on the
counter. Staring back at her was the unmistakable tint of fake
currency.

"Goddammit!" Rose slammed her fist.

Amy whipped around and set down a china teapot she'd
been dusting. Rose held the counterfeit bills to the light,
illuminating the bad ink.

"Ray paid us with his funny money. Of course! That jerk
and his flea-bitten hounds. Why hasn't he been arrested yet?"

"Because he's armed to the gills," Amy pointed out the
window at the gun rack on his truck. "Have you seen his cabin
lately? It's a military compound. They'd need an entire
S.W.A.T. team to take on the Beanes."

Rose frowned at Ray lingering beside his truck, his dogs
barking at him in a chorus. Instantly, all the shame she'd

recalled from her teenage years came rushing back, billowing inside till she was sick to her stomach. She grasped herself around the waist, but she couldn't stop feeling like a thirteen-year-old again, the kicking girl at school, unable to defend herself with Laurel's smarts or powerful right hook. All she could do was stuff the rage that clenched within her like a fist. "God," she sputtered, watching Ray kick one of his dogs, "sometimes I wish I could knock him upside the head."

She'd barely uttered the words when she spied Vincent on the boardwalk of the Magpie Saloon. He smiled as if he'd heard her thoughts on a stray breeze and touched the red bandana around his neck. Out of the blue, Rose felt fatigued. At first she thought it might be her bad temper, draining her energies. Then she heard a peculiar, roaring sound. It grew louder, as though her emotions had somehow accumulated into a force that drove the wind. Rose glanced outside at the dark clouds that began to gather, eerily matching her mood.

"Oh my gosh, do you hear that crazy sound?" Amy covered her ears. "It's like a freight train—"

Rose joined her at the window, watching an enormous dust cloud roll into town, churning grass and leaves into its dark maw. It was like a giant tumbleweed, as tall as the Rainbow's End Cafe, moving with the force of a boxing glove as it headed straight for Ray. Panicked, Ray struggled with the key in his truck next to the post office, dogs scattering in all directions. Before he could swing open the door, the roiling cloud swallowed him in its path. His truck windshield exploded, sending glass everywhere, and Ray's body was lifted and thrown down onto the boardwalk like a lifeless puppet. Sweeping over the post office, the cloud banged the door and window panels into a frenzy, then rolled out of town.

Rose and Amy dashed into the square, wind spinning their hair into knots, and bulleted to where Ray lay face down on the boardwalk with the post office sign beside his head. "It must have fallen!" Rose called out, so weak her fingers trembled. They turned him over to examine the nasty lump on his forehead. Rose grasped his wrist and checked his pulse. At first she couldn't feel a thing, then only the faintest heartbeat. "I don't know if he's conscious."

"Then do mouth-to-mouth!" Amy flapped her hands. "Like you did with Laurel!"

Rose recoiled at the uneven stubble on Ray's chin, the foul smell of his skin, quite certain he hadn't bathed in weeks. "Why don't you?"

"Because I don't know how!" Amy squealed. "Hurry, there's not much time!"

"I can't believe I'm doing this." Locking her lips to Ray's, Rose tried desperately to ignore the taste of stale tobacco as she blew into his lungs. She pulled back to study his still face, unable to tell if he was dead or alive. Gritting her teeth, she sealed her lips for another breath, when she felt him clutch her neck and sweep his tongue around hers for a kiss.

"Couldn't wait to get your hands on me, eh honey?" Rays said in a hoarse voice, coughing.

Rose gagged and dropped his head onto the boardwalk. "You wicked, wicked old man!" She pointed at the post office sign. "You got caught in a freak wind storm and that sign walloped you. As far as I'm concerned, you deserve it for passing bad money in my shop."

"Is that what happened?" Ray edged up on his elbows, woozy. "All I remember is a weird dream. I was on an island, and a little girl came up to me and held out a potato. She sang a song."

"W-what did you say?" Rose's legs began to shake. She leaned her hand against a pillar on the boardwalk.

"You heard me. She sang a song—wish I could remember how it goes." He pressed his fingers to the lump on his forehead. "She told me it was a healing song. It worked on potatoes, and it might work for me, too, if I stopped being mean to her mommy. "

Rose felt as though the air had been ripped from her lungs. She rested her hands on her knees when she happened to glance at the Rainbow's End Cafe. There, she saw Crystal on the front porch. As the wind tousled her hair, she raised her arms and began to spin.

❧ 14 ❧

Sitting at the kitchen table the next morning, Rose's hands were clenched around a coffee cup like a life preserver. Taking methodical sips, she felt weak as she stared at another potato that had mysteriously appeared on the kitchen table. It looked just like the one her daughter had given her in a dream. Could it possibly be the potato Ray had mentioned? She kneaded her forehead, quite certain the notion was batty. Nevertheless, it didn't resemble any of the ones in the sack that she'd dragged with her from Winnemucca, which she'd dumped into a corner of the kitchen. Those were Idaho Gold, with light brown skins and broad, starchy centers, each one big enough for two people. Rose rolled the small potato in her palm. Its skin was gray and the moist soil that clung to it smelled fermented and mossy, like peat. She set it down and studied the other items she'd discovered on the table that morning. Beside the bean pot was the first potato she'd found and a seashell, along with her great-great grandmother's diary and Crystal's bracelet. To Rose, their arrangement in a loose circle looked like some kind of puzzle, silent clues to her daughter's soul—not the little girl she used to know, but the enigma she had become now.

Rose picked up the crystal bracelet and toyed it with her fingers, holding it up to catch the morning light. Prismatic colors scattered over the kitchen appliances, reminding her of her fractured thoughts. Although it defied logic, ever since she'd arrived in Ophir Creek, her life seemed to intersect with a strange dream world beyond her comprehension. It was a place of shadows and myth, lightning flashes and magic—a land where children played happily and women dared to fall in love. Could such a world really exist for her and Crystal? Lately, her dreams seemed to spread a ray of hope. But then how on earth did Ray find his way to the island? Deep in her heart, Rose felt twists of both confusion and envy. She snuck a peek into her coffee cup to catch a glimmer of insight that might sort out her thoughts. All she saw was her own reflection, eyes befuddled.

Rose frowned, knowing better than to discern her own circumstances from a coffee cup, and turned to Crystal. Without much fuss, her daughter had complied with the morning routine of getting dressed and brushing her teeth after breakfast, and now she was sitting cross-legged on the quilt on the bed. Her fingers were tracing spirals over a quilt square, brows furrowed. What are her thoughts during these moments? Rose wondered, longing to decipher her daughter's heart. When Crystal rocks back and forth or spins feverishly in place, does she have dreams, too? Rose strained to hear any stray sounds Crystal might make, as if a gurgle or a click of the tongue might represent a Morse code that she could translate. But her daughter was as quiet as the elk that nibbled on the grass in the town square in the mornings with dew still on their backs. Closing her eyes Rose stretched her hand toward Crystal, wishing she could somehow pierce through a barrier, when the morning hush of her apartment was jarred by the slam of the front door. She got up and peeked past the bedroom curtain, where she saw Amy standing with a cannon ball in her arms.

"Good grief, what are you doing with that?" For a moment, Rose wondered if Amy was crazy enough to exchange her crystal ball for one made of iron.

"It's an antique!" Amy set the ball down on the floor with a thump and wiped the sweat from her forehead. "I finally found something that our male customers might like. You know, we can only sell so many teacups and doilies to little old ladies—it's nice to have stuff for the mountain guys. Besides, if you don't like it, we can try dropping it from the roof on Ray Beane."

Rose trembled at the mere mention of his name. She was afraid to spill the truth to Amy—afraid even her closest friend might think she'd lost her marbles. Amy was too busy panicking yesterday to hear Ray mention his dream, and she probably didn't see Vincent's peculiar behavior before the wind storm. Yet bottling up her observations made Rose feel painfully alone. She stared at the rusty cannon ball that looked as heavy to her as her own thoughts, mulling over her secret. *Even if Amy does think I'm nuts, she'd never make fun of me, and the worst that can happen is that she'll launch into her psychic drivel.* Rose cleared her throat, hoping her friend might offer a little insight. "Listen, Amy, I need to talk to you about something."

"Sure, shoot." Amy opened the bakery case to grab one of yesterday's cheddar scones. She stuffed a hunk into her mouth and chewed like a squirrel.

Rose kneaded her hands. "I mean seriously, Amy. Let's sit down at the table."

Amy tilted her head, puzzled. "Honey, if you don't like the cannon ball, no problem. It only cost five dollars at a garage sale. We can always use it as a door stop."

"No, that's not it." She sat down. When Amy joined her, Rose clutched her hands beneath the table to hide her nerves. "It happened again."

"What?" Amy asked between chews.

"That whole thing yesterday with Ray Beane. It wasn't an accident, I swear. I was so angry at him—fit to be tied. I just wanted to pelt him." Words streamed from Rose's mouth with a fervor she couldn't restrain. "And that's when I saw Vincent across the street. The second he touched the red bandana around his neck, it was like he was touching *me*. I felt a dark energy tighten in my stomach, and then WHAM! A raging wind comes through and shoves Ray's face into the boardwalk." She folded her arms, bracing herself for her next confession. "I know it sounds crazy, Amy. But on top of everything, when Ray woke up, he told me he had a dream about Crystal." She stared at the cafe table, searching for answers. "I hardly know what's real and what's imaginary anymore. It feels like the whole world has gone topsy turvy."

Amy stopped chewing and set her scone on the table. She gave Rose a pat on the hand. "Sweetie, Ray was probably delirious. Besides, if ever a guy deserved to be pummeled by natural forces, it's Ray! You were just a witness to the inevitable resolution of bad karma. I keep telling you, what goes around, comes around—and Ray Beane certainly had it coming."

"But Amy," Rose persisted, "the minute the wind came I felt weak, like my knees were going to buckle—the same way I felt when Laurel was battered by hail. I swear, it's like Vincent somehow sucked the worst emotions out of me and turned them into a violent weather pattern. Did you know when he was in the shop yesterday, I peeked into his coffee cup? I saw dark clouds, and then a lightning bolt. I haven't a clue what it means, but don't you think that's weird?"

Amy folded her arms. "No. I don't think it's weird at all. I think it means love is finally striking your life and you're too chicken to let it happen. After all, why do you keep blaming Vincent for everything? You just met the guy."

"I know!" Rose snapped, so bewildered she was nearly in tears. "But he keeps showing up whenever terrible things happen."

"Well that's convenient," Amy smirked.

"What?"

Amy returned to picking at her scone. "To have a handy scapegoat for all of those feelings you're afraid of. So you project them onto Vincent, or onto dark rain clouds, or whatever else happens to show up in your environment. Rose, hasn't it occurred to you that ever since you got back from Winnemucca, you've been completely shut down? You're like a walking iceberg, so withdrawn that you're afraid to feel anything. I'm not saying it isn't natural, with everything you've been through." She met her friend's gaze with compassion. "But think about it—what if Crystal is merely imitating her mother? Maybe if you're brave enough to come out of your shell, she will too. Isn't it time to start setting a better example?"

Rose sat up straight in her chair. "What do you mean? The doctors said—"

Amy held up her hand. "I know, you told me. And sure, maybe it's all true. Or maybe it's a great excuse not connect with your daughter—or anybody else, for that matter."

"Are you insinuating I'm using my daughter to insulate myself from people?"

Amy brushed the crumbs from her hands. "No, I'm not insinuating at all. I'm telling you that straight up. Look at yourself—you hardly ever flirt with guys who come into the shop, and getting a smile out of you is like pulling teeth. Lighten up, Rose! The way you've been acting, I bet you'd do anything to wriggle out of gold hunting with Vincent this afternoon, even if it means conjuring up stories about strange dreams and freak weather patterns. Listen, honey—I'm as fascinated by psychic phenomenon as the next person. But I don't use it to avoid life. You don't fool me, Rose. Love scares the bejeebers out of you."

Rose gripped her knees beneath the table, breathless. She couldn't believe Amy was talking to her like this. Behind the celestial outfits and jangly earrings, she'd always suspected her friend had a core of steel that belied her flaky image. But did Amy really believe Crystal was mimicking her mother's aloofness? Rose stared out the front window at the tall pines with the morning sun glistening off their needles. What if

Amy's words were true—what if she had been using her daughter's problems to stay in a rut? Is that what her dreams had been pointing to? Tears collected in her eyes.

"Sweetheart," Amy said gently, "I wouldn't be a good friend if I stood by and watched you throw away a chance at love. Something tells me Vincent doesn't give a damn about gold—he just wants to spend some time with you. What would it hurt to entertain him for one afternoon? And in case you haven't noticed, I'm capable of babysitting Crystal by myself. We're great finger-painting partners, you know. Where is she, anyway?"

Rose glanced at the back bedroom, where she'd been keeping a steady eye on her daughter. Crystal was still on the bed, now rocking methodically in place. Rose got up to head to the back, and Amy followed. They watched Crystal for a moment, her blonde hair lightly swinging at her shoulders. Though her expression appeared vacant, her hands clung to the quilt with a fierce grip, as if it were a lifeline. Amy smiled like the behavior was perfectly normal. She turned to Rose.

"So, what are you going to wear today?" Before Rose knew it, Amy had opened up the trunk at the end of the bed and was sorting through blankets, faded t-shirts and overalls. At the bottom, she spotted the green dress. "This is perfect!" She held it to Rose's shoulders. "You'll look like a fairy princess."

"Don't be ridiculous," A flush of embarrassment bloomed on her cheeks. Rose recalled the evening she'd put on that dress, only to run into Vincent on the front porch. Even she had to admit the way he looked at her under the stars was pure enchantment.

"I'm not being ridiculous—it's beautiful! Don't worry, with

hiking boots and a jean jacket on top, you'll still look like a
mountain chick. C'mon, just try it on for me." Amy's lips
curled into a sly smile. "I promise that if you wear this today,
I'll never bother you about men again."

"Deal!" Rose yanked the dress from Amy's hands. She
studied the shimmering green fabric, figuring that if she
tucked it into her jeans carefully enough and covered it with an
old jacket, Vincent would hardly notice what she was wearing.
Then she'd have Amy over a barrel—no longer could her
friend bug her about her love life. It was a small price to pay to
keep Amy from prying.

Rose peeled off her flannel shirt and slipped on the dress
over her jeans, turning to see if her daughter might notice.
Crystal continued to rock in place, her eyes in a trance.

"Oh my gosh, it's gorgeous!" Amy gushed, looking her up
and down. "Who cares if you find gold today—you'll break
hearts with that one. Oh sweetie," she grabbed Rose for a hug,
rustling the silky fabric, "I just know good things are gonna
happen. It's time for you to blossom."

"Really?" Rose was surprised at the fragile hope in her
voice. Maybe Amy has a point, she thought. Maybe I have
been too hard on Vincent because of my fears. Everything had
been so confusing lately—her dreams, her daughter's behavior,
even the erratic weather—and inside it made her feel stretched
as thin as a ribbon. Perhaps a little fresh air this afternoon will
provide some perspective, she considered, smoothing the
wrinkles on the front of the dress and admiring its ethereal
texture. She turned to her daughter on the bed.

"See honey?" Rose stood a bit taller with her shoulders
back. "Mommy's got on that pretty dress you liked. I'm going

to venture out today." She gave Crystal a reassuring stroke on the forehead. "It's okay, we can both be brave now. The world is safe for us."

Without returning her gaze, Crystal stopped rocking. She crawled down from the bed, as though she'd heard her name called by someone Rose couldn't see, and scampered into the shop. Rose trotted after her, only to find her daughter with her hands plastered against the front window. Crystal's stare was fixed on the town square. She tapped on the glass.

"What is it, darling?" Rose saw nothing unusual outside. She assumed the tapping was another repetitive motion that soothed her daughter, and she began to wonder if seeing her mother in a bright dress had been too much for her. "Is something wrong? Does my outfit bother you?"

Crystal ignored her and poked at the window pane. Sighing, Rose felt baffled again by her daughter's mannerisms. She leaned to give her a hug, when she saw Crystal place her palms together on the glass and wiggle her fingers like wings. At that moment, Rose spotted a raven limping toward them in the town square. It reminded her of when Vincent shot a rock at a bird, sending chills up her spine.

"Do you think that's your raven, honey? Is he hurt?"

Crystal remained still. Rose watched the bird, feeling pity for his lumbering gait, certain now he must be her daughter's pet. He had the same gentle eyes, the same way of cocking his head when he approached the shop as if he knew he was near friends. "Should we go help him, sweetie?" Rose gazed into her daughter's face, hoping she might show recognition for her companion, but Crystal appeared listless. Growing impatient, Rose picked up her daughter and carried her outside, setting her feet down on the grass. "C'mon dear," she urged, "let's see if we can get him to come to us." Rose stretched her arm out to the raven in the morning sun, watching the light glisten over his shiny, black wings. "Here, bird!" She turned to Crystal. "Can you say bird for me, sweetie? Birrrrd?"

Crystal grabbed the hem of her mother's dress and gave it a firm tug.

"Man."

"What?" Rose grasped her daughter's shoulders. "What did you say?"

The raven cawed. Her daughter stared intently as if he'd spoken to her. She tugged her mother's dress again.

"Man," Crystal replied.

"I tell you, big breakthroughs are happening today!" Amy smiled, sitting cross-legged on the floor and checking her watch. It was nearly two o'clock in the afternoon, and Vincent was due any minute. "First Crystal says another word, and now you're going out on a date!" She clasped her hands with smug satisfaction and returned to carving a pumpkin on a sheet of newspaper. Amy tilted her pumpkin to show Crystal how to scoop out the seeds, regardless of whether the child responded, her eyes bright from sharing the activity. After carving a gap-toothed smile into the jack-o-lantern, she held up her knife victoriously. "See what happens when you move beyond your boundaries a little? Miracles!"

"Yeah, miracles," Rose replied as a nervous pit swelled in her stomach. That's exactly what she felt she needed right now

—some miracle to help her find gold. She glanced at the raven in the cardboard box that she'd lined with a cozy blanket, her daughter sitting on the floor beside him like a faithful nurse. Although she was ecstatic beyond measure that Crystal had spoken again, she still felt burdened by the upcoming trip. If only she could cuddle Crystal on her lap all day and watch for more signs of words—that would be her idea of· heaven! Yet she'd already promised Amy she would go. Rose cursed under her breath—sure, the trip meant stepping out with the best-looking man in town, but a little voice inside her head kept reminding her that she was an imposter. All morning long she'd been tidying the shop, polishing silver and dusting china to keep her mind off the excursion. The truth was, she didn't have the faintest idea how to find real gold. And in spite of Amy's urging to channel her father's energy, Rose knew her dad had never been very successful in that endeavor either. She rubbed her hands together, trying to ignore the sweat that kept moistening her palms.

"Amy," she finally said, "what if a miracle doesn't happen —what if I can't find gold?"

"Then just pretend!" Amy grinned, holding up the jack-o-lantern to Crystal. "And don't you dare come back until you two have kissed."

"You're impossible!" Rose scanned her outfit, rubbing the fancy fabric between her fingers. "Won't Vincent think it's overkill if I wear this?" She tucked the bottom of the dress into her jeans before Amy could object. "I'll look like I'm throwing myself at him."

"So," Amy wiped pumpkin seeds off her hands with a moist towel, "just tell him you're testing the outfit for

Halloween—all you need is pair of wings." She got up and approached Rose, frowning at the way her jeans bulged over the satin folds. "Here," she moved the sleeves off her shoulders a bit, "this will make you look more feminine."

Rose reluctantly allowed her friend to fuss over her, feeling as frilly as Scarlet O'Hara before a ball. Yet she was surprised by how sexy she looked in the mirror, how well the bodice of the dress hugged her curves and complimented her green eyes, and it unnerved her. She yanked the sleeves back up to her shoulders when she saw Vincent's face appear in the glass. Astounded, Rose rubbed her eyes. Her mother had always claimed your lover's face would appear in a mirror near Halloween, if you stared at it hard enough, an old Irish country legend that made young maids' hearts flutter. Rose had never taken the notion seriously before—yet here he was, staring like they were destiny.

"I liked it better the other way," Vincent remarked, tugging the sleeves off her shoulders again. For a hallucination, his fingers felt far too real. "See?" He pointed to their reflection in the glass, his gaze running down her throat to her cleavage. "You look enchanting."

Whipping around, Rose grabbed her jean jacket from a chair and slipped it on like he'd caught her naked. "I-I didn't hear you come in." She suddenly remembered she'd taken the harness bells off when she'd polished the knob that morning. Vincent must have stepped in quietly, she thought, spotting the sparkle in Amy's eye. Her friend appeared all too willing to allow him to sneak up on her.

"You were expecting me, weren't you?" Vincent tapped his watch. "It's two o'clock."

"Uh, sure," Rose confirmed, unable to quell the tremor in her voice. She was about to give Amy instructions for watching Crystal when Amy carried a pumpkin to her.

"Don't you worry about a thing!" Amy fended her off. "Me and Crystal are going to finger paint and carve pumpkins for the porch. Gotta be festive, you know." She pointed at the door. "Now you two get out of here and find gold."

"We'll give it our best shot," Rose replied hesitantly, grabbing a forest map from the counter. Her gaze met Vincent's with apology already in her eyes. "But I can't promise anything. The rest is up to fate."

"My favorite word," Vincent smiled. Rose startled when he took hand—his grip felt strong and purposeful. "Just lead the way."

As they headed for the door, the raven cawed. He thrashed wildly in the cardboard box, wings flapping in alarm. Crystal covered her eyes and rocked in place. Letting go of Vincent's hand, Rose gave him a dark look.

"I saw you injure that poor bird." She set her hands on her hips. "When you were in the town square, you bruised his leg with a rock. He's my daughter's pet, you know."

Vincent raised his brow, amused. "How do you know he's injured—because of a pretend limp? Maybe he's just playing on your sympathy. Scavengers have all kinds of tricks for scamming free meals. And look, you've even give him a bed." Vincent grasped Rose's hand again, kneading it gently. "If it were me, I wouldn't allow my daughter to be so close to a flea-bitten bird. They're notorious for spreading disease."

Rose's eyes narrowed, irritated by his self-righteousness. Crystal had bonded with the raven from the start. And he meticulously cared for his feathers, always fluffing and preening them—he was certainly cleaner than Ray Beane's hounds. But more importantly, Crystal needed him, even if he was wild. Together, they'd formed a connection that helped draw her daughter out a little, and that alone was worth defending. She yanked back her hand.

"I think I know what's best for my daughter," Rose insisted. "Besides, a little flea powder does wonders. And it's only for a little while, until the bird heals. As soon as he gets better, I'll let *Crystal* decide if he should go."

Rose grumbled to herself while driving the old truck along a winding mountain road. The route was so dusty she could hardly see, and she was embarrassed by the rips in the truck seats and the odor of stale cookies and French fries that had gotten lost in the cracks. For the first twenty minutes, she barely spoke to Vincent, annoyed from their spat over the raven. After all, everyone in Ophir Creek had some kind of eccentricity—why'd he get so uptight over a stray bird? Despite her surly attitude, she noticed the casual way he relaxed his elbow out the passenger window, breeze dancing through his blonde hair, looking entirely content. His blithe expression irked her to no end. Didn't he know their venture was a boondoggle? She could hardly wait for the trip to be over. When they rounded another bend, she spotted a familiar place—a creek bed near the top of the ridge where her father used to take naive gold seekers. She stopped the truck.

How did I let myself get roped into this? Rose fretted as

she killed the engine. "Okay, we're here," she announced with mock confidence. She hopped out of the truck, avoiding Vincent's gaze and marching briskly toward the creek bank.

"Shouldn't I bring some tools?" Vincent called after her.

Rose turned around and caught him laughing, holding up a pick and a pan. She straightened up as if it were her idea along. "Of course," she backpedaled, "I, uh, I meant to tell you that."

With a few long strides, Vincent met her at the water's edge. They listened to the musical tones of the creek, and Rose studied the reflections on the water, desperately wishing she had a better plan to find gold. When she snuck a glance at Vincent, the sun glistened off his hair and warmed the color of his deerskin jacket, making it look as soft as butter. In the rays of light that wove through pines, he was so handsome he took her breath away. Standing there among the trees, with his broad shoulders and long limbs, he reminded her of one of the ponderosas, tall and imposing in his silence, with no need to mark the time with words. Rose wished he would ask her questions so she could finally take her eyes off him and pretend to be some kind of authority—anything to quell the yank of her heart that had already begun to make her feel uncomfortable. Clasping her hands, she ran through a brief litany of lies that she'd memorized long ago, hoping to keep him occupied. They were the kinds of things her father used to say so that customers would remain distracted—mining legends, prospecting superstitions, old wives' tales—each a fabrication designed to foster gold fever.

"So," she elaborated, "we have to start at this creek with the sun on our backs and follow it carefully to those big granite

boulders at the top of Rook Ridge. Did you know at nighttime
they point to the North Star? Which holds a special magnetic
attraction for precious metals? Anyway, if we keep our eyes
peeled, we'll find gold flakes that have settled along the creek
bank. See?" she pointed at the small crystals of mica that
glittered in the afternoon light, "it's like fairy dust showing us
the way." Rose walked up a narrow trail along the creek. She
assumed Vincent was following, but she didn't dare check.
Scanning the creek, she neglected to notice a slippery rock
beside the bank. Her ankle turned and she lost her balance,
stumbling knee-high into the water. From behind her, she
heard laughter.

"Oh, this is part of the tour!" Rose wished she could die.
Water stained her jeans up to her thighs, so she cleverly kicked
the soil from the creek bottom with her boot. "See all the shiny
particles?" she pointed out, knowing it was only mica. "We're
getting close—"

"No we're not," Vincent replied. "Wait up."

Rose's heart sank. She was sure he'd already guessed the
trip was a rip-off. With her luck, he'd probably refuse to pay
for the outing, then spread it around town that she was a scam
artist. Her name would be mud, and she'd lose customers, and
she'd probably end up planting pine saplings in the forest to
make ends meet. Rose sighed, staring at her reflection in the
creek—Ophir Creek, no less. Not only did she not see gold,
she saw herself in dripping wet jeans with a silly dress tucked
in, topped by a faded jacket that made her look utterly foolish
in front of a man who most women would swoon over. You're
such a loser, like your father. What were you thinking?

To Rose' surprise, she heard Vincent sloshing in the creek

behind her. When she turned, she discovered he'd stepped into the creek up to his knees as well. He kicked at the water with the glee of a child, making a big splash. "Look! I think I see gold!"

"Stop it," Rose's cheeks burned. She should have known he was smarter than her father's clientele.

"No seriously." Vincent peered at the gurgling water. He aimed at a fern along the bank, its frond dusted with shiny particles. "We're getting close," he whispered.

"What?" Rose leaned to hear what he'd muttered.

Vincent grasped her shoulders and pulled her in for a kiss. His lips caressed hers, soft and slow, and his hands gently ran up her temples as if he were grasping a treasure. He cupped her face. "Now we're really getting close, just like you said."

Breathless, Rose wanted to pull away. She wanted to dig a pick into the dirt and be the showman in control again, to tell lies about panning on a full moon while jumping on one leg and singing rhymes backwards and all the stupid things her father would say to be master of the performance. But when she opened her lips, the words didn't come. Instead, Vincent's mouth enveloped hers. His hands roamed up the silky fabric of her dress, curving along the seam at her waist and seeking the fullness of her breasts. Rose drew a deep breath, unable to decide whether to break free or surrender, when she realized it was no longer up to her. She couldn't think anymore in logical words or sentences. Only in smells and sensations, her mind reeling between the scent of his skin and the aroma of his leather jacket as his lips descended to explore her throat. She already felt lost in him, submerged in water with shiny flecks of gold all around, and she couldn't stop pressing against his back, pulling him toward her as though he could be devoured. Her own appetite shocked her. She wondered if this hunger had been dormant all along, welling up for ages like a volcano, or was it something that simply exploded, like the dynamite they once used to find gold? Either way, she could hardly believe she was standing knee high in Ophir Creek with her arms wrapped around a stranger. The wind picked up, whispering through aspen leaves, and for a second she peered at the tall, granite stones that loomed before them at the top of Rook Ridge. Gathering her wits, she wriggled free from Vincent's grasp, reminding herself of the purpose of the trip. She stepped out of the water, boots squirting from the seams. Rose cleared her throat. "W-We have to reach the summit," she mentioned dryly, as if nothing had happened.

"I thought we already did." Vincent grinned, following after her.

In spite of herself, Rose smiled. She tried to be business-like as she hiked with sloshing steps to the top of the ridge and entered a shaded glen. There, the granite boulders stood in a circle around them like an ancient sundial, or perhaps a mysterious map of the stars. She hadn't been to this ridge in the daytime since she was a child, when she still believed that fairies fluttered at twilight and the wind held secrets just beyond her grasp. But now, it seemed eerie to be in the same place where her ancestor had once searched for gold—and nearly lost her life by the hand of a crazy lover. Yet one more foolish woman, she thought, just like me. As the breeze wove between stones, lightly moaning through the ponderosa limbs, Rose couldn't help feeling as if the place were charged with presence. Could it be the spirit of Corvine O'Dannan, still wailing softly in grief? Or worse, the ghost of her cruel lover, promising revenge? Rose shivered and closed her eyes, taking in the sound of the wind and the afternoon smell of vanilla that came from the warm sap in the pines. When a stiff breeze rifled her hair, she lifted her arms like wings.

"This is it," she said humbly, no longer keeping the pretense of being in control. "This is where my father always thought he'd find gold." She let her hands fall to her sides. "But he was crazy, you know. Both of my parents were, just like my great-great grandmother."

"No they weren't," Vincent assured, wiping a stray lock from her forehead. "They were dreamers, like us."

Tingles skittered down her neck at the word "us." Her emotions floated somewhere between guarded excitement and full-blown fear. In spite of Amy's urging for her to open up, she couldn't help allowing caution to sober her mood. After all, she'd barely survived Jake, and the last thing she wanted right now was another comet to collide into her life.

"Listen Vincent," she said flatly, "I'll admit you're a hell of a guy, and any woman could get carried away with you. But the point of this whole expedition is to find gold. And unless you've got a few magic tricks up your sleeve, the fact is, I've never seen any around here. It's all a big story that's gone on for years, and I'm sorry I pulled you into this. I certainly don't expect you to fork up any kind of payment." Rose thrust her hands into her pockets and gazed at the tall stones. "So why don't we just rest here for a minute and call it a day."

"Or night?" He reached up to touch her cheek.

Before Rose could catch her breath, he had absorbed her again in a kiss. His hands grasped her back, and she felt as if she were falling—falling into clouds—when she realized he had pulled her down into the soft coolness of the forest floor. His chest felt hard against hers, and the muscles on his arms were rope-like as they traveled from her waist to her hips.

"Don't ever let go of me, Rose," he whispered in her ear. "I couldn't endure that again."

"Again?" She perched on her elbows. After the initial rush of senses when he kissed her, she began to feel light headed and her limbs grew weak, even achy. Rose shook her head as if dispelling a fever. "What do you mean, *again*?"

"You know, forever after," he smiled and kissed her cheek. "Like in fairy tales. You're mine, Rose."

"But we've just met." Puzzled, she brushed the pine needles out of her hair, studying his face.

"Well, that's the reason we can take things slow. We have all the time in the world." He pressed his lips to her forehead. "Time," he whispered, "what a foolish concept."

Rose glanced at his face, and for the life of her, it seemed the longer he held her, the more his cheeks began to glow. His skin became radiant with energy, almost electric. In the shade it seemed peculiar, and she wondered if maybe it was perspiration from the warm afternoon, or if there really was something to Amy's stories about auras. Perhaps he was so taken with her that she could actually see their kinetic attraction. Yet strangely, all she could think about was allowing her eyes to slip closed to embrace the dreaminess of sleep. Her thoughts became cloudy, though they hadn't been hiking very long, and she felt fatigued, as if his attention drained her. It's all too much, too fast, she thought—I barely know this man.

Nevertheless, Rose couldn't bring herself to stop his

fingers from tracing the contours of her dress as delicately as though he had sculpted her himself. Nor did she halt the kisses that caressed her forehead and lips, moving down her neck to the tender places along her shoulders. His hands roamed her body as if he were already familiar with each curve of flesh and angle of bone. His assuredness made her tremble, and he seemed like no stranger at all—more like an old lover who'd come back to taste her softness again. Is this the man from my dreams? she wondered, recalling the island, the way the man in the long, dark coat had kissed her, sending her nerve endings on fire. She had to admit, the two men looked nearly the same, though Vincent's eyes were a riveting blue, and the island man's were dark as a raven's. Yet both of them were handsome enough to send her heart into a tailspin. But then why am I so tired? she pondered, barely able to keep her eyes open. In her dreams, the island man's touch was exhilarating, so charged with desire that she felt like she could lift her arms and fly. But here, she seemed to be losing herself by the minute. As Vincent undid the zipper of her jeans and slipped his hand inside her dress to circle her belly button, she grew uncomfortable, afraid that soon she might abandon herself to sleep—or something more. She stopped his him, forcing herself to stay alert, and edged away. Then she felt something rocky press into the small of her back.

"What's this?" Rose slipped her hand beneath her dress. Underneath a layer of pine needles, her fingers detected a corner of fabric embedded in the dirt. She rolled and pulled it up like a potato from the soil, setting it down between them. Brushing off the loose dirt, goose bumps danced down her arms. It was a red bandana, the corners tied together in a knot. The sight made Vincent smile.

"Go ahead." He picked up the bundle and put it on her lap, its contents making an awkward, clinking sound. "Open it. You never know what you might find deep in the woods."

The wind whined through pine trees, and Rose undid the knot in the bandana. She didn't know why, but her fingers were shaking. She glanced at Vincent, letting the corners of the bandana fall open. Gold coins spilled over her dress, trickling to the forest floor.

"Vincent!" She picked up one of the coins—it was dated 1863, with an image of an eagle with outstretched wings. At one time, her great-great grandmother would have claimed such an omen meant new love. But Rose knew better. The coin looked like the one Jake had given to her years ago at the Magpie Saloon—when he'd gambled for her heart and took so much more.

"I told you we'd find gold," Vincent whispered proudly. He cupped her cheek and kissed her, swirling the coins like leaves over her silky dress. They clinked together as they rustled the green fabric.

There had to be at least two dozen coins, each made of solid gold, worth hundreds, if not thousands, of dollars. "My God," Rose said, "where did these come from?"

Vincent picked one up and flipped it in air. He caught it and studied the eagle's wings, eyes twinkling. "Who knows, maybe it was buried here a century ago to avoid the tax collector. Or perhaps a woman hid it from her lover." He winked. "After all, the legend always said Corvine O'Dannan found her fortune on this ridge."

Rose picked up the bandana in disbelief. Its color was too vibrant to have been in the ground for long. She glared at Vincent, catching the mischief in his eyes. "Or maybe you buried it. For Christ's sake, Vincent," she stood in a huff, "how stupid do you think I am? Where on earth did you get these?"

Vincent untangled a few leaves from her hair. "Well," he admitted, "not all card players who come to my saloon are as smart as they think they are. Too bad for that coin collector." He picked one up and tried to bite it between his teeth. "I think they're real. Consider them payment—for your time, I mean."

"Listen, Vincent," she kicked at the pile of coins on the ground, "I might be poor, but I'm not for sale."

Vincent gazed at her with such fierce longing that it startled her. His eyes appeared deep yet lustrous, as though they were more than a mere blue but actual jewels with facets, each one reflecting back desire. At first his glance was exhilarating, yet something about the familiarity of it shocked her. In his eyes was a piercing possessiveness, as if in that moment he already knew all of her vulnerabilities and had drawn a map to the recesses of her heart long ago. Rose swallowed hard, trying to dispel the force of his gaze.

"L-Look," she struggled, feeling like she was attempting to break free from the gravity of a large star, "I'm not going to be your next girlfriend. Whatever this is, it's just for the moment, all right? We're both adults here—it doesn't have to mean anything. Besides, I have a daughter to go home to."

"But what if I could make this moment last for eternity?"

Vincent absorbed her face as he traced her cheek with his finger, making her shiver. Rose jerked away and folded her arms, taking a step back. "I-I don't believe in forever anymore."

Vincent smiled like she was delirious—as if he'd planned her reaction beforehand and it was only a matter of time until she stepped in line. He wrapped his arms around her, pulling her close.

"Don't be silly, Rose. Forever's already here," he said with a finality that frightened her. Hungrily he kissed her lips, running his hands with a rough force up her spine as he wedged his leg between her thighs. Groping her breasts, he kissed her again and again to the point of pain, his fingers pressing bruises into flesh. Before she knew it, he'd gripped her by the shoulders and shoved her to the ground, standing over her with pride. "You couldn't stop it if you wanted to."

❧ 15 ❧

Rose scrambled to her feet and decked him.

Her fist met Vincent's chin with a furious uppercut. His neck snapped back and his eyes flared, like he never thought she had it in her. Guess it runs in the family, she rubbed her knuckles in honor of Laurel. But then Vincent's lips stretched into an eerie smile. Turning on her heels, Rose dashed down the ridge, his laughter trailing her heels.

"Aw c'mon honey, can't you deal me a better blow?"

Rose refused to look back. With every step she took, she heard magpies cackling in the trees. The wind through aspens heralded danger, leaves quivering with a sound that reminded her of hisses. It was as if there was something dark in the air that mocked her as it closed in, and the whole experience set her nerves on edge. By the time she reached her truck, she hugged the old, rusty blue hood in relief. She hopped in and started the motor, racing home to the Rainbow's End Cafe.

When she parked in front of the shop and cut the engine, her face was dripping in tears. Rose leaned over the steering wheel, trying to pull herself together before she faced Amy. How could she explain herself? Sure, Vincent had been too rough. But some might say every woman in the county would go for a roll with him in the woods—lighten up! Yet something about his aggressiveness shook her to the core, as though he'd already determined every move she'd make and there was nothing she could do to stop him. Even now, as she sat alone in her truck, she felt like an invisible net clung to her, ready to choke off her spirit.

Am I making too much of things? Rose peered with tear-stained eyes out the windshield. All I wanted was a pleasant afternoon—a day to prove I'm not stuck in a rut and can handle being around men again. She opened the glove compartment and dug for a tissue, hoping to erase evidence of her distress. "Snap out of it," she berated herself. "Just walk into the shop with a happy face. Give Amy a smile, tell her everything went fine, and let it go—that way she won't ask questions. Remember, you never have to see Vincent again if you don't want to."

Rose got out of the truck, when she heard a scream—it was Crystal. Running to the front door, she threw it open in shock. The shop was in ruins. Tables were turned over with pumpkin pulp smeared on the walls. Paint was everywhere, not just in splotches, but frenzied depictions of thunder clouds and spirals. It reminded Rose of that night when Crystal ran away, and she'd drawn mysterious images over their bedroom. She spotted Amy in a corner with Crystal huddled in her arms. When Crystal saw her mother, she began to thrash.

"Crystal!" Rose darted over and hoisted her up, humming until her breathing calmed. "What on earth happened?"

Amy brushed pumpkin seeds from her skirt, hands trembling. She appeared exhausted and rattled at the same time, as if she'd witnessed a train wreck.

"I-I don't know. We were doing fine till half an hour ago, when Crystal lost control. She and the raven went crazy, knocking items off shelves and throwing things. When I tried to calm her, she grabbed a paint pot and smeared patterns all over the walls."

Rose kissed her daughter's cheek and set her to her feet, holding her close to make sure she was steady. She twisted her watchband—half an hour ago? That was when Vincent began kissing her on the ridge. She spied the raven perched on an oak barrel, feathers standing on his neck. He lifted his beak defiantly and glared as if she'd betrayed him. Unnerved, Rose hugged Crystal and studied the havoc in the room. Could they possibly have sensed something about Vincent? She remembered her dream on the island, how the peasant woman and Crystal seemed to understand what was happening in her world, their connection transcending time and space. But that was a dream, merely wishful thinking. She rubbed her forehead, when Amy grasped her arm.

"Rose," Amy said gravely. "What happened out there?"

A lump knotted her throat. She released Crystal and walked to a wall, tracing her finger along one of the jagged lightning bolts. It sent goose bumps down her arms.

"W-We just took a hike. When we reached the ridge, he started kissing me too hard, saying weird things like we belonged together forever. And he tried to play a trick on me with gold coins. It was scary because they were the same kind Jake had given me after a black jack game once, when we were barmaids at the saloon."

"Jake?" Amy headed to a black thunder cloud on the wall, squinting at Crystal's frantic brush strokes. "You know, sometimes children have hunches about things we can't—or won't—see. They don't dismiss them in favor of logic. Tell me something," she wrung her hands, "was Crystal afraid of her father?"

Rose hugged her arms. She didn't want to think back to that time, to go over the details that had crushed her heart to dust. That's why she'd come to Ophir Creek—to escape the past. But no matter how far she ran, it always felt as near to her as her own heartbeat. She closed her eyes for a moment. "Yes," she admitted, "toward the end, I think she was. Who wouldn't be? Jake's behavior was so erratic. It got to the point where even the sight of his red bandana on the kitchen table was enough to make her squeal."

"He wore a *red* bandana?" Amy turned pale. "Just like Vincent?"

"I told you that already. Don't you remember? During that stupid love spell you pulled a bandana out of the bean pot, and I threw it into the fire because it reminded me of Jake—"

"Rose!" Amy grabbed her shoulders. "What were you thinking of that night? When we were doing the spell?"

"How should I know?" Rose brushed off Amy's grasp. "I was half-drunk and pissed off at Laurel! What are you driving at?"

"You've got to remember!" Amy paced briskly across the

floor. Clutching her forehead, she pointed at the stove. "We were sitting together in front of the fire. And I made you repeat the spell: Wish I will, wish I might, I call my wish to being tonight. What were you thinking when you said that?"

Rose stared at the mouth of the old Foster, as black as a cauldron and filled with ashes. At first, all she could recall about that night were the shots of whiskey she and Amy had polished off, which had made her woozy. But then she remembered feeling washed up because it was her birthday. When Amy started the spell and urged her to imagine a dashing new lover, her thoughts drifted to Jake, to the eerie way he always had of seeping under her skin, even when she resisted. Was that the price of true love? She hadn't meant to dwell on bitterness, but when she'd tried to banish him from her thoughts, the wind blew out the candle. The spell was over.

Rose shuffled against an unsteady plank on the floor that creaked beneath her feet. "Well, to tell the truth, I couldn't stop thinking about Jake. I'm sorry—I had a dream about him when I first moved here that I couldn't shake. It was like he was still around, haunting me and Crystal. That's half the reason I drank so much. But what does it matter now? We were just playing a game."

"Game!" Amy collapsed on a chair and stared with hopelessness at the cast iron stove. "I don't believe it," she moaned. "How could this have happened?"

"What? What's wrong?" Rose sat down beside her.

"Honey, did it ever occur to you that we might have conjured the wrong guy? Maybe when you thought about Jake and burned that red bandana, it acted like a calling card—"

"That's ridiculous! Only a few hours ago you were convinced Vincent was the best thing that ever happened to me. Now you're saying he's Jake? They don't even look alike— well, okay, maybe the blonde hair and lanky physique. But Amy, the last time I checked, men don't just return from the dead and show up in the mountains of Idaho."

Amy knotted her skirt, glancing into Rose's eyes like she'd seen a ghost. "Maybe they do, Rose—if they can find the right body to possess." She stared out the shop window as if there were phantoms lurking in late afternoon shadows. "Perhaps somebody was sleeping or passed out drunk, so Jake's spirit could take over. There was lightning that night, remember? A soul exchange could have happened, quick as a flash. Think about it, who's been missing lately?"

The raven erupted in a hoarse cry and lifted his wings to hop down from the barrel. He limped to Crystal, who'd sat cross-legged on the floor, tracing the lines of the wood grain with her finger. When she reached out to give him a pat, he stared at Rose with dark, penetrating eyes.

You know who I am.

Rose wondered if Amy had heard the same thing, but her gaze was steady on the town square. She shook her head. The voice softly returned.

Listen to your heart—we met in our dreams.

Rose studied the bird, the graceful flow of his long, black wings and dark crown feathers, recalling the man she'd seen on the island in the full-length, black coat. He seemed so real in her mind that it was as though the shop had evaporated and she was transported to a place where the cool breeze licked her face and ushered in scents from the sea. For a moment, she dared to close her eyes. All at once she felt wrapped in presence—*his* presence. She could see every contour of his rugged, weathered face, the way the wind tossed his black hair onto his forehead, the dark resonant eyes that could peer into souls. This is silly, Rose thought, trying to shake the feeling. Nevertheless, when she opened her eyes, he felt as near to her as her own breath.

"Chance," she whispered, as if in a trance. She smoothed back her hair, suddenly feeling windblown.

"What?" Amy leaned closer. "What did you say?"

Rose gazed at the raven's eyes, as dark as the pot-bellied stove, but with a sparkle that seemed uncanny for a wild bird. "Chance Murphy."

Amy's mouth dropped. She grabbed Rose's arm. "Oh—oh my gosh. Can it be? The forest ranger said he'd been gone for a while. And he is the right build, if you cleaned him up and cut off all that hair. Who knew Chance could be so disarming—"

"But that's not really him anymore," Rose broke in. "That's—that's—"

"Jake," Amy finished. Her fingers trembled on her friend's arm. "Then where's Chance?" She scrutinized the ceiling of the shop as though he might be floating among the rafters.

Rose bowed her head, feeling nearly numb inside. She stared at the raven on the floor beside Crystal.

Several moments passed before Amy noticed the cast of Rose's gaze, her eyes growing wide. "Y-You're kidding." She leaned forward on her chair to examine the bird's feathers and shape of his wings. "How can you tell?"

Rose tilted back in her chair. "Well, you're not going to

believe this, but there's an island. In Ireland, I think—it's the birthplace of my great-great grandmother. Lately, at night, I keep going there in my dreams, with the help of that raven. When we get there, he becomes Chance. Crystal's there, too, along with Ailís O'Dannan."

"Who?"

"She's an Irish woman, from a long time ago. She says she's Corvine O'Dannan's mother. But the funny thing is, she looks like *my* mother, too, except for the peasant clothes. Oh, it's so confusing—"

"No it's not!" Amy's face lit up. "Your past is present, don't you see? It's crowding in all around you." She got up and hurried to the front of the shop, changing the sign in the window to *Closed* and locking the dead bolt. Then she fished out her crystal ball from an old steamer trunk and set it on the front table, stretching out a silk scarf beneath it to cover the table's edges. "We're doing a past-life regression right now. It's high time to deal with your baggage."

"For crying out loud, Amy! In case you've forgotten, it was your hocus pocus that got us into this mess."

"Exactly! So we need her help to get us out."

"Her?"

"Ailís O'Dannan, silly—your ancestor. She's obviously trying to reach you. You need to find out what she wants." Amy pointed at an empty chair beside the table. "Move it."

"Amy," Rose refused to budge from beside the stove. She cut her gaze to the crystal ball as if it might be something dangerous. "Have we gone crackers? I mean, listen to us— what if we're wrong and Vincent is just a run-of-the-mill jerk?

And Crystal simply had a fit while her mommy was gone? It wouldn't be the first time a toddler has done that. Maybe Chance Murphy is merely another missing person, gone AWOL in the woods. This county is riddled with such cases—"

Without warning, Crystal stood up from the floor and marched over to her mother, climbing purposefully onto her lap. She clutched the green fabric of her dress and burrowed into its folds like a bird who'd found a nest. Rose closed her arms around her daughter with caution. She'd learned months ago not to get too excited by what looked like bonding, because in the very next moment her daughter might wail or push her away. Gently, she leaned her chin on Crystal's head, hoping to absorb the smell of her hair and the warmth of her skin before she bolted.

Crystal lifted her gaze as if she were trying to read her face. Rose could have sworn she saw a glimmer of personality —not the spacey expression looking past her into nothingness, but a fiery spark. Crystal puckered her lips like she was about to scold someone. Tears rimmed Rose's eyes—she recognized the look. It was Crystal's impatient face, the one she'd adopted on her fourth birthday before the accident, when she'd decided she knew everything by now and was tired of waiting for her mother to catch up. Rose fidgeted in her chair. Could Crystal's expression be a cruel coincidence, another disappointment waiting to happen? All at once the voice she'd heard earlier came back to haunt her.

Let go of your fears, Rose. Believe—

The words felt tender inside, like a soft quilt wrapped

around her for both comfort and courage. Rose inhaled a deep breath. With all her being, she wanted to accept her daughter's attention as genuine. Yet whenever she'd done so in the past, she had only met rejection, or worse, indifference. She closed her eyes, and for the first time since she'd arrived in Ophir Creek, she let herself imagine for an instant that Crystal might be all right. More than all right—that somewhere inside she still harbored a wild and passionate heart, capable of loving again.

"Welcome back, sassy girl," she dared to whisper with all the hope she could muster. "I've missed you so."

Rose kept her eyes sealed. Despite her morsel of faith, she was afraid to witness yet another empty stare that would wrench her heart and make her feel lonely to the bone. Just as she feared, Crystal let out a fierce squeal and squirmed from her lap. Her feet hit the floor with a thud as she broke free from her mother's arms. Rose opened her eyes. She watched the familiar sight of her daughter darting away, feeling pinched with guilt for not obeying the doctor's orders to avoid prolonged physical contact.

Why can't I just give up? she wondered, burying her head in her hands. I ought to know by now that hope hurts too much. To her surprise, she heard a foot stomp the floor loud enough to echo through the shop.

"Man!" Crystal huffed when her mother glanced up. She pointed at the bird with frustrated certainty. "Island man." Then she turned her back on her mother and began to spin.

∼

Rose counted the gold stars on Amy's silk tablecloth, wringing her hands as she tried to keep her eyes diverted from the crystal ball. All she wanted was to sit by Crystal's side and record every move, every tiny sound, waiting for another word to escape from her lips. After all, she had not merely spoken this time—she had actually communicated. But how could Rose explain Crystal's brief remark to the doctors? Who would believe that she and her daughter shared the same dream and that their pet raven was really a lost forester? It sounded like balderdash, and Rose knew if she breathed a word about it to anyone, they might both be locked up.

Wriggling in her seat at the front table, she brushed away the heady incense that tickled her nose. She'd already made a quick dinner of hash browns and sausage for Crystal and put her to bed, reluctantly agreeing to Amy's demand for a past-life regression. Rose didn't see much choice after Amy issued her ultimatum. "Either you do this regression, or I quit," Amy had fumed, folding her arms. She'd never seen her so adamant before, and although the prospect of exploring reincarnation scared her, the thought of losing her treasured business partner frightened her even more.

"I'm only going along with this because I can't run the shop without you," Rose confessed as Amy peered into her crystal ball.

"Hush," Amy commanded without breaking concentration. She tapped the ball. "Look into the crystal and tell me what you see."

Rose rolled her eyes. Amy had turned off the lights and put candles around the table, which made the shop reek of burning wicks and patchouli. She studied the reflections of the small flames that danced across the crystal like little flags whipping in a breeze.

"Well? What do you see?"

"Candle flames," Rose replied. "That's about it."

"Good! Now look deeply into those reflections and tell me the first thing that comes to mind. Imagine those golden flames as torches at the doorway of your soul. That door is opening for you—and as it opens, tell me what you find."

Squinting, Rose tried to imagine the flames pointing to something—to anything. No matter how hard she stared, she couldn't pick up other images. There was no door. There wasn't even a window. The crystal ball merely looked glassy. Annoyed, she leaned back in her chair.

"Amy, I'm afraid it's like looking into teacups or coffee mugs. I can't see anything for myself. I'm handicapped that way, like my great-great grandmother."

"Oh," Amy tapped her lip, "I hadn't thought of that." She opened a velvet pouch from the table and took out a rabbit's foot, a smudge stick, and an assortment of silver charms. Holding each one to the candle light, she frowned. She scanned the shop and spotted the raven on the floor, nestled peacefully on a rug. The candles cast a warm glow over his dark feathers, making them shine a soft gold. "Hey, what about that dream you had? You said that whenever you go to the island, the raven always shows you the way. Maybe if you hold him and try to meditate, you can go back there." She got up and scooped the raven into her arms, setting him down on Rose's lap. He squirmed until he became more comfortable, letting out a soft chortle.

"It's all right, Chance," Amy assured him, "we need you right now."

Rose shuddered, still getting used to the idea that the raven was a man she'd actually met. Stroking his feathers, she looked to Amy for courage. "Okay," she closed her eyes, "I-I guess I can give it a shot."

"Concentrate on the dream you had," Amy instructed, taking her seat. "How did you get to the island?"

"Clouds," Rose whispered. She hugged the bird in her lap, and in her mind she saw fluffy clouds over the mountains. At first she was wary, unsure whether she could handle doing this without actually being asleep. Yet so many thoughts flooded her mind—the delight of hearing her daughter's voice, the disturbing hike with Vincent, even neglected shop chores that she should have finished by now. Rose shook her head to ward off events of the day.

"C'mon," Amy urged impatiently, "you've got to focus!"

"Okay, okay," Rose promised, clutching the raven. She attempted to imagine clouds again, but nothing came. Her mind had gone blank.

Don't be afraid, a low voice whispered. *Surrender and let your heart speak.*

Startled, Rose dug her fingers into the bird's feathers. All right, she decided nervously, I'll try to listen to my heart. Emptying her mind of tangled thoughts, she focused on her heartbeat, a steady, subtle rhythm that helped numb her reservations. Then she dared to venture to a secret part of herself, somewhere in the silent shadows between thought and emotion, a twilight place where only her essence remained.

Slowly, her mind became a blanket of fog. She could no longer tell what was up or down, left or right—it was as though she had entered a place between places, a corridor between time. This is where souls take flight, she thought, and she pictured herself among clouds. As she stroked the raven's feathers, she could feel herself being lifted. Everywhere she looked there were clouds rimmed with gold from the setting sun, their moisture cool and slightly icy upon her cheeks. When she turned to glance over her shoulder, she saw the raven flying by her side.

It's okay, a voice assured her in the breeze. *You know where to go*.

Rose smiled a little and released herself to the wind that tousled her hair as her body soared. With the raven as her guide, she carefully maneuvered through swells of air, occasionally reaching out a finger to touch his wing. Before long, they broke through clouds and saw a green island in the sunset. Rays stretched orange and yellow on the beach below, making the sand take on a sheen of gold. Rose spied the stone cottage by the sea, with puffs of smoke rising from its chimney and hovering over the thatched roof. A peasant woman stepped out the door and wrapped herself in a shawl. When she glanced up at Rose, she walked back inside and brought out a little girl. Together, they held hands.

"What do you see?" Amy tapped her arm, but Rose didn't flinch.

"Crystal," Rose whispered. "She's with Ailís on the island. I think they recognize me."

"Ooh, of course they do!" Amy noted. "Keep going—listen for what they say."

Rose struggled to keep her eyes closed and inhabit the

dream world, in spite of her friend's interruptions. She searched for the raven again in her heart, the image hazy at first, until she spotted his wings outstretched among a blanket of clouds. He led the way to spiral down to the beach. Hesitantly, she followed him on an eddy of wind that gently lowered her to the sand. Her feet sank into the granules, and for reasons she didn't quite understand, she felt the urge to unlace her boots and remove her socks. The beach was still warm from the setting sun, and the way the sand enveloped her toes made her feel strangely at home.

"*Tráthnóna maith.*" Ailís called out from beside the cottage. "Welcome back."

Rose picked up her hiking boots and started walking toward them, her green dress swishing in the breeze. She kept her eyes on her tow-headed daughter beside Ailís and took a deep breath. Who was Crystal here—the little firebrand she knew, or someone else? Was any of this real? She felt a wing glide around her shoulder, its feathers soft and tender against her skin. When she turned, she saw the dark raven at her side. In a split second, he changed to become Chance Murphy. His long, black coat flapped in the wind, and he hugged her close.

"Shadows are every bit as real as light," he assured her, limping slightly. He let her go and walked toward Ailís and Crystal. Unsettled for a moment, Rose began to run past him, her feet churning in the sand, not wanting anyone to reach her daughter before her. Breathless, she made it to the cottage, where the pale stones reflected a yellow light from the dipping sun. She was about to hug Crystal and open her mouth to say hello, when her daughter reluctantly stepped forward and held out a teacup. She looked her mother up and down as though appraising a stranger.

"*Fáilte*," she said stiffly.

Rose stepped back, startled to hear her daughter speak Irish. She didn't have a clue what she meant. To her surprise, sparks of envy alighted in her heart. She couldn't help resenting Crystal's mysterious life away from her, even if she did seem healthier on the island. Every muscle in her body wanted to grab her daughter and claim, "She's mine—mine!" And then it hit her. All along, when their lives were held captive by Jake in Winnemucca, she and Crystal had shared a common enemy, someone to band together against. In many ways, it was the basis of their bond, the reason for their cocoon apart from the world. Yet here, she felt as distant from her daughter as a cloud blown over the sea, watching helplessly as she latched on to Ailís. Rose glanced up at the peasant woman, at her dark hair with silver strands and startling green eyes. She knew she should be grateful—after all, her presence had helped Crystal come out of her shell. But she was a usurper, too, someone who'd won her daughter's affection. Ashamed of her reaction, Rose studied Crystal, wondering whether it was possible to repair their relationship, to ever create something normal beyond Jake.

Ailís pointed to the teacup in Crystal's hand. "My darling," she said as if she'd read Rose's thoughts, "let your heart become a safe harbor." She bent down and whispered something in Crystal's ear and gave her a nudge. The little girl bristled until Ailís nudged her again. Sighing, Crystal took her mother's hand and led her over to a bed of potato plants. They appeared vibrant in the setting sun with healthy, green leaves stretching over their stalks. She kneeled down to stroke the plants, her fingers moving tenderly as though they were her companions. Then she sprinkled water on their roots from her teacup. Beside the potato beds were Crystal's belongings in a small pile—her play bracelet and a seashell, along with two small potatoes, like the ones on her kitchen table. The sight of them made her shiver.

"C'mon," Crystal grew impatient. She picked up her bracelet and held it to her mother. "Play with me."

"Play?" Rose accepted the iridescent bracelet. She'd been so stressed lately that her imagination felt as gray as a stone. For months, she'd focused exclusively on the learning exercises for Crystal's progress chart, favoring constructive goals that could be counted, measured, analyzed. Now, she hardly knew where to begin. Anxious, she ran her fingers over her daughter's bracelet beads like a rosary.

Crystal folded her arms. "Don't you know anything? You start by singing the song."

"Which song?" Rose replied.

"You know," Crystal rolled her eyes, "the lullaby."

Crystal began to hum the tune Rose had known as a girl. Together, they sang a few verses, and Rose felt awkward at first, her voice wobbly, until she saw her daughter's eyes soften.

"Look," Crystal pointed at the potato beds. "The plants like it when we sing. It makes them strong." She lifted her empty teacup. "We have to get more water."

Tugging at her mother's dress, she made her follow to a well beside the cottage. Crystal stood on tip toes to peer inside. "You ready?"

"For what?"

Crystal set her hands on her hips, the teacup dangling from her finger. "To see."

Confused, Rose watched Ailís and Chance join her by the well. In the waning light, her daughter dipped the teacup into the water and peered at the ripples she'd made. Rose glanced down to see what fascinated her. As the rings smoothed out and the well water became glassy, Crystal gave her mother the teacup to drink. To humor her, Rose took a sip, when all at once she saw herself in the well as a little girl, a few years older than Crystal. But she was dressed differently than her childhood in Ophir Creek. She had on a flannel skirt and a wool shawl, not unlike Ailís. A raven flew protectively overhead, and she was fleeing across a bed of potatoes that appeared gray and sickly. All around, the air was filled with the sound of barking dogs and screams. As her feet drummed against the earth, the frightened expression in her eyes made her appear lost.

"Why are you so quiet—what's going on?" Rose heard Amy say.

Rose kept her eyes closed so as not to disturb the vision. "I-I think I see myself in the past," she whispered. "Only I'm not dressed like me. And I'm running."

"Really?" Amy replied softly. "Keep going."

Rose gazed into the well again. But this time, Ailís dipped her finger into the water and disturbed the surface. Rose saw herself as someone older—in her twenties, perhaps, in a calico dress, nearly gray with dust. Her face was weary, but she was trotting to keep pace with a wagon out in the desert, like gold seekers who headed west over a century ago. There was a man beside her, blonde and lanky, with a fierce look in his eyes. The intensity of his face reminded her of Jake, and it made her tremble. No matter how hard she tried, she always seemed half a step behind him. Her eyes were frightened, as if she feared she might be swallowed by the desert if she didn't run to keep up.

"How about now?" Amy cut in. "What's going on now?"

"Well, I'm older this time, but I'm still running. Always running. The reason's different, I guess, but the look in my eyes is the same."

"Interesting. Hang in there, honey, and keep talking—I'm taking notes. We'll discuss it later."

Rose forced herself to look into the well again, kneading her daughter's bracelet in her hands. When Ailís dipped her finger into the well one more time, and Rose saw herself on a mountain at night, picking up a red bandana. In the moonlight among a circle of stones lay the body of a man and a raven. Tears streamed down her face while the wind gathered strength, howling as it stole the bandana from her hands. The harder she ran, the more it kept slipping from her fingers.

"C-Corvine?" Rose whispered, frightened. "Corvine O'Dannan?"

"The heart knows no time, *a thaisce*," Ailís replied. With that, she put her arm around Crystal and the two became oddly hazy, as if they were submerged in water. Rose reached out, desperately trying to grasp her daughter's hand, but their forms softened and wavered at the edges until they disappeared entirely. Punching her fists to clutch at thin air, Rose felt a bitter wind brush her cheeks, mixed with the hearth fire smoke from the cottage. All that remained before her was

Chance, standing at the well, his large frame so sturdy that for a second she wished she could lean upon him for strength. His dark eyes poured over hers, and Rose caught a depth of insight in his tender gaze that she could hardly bear. Suddenly, she felt exposed, as if he knew every hope and failure she'd ever tried to disguise, and her heart began to race out of control. She darted away, only to find herself dashing toward the wide, empty beach. As her feet roiled through sand, she prayed that the sheer force of her motion might somehow blur her many lifetimes of failures and losses. When her feet hit icy surf in the dim twilight, she faced a dark horizon big enough to devour her whole.

Be still, the voice of Ailís gently soared over the rhythm of the sea. *When feet come to rest, the heart finds home.*

Rose opened her eyes with a start. Her lap was empty, yet her fingers were still clenched around her daughter's bracelet. In the weak candle light, the raven on the floor beside her bare feet with sand dusted on his wings. It was then Rose realized she'd taken off her boots, like in the vision. She winced, staring at the granules between her damp toes. "Gone," she whispered, "Crystal and Ailís—they're gone—"

To her amazement, the shadows around the raven elongated into a shape at her side, all as a pillar. In a flicker of candle light, they transformed to become Chance Murphy. Rose gasped at the imposing figure beside her and glanced over at Amy. Her friend was so distracted by the notes she was scribbling she appeared spellbound, unable to see either one of them. Rose waved her fingers in front of Amy's eyes, but she didn't blink, protected by some otherworldly veil. In the dim light of the shop, Rose peered again at Chance, who seemed half-made of shadows.

"I'm not gone," he assured her, his roughhewn face warmly lit by candles. He reached out to brush her cheek. The caress of his fingers felt like feathers. "I've been with you all along."

His deep voice rippled inside Rose, saturating her soul like liquid, and it made her quiver. "But-but my daughter," she stammered, "every time I get closer, she slips away. All I want is—"

"To love her?" A brief flush warmed his cheeks, as though the words had slipped too easily from his tongue. He shook his head. But then his gaze swept over her—along the smooth line of her throat and reach of her collarbone, down the delicate bloom of her breasts and inlet of her waist—with such raw longing that it pierced Rose's heart. Twisting his jaw, he appeared to be holding back the yearning of centuries. Chance closed his eyes for a moment, steadying his feet.

"Open your heart, Rose," he urged, "like you did to find the island." He crouched down on his heels and stared with an intensity that it made her tremble. "Just be there for Crystal. Don't you see? For so long, she's been scared—and hurt, and angry, just like you." Gently, he wrapped his large fingers around her hand, and Rose felt his heat pulse into her bones. "If you could make her feel safe again, she might trust you enough to respond."

"Safe?" Rose slipped back her hand as if she'd been bitten. "How on earth can I make anyone feel safe with Jake— Vincent—whoever he is—still around? He stole your body!

What happens if we can't put him back? You might be stuck a wild raven, or—"

Chance stood indignation surfacing on his face. He swallowed hard and raked his fingers through his dark, unruly hair.

"My dear," he declared in a somber tone, "I have been your guard in myriad forms for a hundred tangled lifetimes." A rugged bravery churned in his eyes. "There's no storm that can tear you from me—no rise of the sea or mere human force that can ever come between us. Don't you know by now that I'll always find a way to protect your precious heart?"

Chance's chest expanded with the fervor of his words. His fists tightened as a sober dignity emerged in his eyes. Then he glanced down at his long, frayed coat, worn to shreds in places, and at his filthy, battered boots. "Besides," he added, "the animal world has always suited my kind. Souls like me, we live best in wildness—"

He grasped her elbow and easily lifted her to her feet. "It's that same wildness I see in you, sometimes—the wide, open sky in your eyes, the deep, uncharted forest in your heart. We're untamed, you and I. Did you ever consider, Rose, that you might have done me a favor? That your spell released me from the burden of trying to be human?"

Rose flinched. "Is that why I always keep running?" she said, afraid of the answer. "Because I'm—we're—twixt?"

"No," Chance shook his head. He stared hard at her silhouette that shivered on the wall each time a candle flickered and turned to face her. "You run because you don't own up to your own power. To stand and claim what's rightfully yours. That's the only spell that needs to be broken, Rose."

In that instant, Chance's brown eyes burned into hers, and a wince crossed his face, so incongruent with his usual stoic front. All at once, she realized he might feel as much anguish over her as she did over Crystal—for he knew intimately what it was like to be so very close, yet a world apart from the one who'd captured his heart. Tears stung her eyes, beyond her ability to blink them back.

Chance traced the path of a tear that had slipped down her cheek. He cupped his palm to her face—it felt warm and strong.

"Don't be ruled by fear." His lips were so close she could feel their warmth. "The curse isn't about Jake, Rose." His dark eyes penetrated to her very soul. "It's about *you*."

Denial ripped through Rose like lightning crashing through clouds, and it sent her raging inside. But I never wanted any of this! For my life to fall apart! For my own daughter to be lost to shadows—

Chance remained silent. He took a step back and folded his arms, allowing emotions to storm through her. Thunder rolled outside, and for a moment he closed his eyes, as if he could feel the low rumble within him. Then he squared his shoulders and lifted his head to his full height. His silhouette swelled into a dark imprint that filled the entire wall.

"I don't care what the hell comes against us anymore," Chance said gravely. "There comes a time when you decide who you are and what you stand for—all of these twilight notions be damned. And nothing and no one is going to steal what belongs to you. Including your own soul, Goddammit—"

He clutched her face and kissed her with a force that nearly knocked her down. Rose felt thunder drum through her being—wave upon dark, rising wave—as though the power of the midnight sky had poured into her and was shaking her to her core. His lips consumed her cheeks, her forehead, her throat, until she felt like her bones had melted onto the floor. Just when she thought she might collapse, she dared to link her arms around his neck and pour herself into him, as if their souls could somehow combine into one hungry being. Her lips sought his with a kiss that seared through them both, until they were at last forced to break for air. Rose leaned against his weight, reeling.

Chance pressed his cheek against hers. Then he released Rose, steadying her shoulders until she regained her composure. With a firm grip, he took her by the hand and led her through the shop. When they reached the back bedroom, he paused to take in the sight of Crystal in her sleep. Quietly, he steered Rose to the child's bedside. In the soft moonlight that sliced through the window, her daughter was nestled comfortably under the quilt, clutching her favorite stuffed coyote, her sleep as peaceful as the stars that winked overhead. Chance stroked Crystal's forehead with surprising familiarity, his fingers following the curve of a stubborn cowlick.

"Stop being afraid, Rose." His voice was deep and threaded with challenge. "Love her for who she is now, not for who you need her to be."

With that, he turned to the bedpost and removed the photo of Crystal that Rose had tacked up—the one of her daughter's perfect smile on her fourth birthday. Holding it at eye level, he boldly ripped it in half.

Rose sucked air as if she'd been slapped. Ignoring her, he tore the halves into pieces and scattered them to the floor.

Quickly, she bent down to scoop them up, fingers working in a frenzy like she might somehow put her daughter back together, when his hand stopped her. Chance grabbed the pieces and threw them aside like confetti. He pointed his long arm to a stack of papers on the kitchen table.

"And for God's sake," he commanded, "burn those damn progress sheets."

16

S itting alone on the boardwalk in front of her shop at sunrise, Rose gazed at the old storefronts in the Ophir Creek town square. She squinted, watching the buildings become hazy between her lashes, half-expecting them to disappear if she blinked hard enough. In spite of the fact that it was chilly and the boardwalk had a dusting of frost, she felt utterly numb, unable to detect any nuances of temperature. What's real now? she wondered, shaking her head. This dusty old town—this life? Ever since Amy's regression, it seemed like her world had become a house of mirrors, with the past, present, and future all rolled together into one bewildering ball. Rose gripped the boardwalk's edge, her knuckles braced against the wood. And what's mine to hang on to? A thin voice floated by.

Nothing but love.

A bird cawed and Rose glanced up, spotting two ravens perched on a telephone wire. One was tall, even lanky, with disheveled feathers and a distinct sparkle in his eye. The other was smaller, more graceful, its feathers neatly groomed and streaked silver at the tips. Chance and Ailís? She tugged her jacket tighter, unsettled at the idea of winged visitors. After all, could she really believe she was Corvine O'Dannan once? An obscure Irish peasant who was superstitious about birds? Or did they simply share the same pattern, an urge to run from their problems by picking the wrong man, as if it were a defect embedded in the family DNA? Amy had told her that at the soul level, it didn't really matter. The important thing was to transcend her hang-ups. Meditation, aromatherapy, affirmation chants—all of these would be of great help, Amy claimed. Along with hiding the car keys each time she felt like running.

Rose threaded her fingers through a lock of hair, brittle from frost. Dealing with the past might be one thing, but right now there was a more pressing problem on her mind. Namely, what to do about Jake—aka Vincent.

"Well, you can't kill him," Amy had said last night after the regression, "it's against the law. Not that anyone would rat on you in this town, and there are plenty of places to dump a body out in the wilderness. But that only reinforces the cycle. We need to break the pattern. So what did Ailís tell you in your vision?"

"She said, 'When feet come to rest, the heart finds home.'" Rose threw back a stiff shot of whiskey that Amy had poured after their session. "Whatever the hell that means."

Amy patted her arm. "It means make peace with yourself, honey. And don't plan any more escape routes." She filled a shot glass for herself as well. "But just to be on the safe side, I think we'd better explore a few banishing spells. You know, something to send Jake back where he came from. Does your ancestor's diary have any clues?"

Rose shivered. It always spooked her to resort to the diary for anything beyond kitchen recipes—though she'd certainly been tempted a few times. "I don't know," she replied wearily. "Whenever I've gotten desperate in my life and searched the diary for direction, it made no sense to me. It's like the symbols are another language, and I don't know the code."

Mercifully, Amy had dropped the subject, aware Rose was exhausted after her regression and in no mood to haggle over spells. But now, as Rose brooded on the boardwalk, all she could think about was the diary and the secrets it held. She slipped her hand into her pocket, where she'd stashed the small book when she got up that morning. She ran her fingers over the weathered binding and glanced up at the ravens.

"Okay," she called out to the birds on the telephone wire, "if I promise not to run this time, will you help me?" She pointed to her truck parked in front of the shop. "I mean, nothing's stopping me from loading up Crystal right now and driving to another town. So I'm totally trusting you two." She aimed at the Magpie Saloon. "If you want me to stay," she shook her finger in challenge, "he has to go!

"Who are you talking to?" Amy stepped onto the boardwalk, yawning. She was still in her pajamas—bright purple flannel speckled with glittery stars and crescents, red curls cascading over the collar in a mess. She let the front door slam behind her.

Rose stood to her feet, embarrassed. She'd asked Amy not to leave her alone last night, since the whole experience had left her rattled. The old bed in the back apartment was big enough for three, but Rose hadn't expected her friend to rise so early. "I-I wasn't talking to anyone. I just—" she paused, realizing it was more work to lie than to fess up. "Oh all right," she nodded at the telephone wire. "I was talking to *them*."

"Good for you," Amy smiled, "maybe they'll give us some pointers. You know, I've been mulling it over this morning. And I think if we want to get rid of Jake—uh, Vincent—the first thing we need to do is dig up that potato wish seed. Remember from the love spell? Where did you bury it?"

Rose pointed to a spot at the side of the building. In a flash, Amy went back inside and returned with her coat on and a shovel in her hands. "Here you go, sweetie," she handed the shovel to Rose. "Dig."

Rose stepped off the boardwalk and began to slash the spade into the frosted earth. With each strike of her shovel, she cursed under her breath, imagining she was hacking Jake into a dozen pieces. Finally, she spotted the potato in the small hole she'd created. Bending down, she wrenched it from the soil with her hands and held it up to Amy.

"Now what?"

Amy scratched her head. "Well, it's probably not a good idea to re-bury it anywhere—it might sprout or get dug up by one of Ray's hounds. God only knows what kind of spell that would unleash."

Rose gazed suspiciously at the potato in her hand. "How about the garbage disposal?"

"Perfect," Amy replied.

They returned to the shop, careful not to disturb Crystal who was sleeping in the bedroom as they tiptoed through the back apartment to the kitchen sink. Rose was about to stuff the potato down the drain when Amy stopped her.

"Wait, shouldn't we say a little jingle?" she whispered. "Like wish I will, wish I might, take back this spirit from my sight—something to cement the process?"

"Sure, I have just the thing," Rose flipped on the garbage disposal. She guided the potato through the blades and turned on the faucet to wash down the pulp. Glancing through the kitchen window at the Magpie Saloon, kitty-corner from her building, she closed her eyes.

"Go to hell, Jake," she hissed.

Despite the fact that Rose and Amy had banished the potato to the netherworld of Ophir Creek's septic field, Vincent remained a sparkling presence in town. He always called out a boisterous greeting to the women when he opened the saloon, and throughout the day he could be spotted chatting up locals and laughing so heartily his voice echoed across the square. Each time Rose saw him flash his charming smile, she wanted to vomit. His hair still had that infernal shine, and he remained as impossibly handsome as he did that first day she met him. In desperation, she talked aloud to the ravens that hung around her porch, wondering if she'd become unbalanced. Yet each time she swallowed her pride and asked for their advice, they merely swooped to her side and tapped their beaks at her pocket, releasing such harsh caws that it made her head throb.

At first Rose thought they might be hungry, so she obliged

with fresh baked items from the shop. Then she realized they were pointing to her great-great grandmother's diary. Finally, she sat down on the porch and pulled out the book, opening it to a page of kitchen ingredients. Rose studied the drawings of herbs and vegetables with an occasional nut or spice thrown in, when she spotted weather patterns etched in the margins— lightning bolts and clouds, along with fluid dashes resembling the motion of the wind. Even more intriguing were the hatch marks at the bottom. Her heart pounded wildly at the confounding symbols, for she knew full well that they must indicate more than mere recipes. Biting her lip, Rose faced the prospect that Amy could be right—if a misguided incantation had gotten her into this mess, then perhaps a new spell from the diary was required to get her out.

Amy, of course, was only too happy to agree. For the next several days, they searched the diary for creative ways to get rid of their unwanted neighbor. They pored over the symbols on the pages, wondering if rosemary leaves could be used for banishing, chicken gizzards for soul replacement, or if garlic really could ward off evil spirits. No matter what recipes they tried, however, their concoctions smelled like motley stews— too foul for even Ray Beane's hounds. To make matters worse, there was no guidance for words to chant or spells to cast, only the figures in the margins that seemed to add more riddles than they solved. After half a dozen failed attempts at cooking strange brews while reciting a mantra or two for good measure, Amy got fed up and decided to wing it a little.

"Listen," she said impatiently by midweek, "we're not exactly getting anywhere here, so we're going to have to take our efforts outside. It's time to be aggressive, Rose! Let's carry this pot and sprinkle the ingredients around town for protection. Then, I don't know—we'll repeat the word O'Dannan a few times. Maybe a violent storm will strike the Magpie Saloon and send Vincent packing. What do you think?"

"I-I'm not sure." Rose waved the stench of their latest formula away from her nose. "Nothing we've done so far has had any effect. I mean, look across the street—his damn light is still on in the saloon. And with the blue moon coming in a few days, the tourist traffic has tripled going at his place! Just my luck," she scanned her overalls that were splattered with green stains, "the one night of the year that celebrates my ancestor, and it makes *his* business boom."

"Then what have we got to lose? The worst that can happen is that people will think we're nutty—hardly a crime in this town."

Rose had to admit Amy had a point. Things couldn't possibly get worse, and maybe they were on to something. She glanced outside at the ravens who sat on the porch. They'd bristled their crown feathers lately and wagged their heads, but she wasn't sure if it was a commentary on her spells or a reaction to the cold weather. At one point, she even heard a voice whisper, *You're not listening,* but her racing pulse drowned out the rest of the words. The truth was, she was scared—far too petrified to pay attention to telepathic notions from birds. She didn't have another worthwhile strategy for expelling Vincent, and at least Amy had come up with a plan. Frustrated, Rose picked up Crystal, ready to try anything as long as it was legal. "Okay," she relented, "let's move."

Rose carried her daughter through the front door,

following Amy who held the pot of stew and sprinkled droplets from a ladle onto the town's boardwalks. Rose prayed none of the locals would spot them, because she couldn't imagine a good lie to cover their tracks. What could she say—the boardwalks needed watering? Surely Ray Beane would be the first to point a finger and laugh, and God only knows what would come out of Harriet Brimley's mouth. Embarrassed, she stared at her feet and pretended not to notice Amy's splashes as they proceeded around the town square. When they reached the corner of the Magpie Saloon, Amy turned to face her.

"C'mon!" She set the pot down. "You need to participate more. Why don't you sing a rhyme, since you're a descendent of the O'Dannans? Or call out your ancestor's name and ask for power?"

Rose stroked her daughter's forehead. She studied a damp spot on the boardwalk that filled the dry air with the smell of turnips and beef stock. The ravens called out in alarm.

"Amy," she coughed, "are you *sure* we're not going to attract raccoons or bears with this stuff? People will get angry if their garbage is strewn all over town." Crystal began to wiggle, so she set her to her feet.

"What choice do we have? At least try to offer a prayer or something."

Rose pressed her palms together. "All right, all right. O'Dannan!" she burst, feeling awkward. "No, no, it has to be sincere." She closed her eyes and let a prayer roll off her tongue. "Oh God," she said from the bottom of her heart, "we need all the help we can get to free us from this mess. Please do something—anything—about Vincent—"

Before she could finish, Rose heard boot steps echo against the boardwalk. Her heart tightened like a vise—she used to feel the same way whenever Jake came around at night. His presence always had the power to crush air from her lungs, even when he hadn't touched her. Opening her eyes, she braced herself, spying Vincent beside Amy in front of the Magpie Saloon.

"Sweetheart, am I to believe you're *praying* for me?" He smiled and brushed a lock of hair from her forehead, allowing his fingers to linger. "Don't you know that all a man really needs is the sight of a beautiful woman? Restores the soul."

Rose jerked away. Hugging Crystal close, her heart pounded as she scrambled for words. "Well, um, that's why we stopped by," she backpedaled. "You know, to be polite and say hello—"

"And to deliver fresh soup!" Amy cut in. "See," she pointed at the pot, "it's an heirloom recipe—beef and turnips with a dash of mint, the herb of hospitality."

"Then why are you sprinkling it all over town?" Vincent glanced at the semi-circle of splashes that moistened the dust around the square. He peered up at the ravens that glared at him from a telephone wire. "You wouldn't be trying to put a hex on me, would you? I've heard stories about you two."

"What stories?" Butterflies skittered in Rose's stomach.

"Well, that you believe in all kinds of fanciful things—like fairies and magic potions." He leaned forward to whisper in her ear, "And wild knights to the rescue on a blue moon."

Vincent gave her a wink, and shivers ran down her spine, as if he'd pressed a bruise that she'd hoped to conceal. She couldn't help noticing the rope-like muscles that rippled beneath his flannel shirt every time he shifted his weight. Something about his casual grace always derailed her, though she tried to ignore it. If she didn't know better, she would have pegged him as a bronc rider, with that cat-like quality that could defy gravity yet still whisper for a woman's touch. For a split second, she lost herself in the thought of running her fingers along his arm, as though the hike had never happened —as though it had simply been her warped imagination that could ever judge him as anything dangerous. But then she glanced at his blue eyes—though shiny, they appeared as hard and cold to her as sapphires. That's Jake all right, she thought, recognizing the mercenary look. As sure as we're standing here breathing.

"Listen," Rose wrapped her arms around Crystal like a shield, "there are always rumors floating around this town. But the real reason we came by is to give you your money back." She slipped her hand in her pocket, relieved to find her truck keys and a wad of bills still stuffed inside. "Here," she put the money in his palm, "this is the deposit you gave us for that hike the other day. Like I told you, the gold legend is bullshit."

"Really?" Vincent countered like he'd caught her in a lie. "Who says I didn't find gold?"

"Wh-What do you mean?"

"Well, you're not the only one who knows how to find treasure in this town."

With a mere tilt of his head, Vincent's eyes relaxed into hers like an old lover's, as comfortable as the flannel sheets on her big feather bed. The coldness evaporated, and he felt as near to her as her own skin, even though he was a step away. An inexplicable warmth caressed her heart, despite the cold weather, as though he'd pried through a secret window and lit a flame while he quietly tiptoed through her soul. His eyes were soft, welcoming, holding the same promise as a cozy armchair. Rose longed to ease into his gaze, to forget for a little while about spells and curses, past-life mistakes and nosy ravens, when she felt Crystal stiffen against her arms. Shaking her head, Rose's legs became unsteady. How does he always get to me? she wondered angrily, amazed at his sleight of soul, the quicksilver way he went from being an icy stranger to an easy confidant who could light the darkest corners of any woman's heart. Backing up with her arm tight against Crystal, she shot a glance at Amy and prayed to God for help with conjuring an exit plan.

To her surprise Vincent kneeled on the boardwalk and grasped Crystal's hand. "Her hair is so golden in the sun," he rubbed her small fingers, "just like wildfire." A breeze picked up, curling wisps of her daughter's hair, and Vincent smiled as if it had arrived on schedule. He cupped Crystal's chin before Rose could slap his hand away. Thunder rolled, and as Crystal squealed and grabbed for her mother, a slice of light pierced the horizon in broad daylight.

Lightning disappeared behind a bank of clouds. Within seconds a black plume of smoke arose above the trees, blooming into an ominous mushroom. "Forest fire," Rose muttered. She yanked Crystal into her arms, cradling her face as though Vincent had scalded her. "Don't you dare come near my daughter!" she spit out, noticing billows of smoke seemed to rise with her anger.

Vincent stood and looped his thumbs into his jeans. "Now, now," he warned, "don't get too cocky on me. You wouldn't want it to rebound on you. Remember the golden rule: Do unto others, sweetheart."

He picked up the soup pot, walking a few strides along the boardwalk before he turned around. "Oh, and thank you, ladies," he opened the lid to peer inside, "for everything." Taking a whiff, he cast an icy stare at the women that could freeze them into place. "You can damn well bet I'll return the favor."

17

S mall flames flickered in the wood stove and made shadows leap against walls, filling Rose's heart with dread. She sat on a rocker in the darkened shop after putting Crystal to bed that evening, wishing her chair's rhythm could lull her into a sense of calm. The creaking wood only jarred her nerves. Though she was worn out by the crush of tourists who filed into the shop for gold supplies before the blue moon, she couldn't stop brooding over the morning's events. Vincent's behavior frightened her far more than his advances on their recent hike. Out on Rook Ridge, he still seemed to think he could fool her, buying favor with poker winnings and gold coins. But now, he'd moved straight on to intimidation. Just like Jake used to do, she thought, whenever he couldn't get his way.

Rose glanced past the curtain to the bedroom, afraid to let her daughter out of her sight. What bothered her most was the way he'd touched Crystal and a lightning bolt had struck—the same way he'd rested a hand on her before Laurel and Ray were injured. It was as if he knew he could cause catastrophe by tapping into their most primitive emotions, especially anger or fear. She huddled beneath a wool blanket, pulling it up to her chin. What does he want from us? Her mind reeled with paranoid possibilities. Drug runners? Love slaves? Or just more pawns in small-time gambling rings, the kind Jake always had his fingers into? Rose knew he was up to something, but exactly what it was, she couldn't decipher.

A hiss erupted from the stove as the last ember folded into dying coals and snuffed out. The nearly full moon highlighted the shop with platinum hues. Rose was afraid to turn on the lights—afraid that Vincent might see her from across the street or slither up to her building and peer into windows, tormenting her from shadows. In just a few days, the blue moon would rise on Halloween, and she knew that at midnight it would seem like daylight outside. Where can we hide then? Where can anyone hide to protect themselves from him? He had become more than just a man now—he was a dark and cruel resurrection, unbridled by the limits of ordinary beings. And if they were right that he was Jake inside, then there was no doubt he wanted *something*.

Traces of smoke wove through the air—not the aged, wood smoke from the pot-bellied stove, but a raw, bristling aroma that crept under the doorway of the shop and permeated the room. Rose shuddered beneath her blanket. It was the smell that residents of Ophir Creek dreaded most— the sure sign of a forest fire not far away. Firefighters had been dispatched by the county earlier that day and had successfully contained the blaze, but the lingering odor of destruction was a reminder of what she was really up against. There was no question in her mind that Vincent's dark energy had caused the lightning, yet she felt powerless to stop him. *How can I face this man if I don't even know what he's after? For Christ's sake, it took me five years to stand up to Jake, and he nearly destroyed Crystal. There's a price to confronting him—a price I don't know if I can pay again.*

"I can't do this alone," Rose whispered in darkness. "I'm not strong enough—no one is."

You're not alone, a voice replied from the shadows. *Remember —we are always with you.*

Too fatigued to react, Rose let the words pass through her like a woman on the verge of a dream. She glanced around the room and spotted the raven tucked behind the wood stove in the pale moonlight. Chance? she whispered, unable to wrap her thoughts around the paradox of his presence. The raven hopped to her and jumped on her lap, nestling into a fold of the blanket.

Courage will come, he promised, *when you dare to believe. Close your eyes—be still.*

She allowed her lids to fall, more for the relief of sleep than to listen to the eerie chortlings of a bird. With all of her being, she didn't want to be Rose from Ophir Creek anymore —to bear the weight that had chased her for as long as she could remember, reducing her heart to ash. All she wanted was to stop the treadmill she'd created with Jake—a waste that haunted her still. "Can't I start over again?" she whispered. "Can't I ever clean this goddamn slate?"

Smoke filled her nose, this time laced with the smell of something musky and old, like roots embedded beneath an ancient tree. The warm complexity of the aroma embraced her, reminding her of a cozy nest, yet something about it infused the air with mystery. Rose opened her eyes. Rather than see the wood stove, a small turf fire burned before her within a blackened hearth. She was inside a humble, one-room cottage, its walls lined with speckled stones. Her daughter sat at a rustic, wood table in the center of the room, painting pictures by firelight. In a corner, Ailís O'Dannan was at a spinning wheel, quietly threading wool. Neither of them looked surprised to see her. They continued their tasks, humming the same lullaby. Rose scanned the cottage, where she saw a simple chair and a broom in the corner along with homemade toys on the floor created from scraps: a stuffed linen horse with straw for a tail, a yarn-haired doll with a tiny wool shawl, even a raven made of black flannel. But what really caught her eye were the colorful paintings on the walls. They were not depictions of natural calamities, like the thunder clouds and twisters that Crystal had smeared at home. Instead, they featured sunshine and rainbows with flowers reaching their leaves to the sky. Rose stared at the detailed brush strokes. Far from being the work of an angry or regressed child, these were the expressions of a thoughtful four-year-old. Their sheer vibrancy brought tears to her eyes.

"Crystal," she gasped, sitting down at the table next to her, "look what you've done!" She picked up a painting that sat drying on the table, awed by its confident design. The composition was balanced yet creative, colors arranged in a striking harmony that surprised her. She was about to voice her admiration when Ailís shot her a mindful look. In that moment, Rose recalled her caution to simply *be* with her daughter, so she resisted the urge to direct activity like she always did at home. She watched as Crystal made her own color choices, and for the first time since the accident, she didn't steer her to make hard-edged, geometric shapes outlined by the learning exercises. She simply observed her daughter's brush flowing with daring strokes.

"What are you drawing, sweetheart?" she asked, hoping not to disturb her process.

Crystal pointed to a woman she'd created beneath a rainbow. "I'm drawing you. Grandma says we have to make a better picture so you can heal."

"A better picture?"

"Yeah," Crystal replied, a bit impatient. "Where nothing's broken. See?" She tapped a red heart she'd painted on the woman's chest. "All the pieces are there."

Rose winced, troubled by her daughter's assessment, yet stunned that they were actually talking. Crystal was engaging in conversation with her—one that made sense! Choking up, she swept her fingers across her eyes to keep back tears. How many nights had she prayed for such a miracle? She knew the number—exactly two hundred and eight, each prayer murmured before midnight, when she pressed her hands together in the darkness and begged God to bring her baby back. Impulsively, she clutched her hands beneath the table to say a silent thank you to any spirit who might listen. This is all I want, she confessed, closing her eyes. Please let this moment last—I don't care if I ever go back. Please let me stay in a place where everything is whole.

Opening her eyes, Rose watched her daughter's nimble fingers dip her brush into small paint pots—the same ones she played with in Ophir Creek. How they got here was a mystery, but then, everything about the island left her befuddled. Scanning the painting on the table, she wondered why Crystal had portrayed her mother alone, without herself in the picture. Was it a statement? Didn't she see herself in the same world as her mommy? The thought made her heart lurch, and she pointed to the picture.

"What about you, sweetie? Aren't you going to be in the picture with me?" Rose held her breath.

Crystal rolled her eyes. "I already am. I'm the rainbow, silly. I color the way." She pointed at the washes of color she'd made and held up her bracelet, flashing vibrant hues around the cottage. Then she waved her wrist so that instead of fragments, the colors flowed in a stream. "See, Mommy? The colors were never really broken. Only you were."

How could a four-year-old perceive her so clearly? Crystal's words stung Rose's heart, launching a battle inside. *Can't she see how hard I try? I know I've got flaws, but doesn't Crystal realize that I want everything for her?* Gritting her teeth, it took all of her willpower not to become defensive. "Honey," Rose said tactfully, "why haven't we talked like this before? Why aren't you this way at home?"

Crystal set down her brush. She turned to her mother. "Because you're still not there."

Rose felt like her heart halted. She glanced at Ailís for support. The woman stopped spinning and stood from her chair. She walked to Rose with solemn strides and placed a hand on her shoulder.

"Home is now, my darling. Not in the past, buried in pain, or in the future, in your hope for change. This moment."

Stroking Rose's cheek, her fingers were warm and soft from the oils in the wool. "Love is our birthright, *mo stór.*" With that, she folded her arms around her, and Rose felt as if she'd been absorbed into downy wings. Rose closed her eyes, and the cottage disappeared—everything disappeared—except for the distinct feeling that for once in her life she was where she needed to be. The sensation was so foreign to her that she prayed it wouldn't fade. Rose settled her feet firm against the floor. She wasn't sure why—all she knew was that she yearned for something solid.

Soft, warm lips pressed against her cheek. When Rose opened her eyes, Crystal was a mere breath away. Trembling, she realized her daughter had kissed her. In spite of quaking hands, she wanted to grab Crystal, to hug her so close that their hearts might melt as they took synchronized breaths, never to be separate again. But something inside told her not to dictate the moment, to simply accept her daughter's tenderness as a gift. Reaching up, she caressed Crystal's forehead and stared into her eyes. They were no longer dead, but alive and flickering, bright as a candle. "Thank you, sweetheart," Rose whispered. It was then she noticed a small stack of papers at the edge of the table. They were Crystal's progress sheets from Ophir Creek. Ailís picked up the bundle and handed them to her, glancing at the fire.

Rose knew what she wanted—for her to destroy the sheets, like Chance had mentioned after the regression. The very thought disturbed her to the core. The exercises had been her security blanket—a paint-by-numbers plan created by experts that she could follow to pretend she had control over her daughter's destiny. If Crystal could draw a square or a diamond on cue, trace numbers and her ABCs, it meant she was going to be okay, didn't it? But if there were no longer progress sheets as a marker, what guarantee was left?

"Only faith," Ailís assured her. "Do you remember how to believe?"

Rose was speechless. She recalled how her mother's tender stories used to inspire her to think anything was possible, if she would only let the mountain breezes lift her imagination. There was joy in her heart then, a warm glow that came from knowing life offered love and delight, not just anger or fear. In those days, her world seemed to have a whole palette of colors. *When did I allow my heart to become so gray?* Rose flinched. She stared at the exercises in her hands, at the harsh, black and white graphs that made life easier to measure. *Am I strong enough to let these go? Can I love beyond the lines?*

She studied her daughter's painting, her bright colors and flowing shapes—something the learning exercises never accounted for. Leafing through the sheets, she stared at the hearth. "If I do this," she asked Ailís reluctantly, "will everything be all right?"

"My child," Ailís stroked the back of her head. "It already is."

Rose closed her eyes for a moment to allow the words to trickle inside her like long overdue rain. With all her courage, she got up from the table and went to the hearth. Clenching her teeth, she unfolded her fingers to let the sheets drop into the fire. All at once she had a sensation of free-falling, letting go of any hold on her future. Unlike the adrenaline she used to experience with Jake—those rushes of emotion that twisted her heart into knots—Rose felt strangely released, a hidden weight lifting from her shoulders. The pages crackled into flames, and the cottage door creaked open, sending a cool gust across the room that made the hearth ashes flutter. Chance appeared in the doorway, his broad shoulders filling the entire frame. His cheeks were ruddy and his hair was windswept from the blustery night. Beneath his long coat, he wore a fisherman's sweater, the same ivory color as the wool Ailís had been spinning. Ailís patted Rose's hand.

"Time to let the little one be for now, *a thaisce*. I'll tuck her into bed." She pointed to a small cot with a blanket in the back of the room. "You have work to do."

"Work?" Rose's voice trembled.

Chance stared at the pages in the fireplace that had wrinkled into cinders. Nodding at Rose, he held out his hand. She knew if she took it, he would lead her somewhere, but she feared where that might be. "It's all right," his voice was softly resonant with swells of the sea, "I'll give you my coat."

He stepped into the cottage and draped his coat over her shoulders, which smelled moist and fragrant from the ocean. Then he wrapped his large hand over hers and led her outside to where turf met sand. The beach was washed silver in the moonlight, with stars glinting over dark waves. Together, they looked up at the night sky and the broad, twinkling canopy of constellations. To Rose, they appeared limitless, a sea of lights she remembered gazing at as a little girl in Ophir Creek. Back then, her mother used to claim that stars flickered whenever a fairy went by. Don't you see them? she would say. The light shimmers through their wings.

Rose blinked, wondering if it was possible to entertain such notions as an adult. Wondering, too, if she could ever allow her heart to be as open as it was then, as open as Crystal's seemed now. Perhaps she'd become too corroded by time, by the wrong company, by her own failures. She shifted her feet on the turf, taking in the scent of the ocean as it broke over rocks. Chance's warm fingers closed tighter over hers.

"Do you really want a clean slate?" he whispered, his challenge rising in her ear as his hand ran up her arm to clench her shoulder. His grip felt firm—even forceful. "Then for God's sake, Rose, recognize when you've finally got one."

She shuddered, pulling the coat tighter around herself. Under the moonlight, Chance measured the puzzled look in her eyes.

"Oh Rose," he said impatiently, "don't you know? Love is all around you." He closed his large arms around her waist and drew her into his chest. Instead of being startled, Rose felt like she'd slipped into a private sanctuary—as though she'd been wandering aimlessly for years, windblown by fierce rainstorms, only to discover a calm, protected place to settle, like a nest. Rose leaned into the sturdiness of his embrace, laying her cheek against his hard shoulder, made soft by the pillowy texture of his sweater. The wool fibers had the same smell of the cottage: traces of cooking spices and peat smoke, along with something warm and inviting—perhaps the tender essence of belonging itself. Rose inhaled deeply, holding her breath for as long as she could bear. She wanted to cling to that scent forever, to bottle it if she could. It was a smell reminiscent of her childhood in the mountains, when her mother was still alive. It was the aroma of feeling *safe*.

Chance brushed his lips against the moist skin of her cheek. But then his mouth sought hers with a boldness that shook her. Suddenly, Rose felt dissolved into a golden pool, as vast as time itself. This was not the stolen kiss of a renegade, but the rightful stake of a soul guardian—a man who knew her inside and out, who had the fortitude to wait centuries for what he wanted, if that's what it took. And who would never, ever let go once he found her. Rose understood that in an instant, as sure as her feet were planted in the turf.

"Chance," her lips swept his cheeks, his eyebrows, his ears. For a second, she pulled back and gazed at his disheveled hair that glinted silver in the moonlight, into his eyes that reflected a hunger as great as the sea. This time, it was her turn to challenge. "Is this really love, or just another strange dream?"

He cocked his head slightly, the way ravens do. Then his eyes poured over her face as if determined to embrace her soul. Gently, he ran his hand along a lock on her forehead and down her temple, easing his fingers around her chin and up her cheek to complete a circle. For a moment, Rose wondered if he was trying to read her, in the same way he used to examine tree rings deep in the forest. Or perhaps he could see their future somehow, like her great-great grandmother who once peered into teacups. Chance leaned his forehead against hers, cradling her cheekbones in his hands. Drawing a deep breath, he sealed their lips—not just for a moment in the moonlight, but until the two of them burned inside for lack of air.

"My darling," he broke away, gasping. "Don't you realize dreams are the songs our souls sing to find their way home? I have loved you beyond what time can measure." For once, she knew it wasn't a slick line or gimmick, dropped at just the right moment to prey on her hopes or fears. It was a promise as enduring as the sand and sea itself.

Rose had never seen a man like this, certainly not her father. She searched his face beneath the stars, the way his eyes could look soft yet concerned at the same time. Yes, he was a dreamer like her, but underneath, his heart was solid like the granite pillars that reached for the sky on Rook Ridge. For the first time in her life, Rose realized she was standing with a man who wouldn't leave. Impulsively, she kissed his forehead, his cheeks, his lips—relishing the salty spray that clung to his skin, the sweet yet earthy aftertaste that lingered on her tongue. She smiled, realizing he tasted like—*home*. Running her hands through his hair, she threaded her fingers through his cowlicks.

"I love you, Chance—do you hear me?" She clutched his temples, swiping another kiss that filled her soul to the brim. "Why did it take so long for me to find you?"

"Because you had to find yourself first," Chance replied, his lips warm over her cheeks. He lifted his gaze to the silhouette of a mountain in the distance, backlit by the moon. It loomed darkly before them like a blockade. Grabbing both her hands, his grip was so firm it was nearly painful. "Rose, do you understand why that man tried to seduce you—then intimidate you?" He spread out his fingers over hers like wings. "He wants to keep my body, to stop you from sending him back."

"Me?"

"You have the power—it says so in the diary. Haven't you noticed how he soaks off your energy? The hail, the thunder storms, the wind? He has nothing by himself, only what he can steal from you. But if you don't make the switch by Halloween, you'll have to wait twenty years for another blue moon."

Chance stared at his feet, lingering for a moment over the moonlit sand before he shook his head. "Rose," he paused, "I don't know what will happen to me when you send him back."

His words were a sword slicing into her heart. Her mind began to race through possibilities. Perhaps a soul exchange might leave him crazy again, "fairy struck" as the townspeople called him—a mountain man who wandered the woods in circles. Or worse, maybe the shock of the transition would extinguish his life. Rose wove trembling fingers through his, gripping him firm.

"I don't care what your mental state is, Chance!" she declared. "As long as I have your soul. I'm not giving you up—not ever." She scanned the roiling sea that tried in vain to swallow the shore. "Why don't we just stay on the island?" she urged. "Crystal is healthy here, and you—you're normal. Everything's perfect now. We could do this—we could make it work!" She seized his face and kissed him with a vehemence that shocked her, as if she hoped she could seal his heart to hers.

Chance pulled away and gently rested his finger to her lips. "Because, my love," his deep was voice tinged with sadness and the thunder of the ocean breaking over rocks, "we'd always remain 'twixt."

He gazed at the horizon where the dark expanse of the sea met the sky. "Don't you understand? That's what Ailís has been trying to show you all along, to help you overcome. No one can live in twilight forever. Regardless of what the legend says, there comes a time when you have to claim a home for yourself. That moment is now, Rose. And to do it, you need to heal."

"But I'm fine!" she replied. "And Crystal's fine—you saw her."

"Then where else has your heart been bruised and broken? Who makes you hurt so much inside you try not to think of her, or even utter her name?"

Rose shrugged. "I don't know what you mean."

"As I recall, she's not on speaking terms with you."

A burning sensation overtook Rose's cheeks. He meant Laurel.

Chance cupped her face in his hands, gazing into her eyes with an alarm that startled her. "Listen to me, Rose," he softly stroked her cheeks with his thumbs, "you need all the support you can get to face him—and Laurel is the key. Go see her in Boise. Be big enough to mend your fences for a change. And take the diary with you. Laurel knows far more about those drawings than she lets on."

18

A black scar stretched over a hillside beside the highway. A thick layer of smoke pressed down on the charred pines, stripped bare of their needles. Remnants of the recent forest fire made Rose wince as she drove her truck along the mountain road. It was as if Vincent had left his calling card for everyone to see—one of destruction and waste, blistered hopes and dreams. Rose gripped the steering wheel tighter, stroking the diary in her lap with her free hand. She remembered how much Laurel hated the book, how it represented everything she thought was wrong with their family. "All dreams and no drive," Laurel used to say bitterly, whenever she laid eyes on it. But as Rose gazed over the scorched landscape, she felt deeply compelled to contact her sister. If Laurel knew how to comprehend the diary's symbols, as Chance suggested, then a trip to see her was more than justified—it might be the only hope she had left.

Amy had offered to babysit Crystal for the day, promising to keep her safe from Vincent as she eyed a shotgun in the corner of the shop. So, in spite of her trepidation, Rose departed after the morning coffee rush to make the one-hour descent to Boise. She knew she was taking a big risk, particularly since her visit was unannounced. But she feared if she told Laurel she was coming, her sister might barricade the door—there was no telling how long she could bear a grudge. *After all, the last time she saw me,* Rose thought, *she got pelted by hail and slapped in the face. And now I expect her to welcome me with open arms?*

Rose heaved a sigh, revisiting Amy's words before she left: "Why don't you just ask Ailís what the symbols in the diary mean? Go into a trance and listen to what she says about getting rid of Jake's spirit? Then you won't have to deal with Laurel."

"If Ailís had wanted me to know, don't you think she would've said so by now?" Rose had replied, her voice skittish. "Or mentioned something murky, like 'The power lies within'?"

The truth was, of course she'd asked Ailís! Rose had gotten down on bended knees while Crystal was asleep and begged with all her heart for answers. In her despair, she didn't float to the island on a winsome breeze where ready solutions were etched into clouds. Soaked in tears, all she experienced was a peculiar warmth spreading over her like a wool shawl had been wrapped around her shoulders. When she glanced up, Ailís was nowhere in sight. The room was empty, but for the sound of her daughter's breaths in the night and the faint smell of wild roses, scented by the sea. Rose bowed her head, shaking. Deep inside, she suspected Chance was right about her need for healing. No amount of fairy diaries or magic potions could shore up the cracks that had been splitting at her heart for years. If it was true she had to be whole in order to forge the courage to face Jake, like Chance had said, then ready or not, she knew it was high time to repair her life.

And that meant facing Laurel.

Rose shifted her truck into higher gear, speeding down the highway that sloped toward the low foothills of Boise. Up ahead, the landscape became uncomplicated and treeless, covered in dry, blanched grass. Rolling past gas stations and strip malls that began to litter the roadside, there were no mountain vistas or thick forests to gaze at anymore—only crisp houses with white picket fences and manicured lawns that defied the arid landscape. Rose wondered how Laurel could stand to live in such a controlled environment after growing up in the lush wildness of their mountain home. When she turned onto the lane of Laurel's subdivision, it all became clear. A sign at the entrance said *Sunny Retreat Estates: For the Life of Your Design.*

That's *so* Laurel, Rose sighed—to live on a street that holds no surprises, where each house on the block looks the same as any other, with shrubs trimmed neatly in a row. She checked the address she'd left on the dashboard and navigated her truck toward Laurel's stately, Tudor home, careful to parallel park on the road. Rose didn't dare enter Laurel's driveway for fear that her sister might spot her too soon and order her to leave. It would be easier to surprise her at the door, even if she did refuse to open it. With Laurel, ambush was better than etiquette, because at least then Rose might get a word in before Laurel called the cops.

Heart thumping, Rose cut the engine. She hopped from the truck and walked to Laurel's door, noticing the perfect splashes of orange mums that lined the driveway, the only homage to the autumn season. The homeowner's association probably bans decorations, Rose thought, shaking her head. Sucking up a deep breath, she was about to knock when the door swung open wide with enough force to create a draft. Laurel stood with the screen door between them like a blockade. Hands on her hips, she looked Rose up and down, paying particular attention to her soiled hiking boots.

"What?" she demanded.

Rose was lost for words. How could she explain her predicament in a sentence or two? Her gaze sank to her feet, reminding her of junior high when she got caught with cigarettes in the bathroom, and she had to get Laurel's signature on a release form before she returned to class. Words had failed her then, too, but as soon as Laurel spotted the school letterhead and smelled the smoke in her hair, she'd guessed what happened. Will the smoke of my failures betray me this time, too? Rose wondered. Can she sense the mess I've made with yet another man from Ophir Creek?

Without speaking, Laurel edged open the screen door and scrutinized Rose's face. She pursed her lips and shook her head. "Man trouble again," she sniffed like was the broken record of her sister's life.

Rose's breath hitched. For a woman who roundly dismissed psychic gifts, Laurel's powers of observation bordered on spooky. Despite the years of tension between them, in that moment Rose felt oddly less defensive than usual in her sister's presence. It was comforting to be near a person who knew her so well that all she had to do to read her problems was gaze into her eyes. After everything they'd been through, they still had a history together. Wasn't that worth something?

Rose shuffled her boots. Before she'd arrived, she'd rehearsed several versions in her head to justify her dilemma. Now, they slipped from her mind like leaves down a river. Silently, she pulled out the diary from her pocket and rubbed it between her hands.

"Help me," she said. "Please—"

Laurel's jaw tightened, lips pressing into a line. She folded her arms to appraise her sister, stiff as a pillar. Nevertheless, Rose thought she saw her steely eyes soften a little.

"I need you," Rose whispered.

To her amazement, Laurel gestured for her to step inside. She'd never entered Laurel's new house before—the one she'd bragged about in letters for a year. Rose moved over the threshold into the plush living room, complete with a cascading chandelier, gold velvet upholstery and matching brocade curtains. If she didn't know better, she would have sworn it was a hotel lobby.

"Take off those filthy boots," Laurel ordered with the same tone from their teen years in Ophir Creek. Rose couldn't help smiling a little at her sister's bossiness. As she unlaced her boots and let her stocking feet sink into the downy, white carpet, she was struck by how pristine everything in the house appeared. Nothing suggested anyone else lived here—no jacket draped over a chair or newspaper loosely folded on a table. Not even another pair of shoes by the door. The house appeared hollow, a shell waiting for their voices to echo off walls.

"Would you like a cup of tea," Laurel issued a command, not a question. Rose knew she had no choice—Laurel would get it for her regardless of her reply. She sat down on a chair, aware her sister probably just wanted to show off her newest china. When Laurel returned with an ivory teacup rimmed in gold, it took everything Rose had not to roll her eyes. For Christ's sake, she thought, it's ten thirty in the morning—do we really need fine porcelain at this hour? Nevertheless, she accepted the cup graciously, setting the diary down on her lap.

Taking a sip, Rose was disturbed by an unwelcome reflection that appeared in her cup. It was Tom, Laurel's portly husband, with an auburn-haired woman in a tropical location, like Hawaii or perhaps Mexico. They were walking hand-in-hand on a beach at sunset. Rose diverted her gaze, hoping Laurel didn't notice her discomfort. When they were little, she and Laurel used to play endless guessing games—a contest Rose always won if she had a glass of liquid nearby. Soon, Laurel figured out her sister had a special gift, just like her stepmother, and she refused to play the game anymore. But that didn't mean Laurel had forgotten anything. Her competitive streak made her keep track of other people's talents, particularly if they'd ever dared to show her up.

Laurel sat down on a sofa across from Rose and narrowed her eyes, suspecting what her sister might have seen. Her gaze became so piercing Rose's forehead broke into a sweat. Laurel crossed her legs and pressed her taupe wool skirt flat over her knees, then folded her hands onto her lap.

"Don't try to push your mumbo jumbo on me," she

warned in a preemptive strike. "I saw you peer into that teacup. I know what's going through your mind. A blind person could tell you Tom's not here. He's—on a business trip." Laurel's voice sounded flintier than usual. "Of course, he's always on a business trip, right? We have to afford a house like this somehow." She ran her hand through her pale, cropped hair. "So what is it you came to tell me, Rosie? And why on earth did you drag that with you?" She pointed to the diary on her sister's lap.

Rose gripped the book tighter, as stuck for words as she'd been on the porch. In spite of her unease, she found it impossible to dwell on herself and her own problems for once, no matter how pressing and bizarre they seemed. Gazing at her sister's stoic face, pinched at the edges from strain, her heart wedged open a little. All she could think of was the shame and grief Laurel must feel, knowing full well that her husband was cheating. Her sister was far too sharp for the convenience of denial—surely she'd seen the credit card charges from exotic places, or smelled an unfamiliar fragrance on his clothes and skin. Shifting in her seat, she stroked the diary with her fingers. To her way of thinking, Laurel had always been the perfect one who unerringly made the right choices, regardless of the eccentric influence of their family. It had never occurred to Rose that behind Laurel's manicured demeanor was a person who could lose her way in the thunderstorms of life. That she was, in fact, as fragile and vulnerable as any other girl who came from Ophir Creek.

Rather than answer her sister's question, Rose closed her eyes for a moment and prayed. When she glanced up, she caught the lonely ache in Laurel's eyes, the lines of worry that creased her forehead, and it made her wince. Had that pain been there all along, since our father left, and I simply never noticed? Or is this new hurt particularly raw?

To Rose's surprise, tears welled in Laurel's eyes, even as she straightened her back and lifted her chin to a more regal position. Blinking quickly, she turned from Rose, her gaze resting on a picture of Tom on an end table. In the photo, Tom appeared to be accepting an award. His grin was broad and there was a poised, auburn-haired woman behind him who smiled as if she'd been vindicated. Laurel darted her eyes.

"Well," she muttered, her voice crackling, "guess you're not the only one with man troubles. Must run in the family."

Rose's heart surged. She wanted to leap from her chair and hug Laurel, to let her cry on her shoulder and be the kind of sister who could be an anchor for once, instead of the habitual washout. But something inside reminded her that her sister prized dignity above all things, and her desire to hug her might be a selfish act. Let her be, Rose decided gracefully—give her the space to unravel her own heart. In an unusual moment of restraint, she forced herself to remain in her chair, allowing her sister's feelings to run their course.

Laurel turned over the photo on the table and brought out a tissue from her pocket. Smiling defiantly, she swept it across her face, lashes fluttering as though she'd merely gotten lint caught in her eyes, not tears. She stuffed the tissue back into her skirt.

"Y-You know," Laurel began, then hesitated. Rose was surprised to hear her falter over words. "The other day, I came to a realization after that hail storm. While I was unconscious, I dreamed I was transported to another place." She drew a long breath as if gathering strength. "It was an island I'd never seen before. And there everything became clear to me. That's when I made the decision to try a separation from Tom."

She focused on her patent leather shoes. Rose could tell Laurel was fighting back more tears. "I just couldn't be a potato wife anymore. I mean, my God, did you know I actually used to go with him to conferences?" She glanced at a row of brass plaques on the wall, each one etched with the image of a tuber. "Russet Burbank, Yukon Gold, Dakota Pearl —Christ, I can name every variety by heart." She shook her head. "I hated those meetings and cocktail parties. You never met any real friends—everyone was just a stepping stone for Tom's career. Including me, I guess. Somehow, I thought if I did everything perfectly, it would make our lives better. But it didn't."

Laurel stared at Rose with red-rimmed eyes, gaze unwavering, daring her sister not to feel sorry for her. "I know you might not believe this, but that was the reason why I tried to get Crystal into a program. I just wanted to help, to make everything right for once—maybe even create a fresh start between us. That's why I kept paying the electric bill on Dad's old place all those years. Because I hoped you might come back. I always felt guilty, you know."

"Guilty? About what?" Rose asked, floored. Ever since their father had left, there was no doubt in her mind that her sister had tried to do everything for her—even if it was with a severe hand.

"Because I let you run off with Jake," Laurel confessed. "A lost, motherless young woman, with a man who had crash and burn written all over him. Anyone could predict how that was going to end up. Why'd you do it, Rosie? Why on earth did you trust him?"

Rose's cheeks grew hot. She'd never considered how much pain her absence had caused her sister, adding to the depth of her grief and those rows on her forehead. Squirming in her chair, she searched her heart for an answer to the question that had plagued her for years. I took off with him because he was handsome. Because he made me feel more alive. Because he promised me the stars. These were the lies she'd always told herself, the ones she repeated like a recording in her mind to avoid thinking about it for five long, lonely years. Buried in a dusty corner of her heart, she knew those rationales weren't even close to the truth. She glanced at Laurel, envying her sister's courage, the way she'd always confronted her fears head-on. Clutching the diary in her lap, she tried to absorb a bit of solace.

"I did it because—because I'd lost hope," Rose confessed, "and that scared the hell out of me." It was the first time she'd admitted the real reason to herself, let alone to anyone else. "I guess I never thought I had the power to change my own life, to make anything truly better. Running away was easier than facing the fact that I was going nowhere. The thing is, if it hadn't been Jake, it would have been somebody just like him. As long as he was charming and had fast wheels. Of course, I only managed to make things worse."

"What do you mean? You have a daughter now."

Rose caught the longing in her sister's eyes. She'd never considered before that Laurel might really have wanted a child —someone who could love her back in a marriage that had gone stale. Was she unable to conceive? Or was Tom simply not around enough to father a family? Rose didn't have the heart to ask. "Laurel," she asked nervously, "do you seriously believe Crystal needs a residential program?"

"Not anymore," Laurel glanced at the diary on Rose's lap, weighing her thoughts. "I know this sounds strange," she paused to choose her words carefully, "but during that hail storm, your daughter appeared to me while I was knocked out. She was on the misty island with a woman who looked a lot like your mother."

Laurel clenched her hands together, and Rose could tell she was struggling inside. "The woman told me I didn't need to be afraid anymore. Everything would fall into place if I would just let go—allow things to run their course."

Her face softened a little. "Then Crystal took me by the hand and showed me her potato plants, how she waters and sings to them, and they bear fruit in their own time. I know it might seem crazy, but afterwards, I felt like Crystal had touched me somehow." She glanced up at Rose with a sincere gaze. "You know, it made me wonder if she's fine in her own way. I just didn't know how to see it before."

Stunned, Rose tried to contain the lump swelling in her throat. Her mind reeled, unable to reconcile the two worlds that kept colliding on her—one of ordinary flesh and blood, and the other of misty island visions and dreams. Speechless, she watched Laurel open a drawer inside her coffee table and pull out a photo.

"In my dream, your daughter gave me this picture." Laurel cradled the photo in her hands. "When I came home later that day, I found it on my kitchen table. About scared me to death —I have no idea how it got there."

Laurel patted the sofa cushion next to her. "Here, Rosie," she lifted her eyes with a welcoming glance. "Come see."

Cautious, Rose stepped to the sofa to sit down beside her, setting the diary on her knees. She felt awkward with Laurel's warm body next to hers, the two of them sitting quietly in the morning light—like when they were children and used to sleep in the same bed until her mother called them for breakfast. They hadn't been this close in years. Yet everything was different this time. Rose used to think she knew Laurel, the one who always insisted that life be a straight line, no room for dawdling or daydreams. Now, her sister was a paradox—someone who actually listened to a vision. How can this be the same person who refused to believe in fairy gifts? Rose wondered. Who used to say my mother was moonstruck?

Laurel grasped Rose's hand, holding up the snapshot for her to see. It featured the two of them as little girls alongside Rose's mother. Rose didn't recall seeing the photo before, or any others like it for that matter. Her family rarely spent money on film processing, and sometimes their lack of memorabilia made her feel historyless, with only her mother's stories and the O'Dannan legend to cling to. She studied the snapshot of their past where she and Laurel wore frilly dresses with homemade wings, sprinkled with glitter. They held up jack-o-lanterns, proud that they'd carved them for Halloween. In the sky were tints of red and blue and yellow, as if someone had dribbled watercolors onto the photo by accident. What struck her most was the smile on Laurel's face—she grinned from ear to ear. Rose had never seen her so happy.

"I don't know if you remember this," Laurel continued,

"but your mother used to live for Halloween, like it was Christmas or something. She called it the Celtic new year."

Laurel laughed a little, staring at the woman in the photo with the embroidered peasant blouse and frayed bell bottom jeans, a string of homemade beads around her neck. Her long, black hair with wisps of gray was braided with feathers, and her expression appeared warm and generous. "God, she was kooky," Laurel smiled. "She had this silly notion that Halloween was a time when the veil was thinnest between worlds, and if you wanted, you could contact fairies or the departed. Do you remember how she made us go on a fairy hunt that afternoon?" Laurel tapped the photo. "We actually found an old teacup in the woods. She claimed it was the fairies' blessing."

Laurel's eyes became misty, and she gently slipped her arm around Rose's elbow, drawing her close as though they were links in a chain. She gave her arm a squeeze, and Rose suddenly realized that all along, Laurel must have loved her mother as much as she did. She probably criticized her over the years because she was devastated by her loss. Rose understood the reaction too well—at least anger felt stronger than crumbling inside. No one else brought so much wonder to their lives, with a sense of imagination and whimsy that was always laced with wisdom. Rose gazed at her mother in the photo. Her eyes were sparkled and her mouth was slightly open, as though she were about to say something important when the picture was taken—something that had been lost through time. She wove her fingers through her sister's hand, pressing them warmly against her palm.

Laurel leaned her head onto her shoulder. "Rosie," she whispered, "why did she have to leave us?"

Rose turned and hugged her tightly, knowing it was one of those mysteries, like the island, that might require an eternity for an answer—if mere mortals could ever access such knowledge. She swayed with her sister in her arms, relishing the soft warmth of her hair, cheeks that were nearly as smooth as Crystal's. All she could do was glance at the photo again, her heart wishing she could reach through the picture. Grasping the photo from Laurel, she turned it over to see if it might have a date. She found an inscription in her mother's hand: *To my darlings. We will be with you.*

Goose bumps alighted on her neck. She cupped her sister's face. "She didn't leave," Rose said, showing her the back of the photo, "we just stopped listening." She held up the diary. "Laurel, since you were older, I know you remember more of what mother used to say—you know, about the diary and the quilt patches, how they all had special meaning."

Laurel nodded, a bit confused.

"I need you to show me how to read this." She stared at the book in her lap. "He's back, Laurel."

Her sister squinted. "Who's back?"

"Jake," Rose said. "And you've got to help me get rid of him."

19

A dark line of birds led the way up to the mountains. Gazing out the windshield of the truck, Rose steadied her eyes on the winding road and tried to ignore them, anxious over what such an omen might mean. Beside her, Laurel wriggled uncomfortably on the seat, avoiding the rips in the old leather cushion. She'd never ridden in Rose's truck before, and she was careful not to rest her feet near the broken butter cookies on the floor. Brushing crumbs from the dashboard, Laurel stared through the windshield at the row of birds and cleared her throat.

"Rosie, do you *really* expect me to believe you conjured up Jake from the dead?"

"It wasn't on purpose!" Rose was still amazed her sister had agreed to go home with her. "I had a bad birthday, remember? You came to the shop and we got into a fight. When Amy and I got tipsy later, things just happened. You know how she is with a candle and a few spells—"

"Honey," Laurel cut in, "you're starting to resemble Fannie Thistlewaite. Do you have any idea how crazy this sounds?"

Not half as crazy as falling in love with a man who moonlights as a raven, Rose thought, gliding her fingers over the steering wheel. She'd only filled Laurel in on half of the story—the part that most required her help. Rose didn't have the nerve to tell her about Chance. Her heart was too raw and their love seemed too precarious—she feared their bond might somehow evaporate if she mentioned it. After all, he'd only kissed her in shadows and told her he loved her on the island. What if, in her normal waking world, the same rules didn't apply? Perhaps a romance like that was only for fairy realms and twilight, old Irish cottages where hearth fires still burned. Not in the broad daylight of Idaho.

"I thought you said you were ready to be open minded," Rose scolded Laurel. "You saw the island, too, remember? Why would either one of us make this stuff up?"

"Because we're lonely and unstable." Laurel clenched her hands. "Sorry—it's just that, well, this is all new to me. I'm not like you and your mother."

"Believe me, it's a stretch for both of us." Rose lifted her gaze, unable to ignore the birds any longer. She poked a finger at the windshield. "Laurel, is it my imagination, or are those birds leading us back to Ophir Creek?"

Her sister's eyebrows creased. She studied the sky with a brooding look on her face. "He loves you, doesn't he?"

"Who?" Rose's temples began to pound.

Laurel's eyes followed the birds as their line swayed with the curve of the road. "The raven man."

"You saw *him*, too?" Rose set her hand on her shoulder.

She jiggled it harder than she meant to. "What did he tell you?"

"That you care about me." Laurel was quiet for a moment. "He said the reason we fight so much is because we're afraid to admit that to each other. If I didn't know better, Rosie, I'd say that was him leading that line of birds. Looks like he's been guarding you for a very long time."

Tears came to Rose's eyes. She didn't know if she could bear to hear any more. "Laurel, have we lost our minds?"

Laurel reached up and curled Rose's fingers inside hers. "I'm so jealous," she whispered.

"Of what?"

Laurel squeezed her hand. "He told me he'd do anything for you. And from the look in his eyes, I got the impression he'd give his life if that's what it took to fix things." She stared down at her skirt. "I didn't mention this before, but he was the one who escorted me in my dream to the island through the mist, changing shape as he went. It was strange, like he was, well—"

"Twixt?"

"Yes, that's it." Laurel gazed at her sister. "Oh Rosie, if we're not crazy, if any of this is real—and a man can love you that much across time and space—well, that's the stuff dreams are made of. I wouldn't even begin to know how that feels."

Laurel let go of her hand and picked up the diary between them on the truck seat. Flipping through the pages, she hesitated at an image of a gold nugget with a red heart at its center, carefully drawn in ink and filled with faded watercolors. She held up the book to show her sister. "Rosie," she said with surprising firmness, using the same tone she used to scold her with as a teenager, "to be truly loved is a precious gift. I don't care anymore where it comes from—it deserves to be cherished for as long as it lasts." She set the book down carefully on her lap, rubbing the empty place on her finger where her wedding band used to be. "Whatever you do," her voice cracked a little, "don't blow it."

When Rose and Laurel rolled up to the shop, Amy was standing on the porch alongside Crystal, both of them wearing wings. Rose could tell the wings had been created from cardboard and craft glitter, fastened onto their bodies with elastic. Laurel glanced at Rose like her business partner had been doing drugs.

Amy shimmied her shoulders to make the wings flutter. "It's good for business!" she proclaimed, holding up a Rainbow's End brochure. She pointed to the fairy on the cover. "With the legend and all, everyone wants to see a little magic this time of year."

"Right, magic." Rose stepped out of the truck and shuddered when she noticed the line of birds that had led the way home now made a loose circle over the town square. Their shadows formed a dark ring on the dry grass before it slowly dissipated. Feeling edgy, she grabbed Crystal's hand and opened the front door. Amy slipped in ahead of her, careful not to brush her wings against the threshold.

"A boy scout troop came through for lunch." Amy pointed to the picks and pans spread on the floor. "You'd be so proud of me," she swished the hem of her floaty skirt, "after they ate sandwiches, I actually gave them a panning demonstration like

I knew what I was doing. It went okay, considering it must be the first time they saw a grown-up wear wings."

"Wouldn't bet on it in this town," Laurel sniffed.

Rose rolled her eyes and picked up Crystal, cautious not to crumple her wings. She smiled at how adorable she looked, her blonde hair complementing the gold glitter. For a second, she imagined how the two of them might look if they wore wings for Halloween, like she and her sister had done in Laurel's photo. They could put on dresses with flowers and hike to the ridge for a fairy hunt, the way she used to do with her mother. The thought made shivers run down her spine— she hadn't realized it at the time, but her mother had been doing far more than playing games. She was trying to teach them things, lessons that might help them get through times like this. A broken circle of ravens means change is coming— never step into a fairy ring unless you know what you want— only true love leads to gold. In those days, such words sounded like nonsense, catchy riddles to keep two little girls amused. Now, they were still riddles, but Rose viewed them in a more serious light. Her face grew stern.

"Amy, Laurel's come all the way from Boise to help us with, well, our dilemma. She's going to try to translate the diary."

"Really?" Amy's wings trembled.

Laurel nodded with a somber look, daunted by the task. She stepped over to a cafe table and set the diary down, opening up the delicate pages. Rose carried Crystal to her play area and placed her on a chair next to her construction paper and crayons. When she returned, Laurel pointed at a picture of a wheel.

"The way I remember it," Laurel circled the wheel with

her finger, "your mother claimed these pictures are a kind of code, which are meant to be passed down as knowledge through generations. Each symbol has a correlation in reality, but it's *different* than what most of us understand. It's the reality of the 'twixt—those who are forced to straddle two worlds."

"Two worlds?" Amy looked intrigued.

"Yes." Laurel had a strained expression on her face that Rose didn't quite understand. "The twilight realm of the Tuatha de Dannan and the ordinary life around us. Rosie's mother said for the 'twixt, nothing is ordinary." She glanced out the window at the ridge that loomed over the small, western town. "On certain dates of the year, your mother would hike to the top of Rook Ridge at dusk to pay homage to the seasons. Like Beltane in May or Samhain in October. She called them 'spirit nights,' those shifts between spring and summer, fall and winter, when she thought fairy powers were more accessible. Somehow, it gave her a kind of sustenance, as if the wind and rocks and trees nourished her. She always came back radiant, talking about the energy behind the moon and how time moves in circles."

Rose recalled how lively her mother always seemed when she returned, wearing her black coat of feathers, her head full of ideas for how her daughters could celebrate the seasons. She had an amazing way of turning everything into play, imparting her gentle wisdom with songs and games. Remembering her made Rose's heart feel full, and she could almost hear her mother's voice, somewhere between the rays of daylight and shadows in the shop. But each time she wanted to pin down the words they eluded her like dandelions seeds on a breeze.

Laurel tapped her arm to bring her to attention. She pointed at the spokes on the wheel in the diary. "These lines represent winter, spring, summer and fall." She flipped to another portion of the book. "The diary is divided into parts —each one belongs to a season and has recipes that go with it." Laurel gazed at a page filled with acorns and leaves, then turned to a picture of a fire burning in a hearth. Beside it were drawings of potatoes and onions, a brown dairy cow. "See? This whole section is for autumn. The recipe here is for Champ—mashed potatoes with milk and onions. It's supposed to bring harmony and warmth to the home." She flipped to the next page, featuring a cake with charms beside it. "And this is Barmbrack cake. Do you remember that one? Your mother used to make it for Halloween. It has dried fruit, and she'd put small charms inside to surprise us."

Laurel's eyes twinkled. "It was the most enchanting game. If you found a coin, in the coming year you'd prosper. A thimble meant you'd be a spinster, and a ring hinted you'd be married soon." Her gaze shifted to her left hand, dimming a little. "But that's not the same thing as finding true love. For that, you'd need to uncover a gold heart."

Laurel glanced up at Rose. "And this," she tapped the page, "well, this is the spooky part."

Drawings of dark storm clouds over a rainbow circle were featured on the paper. The clouds had jagged edges in the middle, like they'd been torn apart. "On Halloween night, or Samhain," Laurel continued, "your mother claimed the veil between this world and the next is as thin as a cobweb. It's the start of the Celtic new year, a time outside of time, when you can contact the dead, predict the future, and—"

"Do a soul exchange?" Goose bumps prickled Rose's skin. "How do you make that happen?"

Laurel became quiet. She got up and walked to the back bedroom and brought out the family quilt. On it was a patch just like the one in the diary, with storm clouds appliquéd in gray flannel and a circle below them embroidered in colorful chain stitches. Rubbing the patch between her fingers, she compared it to the drawing in the diary. Laurel's eyes grew moist. "I—I'm not sure," she stammered. "This is all over my head."

"How about if we use a lightning rod for a soul exchange?" Amy trotted to a corner and picked up a wrought-iron pole with a star on top, dipping it into the air like a metal wand. "Belle Crawford sold this to me this morning for five bucks. She said it used to be on one of her lover's cabins—in this life, not a past one."

She touched her finger to the star's sharp edge. "Ouch! Anyway, we could take it to the top of Rook Ridge, and maybe Rose could use her emotions to get the storm clouds going. If we poked her with this star, she might even get fiery enough for a really big thunderhead! All we'd have to do is lure Vincent up there, make sure he stands next to the rod when lightning strikes, and ZOWIE!" "No more Captain of Darkness."

Rose and Laurel regarded her with skepticism. "Okay, if that doesn't work," Amy offered, "Larry has a battery-operated generator that I've heard can spark electricity. I don't know much about physics, but we can use all the help we can get, right?" She pointed the lightning rod at the women and jabbed it in air. "Maybe we could give Vincent a nasty zapping that will send him packing—"

"Amy," Rose sighed, "we haven't had the best of luck with your ideas lately. And besides, there'll be hundreds of gold seekers on the ridge during the blue moon. We can't afford to zap the wrong person."

"But don't you see?" Amy pressed. "All we have to do is show up on Rook Ridge, and pow! Everything will come full circle. Just like the legend of Corvine O'Dannan."

"But the legend ended in *tragedy*." Rose shivered as she studied the storm clouds on the diary page.

"Well," Amy clasped her hands, making her charm bracelet dance, "how about a new potato spell? We could correct the situation by focusing on reversals! I learned this at the commune—first, you repeat every step you did, only backwards…"

Rose couldn't help tuning out Amy's enthusiasm for her newest idea, her gaze drifting to the Magpie Saloon. Inside, a murky silhouette stirred about the bar. She knew it was Vincent because of the effortless grace in his movement, the way his presence, even in shadows, seemed to dominate the building. Hugging her arms, she feared what might preoccupy him in mid-afternoon, what new scheme he was planning this time. In that moment, the grass on the town square darkened to the color of ink. Large, gray clouds had collected in the sky to match her anxiety. Must be a storm coming. The shadows on the lawn seemed to swell with her thoughts. Amy's non-stop chatter about hexes and spells began to grate in her ears, becoming unbearable.

"Amy! Don't you get it?" Rose shook her shoulders. "This

isn't a silly parlor game! If we don't succeed," she spun her around and pointed at the dark figure in the saloon, "I might have to deal with that man's walking evil for God knows how long—maybe lifetimes."

Amy's eyes grew wide, and Rose could have sworn she saw her wings droop. Her friend studied her ruby boots on the floor before raising her chin.

"You're right. It's not a game—if you *believe*," Amy countered with a conviction that pierced Rose. "A little faith wouldn't kill you for a change."

"Oh God, I'm sorry," Rose blurted, clutching her forehead. "It's just that—we can't spend time on experiments right now." Tears dampened her eyes, matching the rain that began to patter outside.

Laurel rested a hand on Rose's shoulder. "So that's him, huh?" She stepped closer to the window. "Inside the saloon without a light on? Strange.".

Rose caught her sister's gaze that could freeze fire. Laurel had never liked her former husband. It wasn't just the slick attitude and tattoos—it was his possessiveness. She remembered, toward the end, how she'd written a letter to Laurel complaining about Jake's need for total control. "Crystal and I are just objects to him," she had scribbled desperately, "something to own, like gold coins or diamonds, not souls to love. He doesn't seem capable of extending his heart without chains attached." The shadow in the saloon shifted near the front window, as if he knew she'd been talking about him. All at once, the saloon door slammed shut on its own, making the hair stand on the back of her neck.

Laurel peered at the lightning rod in Amy's hand, then

back again at the dark figure. She sat down at the cafe table and leafed through the diary before staring off into space. "No," she shook her head. "This is exactly what he wants—for us to waste all of our energy on spells or methods to spark electricity. Don't you see, Rosie?" She searched her eyes. "He wants you to behave irrationally, like you did before, so he can use your emotions against you. Remember, five years ago, how you left Ophir Creek with him out of fear—fear that this town was going to swallow you whole and spit you back into the dust, old and alone? He did a mind game on you, acting like he was your only salvation."

Laurel stood and grasped her sister's arm. "Think about it. He never encouraged you to open a shop like this, or to teach school, or to learn to fly an airplane, or any of a hundred things you could have done. No, he dragged you off to Winnemucca and made you rely on him. You said it to me yourself this morning in my living room—you didn't think you had the power to change your life, so you needed him. It's the same old game all users prey on." She stroked her ring finger. "If they can keep you in a state of weakness, they can drain you of power. So we've got to think—what *isn't* he expecting you to do?"

Rose searched the knots in the wood floor, thoughts running in circles. Try as she might, she didn't have clever ideas for outfoxing her former husband. It didn't help matters that the sound of Crystal's rocking at the craft table distracted her, when she heard Crystal break into a gentle hum. Her daughter got up and taped one of her crayon drawings to the wall. It was a picture of a family inside a cottage, circled by a rainbow. She held her crystal bracelet to the sunlight and began to spin, making colors float across the room. The fleeting hues danced off the antiques and appliances in the shop.

"That's it." Laurel picked up the diary and compared it to the colors that glided along the wall. Stepping over to the drawing, she reached out to caress Crystal's hair. Rose was touched when she saw Laurel's mouth slip into a smile with no complaint from Crystal. Her sister turned around.

"This is brilliant." Laurel pointed to the people in the cottage in Crystal's drawing. "That man over there—he's not expecting us to sit tight, unafraid—like a real family. And I'm quite sure he wouldn't believe you'd hold your ground. What if, tomorrow night, we just bake a Barmbrack cake for Halloween and celebrate, business as usual?" She shot a glance at Amy's charm bracelet as if it were source material. "We could throw in every charm we find, anything that might speak of home and hearth and happiness. You know," Laurel headed to Rose, holding up the book, "before Ailís O'Dannan passed away, she gave this book to Corvine as her legacy so she'd know how to be grounded in the new world. But Corvine didn't understand that. She kept on running. It's time for you to change the pattern, Rosie. It's time to stay put and claim what's yours."

Amy nodded, her wings jiggling in affirmation. "That's right! Like I always say, the only way people overcome past lives is by facing their issues. Maybe the most radical thing you can do is keep your feet planted."

"Planted?" The concept was so new to Rose. She'd never *not* run from her problems before, and the thought made her heart palpitate. When she gazed at Crystal at the craft table, with her delicate blonde hair and charming wings, she nearly melted. She remembered the potato plants her daughter had tended during her island visions, and Ailís's words came floating back: *When feet come to rest, the heart finds home.* Rose shook her head. That sentiment was so lovely, the kind greeting cards are made of. But what if it didn't work?

"Laurel, I know I'm the last person on earth who you'd expect to be practical at a time like this. But what if your idea doesn't succeed and his spirit refuses to budge? Then what do we do?"

"Well," Laurel's her eyes flickered, "we both know where Dad used to keep his pistol—under the bed."

A tremor worked its way down Rose's spine. She spied the silhouette in the Magpie Saloon again, certain it was time to tell her sister the truth. "Laurel, that man you see out there, that's Chance's body he's stolen. I don't know how he changed the color of his hair and eyes—but if we shoot him, we might kill Chance."

Laurel's mouth dropped, her gray eyes as flat as stones. For once, Rose could tell that her sister didn't have a clue how to fix things—no ready response that cast the world into a clearer light, no plan of action that merely required good sense and willpower. She had only the empty silence that weighed upon them both.

"L-Let me get this straight," Laurel enunciated her words, "your former husband took the raven man's *body*?" She clutched her head and moaned. "Oh Rosie, how on earth do you create these messes?"

Rose didn't have the guts to tell her sister the situation was far worse than she let on. Even if everything worked out, and they somehow managed to return Chance to his rightful body, he might still be fairy struck, his mind wrapped in circles. She closed her eyes, certain by now any love that came her way would have to be doomed. When she dared to open them, she found her fingers had twisted the edge of her flannel shirt into knots.

Squeals of laughter rippled across the town square as a group of children darted from the rain onto the boardwalks. They wore colorful costumes—little pumpkins and ghosts, vampires and witches, each one with an orange paper sack for candy. Rose had heard Mrs. Dingle volunteered to take some of the mountain children trick-or-treating early this year, since Ophir Creek was bound to be flooded with miners on Halloween. Of course, Rose wanted to bring Crystal along, but then thought better of it, unsure of how she might handle the commotion. So she'd resigned herself to making caramels ahead of time, now sitting in a jack-o-lantern bowl on top of the counter.

Rose watched the children shake themselves off from the brief shower and approach the Magpie Saloon. With her usual brisk manner, Mrs. Dingle huddled them under the overhang like little chicks. All Rose wanted to do was tear across the street to warn her that there was a monster inside. But she knew such behavior would seem ridiculous, given Vincent's effervescent charm, and she was forced to merely stare at the building, fingers clenched.

Mrs. Dingle helped a little boy in a bat costume stand on his tiptoes and rap the brass knocker on the saloon door. Moments later, Vincent appeared with a smile as wide as the town square. He held out a bag of candy and waved at the Rainbow's End Cafe like he had an audience.

Laurel's eyes grew wide. "Well I'll be damned, he *does* look like the raven man from the island. Except for that shiny blonde hair—"

"Oh my gosh," Amy clicked her fingernail against the window pane, "Ray Beane just joined them. With his kids instead of those hounds. At least he finally let them see daylight."

Ray's ragamuffin children eagerly held up trick-or-treat bags to Vincent. Their hair was tangled and their costumes had stains, reminding Rose of the way Chance looked when he first came to her shop. Ray's daughter wore a disheveled princess outfit with a mismatched skirt and blouse, a bent tiara tilted on her head. His two sons were soiled trappers in coon-skin caps with rifles that looked all too real. Rose cringed. These weren't the darling, homemade costumes her mother used to create for her and Laurel, with delicate wings that made them feel like real fairies for a day. Rumors had circulated around town that Ray's wife was agoraphobic hadn't left their cabin for months. From the looks of it, her children weren't getting out much either.

As the group turned toward the Rainbow's End Cafe, Amy shot a stiff glance at Rose. Rose knew she'd rather be dead than let Ray set foot in their shop. But as the children advanced, she stole a glimpse at Laurel. It wasn't so long ago they were like the Beane children, after their parents were gone. She could never forget the threadbare clothes they wore to school and the watery soups for meals, their daily struggles to negotiate a hard-scrabble life. She grasped Laurel's hand—

it still had the warm strength of that amazing teenager who helped her survive tough times. Letting go with a squeeze, she moved to the counter to grab the jack-o-lantern of caramels, then went to the door and opened it with a smile on her face.

"Hello, honey," Rose greeted Ray little girl, the first of the children to reach her porch. She couldn't have been more than four or five, with blue eyes the color of chicory blossoms. "Welcome to my shop. Would you like a caramel?"

The girl nodded, nearly losing her tiara. Rose caught it and it straight. The girl's brothers joined her, and she held out the jack-o-lantern.

"Good afternoon, Ray." Normally, she would have added a cutting remark, but hesitated, deciding to be generous for the children's sake. "I suppose you want a caramel, too."

Rose expected him to dive into the bowl with a thankless grunt. Instead he kindly helped Mrs. Dingle onto the porch while the rest of the children scampered past them. "My little Evie brought you something," he mentioned with a softness in his voice that surprised her. "Go ahead, sweetheart, show her."

Ray's little girl pulled out a folded piece of paper from her skirt pocket and handed it to Rose. She opened it and gasped at the crayon drawing of a green island with a rainbow.

"I told her about that dream I had the other day. You know, while I was knocked out from that big wind." He tousled his daughter's hair. "Afterwards Evie said your little girl appeared in her dreams, too. She promised Evie her mommy would heal, if I would start being nicer to her. She said that's how you fix broken mommies."

Ray spotted Crystal at the craft table in the back. "Look,

honey," he patted Evie's shoulder, "there's your angel friend. She's even got wings."

Rose choked up when Evie ran to her daughter at the back of the shop, handing her the caramel from her trick-or-treat bag. Crystal quietly accepted the candy while Evie sat down and began to scribble with a crayon like she'd expected to be her playdate.

"Ain't that something?" A sparkle shone in Ray's eye. "Evie's never seen her before, and they act like old friends. Did I mention Gloria stepped outside our cabin yesterday? First time in ages. She let the sun warm her cheeks for a while."

Children in costumes scurried around the shop while Laurel tried to protect teacups on the shelves from crashing. "I tell you, something's going on around here," Ray said. Maybe something good. The way you opened this shop in our dried-up old town, welcomed folks when they couldn't pay. You've really helped change things, Rose. People actually talk to each other now, like real neighbors. Which reminds me," he rifled through his pocket, "I meant to pay you for that meal the other day. I mean, with legal tender." He held out a crumpled five-dollar bill dusted with lint.

Rose recognized the green print as legitimate this time—it might be the only cash Ray had. After his lay-off at the lumber mill last year, money had been tight for the Beanes. She waved her hand. "Oh, that's all right. Consider it, you know, a neighborly gesture." Rose's mind reeled from the idea that Crystal might have helped her mend a bridge. "W-Would you like something warm to drink?" She smiled at Mrs. Dingle, who instructed the children to sit cross-legged on the floor. "We've got hot apple cider." Rose lowered her voice to Ray.

"Don't worry about the bill today," she said gently. "For Halloween, it's free."

"Does that go for me, too?"

The sound of Vincent's words made her whip around. He stood in the doorway in a gust of cold wind that burst into the shop. His deerskin jacket was dappled from rain, and he smelled of smoke with a hint of something vaporous, like gasoline.

Rose kept her eye on Crystal, straightening her shoulders.

"The cider is for children. "You're a bit old for trick-or-treating—"

"Don't worry. I'm not looking for hand-outs—"

"Then what are you looking for?" Quickly, Rose maneuvered between Vincent and Crystal, her body a ready shield. She fired a glance at Laurel, watching her porcelain jaw tighten as she lifted her chin. Laurel's stalwart presence and pale hair made her appear regal, an ice queen in the front window light, and for the first time in Rose's life she appreciated how intimidating her sister could be.

"Well, I just stopped by to say thanks for the soup the other day," Vincent mentioned lightly, shifting his gaze to Amy. He rolled up his jacket sleeve and flexed his arm, flashing an easy grin. "Made me feel like superman. A good meal does that, you know."

"Wish we'd put arsenic in it," Amy muttered, before Rose shot her a warning look.

Nervously, Rose stepped behind the counter and pulled out a ladle, nodding at Laurel to help guard Crystal. She set out paper cups with smiling ghosts on a tray and began to serve cider from a pot on the stove. All the while, her eyes measured the distance between Vincent and her daughter, monitoring his every move. She set a stack of cookies beside the cups.

Mrs. Dingle looked weary, so Amy passed out the treats for her, sitting down with the children when she finished. Laurel remained a watchdog beside Vincent, gauging his degree of threat. At first she seemed fixated on his face, searching for signs of the man she'd known who'd stolen her sister from Ophir Creek. Then she spotted a gun in a leather holster on his belt. In a flash, she grabbed the revolver and turned it over, brazenly emptying the bullets into her pockets. Rose smiled— for as long as she could remember, Laurel had always been gutsy.

"Do you have a license for this?" Laurel sniffed.

Vincent let out a laugh. Faster than she could blink, he gripped Laurel's arm with a power that made her skin burst white beneath his fingers. She flinched in pain.

"Who gives a damn in this town?" He removed the gun from her hand and slipped it back into his belt. "Every prospector in the county packs a weapon, in case somebody tries to jump his claim."

"Claim?"

"Haven't you heard?" He gave her a wry smile. "There's gold in them thar hills."

Laurel rolled her eyes. "Oh that's just a story." Nevertheless, she kneaded her arm with a wince. "We've dealt with that nonsense for years."

"Is it such a burden?" Vincent sauntered up to the counter. He set a wet cowboy boot on the rung of a stool and leaned his elbow on the butcher block surface. "After all, this is a gold-panning business. And the O'Dannans have a remarkable knack for making discoveries—surely that entitles you to feel special, doesn't it? But I suppose such a gift can make you feel isolated sometimes." He dipped his chin thoughtfully. "I think I know how that feels."

His eyes locked on Rose, and his gaze became soft and receptive—vulnerable, even—the way people often did when they hoped she'd read their futures. For a split second, she noticed his large, blue eyes appeared far more lost than sinister, with a tender, almost wounded quality that could pierce he coldest heart. Rose gritted her teeth, recalling how pity had always been Jake's stock-in-trade, his last-ditch ploy to wear her down. Cursing under her breath, she turned her back on him, only to see him abruptly walk over to Crystal.

"Hey sweetheart," he called out with the assurance of a man addressing his own child, "would you mind coloring a pretty gold map for me? I promise to use it for prospecting."

Rose's heart lurched, and with all of her being, she wanted to set her hands on his shoulders and tear him to pieces. She stumbled past an oak barrel and a sluice box on her way to Crystal when she felt Laurel grab her by the arm and twist it, just like she used to in the school yard to make her behave. Confused, Rose turned and stared at Laurel, at her firm chin and poker face, devoid of any emotion. Laurel's eyes met hers, and in her gaze was a determination that left Rose breathless. "Whatever you do," Laurel hissed in her ear, "*don't react.*"

Rose nodded, finding it nearly impossible to squelch her panic at seeing Vincent near her daughter. Her whole body trembled, and in spite of her effort to gulp down emotion, dark clouds gathered ominously outside. With a mere brush of his hand over Crystal's forehead, the floor shook beneath the cafe. In seconds, teacups rattled on the shelves and old tins and mining pans began to tumble down with a clatter.

"Earthquake—children, duck your heads!" commanded Mrs. Dingle. She spread her arms over the small group and made them squat down in a huddle. Ray grabbed his daughter from her chair and dove beside them, while Amy pushed back a saddle rack from falling and wrapped her arm around Mrs. Dingle.

"Crystal!" Rose saw her daughter at the craft table pull away from Vincent, twisting her mouth and spooling her crayons in fury. She writhed to break free of Laurel, but her sister held her in a vise. To her astonishment, Laurel began to hum a lullaby in her ear, the one her mother had taught them in childhood. Laurel hugged her close and sang with a sweet lightness, as if it were her favorite tune in the world. Tears brimmed Rose's eyes—she didn't think her sister had even remembered that song. She gazed into her eyes, catching a sincerity that broke her heart. Clearing her throat, she clutched Laurel's hand and joined her in the melody. With every note, Rose felt emboldened, and as their voices twined across the room, the tremors ceased and a soft peace settled over the building. A raven cawed brightly outside just as sunlight burst through the window, sparkling on the tins and mining pans that had fallen to the floor. Crystal stared at the twinkles and smiled.

Ray lifted his head from beside his children. He glanced around the shop, squinting at the items on the floor to test gauge if they were settled. His face broke into a grin. "Would you look at that?" he marveled. "The quake stopped and the sun came out." He winked at Rose and gave his daughter a hopeful squeeze. "Maybe your mommy will go outside for us again."

As others dared to peek up, Rose smiled defiantly at Vincent, marching to Crystal at the craft table. She wanted to cover her in kisses and let out a whoop that they'd defeated him for once, but she knew what she had to do. Nuzzling her daughter's cheek, she drew a deep breath and swiveled to face Vincent.

"Leave," she pointed to the door, "this minute. And don't ever come near my shop with a gun again, or I guarantee I'll have your ass thrown in jail."

Vincent returned her demand with a gaze that could bore through steel. Then he leaned so close she caught his scent, which still smelled strangely of vapors.

"Fine, darling," he whispered, "if that's how you want to play your hand."

With that, he gave her an odd smile, as though he'd just lassoed the stars, and he turned and quietly left the shop.

That night, Rose snuggled beneath the old quilt, relishing their small victory. At least they'd stood up to Vincent, and no matter what happened in the future, she could be proud of them for that. Burrowing under the bedcovers, she felt the warmth of Laurel's body next to hers, in a borrowed pair of pajamas, just like when they were little and used to huddle during storms. Now, they were together to boost a different kind of courage. Silently, Rose stroked a lock of Laurel's hair in the dark, as smooth as Crystal's, and for a second she envied the features they shared —the rosebud lips, perfect cheeks and soft, ivory tresses. With both Crystal and Laurel by her side, she felt more whole than she had in ages. Her life had finally come full circle, and she was blessed to be surrounded by those she loved most— connected, it seemed, by fringes of hair and edges of flannel. She studied the two of them sleeping, their bodies curled into folds of blankets, the quilt rising and falling with their breaths.

A few weeks ago, she never would have imagined she could patch things up with her sister, after so many years of bitterness. And it was all because of Chance—

Chance.

Rose scanned the room, wondering if the raven was somewhere in shadows, or perhaps perched on the old trunk at the base of the bed. She hadn't seen him since he appeared to lead the line of birds on her drive from Boise, and sometimes she wondered if he remained outside to hurl stones on Vincent's head. Even so, she hoped he might have snuck into the shop, as he often did when she wasn't looking. Wriggling from beneath the quilt, she was careful not to wake up Laurel and Crystal as she stepped onto the creaking floorboards. She walked cautiously around the apartment and whispered his name, checking behind curtains and underneath a heap of laundry before stepping into the shop.

"Chance," Rose murmured, feeling a bit silly, "are you here?"

Darkness weighed heavily around her. She squinted, allowing the moonlight from the front windows to help her navigate the shop. After peeking in the usual places—a roost he frequently made high on a shelf or underneath the front table where he liked to scavenge for crumbs—she began to doubt his presence was nearby. Then she peered at a particularly black shadow beside the bakery case. When she tapped her foot next to it, the darkness didn't budge.

"Chance, can you hear me?"

Nothing but silence, until the sound of her own stomach growls disturbed her. Rose walked to the fridge and opened it to the glow of a harsh electric light. Inside was a bowl of mashed potatoes, an expired carton of milk, the usual odds and ends from the day's baking. She spotted a few fairy cakes in the back—the lemon frosted ones that were supposed to help you see fairies—and uncovered the saran wrap to take a greedy lick of icing. From somewhere in the darkness, she heard a familiar voice.

I'm with you, Rose—

She whipped around to no one was there. "Chance?" she whispered eagerly.

In a band of moonlight she caught a glimpse of a shiny, black feather on the floor. Stepping closer, she picked it up, only to spot another, then another. Gathering the feathers in her hand, she realized they formed a line, like bread crumbs, leading to the cafe table. She walked to the table and glanced down, spying a pair of wings Crystal had crafted that morning with Amy, glittering in the moonlight. They looked magical, and she couldn't help recalling those times she used to spend with her mother and Laurel, searching for fairies at twilight. Soft, rustling leaves, flickers of forest light, sparkles off creek water when you least expected it—those had been the most enchanted moments of her life, until she'd had Crystal. Rose reached out a finger to touch her daughter's wing, caressing a memory. She swore she saw it quiver…

Go ahead—put them on, the voice urged. *Tonight we can fly.*

Rose's cheeks flushed, her lips curling into a smile. She slipped the wings on over her shoulders, hoping Laurel wouldn't wake up and see. Nevertheless, she couldn't find the raven anywhere. Longingly, she stroked the feathers in her hand. "Where are you?"

Close your eyes, the voice said. *Believe*—

Easing her eyes shut, Rose tried as hard as she could to feel his presence. She imagined the softness of the feathers as his windswept hair, tinged with sand, which he was just waiting for her to touch. He would smell fresh, she thought, like seaside air, with hints of wild roses and turf fire smoke. She inhaled deeply, wishing she could breathe him in for safekeeping, when she felt the feathers slip from her fingers…

Slowly, a feather traced her cheek before it curved along her jaw and caressed her throat. Soft as a whisper, it glided along her collar bone. The feather whisked down to the swell of her breast and paused before she felt Chance's lips press against hers. Gently, he stroked her hair as he kissed her. Rose opened her eyes. Before her, illuminated in the moonlight, was a tall man with dark, unruly hair and a black overcoat. His brown eyes drank her in as though the very sight of her nourished his soul.

Rose was about to speak when he put the feather to her lips. He took her by the hand and held her close, humming as he moved his hips, imperceptibly at first, then with a little more fervor, so that before she knew it they were waltzing. She allowed her head to fall against his shoulder, wings bobbing as the two of them dipped and swayed. Inside, however, she had to giggle—here she was, in her white flannel nightgown and wool socks, dancing with a man who clearly could use a few lessons. His movements were awkward at first, like someone unaccustomed to wooing women, and his jerking strides made her feel like she was attached to a darting shadow. He's so different from Jake, she thought, whose smoothness used to work as effortlessly on her as his smile. How many times had he waltzed her through smoky bars or clanging casinos, purring lies that only made her feel weaker by the second? Rose had lost track long ago. Instead, Chance clutched her hand a little too hard, his wrist rigid as he tried to overcome stumbling feet. He let out a small cough each time he missed the rhythm, wincing and ducking his rugged chin. Chewing his lip, every motion in his body betrayed the lonely mountain man he truly was, but his dark eyes told her he gave his heart for keeps.

Wouldn't have it any other way, Rose smiled as she rested her cheek against his chest. His coat rustled with their rhythm, and in its swishes she could almost hear the lapping waves of the sea. Soon, his gait became more confident, and slowly she began to feel swept up in his motion as if floating on a tide. Is he really here? she wondered, dusting off the sand from his lapel. Or am I so desperate I've lost myself to dreams? Rose reached up to touch his cheek for assurance, when she felt his large hand grip hers. The determination in his grasp made her heart surge like she had boarded a ship that had finally set its course for home.

Chance smoothed the hair from her forehead and cupped her face. "Look into my eyes." He halted their movement. "What do you see?"

Rose wasn't sure what he meant—was he asking her to predict their future together? How could she, when after tomorrow night she didn't know who he would be? Vincent or Chance? She glanced into his eyes, shiny in the moonlight. "You know I can't see the future for myself."

Running his fingers through her hair, he twirled a strand like fine silk. "But you can dream." He took her by the hand and opened the front door to lead her to the porch. Above them, the nearly ripe full moon washed the town square in silver, and splashes of stars winked in the sky like fragile hopes. Chance slipped his thick arm around her waist, careful not to disturb her wings. "At least for one night," he said, "dare to *dream* with me."

Rose nodded, swallowing hard. For years she'd been reluctant to consider her future, especially after her possibilities had been beaten down by Jake. Day-to-day survival was the most she could hope for in Winnemucca, where dreams withered like tender blossoms in the relentless desert sun. But it wasn't a life—it was merely an existence. Now, she didn't want to let that happen to her anymore, or to Crystal. Positioning her feet squarely on the porch, she stared at Chance.

"This is what I see." She grasped his shoulders and looked into his eyes with as much courage as she could muster. "I see love and light all around us. And for the first time in my life, I'm not going anywhere."

Chance smiled. "Of course you are." He grabbed her by the hand and leaped from the porch—

All at once, the moon appeared closer, so big Rose thought it might swallow them, and Ophir Creek steadily became a small cluster of lights as far away as the stars. Rose gasped, realizing the town had edged from their sight. She studied Chance's coat, flapping in the breeze, trying to detect where he might have sprouted wings. But there were no bulging feathers or wingtips in view, no mysterious modifications into a wild bird—only a man beside her whose grin rivaled the stars. Stretching out her hands, she felt the force of an unusually warm current suspend them in flight. Had Chance somehow learned to influence the clouds and winds, like her great-great grandmother? He shook his head and laughed.

"Twixt hearts are full of surprises," he remarked mischievously, "when the moon is right." He tweaked her chin. "I thought you'd know that by now—"

Gripping her tight around the waist, he steadied her beside him and tilted her shoulders so they floated upright before an incandescent moon. Chance's face, though hard and weather beaten at the edges, radiated like an angel's. Rose slipped her hands to her cheeks, wondering if they might emit heat from his reflected glow. He chuckled and grasped her fingers, curling them into his. This time, when he led her in the dance, his movements were as light and graceful as the wispy clouds that collected at their feet like lace. A soft breeze whisked Rose's hair, and despite their altitude, she felt safe in his arms —aloft, it seemed, by their own delight.

"Chance," she smiled, "are we hallucinating?"

"I don't know!" He gazed at the moon. "Do we care?"

He pressed his cheek against hers, gently spinning her among thread-like clouds that were so sheer they were almost transparent. Rose giggled, and for the life of her, she thought she could hear music. It was soft at first, seeming to vibrate from her own chest. But as the notes began to throb in her mind, she saw soft lights glitter all around them. Their twinkles resembled stars with fleeting colors, like the reflections that danced off Crystal's bracelet.

"They're here," Chance whispered proudly, "all around us. They're attracted by our joy."

"Who?"

He hugged her close. "The good people. See?" He pointed at the glimmering colors. "They've been waiting for you—"

Mystified, Rose watched a trickle of hues stream past them in a graceful swirl. Flashes of red and blue and yellow reflected off Chance's face, making him look more alive than she'd ever seen him. No longer the desolate man of the woods or a windswept island, he appeared as fresh and illuminated as the moon. His dark eyes sparkled, yet even as they swayed together in the gentle breeze, his expression slowly began to stiffen and grow stern.

Chance searched her face as if memorizing her features— the curve of her chin with two freckles on the left; the line of her lips, a bit full on the bottom, the mossy green eyes that appeared liquid in moonlight. Sweeping his fingers along her brow, he rested his palm on her cheek. "This could be our last dance together," he opened the front flaps of his coat to snuggle her inside. He hugged her so close Rose could feel her ribs press against his chest. Greedily, he grasped her temples.

"I love you, Rose." He stared into her eyes. "Not just on the island, or in the forest." He paused and glanced at the floating colors that still hovered around them, vibrating soft melodies. "Or even among fairy lights and stars, but everywhere you move and breathe. No matter what happens," he promised, stroking her cheek, "you have my heart."

Then he kissed her with such force that she imagined he might breathe her in, and the white glow of their merged souls would melt into the moon. From that moment, she thought, when people looked up at night, they would see the silhouette of two 'twixt dancers who'd finally found each other, their bodies entwined for all time. Rose ran her fingers along

Chance's face, hesitating over his long scar, wanting to etch his features into her heart the way pictures had been drawn in her great-great grandmother's diary. As they kissed, she closed her eyes and listened—listened to the very way he inhaled and exhaled—hoping to hold the rhythm in her soul. Touching her hands to his chest, she reveled in the rise and fall of his lungs beneath his wool sweater—proof to her that he was real, that everything around them was real—when she felt his lips release hers. He burrowed his hand into his coat pocket.

Chance pulled out a small seashell and held it up to the colors that undulated even more brightly in the night sky, as if swelled by their kisses.

"Your daughter gave you tokens from the island," he said. "Seashells, potatoes, her paintings. She told me they were her hopes. Little ways of connecting with you, I guess. Well, I want to give you something, too, Rose. Something more than feathers." He slipped the seashell into her palm and closed her fingers. "I want to give you back your dreams—"

Rose's eyes misted as he put his arm around her shoulder and glanced down. They descended to the tops of pine trees until she could once again see the lights of Ophir Creek.

"I dream of you and me and Crystal by the fireplace," Chance pointed to the Rainbow's End Cafe. "With a pot of stew on the stove, the three of us wrapped together in that dusty, old quilt." He kissed her softly. "We're warm and safe and happy. And in the mornings, I'll walk Crystal to school before I go to work. And on weekends, I'll teach her how to read tree rings and listen to the wilderness." He grinned slightly. "If she's anything like you, she'll always have that touch of wildness in her."

Chance twirled her in air as they drifted over treetops. Her wings fluttered, and he slowed her spin to a stop. "And at night, Rose," he ran his hands over her temples, "I'll wash your hair in mountain rainwater, and unravel every silky strand before I kiss your skin all over until you tremble. And then we'll make love, long and slow, under an alabaster moon, our bodies bathed in starlight, and we'll dream. We'll dream and dream, and never stop dreaming—"

Heaven, Rose thought. He's just described my idea of heaven. She arched her back, feeling her wings shudder in the breeze. Above her, she could still see colors dangling like painted stars, their music a gentle hum in her ears.

Chance gazed at the twinkling hues as if he'd already begun to miss them. He grasped Rose's fingers and held them out to touch a fleeting bit of yellow that appeared lost and was skittering past their shoulders to join the others. When Rose made contact with the sparkling color, a warm and invigorating feeling sped up her arm. Surprised, she touched her finger to her lips—it tasted like the lemon fairy icing! Another one passed, less hurried this time, as though it might be curious. Rose extended her hand cautiously, when the orange color dashed forward to meet her touch. Again, she brought her finger to her lips and a taste filled her mouth. It was a complex blend of spices with overtones of both sweet and nutty flavors, like her mother's Barmbrack cake— something she hadn't savored in ages. Rose glanced at Chance in astonishment as the feeling surged up her arm and began to embrace her entire being. It felt warm and full inside, like a hug from her mother on a late afternoon, perhaps after a tea party in the forest. Or like having her hair brushed by her sister in the bright sunshine. Or like doing nothing at all, just lying in a heap with her loved ones on the family quilt. Is this a trick of my mind? she wondered, watching the orange color flitter away. Or had the fairies somehow recorded every joy she'd ever known, somewhere in the annals of the cosmos—all those little moments that she'd thought had been extinguished under the harsh Winnemucca sun? Rose tried to read Chance's face for the answer.

"It's all here, Rose," he assured her, the colors reflecting across his cheeks like a kaleidoscope. "Everything good and true you've ever known. All you have to do is reach out and remember. We'll always be with you—"

Goose bumps ran down Rose's spine at his words. He cradled her elbow to steady her and guided their feet to settle on the wood planks of the porch. Glancing back at the moon, he lifted his chin as if it had called his name. "Rose, I don't know what will happen tomorrow night," he confessed. "I could return to my body, my mind a scramble, or worse." He studied his feet as though it might be the last time he would see them. "But I do know this: if I do everything in my power to return to the daylight people, Crystal will too. She just needs someone to go before her, to show her the way home."

Tears trickled down Rose's cheeks, beyond her willpower to make them stop. It wasn't just the possibility of losing her lover at the brink of a full moon, when she and Chance had barely started. She glanced at the seashell resting in her palm, so similar to the one her daughter had given her. More than anything, more than all the handsome strangers, full moons and fairy lights the world had to offer, what she wanted most was to have her daughter back, as sassy and whole as she'd been before. Rose knew Crystal had shown signs of improvement, baby steps to test the waters, perhaps. But nothing was certain, only that her heart lurched each time she caught a glimpse of the girl she'd known. Closing her eyes, she rubbed the seashell in her palm and prayed with all her heart that her daughter might once again be hers. Not a twilight child, snared between two worlds because of damage or fear. Rose pictured a child of the sun, light glinting off her cheeks and curls—a bold child who'd brag about her adventures when her mother smiled and asked about her day. A child who wanted to be with her. A child who would stay.

Please God, Rose prayed silently, please—please—help me to be worthy of my angel—

A raven called from a tree limb overhead, its voice thick and resonant. Soon, a group of birds descended on the grass in the town square. They assembled in a circle and began to chortle like members of a midnight council. Chance nodded.

"Rose," he said in a solemn tone, "Laurel's told you the truth, as much as she could handle, anyway. She's right—you don't need thunder and fireworks to do a soul exchange. But you *do* need the help of the good people. Believe, Rose. Believe enough for you and me and Crystal, and our future—"

He stared up at the last of the flickering colors that hovered in the sky like northern lights. "And ask Laurel about the fairy ring. There's something she's not telling you."

21

Rose awoke the next morning to the smell of smoke. At her window, two ravens pecked on the glass, one with feathers tinged gray. She untangled herself from the bed, slipping her arm beneath Crystal's elbow and unfolding a knee from Laurel's shin to step onto the floor. Tiptoeing across the wood, she made her way to the kitchen window where she discovered Rook Ridge was on fire, smoke billowing from its peak. Panicked, she hastened through the shop to the front porch, only to see particles of ash floating through the town square like grim confetti. A gas can sat on the boardwalk with a page torn from the diary stuffed into its nozzle. Prying the page loose, she stared at its charred remains. Between burn marks and flakes of ash were the faint hues of a rainbow circle.

He's already winning, Rose realized in horror. She recalled Vincent's peculiar smile the day before in the shop, how he smelled of vapors. At the time, she'd assumed he'd been working on a car, never dreaming he'd conjure such devastation. Trembling, she glanced at the gray smoke that threaded between buildings like a fog. Rather than the usual sights of townspeople opening the post office or the local museum on a Wednesday morning, Ophir Creek appeared desolate.

Across the street, Vincent emerged from the haze as if he'd been waiting for her. He stepped off the boardwalk and stood tall in front of the saloon, reminiscent of a gunslinger from the gold rush days, with smoke creeping around his feet like dust kicked up from wagon wheels. Heart drumming, Rose half-expected him to draw his gun from his belt, and she ducked her head behind a wooden porch column. Vincent folded his arms and laughed. Something about the sound of his voice reverberated inside her, making her feel nauseous and weak at the same time. She thought she might have inhaled too much smoke, when a magpie landed on the boardwalk and squawked at her. The bird strutted several paces, flashing its wing bands in the air like victory flags. A voice trailed the smoky breeze.

Give up, aisling. It's destiny. Remember what they used to say in the old country—time moves in circles.

Bewildered, Rose peeked from behind the porch column. It wasn't Vincent's voice she'd heard, nor was it Jake's or even Chance's. The sound lilted in her ears as if it had echoed from the shores of Ireland. Her eyes narrowed at the man in the street, watching the smoke obscure his frame and then lift. Sparks ignited down her spine—all of a sudden, he didn't look like Vincent or Chance anymore. His hair was still blonde and cowlicked, but his face was different: ruddy and freckled, with a wide forehead and a thin smile, as though he harbored a secret or perhaps a riddle. Somehow, deep in her bones, Rose recognized him. She searched her mind frantically, when she remembered the lit candles and incense beside Amy's crystal ball a week ago, the feel of the raven's feathers in her lap. She'd seen this man in a vision, while supposedly going over her past lives. Corvine O'Dannan's lover? Her heart pounded wildly as he tied a red bandana over his face to deflect the smoke.

"R-Rory?" she whispered, feeling like the cadence of her voice came from someone else—someone from a long time ago.

I told you. He stepped toward her. *It's never over between us.*

His words resounded in her chest to the rhythm of her breaths.

You made a promise to me once in a garden. Eternity is a heartbeat, you'll see.

Coughing, Rose's throat constricted as if he'd managed to reach his fingers through the smoke to close around her neck. She struggled for breath, clutching at her chest while she grabbed for the front door, when a jeep parked at the shop with an abrupt squeal of brakes. A firefighter leaned out the window, his face smudged in ash.

"It's raging up there," he called out, voice hoarse. "Everyone's out battling the blaze. Take us all day to contain it, unless there's rain. Too bad for you, huh? Guess you were hoping for business on Halloween."

Rose nodded, glancing at the jack-o-lanterns on the porch, wishing they really could ward away evil spirits. She peered past the jeep to catch a glimpse of the stranger again, but all she saw was smoke.

"I'll—I'll send meals for the workers right away," she promised. She hugged her elbows to hold herself together, her skin ice.

"You all right?" He cocked his head. "You look like you've seen a ghost."

Rose wanted to grab his hand, to beg him to stay with her like a shield against whatever it was she'd seen—surely that would work better than any jack-o-lanterns. But when she checked again across the street, no one was there, as though the stranger had evaporated. The firefighter studied her face, puzzled.

"I-I'm fine." She summoned what little courage she had without coffee to boost her nerves and waved him on. "You be careful out there."

The jeep rolled away, and Rose searched the haze in vain, keeping a firm grip on the doorknob of the shop. She swung open the door to find Laurel sitting at the cafe table, her fingers wrapped around an empty mug. Thankfully, she heard coffee percolating in the kitchen.

"What on earth sent you bolting from bed?" Laurel yawned, stretching out her arms in Rose's red plaid pajamas. She eyed her sister's nightgown. "Next time you step out for firewood," she sniffed, "grab a coat." She walked to the kitchen to pour herself a cup of coffee before the percolator finished. "Look what I found under the pillow this morning." Laurel offered a wry smile and held up her palm. "A seashell. Don't tell me the tooth fairy came by last night."

Rose winced at the reference. Their parents never had

spare cash lying around, so after losing baby teeth she and her sister often found pretty stones or pinecones beneath their pillows. She gazed at the dainty pink shell that Chance had given her the night before, feeling goose bumps alight on her skin. Try as she might, she couldn't reconcile her flight of fancy beneath a glowing moon with the fire that had erupted on Rook Ridge. How could both incidents have happened in one night, with the freest moment of her life coinciding with flames? She knotted her hands into her flannel nightgown. Love and hate had circled back on themselves in ways that boggled her mind.

"It's *him*," Rose blurted.

"What do you mean?"

"Whoever Vincent is," she pointed at the Magpie Saloon, "*whatever* he is—he doesn't want us to go to Rook Ridge, so he set it on fire. He's trying to scare us away, Laurel. There's something up there. Something you're not telling me."

Laurel peered at the smoke out the window and rolled her eyes. "Oh don't be so skittish." Her voice was oddly casual. She slipped the seashell into her pocket and smoothed over the flannel. "This is hardly the first time that ridge has been on fire. You'd be amazed at how fast smokejumpers can contain a blaze—"

Rose held up the singed diary page. Her fingers shook as the violation to her and the O'Dannan legacy sank in. "He stole the diary, Laurel," her voice cracked. "He must have pocketed it yesterday when he was here."

Laurel squinted at the charred page, examining the faded rainbow circle that was still barely visible. Her fingers clenched the coffee cup until her knuckles creased white. Fear surfaced in her eyes—an expression Rose had never seen on her, and it left her rattled. Even when they were alone as teenagers, Laurel invariably put on a composed front, too strong to waste time on insecurity or panic or anything else that might impede her goals. Rose always thought her sister's emotions were as sculpted as her face, and she could be counted on to display fortitude in the face of any calamity, real or imagined. Laurel set down her coffee mug, folding her arms into her waist like bruised wings.

"What does this mean, Laurel?" Rose prodded, afraid of the answer. "What did my mother tell you about the fairy ring?"

"How'd you hear about that?" Laurel stubbornly ignored her and focused on a stain on the floor, measuring its width and contours, till she spotted a mop near the oven. She took brisk strides to grab it and started cleaning—her usual routine whenever she became agitated and didn't feel like talking. Rose cut in her way to stop her. Before Laurel could protest, she snatched the seashell from her pajama pocket and held it up.

"There aren't exactly any oceans around here. It wasn't the tooth fairy who came by last night—it was Chance, and he gave me this seashell from the island. He told me to ask you about the fairy ring."

Laurel's eyes grew wide. She fluttered her hand in air. "I-I don't know what you mean. Besides, we can't waste time dwelling on the past—we've got work to do." She handed the mop to Rose. "This place is a mess—look at that floor." She pointed to the stain on the wood. "You'd better get cracking before the day slips away." Then she hastened to the fridge to pull out lunch meats and condiments along with a loaf of bread. "I'm going to make sandwiches for the firefighters," she declared. "Is that what the man in the jeep asked about? Heaven knows, they'll need provisions."

Rose set aside the mop and marched to Laurel, yanking the butter knife from her hand. "What the hell are you hiding?" She placed the diary page in the middle of a cookbook and grasped her sister's shoulders. "For God's sake, this is our lives—Chance's life—we're talking about."

Laurel stared at the loaf of bread she'd taken from the fridge, suddenly aware she'd squeezed it into the shape of an hourglass. She let go and settled her hands on the counter. Closing her eyes, she heaved a strained sigh as if exhuming a difficult memory.

"Rosie, you were too young to understand, to witness something like that." Her eyes met her sister's. In Laurel's gaze was both resignation and dread. "Sometimes ignorance can be a form of mercy."

Laurel stared at the nicks and cuts in the surface of the butcher block counter. She ran her finger over a particularly deep slice in the wood. "Did you really think your mother died of cancer? Well, think again. Where was the body, Rosie? Why was the casket closed at the funeral?"

Rose dropped her hands from her sister. Her forehead grew uncomfortably warm. She recalled the plain pine casket hoisted on their mountain neighbors' shoulders, how she hadn't even been allowed to touch her mother's cheek one last time. They'd buried her in an old cemetery on a hill by Rook Ridge, the same place where gold seekers had been laid to rest over a century ago. All she could remember was the brutal sunshine on the morning that she had to let her mother go, the way everything sparkled in spite of her tears, until the afternoon gave over to a hard rain. The neighbors claimed that the change in weather was due to the O'Dannan influence, a reflection of the family's grief. "I-I never really thought about the casket before. Everything happened so fast —those days were a blur. I assumed she'd had chemotherapy and didn't look like herself anymore."

Rose's heart quickened at how ridiculous her words sounded. They both knew their family couldn't afford health insurance, let alone expensive medical treatments. When her mother had come home one spring day from Boise with the news that she had advanced lymphoma, her face pale as a cloud as the afternoon became overcast to match her fears, everyone in the family knew what it meant: a certain death sentence.

"There was no body," Laurel declared. "She—just disappeared."

Tears pooled at the corners of her eyes. Laurel brushed them aside before they could slip down her cheeks. "I was with her, Rosie, at twilight. She called it the Tween Time, at the brink from day to night." Laurel stared at the cookbook, glancing at the charred diary page. Her eyes rested on the faded colors. "It's true, your mother was very sick. Her illness made her body weak and her eyes grow dim. She didn't want us to watch her wither away, Rosie, to turn our memories of her into darkness and pain. So she stepped inside the fairy ring and—left."

"What do you mean, *left?*"

Laurel traced her finger over the diary page. Her gray eyes looked worn. "Two days before the funeral," she said in an unsteady voice, "your mother took me to the top of Rook Ridge, to the ring of stones up there. It was springtime, when wildflowers grow bright red and blue in a wide circle. I thought it was the base of where a stand of trees used to be that had decayed. But it was more. When twilight came, she handed me the diary and pointed to this page." Laurel tapped it, blinking back more tears. "She cupped my chin and told me that when 'twixt people step into a fairy ring, there's a possibility that they can return healed. But they might become fairy struck instead—or disappear altogether. The thing is, no one can know for sure. All she could do was whisper O'Dannan before she made the leap. Either way, she said she'd always be with us." Laurel bit her lip to keep from trembling. "She stepped into the ring, and it swallowed her."

"Swallowed?"

Her sister nodded. "Colors circled around, like Crystal's bracelet, and before I knew it, she was gone in a swirl of leaves. The only thing left was the smell of flowers. And music —peculiar, melodic tones I'd never heard before." She grasped Rose's arm with a force that startled her. "It drove Dad mad."

"He was there?"

"No, he was home, taking care of you. I walked back to town by myself in the dark. He had put you to bed, and he was sitting by the stove, waiting for me." Laurel glanced at the old Foster. "When I opened the front door and told him what had happened, he was never the same again. That's why I couldn't tell you, Rosie. I didn't want you to be damaged somehow. Your mother wouldn't let you see the fairy ring because she knew you'd try to follow her—I guess 'twixt people can do things like that." Laurel grasped her elbows. "She knew I couldn't bear to lose you."

Rose buried her head in her hands, her fingers straining against her temples. How could words like this be coming from her relentlessly practical sister? It was all too much, too overwhelming to comprehend. When she peered through her fingers at Laurel to make certain she wasn't delirious, her sister returned her gaze with puffy red eyes, a tightened jaw to prevent more tears. This is no hoax, Rose realized. Gently, Laurel tugged her hands from her face.

"I don't want this reality," Laurel's fingers clenched around her sister's. "But this is the way things are, so we've got to deal with it."

Tingles dashed down Rose's neck and collected at the small of her back. Her sister had uttered those very same words after their father disappeared years ago, when they'd become orphans. Rose blinked like the moment had slipped through time somehow and fallen, as a drop of water, into the well of the present day. Hesitantly, she cleared her throat, which still felt rough from smoke.

"Laurel, if we can find the fairy ring under the blue moon tonight with Chance—I mean, with the raven—perhaps he can change places with Vincent and return to his body."

Laurel dropped her sister's hands, staring at her in disbelief. "Rosie, you told me yourself there's a fire on the ridge. Even if they put it out by noon, how on earth would we find a fairy ring in October? There aren't any flowers this time of year." She gazed at the burnt page on the cookbook. "Besides, without the rest of the diary, I wouldn't know where to begin."

Laurel stared into the smoky light of the front window, running her hands through her cropped hair, which looked neat and straight, even though she hadn't brushed it yet. Hugging her elbows, she focused on the ravens that had collected in the town square. Rose knew what she was doing—she was studying the birds, wondering if they might make a circle or some other kind of pattern that would give them a clue. The ravens remained scattered across the lawn like pepper.

Quietly, Rose joined her sister. Although a few of the birds shifted on the grass, their positions were random, yielding no secrets. With a sigh, she headed back to the kitchen, spotting Laurel's purse with a photo sticking up from the front pocket. It was the snapshot of her mother, and Rose pulled it out to gaze at her willowy frame and wild dark hair, wondering how she could possibly have disappeared to another realm. Did a misty gate arise for her at twilight that only she and the fairies could see? Perhaps a rabbit hopped by, like it did for Alice in Wonderland, leading her to a world unlike any she'd ever known. Rose studied her mother's green eyes, her earnest expression that looked as though she were about to say something, cut short by the camera's shutter. Both she and Laurel stood beside her, holding jack-o-lanterns, with smiles as wide as the pumpkins'. Rose recalled their glee that day, and in spite of her troubles, her mouth slipped into a half-smile. It was then that she noticed them again—the colors in the background sky of the photo. Originally, she'd thought they were drippings of paint that had faded into the paper over time. Turning the picture over, she reread her mother's inscription: *To my darlings. We will be with you.*

"We," she whispered, the memory still fresh of her moonlight dance with Chance, the way colors swirled around them and hovered in mid-air, like they did in the photo. "Laurel," she held up the snapshot, "why did you bring this here?"

Her sister turned, hands squeezing tighter around her elbows. "I-I thought you might want to keep it, Rosie, to put inside the diary. It's the only picture we have of Mom."

Mom. Rose had never heard Laurel call her mother that before. It was always "your mother," "my stepmom," or even "Alicia." She walked to Laurel and pressed her finger to the photo. "These colors in the sky. Do you remember them?"

Her sister ran her toe along a knothole in the floor, nodding with a shrug. "Sort of. It was strange, they seemed a bit like the northern lights, except they often appeared in the afternoons—when we'd been playing too loud and giggling. Mom said that always happened near important times, like Samhain in October or Beltane in May—the days she went up to Rook Ridge."

"What did she call them?"

Laurel squinted at a braided rug by the stove made of strips of cloth that Rose's mother had saved. Her gaze followed the motley weave of colors. "I remember her mentioning the 'good people', whatever that meant. Most of the time she didn't call them anything, really. She just referred to them as 'we', like they were a part of her."

Rose turned over the photo to show Laurel the inscription. "When Mom said 'we will be with you,'" she tapped the colors, "these are the *we*." She paused to study the translucent hues—watery reds and blues and yellows, as if made from molecules of moisture, the kind that reflected rainbows. "They're fairies, Laurel. All along, they were real—just like Mom said. And they came because of our joy." She searched her sister's face. "Why is it so hard to believe?"

Rose expected to see a stymied look on her sister's face. After all, this was crazy talk, like the way Harriet Brimley babbled on about floods that were going to wipe out the wicked, who probably thought the fire on the ridge was God's backup plan. Instead, Laurel gazed at her with weary recognition. Her expression hinted at the fatigue of one who had wrestled for too long with challenging memories.

"It's hard to believe because it's beyond our control," Laurel replied dryly. "Fairies, ghosts, goblins. What next? The Wicked Witch of the West? As a little girl, I didn't need any more surprises. Besides, they steal things."

"Who?"

"The fairies. You have such romantic notions about everything—all pretty colors and gossamer wings. They *took her*, Rosie—don't you see? Look what it did to us, to Pa. They're reckless, nothing but thieves."

Rose scrutinized the photo again, her mind a whirl. However difficult, she understood the fairies had spirited her mother away, irrevocably changing their lives. Yet tucked deep inside a place in her heart lingered a fresh hope, akin to faith, because of her moonlight dance with Chance. Among the swirls of colors, the fairies had recorded every moment of joy she'd ever known, like the strange inscriptions in the diary. Nothing had been lost, no matter how small or seemingly insignificant, and the one thing Rose realized under that big moon was that she mattered—she mattered as deeply to the fairy world as she did to Chance—even if she was just a lowly shopkeeper from Ophir Creek.

She began to wonder if, all those years ago when they spirited away her mother, the fairies had higher reasons, maybe more merciful than Laurel could comprehend. And what if, in their own time and season, they'd brought mysterious blessings as well? She recalled how the ravens had led her back to Ophir Creek earlier in the month, with a long line that went before her on the highway as she drove home from Winnemucca. Everything that had happened since then —Amy's love spell, Chance's transformation, her visits with Crystal on the island—had, in one way or another, brought her closer to her daughter, to her sister, perhaps even to her own soul. Was any of it an accident? Or could there be benevolent energies guiding her, if she was willing? Rose glanced at Laurel, numb for words. She didn't know how to explain her thoughts without sounding as fluttery as Amy or as half-baked as Harriet Brimley. What Laurel seemed to want most now was security—not more ethereal fairy tales.

Rose stole one last peek out the window at the ravens, in case they might have assembled into some kind of order, but their positions were haphazard. "Would you like some breakfast?" she asked Laurel gently. Her sister swallowed a last sip of coffee and held up her mug in reply, gray eyes visibly drained. Grabbing the coffee pot, Rose gave her a refill. While she poured, she heard a soft shuffle behind her, the floor creaking with tiny footsteps. She swiveled to see Crystal entering the shop, dragging along the quilt at her side. It was far too early for her to be up, at least two hours before her usual rising time, and Rose cringed, wondering if their voices had disrupted her sleep. Perhaps she had smelled smoke, Rose thought, and it tainted the edges of her dreams.

"How are you, honey?" she said in a chirpy tone, despite the fact the ridge was on fire. For all she knew, they might have to evacuate soon. She scurried to the kitchen to make sure her daughter had a full stomach before the situation became too critical. "Did you have a good sleep?" She opened the fridge to search for eggs to scramble, then spotted leftover fairy cakes. She set them on the counter and spied Crystal yawning, blonde hair mussed from sleep, which made it look pressed on one side like cotton batting. Crystal ignored her mother's questions and wrapped herself in the quilt, plopping on the floor. She rocked in place, hand tapping the wood as reliably as a clock. Though her daughter had made astonishing strides, the way she clung to her rigid habits sometimes made her seem to Rose as far away as the stars. Crystal stared at the stain on the floor that had preoccupied Laurel, and Rose worried the two of them might share the same obsessions.

She set the fairy cakes in the microwave for a minute until the lemon icing began to bubble. Rose headed to Crystal with a warm fairy cake on a napkin. Hopefully, it will tide her over till I can fix eggs, she thought. She stooped to set down the treat, only to discover her daughter wasn't focusing on the floor stain at all. In the hazy sunlight, on a wooden plank beside Crystal, was a long, black feather.

Rose's breath halted. She couldn't help smiling a little at the reminder of her night with Chance. Lifting the feather, she wove it delicately in air to relive the feeling of flight. Laurel stared at her from the cafe table as if she'd lost her mind, but Rose refused to care. For just one moment, she shut her eyes and allowed herself to feel free again, to feel the innocence she'd known under that big, bright moon. She imagined herself as lively as Crystal used to be before the accident—confident and full of energy, the kind of child who would never hesitate to let an instant of joy infuse her being. Letting the feather fall from her fingertips, to her surprise, Crystal began to giggle.

Rose glanced down. At her feet, her daughter was doing what she always did: rocking steadily and holding up her bracelet to make colors. What was different this time was the peculiar knowing in her eyes. She didn't gaze at the dancing hues on the wall with the usual far-off wonder that mystified her mother. A familiarity had surfaced on her face, as if she were among old friends. Crystal moved her lips, seeming to whisper to the colors. She paused to pick up the feather and glided it over the quilt with a fond caress.

Intrigued, Rose bent down, hardly able to remember the last time she appeared warm or affectionate, unless it was in a dream. She watched Crystal traced an old muslin patch with the feather, pausing over random stains that looked like ink or rust, or perhaps from the huckleberries that she and Laurel used to collect in late summer. Quietly, Crystal stroked the feather over each faded splotch of color. She glanced at her mother—not as the spacey girl Rose had become accustomed to, but as one who actually recognized her. For a fleeting second, Rose thought she saw her daughter smile as she tugged on her sleeve.

"We," she said.

Rose blinked. In her daughter's hushed tone was not merely a word but a shared intimacy—a gentle secret between the two of them. The small utterance so startled Rose she shook her head, wondering if she'd her correctly. Before the accident, she'd always considered Crystal to be impetuous and headstrong, not one given to quiet confidences. Yet here she was, with her liquid green eyes steady upon her face, as if inviting her in. Then, soft as a winsome breeze, Crystal let go of the feather and slipped her fingers into her mother's hand.

Rose stiffened. Had she really seen Crystal smile? Were they actually holding hands? She knew all too well her daughter's behavior could change on a dime—one second she might reach out her fingers, only to yank them back before her mother could blink. Nevertheless, a full minute passed while their entwined fingers grew warm. Cautiously, Rose held her breath and stared at the ceiling, afraid to verify whether their locked hands were real or just her lonely imagination. She let her gaze drift to the paper ghosts on the wall before she dared to glance down.

Crystal's hand was still in hers.

Tears blurred Rose's vision, making the Halloween decorations in the shop blend together like finger paints. Suddenly, it no longer mattered to her that the ridge was on fire, that the town might evacuate, that her neighbor was evil or even that her lover needed his body back. All that mattered was this moment, as beautiful and golden as any color the fairies might reveal. Savoring Crystal's soft hand, Rose cradled it in hers like a precious egg. If only I could bottle this feeling, she thought, careful not to crimp her daughter's fingers. With all of her being, she wanted to kneel down and grab Crystal, to wrap her arms around her and squeeze until they both fell into a heap, laughing uncontrollably, the way they used to before the accident. But she didn't dare. Like a relentless ticker tape, every warning from the specialists came darting back to her mind:

Watch what you do, Crystal can't handle stimulation—
Close contact might overwhelm her—
Sudden movements could spark radical regression—

A tightness enveloped Rose's chest. All at once the room began to ripple, as if she'd stepped back in time somehow and was standing once again by the pool in Winnemucca on the day of the accident. She remembered how her heart had raced and adrenaline pumped through her veins. There'd been no doubt for her on that day—of course she would jump in for Crystal! Wild horses couldn't have stopped her! If bravery came so easily then, why couldn't she allow herself to bond with her daughter now? She gazed at their clasped hands, frozen in place. Her mind danced through a dozen excuses— Crystal's fragile state, the doctors' restrictions, even that Laurel was nearby and might scold her for foolishness. Deep inside, Rose knew she was a liar. She stared out the front window at the gray sky, her throat swelling in fear. All along, those reasons had been nothing but a smokescreen. With her hand stiff against Crystal's, she forced herself to admit the truth: the last time she threw caution to the wind and dove in for her daughter, her whole world collapsed: Jake died and Crystal became a total stranger.

Rose shifted her feet. As long as she never committed, she could always pretend nothing was her fault, the way she had blamed her problems for years on Jake. Now she'd come face to face with what standing on the sidelines had really gotten her—a life locked in limbo, strangled by her fear of losses. She gazed at the black feather on the floor, longing to share with Crystal the freedom she'd discovered under the stars. Then she heard a voice, so quiet it seemed to slip between her thoughts.

Take the leap.

Startled, Rose looked up. There were no ravens beside the front window, no fleeting shadows or glimmers of light to indicate a fairy power had echoed sublime advice. This time, the words came from her own heart. The voice returned, soft as a sigh.

Now, before it's too late.

Rose kneeled down to gaze at Crystal. Her daughter's green eyes were as clear to her as the pool that day in Winnemucca, like a sheet of glass between them. Rose's heart sank, wondering if her window of opportunity had already passed. No, she thought defiantly, I won't give in to excuses this time—she's my girl and I want her back! She wrapped her arms around Crystal and held her—all of her, the girl she used to be and the girl she was now, even the woman she might become in the future. Rose buried her face into Crystal's cottony hair. "I love you, sweetie," she whispered. "Forever and ever and ever."

Biting her lip, Rose dared to lift her daughter high up in the air. She spun her around in a big, reckless circle and let Crystal's legs and bottom land on her hip, just like she always used to do when they played a favorite game they called "magic butterfly wings."

Slowing her feet to a stop, Rose closed her eyes, assuming Crystal might panic and wriggle away, or perhaps go limp entirely. Then she felt her daughter's soft fingers embrace her neck. All at once, Rose thought she heard the sound of shattering glass. When she opened her eyes and glanced into her daughter's face, she saw a mischievous sparkle.

"Weeeeeeeee!" Crystal cried at the top of her lungs, holding out her arms. She waved them briskly up and down, wiggling her fingers for wings.

Stunned, Rose spied a wicked look in her daughter's eyes. Grinning, she drew a deep breath and whirled Crystal with abandon until, with surprising force, her daughter clutched her around the waist and jumped down. Crystal gave her a hard shove, giggling as she tackled her onto the family quilt. Rose began to laugh and cry at the same time, her heart so full of light she thought it might rip at the seams. Engulfing Crystal in the quilt, she treasured her warmth and the soft quivers of the fabric with her laughter. To her, it was the sound and feel of pure magic, above and beyond any fairy enchantment, and she dug her hands deeply into the quilt, filling herself up with the weight of her daughter. The cadence of Crystal's giggles rang in her ears like sweet music. Rose swayed back and forth, tears streaming down her cheeks, when her joy was interrupted by a sharp gasp near the front window.

Laurel stood at the cafe table with her mouth open. At first, Rose thought she was reacting to Crystal's behavior. Then she pointed a wavering finger outside.

"R-Rosie," Laurel stammered, "l-look."

Nestled on the grass in the smoky town square were the ravens in a wide circle. Their black wings were shiny from a gentle rain that had begun to fall, collecting on their feathers like dew. In unison, they began to caw. Crystal sat up and listened to their chorus as if it were a kind of song. She allowed her fingers to slide from her mother's neck and picked up the fairy cake from the napkin on the floor, holding it to her mother.

Puzzled, Rose swept her finger through the icing, assuming it would please her daughter, and took a lick. When she gazed out the window again, a peculiar crease hung in the sky over Rook Ridge, rippling through the smoke like a strange portal.

Rose shook her head.

Suddenly, all she saw was colors.

22

"You saw them, didn't you?" Rose picked her way through the pines and buckbrush in the silver moonlight.

"What, the ravens?" Laurel replied. "Of course, they were in a circle."

"No. I mean the colors."

Laurel fell silent.

"I knew it," Rose nodded, her mouth firm. "You're one of us—you always have been."

Laurel paused on the hillside. "What are you talking about?" She leaned her hands on her knees to catch her breath.

"You're one of the fairy people—'twixt, like me. All along you've seen the colors, haven't you? Even when we were little." Rose glanced at the stars that twinkled across the sky in a coverlet of lights. "I remember how your eyes always traced the treetops every time Mom said the good people were near. You could see them gathering around us—you just wouldn't admit it." She brooded over the memory, folding her arms. "Maybe everyone can see them," Rose added, "if they really want to."

Laurel averted her eyes, but Rose caught the way her lips quivered in the moonlight. Her sister stubbornly brushed off water drops from her slicker as though wiping away her sister's comments. It had rained buckets all day, leaving the charred trees and brush on the ridge thoroughly soaked, with the clouds clearing out by nightfall. Everyone in town had called it a miracle, just what was needed to put out the fire. Except for Laurel, who said it was a curse. Now there was no reason *not* to climb Rook Ridge at midnight on Halloween. Laurel, of course, had protested every way she knew how, pointing out that they might get lost trying to find a fairy ring in the dark, or worse, slip and break their necks in the mud. And how could they guard themselves against Vincent when they didn't even know where he was?

Rose had refused to back down. To her, the rain was proof —Vincent wasn't winning after all. He might have set the fire, but clearly he had no control over the weather. Could she really believe mysterious forces had sabotaged his plans? All she knew was something had happened to her when she dared to play with Crystal that morning. As the ravens gathered in a circle with colors shimmering above their wings, she'd suddenly felt clean and new, as if she'd been baptized somehow. But into what? What curious initiation had happened? Such things were difficult for her to articulate, yet deep in her soul, Rose sensed a release, like she was finally allowing herself to flow with the fairy powers, rather than against them.

Rose steadied her feet on the ridge, gazing at the broad moon shining as bright as a streetlamp. All around, trees hissed that still smoldered from the fire, in spite of the day's deluge of rain. The soot released into the air made the full moon appear wavy and slightly blue. The coincidence was not lost on Rose, and the sight made her pull her slicker tighter around herself. She cleared her throat.

"Laurel, what else did you see in the sky this morning?"

"Nothing," Laurel dug her hands into her slicker. "Except colors. They must've been the northern lights—they're fairly common when there's dust or smoke in the atmosphere." She smirked. "I guess even the cosmos could use a good cleaning."

Rose wasn't fooled by her dry wit. "In broad daylight? Those were more than northern lights, and you know it. I spotted that look in your eye—whatever it was, it scared the crap out of you. Don't lie to me, Laurel. What did you *see?*"

Laurel returned her gaze with a fixed stare, weighing her sister's strength. "Mom," she finally admitted.

She waited for her sister to react, but Rose kept silent, her boots planted firmly in the mud. Laurel drew a deep breath. "She appeared inside a wrinkle in the sky. Only she looked different than I remember—windblown, with a shawl around her shoulders like she came from an old country. And she said something about magic."

"What?" Rose prodded.

"Well, she crossed her arms over her chest and said it's here."

"Here? Like on the ridge?" Rose asked desperately.

Laurel winced and threw up her hands. "I don't know!"

Rose had to hug her for her honesty. She'd never heard Laurel admit she didn't have all the answers, let alone confess to a fairy vision. Fighting back tears, she wondered why she hadn't seen her mother for herself. But perhaps the fairies knew Laurel needed it more. Surely she must have worried sometimes during childhood that her stepmother might not love her as much as her own daughter. This time, Laurel came first. Rose swallowed her pride, allowing her heart to be grateful for the gift. There'd always been enough love for them both.

Rose gave Laurel's arm a gentle squeeze, awed by her transformation in the last twenty-four hours. For a stalwart woman who denied fairy superstitions as simple minded, in her own small way, she'd actually admitted she was 'twixt. *Maybe it's just a phase, before Laurel snaps back to her no-nonsense self.* But Rose didn't care—at least for this instant, high on a windy, ash-strewn ridge, she felt closer to her sister than ever before. She gazed at Laurel in her borrowed jeans and hiking boots with an old lumberjack slicker, looking surprisingly like she used to before Tom got a hold of her. Rose smiled at the fact that she smelled of smoke and damp leaves instead of her usual pricey perfume. The moonlight made her hair shine platinum, and her face appeared fresher and more youthful than it had in years. *No matter what Laurel thinks of all this fairy business,* Rose smirked, *it sure has done wonders for her spirit.*

Weaving around stones and fallen logs, Rose searched the ridge for evidence of a fairy ring. There were no mushrooms to be found in a loose circle, or decayed tree stumps with flowers dotted along their rims. All that was left after the fire was blackened earth and ash, which the wind swirled around them in columns. Everywhere she glanced, black trees stood tall like soldiers at attention, scorched bare of their needles, as if waiting for direction from the moon. Rose studied the dark recesses of the shadows they cast to see if any of them wavered. The slightest motion could be Chance, lingering in shadows, waiting to help her as he did when he found Crystal on that first October full moon. Or it might be Vincent, with his heart as black as the silhouettes, ready to do her in.

A twig snapped, and Rose jumped, nearly losing her balance. She reached out to grab Laurel's arm, unwilling to use her flashlight for fear that Vincent might spot her. No one had seen hide nor hair of him all day. At one point, Amy had snuck over to the saloon to peek through his windows, while Rose and Laurel were up to their elbows making meals for the fire fighters. When she came back, she said the building was empty and dark as a cave. To her way of reasoning, it all made sense. "I bet he's hiding out so he can lay low," Amy explained. "Think about it, if he can't make it past midnight without soaking off someone else's form, then he's got to conserve his energy until that moment. For all we know, he's buried himself in a hole in the ground like the snake he really is, until he's ready to spring."

Then Amy had walked to the shotgun in the corner of the shop. "We might as well face it, ladies. Our only hope is for you to go up to Rook Ridge tonight and find that fairy ring. I'll take care of Crystal here with all the doors and windows locked." Amy picked up the gun and tapped it on the floor. "Don't worry—anybody who tries to fool with me will get a bullet in his butt."

Despite Amy's bravado, Rose trembled with every step she took on the ridge, her nerve endings on fire. Not even Laurel's cell phone worked at this elevation, and she was glad she'd slipped her father's pistol into her pocket. She gazed again at the sky, hoping to see a circle of ravens—or any sign, for that matter—which might direct her path. All she spied was a sliver of smoke that threaded past the moon. The ridge was a wasteland—a vacuum devoid of life. Nothing can survive here, she thought, much less point to a fairy ring.

"Chance, where are you?" she whispered urgently. "We need your help—"

An owl swooped by, wintry feathers gleaming nearly as white as the moon. Startled, Rose listened to its lonely call echo across the ridge.

"Chance!" she pressed. "Don't you hear me? Please show us a sign—"

Rose leaned to peer past a large tree, when Laurel's fingers dug into her arm.

"R-Rosie," Laurel stuttered. "Oh my God. They're here."

It was then Rose saw them. Her hand closed over her father's pistol as one by one they moved through the darkness, walking in weary procession like a slow train. Under the moonlight, their faces appeared as hollow and empty as ghosts caught in search of something they'd lost. To Rose, they were characters from a nightmare, heads bowed to the ground and feet shuffling heavily while pans and shovels clanked against their backs. Shuddering, Rose pressed her shoulder to Laurel's, afraid they might be disembodied souls, still restless over a century after the gold rush. But when she saw their flashlights dart over rocks and embers like flitting spirits, it soon became obvious that these were not phantoms of the past, nor did they belong to a fairy march to herald the coming of Samhain.

These were the gold seekers—and the only reason they were on the ridge was because of the legend.

"When a blue moon rises over Rook Ridge," Laurel sighed, "all those who are pure of heart can make a wish in the O'Dannan name and find gold." She rubbed her eyes with suspicion. "So Rosie, how pure do you think they are?"

"Purely greedy." A chill swept through Rose, and all at once she felt like a fool—surrounded by all of the other fools. She flinched when she heard someone repeat "O'Dannan, O'Dannan" like a prayer. As the person approached, she could tell he was merely a boy, maybe twelve or thirteen, with a patched coat and threadbare jeans and enough rattling gadgets strapped to his back to scare any fairy away. Rose wasn't certain, but she thought he might be one of Ray Beane's sons. She elbowed Laurel to take a closer look. Her sister nodded, then dug into her slicker to pull out a small leather bag. She lifted it to the moonlight—it was their father's old gold pouch.

"There's no gold here, honey," Laurel called out, shaking her head. "If there was, our daddy would have found it a long time ago. Here—" she tossed him the bag, "go home and buy your folks a good meal."

The boy examined the pouch with a disappointed look, unimpressed by its meager contents. He trudged away, followed by the others, but Rose doubted they would give up any time soon. They'll probably move to another part of the ridge, she thought, and keep searching till dawn. She turned to Laurel. "I didn't know you brought dad's gold pouch."

"Oh hell," Laurel shrugged, "I thought it might bring us luck for a change. By the way, I noticed his pistol was missing."

"No it's not," Rose confided.

"Good girl." Laurel gazed at her watch. "We'd better head over to the stones before it's too late."

Laurel tugged her arm, and the two of them stepped carefully through charred forest debris to the circle of boulders that stood high on the ridge. Under the moonlight, their granite was mottled yet shiny, with specs of wet mica glistening as bright as the stars. Rose reached to touch one of the stones, easily twice her height. Its surface felt smooth and cold like Amy's crystal ball, and the thought made her shiver.

"Is this where Mom, you know—"

She was afraid to finish her sentence. When Laurel nodded, Rose crouched to scan the ground for the slightest sign of a fairy ring—a small depression in the dirt, an intriguing array of branches, a shimmer of fool's gold that could be construed as fairy dust. She dug her fingers into the crusty soil and turned it over to watch it crumble through her hands. The exercise felt futile, even ridiculous, and her heart thumped wildly as she glanced at her watch. It was only twenty more minutes till midnight, and she worried that if by some miracle she did find a fairy ring, how could she do a soul exchange without the right souls? For the last twenty-four hours, both Chance and Vincent had been as elusive to her as ghosts. Even if they did appear out of nowhere, what could she do? Pretend to know where to find gold, like her ancestor Corvine, or try to bribe Vincent to leave Chance's body with tales of fairy power? Rose kneaded her forehead, cursing the ashes that fell into her eyes. She grabbed her father's pistol.

"Dammit, there's nothing here!" she fumed, rising to her feet. She glared at the moon, which looked as dead to her now as an empty seashell, and aimed her pistol. "Where are you, Chance?" She cocked the hammer and took a shot. The blast echoed across the ridge, startling Laurel, but Rose refused to lower her arm. "Sure, you say you love me," she waved the gun, "when it's all colors and feathers and fluttery wings. Now that I *need* you, you're nowhere to be found! What kind of love is that? I trusted you!" She fired the pistol again, falling into a huddle as the sound reverberated inside her ears.

Rose buried her head in her knees, tears dropping onto her slicker as the gun's echo faded and the ridge fell silent. She lifted her head to the moon.

"What on earth can I do now?" she sputtered, struggling for any morsel of faith she had left in the smoky darkness. Gritting her teeth, her tears flowed as if her soul had cracked open and poured onto the forest floor. All she could feel, from her head to her toes, was loss—the loss of her hopes, her dreams—even the certain loss of time as her heartbeats counted off the seconds. Exhausted, Rose wiped her eyes.

"No!" She grabbed at her temples, coughing from the lingering smoke. "This can't be all there is. I can't give up— not when we're so close. Chance couldn't have deserted us— he *wouldn't*. He told me to believe, and I've got to—"

Rose studied the barren ridge that appeared as desolate as she felt. All at once, a thought struck her: What if this is what Vincent wants—for his darkness to overwhelm my heart? The sparkle from Crystal's eye that morning came to her, the way her giggles had filled her up inside with a tender hope, like the colors. Though Crystal hadn't made a peep for the rest of the day, Rose stood to her feet, more determined than ever.

"No matter what you do to this ridge, Vincent—or Jake—or whoever you are," she called out, in case he was within earshot, "I'm not going back to a gray life anymore. Crystal and I deserve better—and so does Chance! Do you hear me?" She whipped around, steeling herself for any shadow that might advance. "I swear to God, I'll comb this mountain till the day I die if that's what it takes to find my miracle."

Bracing her shoulders, Rose dared to step forward in the dark, only to feel a cold shock as her foot plunged into a puddle. Startled, she glanced down.

Instantly, colors arose over the water like butterflies. They hovered at first, rising and falling in a dance, then gradually swirling with translucent, abalone hues. Shaking, Rose stared in awe. She peered into the puddle and reached out a trembling hand. As the blues and reds and greens skimmed past her fingers, they felt warm, even tingly, and her heart raced.

"L-Laurel," she gasped. "Come quick!"

Laurel trotted across the hillside and clutched her arm. When Rose bent down to touch her finger to the water, the reflections changed into a face. Rose's breath crimped—the image she saw wasn't her mother, or Ailís, or even Chance. It was Crystal.

"Sweetheart!" Rose cried. Dropping to her knees, she dove her hands into the water. "Are you all right?"

A strained voice filled the night air, seeping into her heart like a breath. *She's with us, love.*

Rose knew that voice—it was Chance. She searched the circle of stones, wondering if he stood in shadows, they way he did on the night that Crystal ran away. "Where are you?"

Where I've been all along, his voice wavered over a gust of wind. *Guarding Crystal.*

Rose heard a small cry. Her daughter's face receded into the puddle and disappeared. Rose dashed her hands furiously into the water, feeling it slip through her fingers. Clenching her fists, she stood to her feet and batted at the colors.

"Where is she?" Rose demanded, taking angry swings. "I don't care if you're fairies—you can't have her. She's mine!"

The floating hues paused, as if suspended by her words, and Rose realized they had formed a ring around her and Laurel beside the water. Slowly, they closed in until she felt their warmth against her skin, even through her vinyl slicker. Despite her rush of panic, an inexplicable stillness washed over her, and she wondered if they had somehow snuggled against her soul. Breathless, Rose folded her arms over her chest to retain the peculiar sense of calm. It was more than peace—it felt deep and strong, as full as the ocean in her island dreams —like the power of love itself. The last time she felt that way was when she was with Chance and they reached up their hands to the moon. In that moment, she knew she could race with clouds or touch the stars—even fall in love with a man who could fly—anything was possible. She studied the shimmering ring around her and Laurel, the way the hues circled their bodies yet infused their hearts at the same time, and it dawned on her that there were no divisions between her and the colors now. They were all made of the same dancing molecules, the same magic. Suddenly, she understood the vision that Laurel had earlier, and she turned to her sister.

"It's here," she patted her chest. "We don't need to search anymore. The magic—it's inside us."

The water was as smooth as glass now, and Rose knew she would take the leap, just like her mother had done all those years ago. It was the same urge she had when she'd hugged Crystal that morning—all she had to do was immerse herself with her full heart, and healing and wholeness would follow. The pull was as strong as that day by the pool in Winnemucca that was forever burned into her brain. She couldn't *not* do it, for she knew whatever lay beyond the moonlit water held the key—she just needed the courage to dive in. Whether or not she could bring about a soul exchange was beyond her grasp, but one thing she knew for certain: somehow the trip would lead her and Crystal home. Rose lifted her boot to jump.

"Rosie!" Laurel held back her elbow. "What if the fairies keep you?"

Rose hadn't thought of that—of the fairies' capriciousness. But if she'd learned anything lately, it was that holding back had never gotten her anything but ashes. She stared boldly at Laurel and lifted her chin. "Then I guess they'll have to take us both, won't they?"

Laurel froze. She scanned the colors that linked around them like the daisy chains they used to make in childhood. She peered hesitantly at Rose as though her face were a map to a foreign land.

"You've got to *believe.*" Rose cupped Laurel's cheek. "Do you really want to go back to a life without these colors?"

Slowly, Laurel shook her head. Then, to Rose's surprise, she clutched her hand with a fierce grip.

"Let's go," Laurel nodded.

With that, Rose wrapped her arm around her sister. At the count of three, she breathed the word "O'Dannan," and they made the leap.

Darkness gripped Rose and Laurel like a fist. At first, Rose couldn't see anything, as if they'd dropped into a black hole. When her eyes adjusted to the dim light, she startled to find herself standing on a wood floor in front of Amy, whose face was washed in fear. She and Laurel were no longer on the ridge—they were inside the Magpie Saloon, surrounded by bar tables and captain's chairs that glinted with an eerie orange light. Through the saloon's front windows, Rose could see her building was on fire, smoke rising from the roof over the apartment kitchen. Laurel squeezed her hand until her knuckles flinched in pain.

"R-Rosie," Laurel stammered. "T-Turn around."

Rose swiveled on her heels. Vincent stood before her with Crystal in his arms. He held a gun.

"He smoked us out!" Amy blurted desperately. "I grabbed Crystal to escape the fire—I had no idea he was waiting for us."

Vincent pulled back his thumb to cock the revolver.

"Welcome back," he aimed the weapon at Crystal's

temple. "God, you're stubborn, Rose. Aren't you tired yet? The endless merry-go-round, eternal chase through lifetimes. Don't you know it's inevitable? I'll *always* be with you. But then, I guess you've heard that before."

A raven cawed and dove at him from on top of the bar with its claws bared, all black feathers and beating wings. Without blinking, Vincent took a shot, his bullet grazing the bird's head and sending the bar mirror into pieces on the floor. Each shard reflected the fire's glow.

"Chance!" Rose cried as Laurel's and Amy's screams erupted in a chorus. They watched the raven flutter to a high shelf.

Vincent smiled. It made Rose shake to see a similar face and body of the man she'd soared with among stars now holding a gun to her daughter's head. Only his eyes were a hard, icy blue, not the soft, welcoming brown she'd come to love. Impulsively, she reached out for Crystal when he thrust the revolver between her eyes. The barrel felt cold and hard against her forehead.

"You see, darling, it's the burden of the 'twixt—we're always caught between dark and light, yin and yang, just like your friend Amy talks about. Without me, you don't exist. It would be like trying to function with only half a heart. That's why I keep coming back—because you need me."

"What do you want?" Rose demanded. She dug frantically into her pockets, emptying bills and coins onto the floor. When her fingers slid across her father's pistol, she smoothed down the pocket of her coat to keep it hidden. "Whatever it is— money, the shop—take it! Just give me Crystal." Despite his weapon, she grabbed for her daughter. Vincent smiled viciously and took a step back, stumbling for a split-second against a wooden crate before regaining his balance.

That's when Rose saw it—a glimmer of it—the gnawing hunger in his eyes before he summoned his confident face again. No matter how assured he pretended to be, Rose knew in that instant that he was always empty, as voracious as what her ancestor Corvine had seen in the gold miners at Ophir Creek. It was the same bottomless desire that made his eyes look like deep pools in the right light—exactly what Crystal had fallen into that day in Winnemucca.

"You know what I want," Vincent's voice was oddly fatigued. "You promised it to me in a garden over a century ago: nothing less than eternity. All you have to do is sit back until that clock strikes midnight," he gazed at an old cuckoo clock on the wall, and Rose could have sworn his words had taken on an Irish lilt, "and this body will be mine forever. Let's just say I'm cashing in on an old bet."

His lip quivered, and in spite of his arrogance, Rose could tell he was bluffing—the slight slouch to his shoulder, the droop to his eyes. With each passing minute, he was growing weaker, not stronger.

"Eternity? What were you going to do, steal Crystal's life force if Chance's body couldn't sustain you after midnight? Take a *child's* body this time?"

"If I have to," Vincent replied. "You're not the only one who reads the diary, Rose. Samhain and Beltane—they're both gates."

He squeezed Crystal's arm, and from out of nowhere the front door blew open with a cruel wind that swirled through the saloon, knocking over chairs and shattering windows before it rushed outside to rattle the building. Laurel and Amy shrieked and covered their heads from the bottles and lanterns that tumbled off shelves, while Rose watched in horror as Crystal's wary expression began to fade. She seemed to be slipping into a coma.

Rose felt cold—a bone-crushing cold, as though her heart had splintered into countless fragments. It was the same way she'd felt six months ago in May, on the day her mother used to call Beltane, when she'd seen her daughter at the bottom of that pool. She cut her gaze to Vincent, who was sparkling with energy now, and for the first time she put the pieces together —what had happened in Winnemucca had never been an accident. He'd attempted to siphon the life force from Crystal then, too. He must have known he was dying from the overdose, Rose thought, so he tried to prolong his life at the height of Beltane. She wondered what page of the diary he'd consulted, what he'd done to make Crystal dash from their apartment and into the pool to get away from him. Rose searched her daughter's eyes, which appeared glassy and lifeless as marbles now, and she understood that all along, while he was Jake, he'd been more than a neglectful addict— he'd been a truly evil presence who thought nothing of trading in his daughter's life to preserve his own. The cuckoo clock on the wall registered eleven fifty-eight. Cautiously, Rose snuck her fingers into her pocket, keeping her arm at her side so Vincent couldn't see, and gripped her father's pistol. Forgive me, sweetie, she said in her heart, hoping Crystal might somehow hear. I didn't protect you then. I'm going to now.

Above her, the raven cawed from on top of the bar shelf.

His dark eyes flashed from the fire's glow, and he stretched out his wings like a man nailed to a cross.

Do it, Chance's voice urged. *When the clock strikes midnight, shoot.*

Before Rose could weigh the consequences of his demand, the raven knocked a heavy crock off the shelf with his claws. It struck Vincent on the head with such force that his knees buckled. Laurel instantly dove at him to grab his revolver while Amy wrestled Crystal from his grasp. Rose didn't have time to think as she raised her father's pistol to Vincent's head.

Running her hand over the top to cock the hammer, she suddenly realized she was about to kill Chance—to kill the love of her life, her partner in starlit dances and magical flights to places she'd never known, both inside and out. He was her shadow, her soul mate, and her heart was about to burst.

"I c-can't!" Rose sputtered. "I can't kill you! Go to the island," she pleaded to the raven. "I'll find you somehow—I swear, I'll find a way to cross time and space where we'll all be safe."

The raven erupted in a haunting cry. Rose shuddered when she heard Chance's voice echo in her ears.

And remain 'twixt forever? Never truly alive or dead—snared for eternity in between? I want more, Rose. And so do you.

The clock struck twelve, and the cuckoo burst from its door and began to sound. Vincent's lips slid into a sick grin.

"I knew you couldn't do it." He let out a strained laugh, though his body began to slump. "Like I said all along—soul bonds can't be broken."

The raven lifted his wings and dashed from the shelf to land in front of Rose. There, he stretched to his full height. In the blink of an eye, he swelled to become the towering silhouette of Chance Murphy.

Yes they can! Chance's voice thundered in Rose's veins. His dark hands grabbed her by the shoulders and shook her. *You decide the direction of your heart—no one else can make that call! Think of that bullet as the lightning rod that can bind our souls forever—if you believe. No more vicious circles anymore. You and Crystal will finally be free.*

To Rose's astonishment, his form passed over Vincent's like a phantom glove, engulfing his body in shadows. Before her eyes, the two men suddenly appeared as one being—light superimposed by dark, blonde hair cast murky with black locks —a confusing duality of both spirits that sent her mind reeling. Chance folded his long, dark arms in a fierce grip around himself—around Vincent—like a man wrapped in a burial shroud.

"Chance!" Rose cried out. "Which one are you?" She waved her gun. "Step aside! Move out of the way!"

NO! Now's the time! Chance demanded with a finality that made her heart want to stop. *For once in your life, Rose, don't choose fear—*

He reached out his dark hand for a split-second to sweep her cheek, and his fingers felt warm, though they looked made of black ether. *Choose ME. When you pull that trigger, you take control of your destiny and say yes to everything we've ever dreamed. Do it, love —do it for me.*

"But what will happen?" Rose squinted to perceive the shadowy outline of his face over Vincent's. "I can't let you go!"

Silently, Chance took one last look at her.

I'll always be with you, he promised. *In the rain that settles on your cheeks. In the moonlight that caresses your face and lights stars in your eyes. In the wind that curls around you and presses you forward, reminding you to be free. Everywhere you live and breathe, Rose, I will shadow your soul for eternity.*

He bowed his head.

Rose's entire body began to shake, tears streaming down her cheeks, when she heard the cuckoo's final call.

"Shoot, Rosie!" Laurel cried out. "For the love of God—"

Rose raised her father's pistol and gripped it with both hands, trembling as she aimed it straight at Chance's forehead. With every fibre in her being, she wanted to step forward and press her mouth to his—to savor the fleeting warmth of his lips for one last kiss—though his form was intertwined with Vincent's and he remained cloaked in shadows. But she knew with only seconds to spare she couldn't delay any longer. Heart breaking, Rose forced herself to stand tall and whisper "O'Dannan," feeling as if she'd surrendered her own soul with the current of her breath.

She pulled the trigger.

A blast pierced the air and she screamed. Instantly, Chance's shadow vanished and blood erupted on the side of Vincent's blonde head, spilling from his temple. He stared her down, icy blue eyes fixed in surprise, like he never thought she'd really do it. In that moment, Rose could have sworn she saw his eyes waver from blue to brown and back again, even as his body convulsed and then stiffened. Stumbling forward, he reached out for her when lightning flashed across the bar like a floodlight. Roof beams and ceiling tiles came tumbling down. Rose couldn't tell where the bolt had struck—if it had sliced through the roof or hit a tree that slammed against the saloon.

All she knew was that as thunder rolled, the dead weight of his body fell against hers, knocking her down. With a crack her head hit the floor, and for a while all she saw was fractured angles and smeared colors, mixed with blood, until everything became washed in gold.

23

Blinking slowly, Rose rested her gaze on the flickering gold flames. Memories ambled in and out of her mind with no particular order—a moonlit flight with Chance, holding Crystal in her arms while colors danced, laughing with Amy over spilled cider that didn't taste very good anyway. But then the impressions took on a harsher turn —her building licked by orange flames, the sound of a gunshot, a searing white lightning strike. Gasping, she remembered the events in the Magpie Saloon and sat up straight, only to discover she was wrapped in a wool blanket on a rustic, wood-framed bed. The small flames before her belonged to a turf fire in a hearth, and they released thin curls of mossy smoke. She coughed and glanced around, realizing she was once again in Ailís's cottage on the island.

Crystal sat at a table in the center of the room, dipping her brush into a pot of paint. Rose's heart lurched and she spun around—Vincent was nowhere to be found. Neither was Chance, or Laurel, or even Amy. There was only Ailís in the corner at her spinning wheel. She hummed softly, hand threading wool while her foot pedaled. Rose threw off the blanket and stood up, woozy. She stumbled to the table to sit down next to her daughter. She wanted to grab Crystal's arm and ask what happened—if Chance survived, whether a soul exchange took place, if either of them were alive anymore or if this was all a dream? Her head ached like it had been cracked in two, and she buried her forehead into her hands to allay the pain. When she withdrew her fingers, she noticed feathery marks ran up her arms and her fingertips were stained with blood.

"Crystal," she feared the worst, "where are we—I mean, really? Will we ever go home again?"

Crystal tapped the page in front of her. At the top, she'd painted gray clouds that were jagged in the middle, split in two, and the rest of the page was blank. She stared at her mother, undisturbed by the blood on her hands.

"It's your turn." She handed her the paint brush.

Confused, Rose shot a glance to Ailís.

Ailís stopped pedaling. She allowed the spinning wheel to come to rest and folded the wool on her lap, laying it inside a basket.

"Samhain is not over, *a thaisce*. The night when the veil is thinnest."

Rose shivered, knowing that meant the departed, like Jake, might still haunt her. She kneaded her hands when she heard her daughter sigh.

"It's not about the old pictures anymore." Crystal pointed to the brush in her mother's hand. "You have to paint the next picture for us, Mommy."

Rose shook her head, not quite understanding.

Ailís walked to the table. She cupped her hand to the back of Rose's head. Her fingers felt warm, even healing, and she smoothed them over the piece of paper, leaving a trail of Rose's blood. "It's time to rewrite the legend, love. Samhain opens the gate for the future and prophecy. What will tomorrow bring?"

Rose tried to steal a glance at the water glass Crystal used to rinse her brush, hoping the reflections might help her, but Ailís moved it aside before she could cheat. She leaned down to Rose's ear. "The picture must come from within."

A blush spread over Rose's cheeks. She gazed at her watch, worried that time might be slipping, when she realized that the hands weren't moving—they had stopped at twelve o'clock. She and Crystal were caught in a time between times—'twixt —on the island. Unsure of how long it might last, she quickly dipped her brush into the paint pot as she'd been told. At first, she attempted to draw herself and Crystal, standing hand in hand like a happy mother and daughter, though gray clouds loomed above them and the paper was stained with her blood. After making ovals for heads and bodies, sticks for arms and legs, she remembered to include hearts for her and Crystal, the way her daughter had showed her once—whole, not broken. Nevertheless, her figures looked stiff and flat, like cartoons frozen in a frame. Swiftly, she added a square around the people with a triangle for a roof to make the scene look homier. In spite of her efforts, her painting appeared harsh, heavily contrasted with black and white, like the learning exercises she used to force on Crystal. Her daughter interrupted her progress and pointed at the characters.

"Don't forget the colors."

Rose nodded. She swirled her brush in water and searched for more paints—but there weren't any, only black. She turned to Crystal. "Honey, where are the colors?"

Crystal smiled, proud to be of help. "They're here," she patted her heart. "Feel them inside. Use your fingers."

Rose checked Ailís, who nodded. "You can do it, *aisling*. You know how. Let them flow, like when you danced with Chance."

Tears trickled down Rose's cheeks. It hadn't occurred to her that all along, Chance had been giving her an education—lessons in dreaming, in believing, in igniting her heart to accept possibilities once again. She closed her eyes, remembering the way his arms felt around her as they swayed beneath stars, how his breath warmed her cheek—warmed her very soul. Her heart felt full then, yet free as a bird, and that's when they'd come, the colors, like lanterns illuminating the sky. Rose reached out to grasp Crystal's hand, clinging to her soft fingers. The feeling made her heart swell, and she pressed her hand to her chest to hold in the sensation. Then she touched the paper. Opening her eyes, she saw a stream of yellow swirl into curls where her daughter's hair should be. She moved her finger and the stick figures acquired warm skin and faint blushes to their cheeks, shirts and jeans of red and blue. Rose smiled. She eagerly stroked their eyes and watched them emerge as emerald pools—O'Dannan green, no less. Then she swept her finger around the house and trees appeared with long, elegant bows framing the scene.

Crystal giggled and joined in, dotting her finger around the house to make bright blossoms and potato plants with healthy stems. For the life of her, Rose could have sworn she smelled the flowers' fragrance and the gentle aroma of pine trees. Astonished, she studied the painting, when it dawned on her that the colors weren't stationary, tinted into the texture and fiber of the paper, the way she usually thought of a child's play paints. Instead, they vibrated on the page, throbbing like beats of her own heart. Her thoughts turned to Chance, and immediately a black raven appeared on a cloud in the sky, without her touching the paper. She wasn't sure, but she thought she saw his wings waver. Rose's breath hitched, mind racing with questions. Was he ever coming back? Was he even alive? She stared at the swipe of her blood that had dried to a deep burgundy on the page and turned to Crystal.

"Help me, sweetheart."

Crystal gently stroked her head and dotted her finger to the painting where her mother's heart was drawn. Rose's blood seeped onto the page, but this time the vivid red pool pulsated in place. "Feel him, Mommy," she urged, "right here." She took her mother by the hand and made her stand to her feet. "Dance."

"What? Right here—right now?"

Crystal nodded.

Bewildered, Rose took a couple of awkward steps from the table and swayed left and right with her daughter. "Like this?"

Crystal stopped. She patted her mother's chest. "You have to really feel him, Mommy—in here." She stood on her tiptoes to reach her mother's face. When Rose bent down, Crystal pressed her fingers to her brows. "Close your eyes and dream," she sealed her eyelids. "Dance with him like you mean it."

Rose's cheeks flushed, a slow burn that worked its way up to her temples before igniting into a fire. She felt silly pretending to dance with a suitor in the middle of an old cottage like a love-struck school girl. At the same time, she was all raw nerves and seared brain cells, wondering if Chance could have possibly survived the gunshot. The pain in her head returned like an ice pick and she winced, when she felt Crystal push against her hips to force her into a waltz. Rose relented with a grimace, trying to keep her mind off the bone-splitting ache in her head. Shifting her feet, she matched Crystal's three-quarter time, the way she had taught her daughter once to dance in their kitchen in Winnemucca. Back then, it was to distract her from the fact that her father had come home high again, strung-out like usual and talking in circles. She used to turn up the music loud, hoping Crystal wouldn't notice his condition, and she always pretended to be giddy, like it was merely a game. And now? While they shuffled their feet on the sandy cottage floor, Rose wondered what on earth they could hope to achieve.

"Dream, Mommy!" Crystal gripped her hands so tightly Rose flinched. "You're his only hope. It's up to you now—you have to believe!"

Rose opened her eyes, shocked to see the indignation on her daughter's face. She shut them again and forced herself to concentrate on Chance, though her last sight of him, folded like a dark shroud over Vincent's body, had pulverized her heart. With all her might, she tried to erase from her memory the bullet she'd put into Vincent's head, oozing with blood, the way his eyes had glassed over and he'd toppled to the floor. Like a playing card, she forced herself to lay the image down in her mind, sealing it with her hand as if on a poker table. Then she imagined Chance's rugged face and windblown black hair, the way his brown eyes flickered when he invited her to dance for the first time in her shop. Drawing a deep breath, she recalled how he smelled of pines and buckbrush, the aroma of sage on a dewy mountain evening. His voice rolled softly like the sea at low tide, and when he called her name, her soul leaped inside, already taking flight.

Rose bit her lip, her legs growing stiff against her waltz. After what had happened in the saloon, how could she picture him with her and Crystal in the future, dancing in a place like Ophir Creek? She shook her head, heart racing, trying to maintain her focus. If he were with them, she thought, he'd let Crystal rest her feet on his boots as they waltzed, his big knees lifting her high in the air, just to make her laugh. Then he'd grab her, giggling, and take them both for a spin, all three of them dancing in haphazard circles to avoid the barrels and tables in the shop. They'd squeal with delight—not only because of their joy, but because he was a terrible dancer! He had two left feet, and he'd step on their toes, his shoulders so wide that he'd lumber them into erratic loops with the rhythm of their dance. And that's when they would come, Rose thought, the colors—alighting all around them like butterflies.

Deep inside, she dared to allow her heart to tingle with expectation, in spite of all that had happened—the accident in Winnemucca, the fire in her building, the gunshot in the saloon—as though such a miracle could ever really be possible. She felt her daughter squeeze her hands, and a soft serenity descended upon her like on the ridge. It felt delicate and sacred, the way newly fallen snow does on your forehead and eyelashes, yet unexpected at the same time, like a blessing. Rose couldn't explain it, but somehow, in that moment, she felt as though her vision could come true—and her lover could return—for the peace began to wrap around her heart with the same warmth and assurance as the O'Dannan family quilt.

In that instant, Crystal wriggled her herself free. Rose felt a feather glide along her cheek, like a wingtip. Her heart raced as a gentle hand sealed over her eyes with strong, rough fingers while a warm breath brushed over her lips, as soft as a prayer. A sturdy arm wrapped around her shoulders, drawing her into the sureness of his chest. Rose gasped, but all she could see was the fabric of his coat, as black as coal, along with weathered buttons, some broken at the edges. Nevertheless, in his grasp she felt her soul anchor to his, reaching a long-sought-for haven. Then their bodies swayed in the same waltz pattern as before, but it was not nearly as flowing this time. His movements were occasionally jerky and stumbling, and sometimes he lost the rhythm entirely. Rose didn't care, as long as those big arms held her forever. But when his heavy boot stepped on her toe, she heard an embarrassed cough.

"You know, unless you're in flight," Rose giggled, "you really can't dance at all."

He laughed, soft and low.

"Look up, darling." Chance lifted her chin so her eyes met his. In their mahogany depth was not the longing of centuries or the wispy twilight adoration she'd become accustomed to, but a love that had finally found its place of refuge. He clutched her temples and enveloped her in a long, warm kiss. "We made it home."

POSTLUDE

Snowflakes fell on Ophir Creek that morning, soft and quiet as feathers. Rose gazed out the window of her shop at the white powder on the ridge, knowing it signaled the end of gold hunting season. Knowing, too, that winter was on its way, with only three more days left before Thanksgiving. Usually that meant there'd be fewer tourists until the skiers and snowmobilers arrived around Christmas, but Rose didn't mind —she was grateful for the time to rest. Inhaling a deep breath, a hush settled in her bones as she scanned the light snow that spread like lace over the town square. Outside, an old raven landed on the porch, its feathers dusted white. It hopped onto the windowsill and rapped on the glass. Rose smiled, studying the bird's gentle eyes before heading to the wood stove to throw in another log.

"When's he coming?" Crystal demanded from her stool at the counter. She sat in front of a painting, wearing a brand-new pair of wings that Rose had fashioned for her with real feathers and flecks of gold. Dipping her brush into a water glass, she clicked it loudly against the sides.

"Oh, a little birdie told me it won't be long," Rose winked at the raven. She stepped over to peek at her daughter's artwork.

"Good," Crystal nodded. "Because he promised me, you know."

"Promised what, sweetheart?"

"That he'd stay with us forever."

Rose's heart fluttered. She shot a glance at Amy, who was hanging decorations—Indian corn, wild turkey feathers, a horn of plenty. She added paper pilgrims to the wall and nodded at her friend with a smile. They both knew Laurel was picking up Chance today from the hospital in Boise, where he'd been recuperating from surgery. The bullet had lodged in the left side of his brain, the part doctors said was responsible for logic and language. Although the operation was successful and he regained consciousness, they reported that his ability to speak and organize vocabulary might be permanently impaired. Every time he tried to utter a word, his voice came out a raspy caw. Nevertheless, after four weeks of convalescence he could dress and feed himself as well as walk down the hallways, so he was due to be discharged that morning with a referral for speech therapy.

Rose had visited him countless times, of course, bringing meals for him and his entire medical team, but she hadn't allowed Crystal to go with her, only Amy or Laurel. She didn't think her daughter could handle being in a hospital setting again, much less seeing her friend surrounded by tubes and pulsing machines. On top of that, there were strict regulations against commotion and loud noises. And unlike Chance, ever since Halloween night, Crystal hadn't stopped talking—and laughing and squealing and bubbling over with more exuberance than Rose could ever have imagined. Be careful what you wish for, she often smiled to herself, but the truth was, she wouldn't have it any other way. The staff psychiatrist was naturally astounded, given Crystal's previous diagnosis in Winnemucca, but he attributed her burst of progress to a case of "selective mutism"—a rare disorder arising from severe stress or physical trauma, which can sometimes disappear altogether with sufficient therapy. He complimented Rose on her devotion to working with Crystal on her learning exercises, and she nodded politely at his assessment. But deep inside she knew the real reason Crystal was talking. It was because her mother was finally listening. After all, they were home now, *really* home, in each other's hearts as well as living space, and that was what had made all the difference.

The psychiatrist was not nearly so cheerful about Chance's prospects. When he'd failed to speak with any clarity, he'd been given a pen and a notebook to communicate his thoughts. According to the psychiatrist, he wrote endless drivel about a misty island in a foreign land, about colors that miraculously changed into birds and people who could fly. And then there was the obsession over dancing—pages and pages about airy waltzes beneath a full moon with a beautiful woman who giggled as they spun their dreams.

"Markedly delusional," the psychiatrist reported, shaking his head. Yet to his surprise, Rose hugged him with such fervor that he nearly choked. When she finally let go, she glanced at the notebook with tears in her eyes. It was all there, clear as a bell—her raven man, his words inscribed for everyone to see in prose that bordered on poetry. These were not the ramblings of a lunatic, but the keen observations of a forest scientist who couldn't help noting everything he'd seen, smelled, and experienced on the island. On these pages were the slow changes of the tides, the delicate star patterns of October, harvest instructions for potatoes, and the behavior of ravens elucidated with an ornithologist's precision. He was both thoughtful and brilliant, yet even she was surprised at the level of detail he'd composed. And, of course, there was also the black-haired woman and her tow-headed girl—"those wild birds who stole my heart"—which he wrote about with an intensity usually reserved for fine treasures. How could he be so lucid now, she wondered, when his mind used to be a scramble? She turned to the doctor and asked if he'd ever heard of madness somehow being reversed. The psychiatrist shrugged.

"Only once," he replied. "A journal published a case about a woman who was electrocuted by a fallen power line. She survived and her symptoms vanished, but such incidents are very rare—neurons are quite fragile, you know."

"So are hearts." Rose gently stroked Chance's forehead while he lay in the hospital bed. What the doctor couldn't have known, of course, was that there had been *two* lightning strikes in Chance's life, both with the power to change lives. One had hit him at the top of Rook Ridge in early October during the love spell, but the other had entered them both inside the saloon on Halloween. As the bolt crashed through the roof and struck Vincent, it came up through the floorboards to Rose's feet, knocking her unconscious as she hit the floor.

Although the event might have altered Chance's brain chemistry, Rose was convinced that the true cause for his recovery was something else entirely. In that instant, when she held his fallen body against her chest and Chance's soul returned, Rose believed that the fairies had granted her ultimate wish: for their hearts to be fused together for all time. After all, now he possessed her clarity and she embraced his wisdom, like one soul spread across two bodies, forever 'twixt. It was a mysterious notion—something she wouldn't admit to his doctors, or even to Amy and Laurel. Rose kept it as her private secret, which she reserved only for her visits to the hospital, when she whispered to Chance late at night in his dreams.

Whatever the truth really was about that night, Rose had a more difficult time explaining why she shot Chance Murphy to local authorities. Tongue-tied, she got lost in descriptions about an eternally evil saloon keeper and her bone-wrenching fear for Crystal's safety when Sheriff Donahue came around the shop to pursue his investigation the following Monday. "Arson and kidnapping!" Amy had finally blurted, after Rose blundered through various justifications. But then Laurel led the sheriff aside and informed him in a clipped tone that the real culprit had been Vincent, who'd set fire to the building and threatened them all with a gun before skipping town. When her sister pulled the trigger in self-defense, the bullet hit Chance by mistake. "You'd better send out an A.P.B. right away," Laurel declared, glancing at Rose and Amy with a twinkle in her eye, "you don't want his kind to ever come back."

Sheriff Donahue merely sniffed as he scribbled onto a

notepad, acting unsurprised. When he'd finished jotting down a few lines, he asked if he could look around the shop. Rose nodded as he methodically made his way through the building, dusting for fingerprints and leaving no tea cup unturned. By the time he'd finished, he stood in front of the three women and shook his head.

"Well, if you ask me," he said dryly, "it was a matter of time before somebody took aim at that son-of-a-bitch."

It turned out that Vincent had beaten the sheriff at poker one too many times, fleecing him for over fifteen hundred dollars, and he was certain the man had cheated. "This whole incident is starting to look like another Ophir Creek feud. I've seen battles like these rage on for years, usually over mining claims. Believe me, they're a pain in the ass—and they cost taxpayers a fortune."

Then the sheriff narrowed his gaze at Rose and rubbed his chin. "So, given your lack of a criminal record, why don't we call it a draw this time—accidental gunfire—and have ourselves some breakfast?" He stole a glance at her bakery case. "That is, if you promise never to bring a gun again to the Magpie Saloon. I don't want to hear one more word about you ladies, unless it's to brag about your cooking."

Rose was so stunned she felt as if her boots had been bolted to the floor. But Amy let out an ear-splitting whoop while Laurel nodded enthusiastically. To Rose's astonishment, her sister even leaned over and gave the sheriff a kiss. The man blushed, but Rose was nearly certain she saw him smile.

"W-why Sheriff—we'd love to serve you breakfast!" Rose gushed. "And while we're at it, we'll set out picnic tables and invite all the neighbors—"

Rose scurried to collect her vintage linen tablecloths and directed Laurel and Amy to help her carry out tables and chairs to the town square. Then they added pumpkins with pretty fall leaves and pinecones for centerpieces. Afterwards, they went around the town of Ophir Creek and knocked on every single door to gather their neighbors for a big harvest celebration.

The reason for their generosity was more than the fact that the sheriff wasn't going to press charges—it was because the entire town had banded together on Halloween night to put out the fire. While Rose had been recovering in the hospital, Amy and Laurel had told her how the neighbors had labored simultaneously like busy bees. Within minutes the flames were gone, before the fire department could arrive. Led by Ray Beane, they employed water buckets and shovels, fire extinguishers and garden hoses—whatever they could get their hands on to stop the damage.

No one had ever seen anything like it. There were the usual town eccentrics like Belle Crawford and Fannie Thistlewaite, but even forest rangers like Sylvie and saloon regulars like Jim Trotter and George Brickman worked diligently alongside each other. And then, to everyone's surprise, an old woman showed up wearing a hunter's cap and a big down parka. She doused the fire with a water bucket and waved a black bible while cursing at the flames. It was Harriet Brimley, coming to the rescue of people she probably considered heathens, and the very sight of her warmed everyone's heart. Because of the townspeople's efforts, only the back corner of the building had been affected, and already Ray Beane had put up makeshift siding to keep out the cold.

He told Rose that with a little more insulation and a few splashes of paint, it would be as good as new.

Rose breathed a sigh of contentment as she studied Amy's Thanksgiving decorations that morning, full of pride. It wasn't because the shop really looked all that different—it still had the same old oak barrels and faded doilies, tea cups and gold pans. Yet it felt more like home now than ever before. She stepped over to the kitchen to pour herself a cup of coffee and leaned over the counter to check her daughter's progress. In Crystal's hands was Chance's notebook, the one he used to communicate in the hospital, opened to a fresh page. At the top, Crystal had painted a large pumpkin with curly vines and leaves framing a list of ingredients. Rose had written a new recipe inside that she'd created especially for Thanksgiving. It was a lot like the Barmbrack cake her mother used to make for Halloween, only the main ingredients were pumpkin, roasted pine nuts, and even a smattering of potato. She called it her Blessings cake, and she topped it with cream cheese frosting and a hint of cinnamon and nutmeg. Rather than baking charms inside, like her mother used to do, she slipped little parchment notes into the batter of all that she was grateful for that year. At the top of her list, of course, was Crystal and Chance, but a close second was the many traditions her family had passed down to her, not the least of which were the quilt and the diary.

Luckily, the quilt had escaped the fire without damage, and to their surprise, Laurel had stumbled across the O'Dannan diary when the women entered the Magpie Saloon a few days after the shooting. It was beside Vincent's cot in the back next to an old oil lamp, with his red bandana curled beside it like a snake.

"He must have used it late at night as an encyclopedia," Rose mentioned at the time, and it gave her chills to know he'd touched it, maybe slept with it to try and absorb its power. At Amy's insistence, the three of them burned the bandana with a lighter right there, keeping their minds free of all thought so that his spirit would have nothing to cling to. When they returned to the shop, they performed a cleansing ritual over the diary using a special smudge stick, which Amy said was laced with the sap from local trees. The shop smelled like Pine-sol afterwards, but Rose didn't care. She was glad to know his spirit had finally been banished, and she considered the bracing aroma a reflection of the fact that her life was starting over, fresh and new.

Besides, Rose decided that Chance's notebook would serve as their new diary now—as much a testament to their lives moving forward as a tribute to the traditions of the past. Like the old diary, it would contain recipes and drawings, and maybe descriptions of an omen or two, but it would also preserve mementos of their current happiness. Of course, Crystal insisted it needed stickers to add more glitter, so without asking, she pasted several of the gold stars her mother used to keep for her progress chart into the notebook's pages. When Rose discovered them, she laughed with tears in her eyes. This was precisely what she had prayed for—the return of her little dynamo, even if Crystal did overpower her with enthusiasm one second and contradict her the next. After everything they'd been through, Rose had learned to cherish all the facets of her daughter, as complex and varied as the colors on her play bracelet, regardless of how contrary she might be.

"Mommy, what's baking soda?" Crystal puzzled from her stool by the counter. Frustrated, she blew on the small mound of white powder that had spilled next to her artwork, scattering it across the wood like dust. She lifted the notebook and brushed it off, showing her mother the bright orange pumpkin she'd finished, her eyes radiant.

Rose smiled at her daughter's painting and tapped the recipe on the page. "It's an ingredient that helps things rise, honey. Without it, our cake would be flat."

"Is it magic?" Crystal peered at her intently. Her wings quivered a little as she shifted her gaze to the bracelet on her wrist, studying its soft colors in the pale, wintry light.

Rose was about to say no. There were explanations for these things—chemical reactions that helped the dough to release carbon dioxide and rise, which she'd learned about years ago in Mrs. Dingle's science class. But then she heard the old raven caw outside, and she held her tongue. "You know, honey, it just might be." Gently, she pried the notebook from her daughter's fingers and handed her a plate of fairy cakes. "Sweetheart," she glanced back at the raven, "do me a favor and set these outside on the porch."

"For the good people?"

Rose patted her head. "Something like that."

As Crystal stepped onto the porch with the plate of fairy cakes, Laurel pulled up to the shop with the old, blue pickup. Its windshield was frosted at the edges with snow, and Rose spied Chance beside her in the front seat. Her heart began to race. All at once, Crystal squealed on the boardwalk and poked her head inside the door.

"They're here!" she shouted, wings jittering. "The good people—they're here!"

Amy clapped and dashed to the front door, but Rose held out her arm to make her stop. With every ounce of her being, she wanted to run outside as well, to throw her arms around Chance and cover him with a thousand kisses, but she held herself back. This is Crystal's moment, she thought—her reunion with a friend she hasn't seen since the first moon in October, except in her dreams. Anxious, she pressed her hands down the delicate green dress she'd put on for the occasion, which Crystal insisted she wear. Then she took a deep breath and grasped Amy's hand, staring through the window as Chance stepped out of the truck. He moved cautiously with a cane, and Laurel walked around to guide him. Before he could manage two steps, Crystal ran up and hugged his knees so tightly he couldn't budge. Chance tilted his head back and laughed. Against doctor's orders, he picked her up, her wings fluttering, and set her high on his wide shoulders with a smile as big as the sky. Tears rolled down Rose's cheeks. Her eyes met his through the window—they were as soft and inviting as when they had danced beneath the moon. Yet as she stared, she noticed her reflection in the glass beside him and Crystal. This time, it wasn't her past or her future she was perceiving—it was her *now*, the kind of present she used to only dream about. Curiously, the closer he walked with Crystal to the shop, the more she felt as if her soul were melting and slipping through the glass to blend with theirs. There was nothing between them anymore—no time or space or distance. Their hearts shimmered in the same pool, the same light. Is this what it really means to be 'twixt? she wondered. For once, she didn't struggle to find an answer. She simply let go of Amy's hand and blew them a kiss.

Rose. Chance's lips made an effort to pronounce her name as he stepped onto the porch. *My Rose.*

Trembling, she turned to glance at the counter. "Let me get it," Amy offered, and she grabbed the Blessings cake and set it on the cafe table. They had baked it the night before for Chance's homecoming, which they intended to serve as the world's most decadent brunch. Such a meal was probably against the doctor's orders as well, but Rose figured they might forgive her this time. Then the harness bells jingled with the sweetest tones she'd ever heard, and Chance swung the door open with Crystal on his shoulders. Snowflakes glistened on his dark hair, and his brown eyes looked to her as if he'd just been born that minute.

"My Rose," he said from deep in his throat, somewhere between a whisper and a caw. Rose wasn't sure if he'd really uttered the words, or if she'd merely heard them in her heart because she wanted to. But then he cocked his head a little, the way ravens do, and he twitched his neck as if he were still struggling with the change of becoming human. His lips moved with an awkward, raspy sound. "Home."

In that moment, sunlight filtered through the clouds and the town square became rimmed in gold. Rose smiled at the abrupt change of weather that matched the swell in her heart. She saw the old raven lift its wings and rise from the porch, nodding at her as it slowly spiraled above Ophir Creek. For once, she didn't search for colors to appear or dash to the

O'Dannan diary to see what it all might mean. She simply stared into Chance's eyes, letting the moment be, with her feet planted on the floor. Gazing at the sunlight that danced on her daughter's curls, she recalled the words from the legend—all those who are pure of heart may make a wish in the O'Dannan name and find gold. Rose wrapped her arms around Chance and gave him a long kiss, resting her head on his chest to absorb his warmth and treasure his breath. Then she smiled and whispered "O'Dannan" so softly that only the good people could hear. Sometimes, she thought, you don't need to try so hard to find gold. All you have to do is let it in.

DISCOVER THE IRON FEATHER BROTHERS SERIES

He's a fierce protector of his land and sacred heritage— and only a strong woman can capture his wild heart.

Buy now!

IRISH LANGUAGE GLOSSARY

The following Irish words, names and expressions are featured in the novel *Twixt* and are listed in alphabetical order. Approximate English pronunciations for the Connacht dialect are in parentheses.

Ailís: (ay + lish) Irish form of the name Alice, meaning noble, kind, honest

aisling: (ash + ling) my dream, my vision, my poem

a thaisce: (uh + hash + kuh) my treasure, my love, my dear

a Thiarna déan trócaire: (a-heerna + jan + tro-kruh) Lord have mercy

bheith idir eatarthu: (veh + idjir +atur-huh) 'twixt, betwixt, between

croagh: (kro + ah) mount, mountain

cuir uait: (kwir + oo + wetz) stop that, not now

currach: (curr + uch) boat

damnú: (dam + noo) damn

damnú air: (dam-noo + wet) damn it

Dia ár sábháil: (jia + awr + sav-oyl) oh my God, God save us

fáilte: (fall + chuh) welcome

mo stór: (mo + stohr) my love, my treasure

sluagh: (sloo + ah) horde of restless dead, vile creatures, soul stealers

súmaire: (soom + air) blood sucker, vampire, leech

tráthóna maith: (trah-no-nuh + my) good evening

ENCHANTED IRISH FAIRY CAKE RECIPE

Makes 1 Dozen

Caution: This fairy cake recipe is featured in the novel *Twixt* and is rumored to help one see fairies. Don't be surprised if you spy flits of sparkling light or hear tinkling laughter and become "fairy struck" with inexplicable feelings of joy…

Fairy Cake Ingredients:
½ cup (1stick) butter
1 cup white sugar
½ cup brown sugar
4 large eggs, room temperature
½ cup sour cream, room temperature
½ teaspoon pure vanilla extract
Seeds of 1 vanilla bean (scrape seeds into batter & discard hull)
1 ½ cups all-purpose flour
2 tablespoons corn starch

$\frac{1}{2}$ teaspoon salt (scant)
$\frac{1}{2}$ teaspoon baking soda
2 handfuls rolled oats

Now here's where the MAGIC comes in! According to your
fancy, add any of the following ingredients that you like (go
with what your heart tells you!):
$\frac{1}{2}$ cup of chopped walnuts/or pecans
$\frac{1}{2}$ cup of chopped dried fruit (such as dates, cranberries,
apple, or apricots)
A few flower petals!
Then wiggle your fingers and sprinkle joyful feelings (it
matters!)

Lemon Fairy Icing Ingredients:
1 (8-ounce) package of cream cheese
$\frac{1}{4}$ cup ($\frac{1}{2}$ stick) butter
2 cups powdered confectioners sugar
2 teaspoons lemon juice
2 teaspoons grated lemon peel (zest)
Several drops of yellow food coloring (to desired color)
(Feel free to add more or less sugar/lemon to taste)

Directions for Enchanted Irish Fairy Cakes:
Heat oven to 350 degrees and line a muffin pan with paper
liners. Cream the butter & sugar in a bowl with an electric
mixer until light & fluffy, then add eggs, sour cream, vanilla
extract & vanilla seeds (discard hull!) and mix until creamy.
Add flour, cornstarch, salt & baking soda and mix at low speed
until just combined (don't overmix). Stir in by hand the with a

wooden spoon the 2 handfuls of rolled oats and any or all of the following: chopped nuts, dried fruit, flower petals & sprinkles of good feeling (remember, this is where *your* MAGIC comes in—so be creative and play!). Spoon the batter to fill cupcakes liners & bake for 20-30 minutes (until a toothpick comes out clean). Cool to room temperature before frosting.

Directions for Lemon Fairy Icing:
Mix cream cheese & butter with an electric mixer & add lemon juice, lemon zest & powdered sugar, beating until creamy. Spread a generous amount on each fairy cake—and if you happen to swipe a lick (like Rose does in *Twixt*), prepare yourself to see fairies! Adorn with flower petals, of course!

ABOUT THE AUTHOR

USA TODAY bestselling author Diane J. Reed writes happily ever afters with a touch of magic that make you believe in the power of love. Her stories feed the soul with outlaws, mavericks, and dreamers who have big hearts under big skies and dare to risk all for those they cherish. Because love is more than a feeling—it's the magic that changes everything.

To get the latest on new releases, sign up for Diane J. Reed's newsletter at dianejreed.com.

www.ingramcontent.com/pod-product-compliance
Lightning Source LLC
Chambersburg PA
CBHW031028030726
47497CB00004B/1045